THE WINTERSTONE MURDER

THE WINTERSTONE MURDER

Book One

THE WOODHEAD & BECKER MYSTERIES

PAUL AUSTIN ARDOIN

Author's Note

**This book was originally published under the title
Ceremony in August 2021.**

I worked for a company headquartered in Milwaukee for several years, and I fell in love with the city, even (especially?) in the winter. Although this is a work of fiction, many elements are based in the history and geography of Milwaukee.

While there is no Anne Askew Chapel and no Kilbourn Tech University, there *is* a fifteenth-century church—the St. Joan of Arc Chapel—that was transported stone by stone to Milwaukee from France. Today, it's situated on the Marquette University campus (and there is a stone in the wall that's colder than everything around it, too). Anne Askew was a real Protestant martyr during the reign of Henry VIII, and the chants used in the anchor ceremony are taken directly from her writings.

Likewise, Milwaukee houses one of the top freshwater science labs in the world. It's part of the University of Wisconsin at Milwaukee.

Sea lampreys are an invasive species that almost killed the

fishing industry in the Great Lakes, and TFM is the real lampricide that has kept the problem at bay for the last seventy years.

Spotted Cow is a real (and delicious) beer that is illegal to distribute outside Wisconsin.

For background on these items and other details of my research, check out my blog at www.paulaustinardoin.com.

Chapter One

THE CARETAKER WAS ALSO A DOCENT. SHE EXPERTLY delivered her patter about the history of the dark old building, but her breaths came quick and short. It made sense, given that she'd come into her chapel the night before and found a dead body in the center aisle.

"Anne Askew," the woman continued, "who gave her name to this chapel—that's her depicted in the left part of the stained glass behind the altar—was tortured before she was burned at the stake." She took a deep breath. "I appreciate you letting me tell you this, Agent Baker."

Bernadette's last name was Becker, not Baker, and she hadn't been an agent since her demotion two months ago. She kept her mouth shut, though. After ten minutes of monosyllables the docent was finally talking, and Bernadette wasn't about to stop her now.

"The police asked me a hundred questions last night, but every time I tried to answer, they cut me off. As if the chapel's history didn't matter."

"You think it's relevant to this case?" prodded Bernadette.

"Look at that shape," said the docent, pointing to the small wooden flags laid out on the outline of where the body had been. "Murder victims are supposed to sprawl, aren't they?"

The woman was right: the posture was odd. Murder victims were most often sprawled or curled up. Here, the flags on the floor agreed with the crime scene photos that CSI had texted to Bernadette's phone: this man had been stretched at full length, either before or after death, arms straight out over his head. It had suggested foul play to the local police. But what did the victim's position have to do with the chapel's namesake martyr?

"You see," said the docent, "Anne Askew was tortured *on the rack*."

Bernadette nodded slowly, following the docent's train of thought.

"She's the only woman who's ever been tortured in the Tower of London," the docent continued. "Maybe I watch too many true-crime shows, but I think someone's trying to make a point."

"A point?" Bernadette's thoughts went in several directions —torture, heresy, apostasy. "What point do you think that is?"

The docent hesitated. "It's not just because of the position of the body," she said carefully. "It's the placement. The body's lying on the Winterstone."

Bernadette thought back through her notes about the Anne Askew Chapel but didn't recall anything by that name. "I'm sorry—the Winterstone?"

The docent, a glint in her eyes, walked toward the wooden flags on the floor, next to where Kymer Thompson's feet had been half a day earlier. "Come here and I'll show you."

"Don't get too close to the flags," Bernadette said, walking from her position next to the rear pew to the other side of the flags, near the arms. Dr. Woodhead wouldn't want anything corrupting the scents where the body was found.

"You can feel it without touching the floor," the docent said.

"Feel what?"

"You see the large stone there, in the center of the aisle? In the center of the flags?"

"The big one."

"Notice it's a lighter gray than the stones around it?"

Bernadette nodded.

The docent beckoned her with one hand and held the other about six inches above the light gray stone. "Put your hand there."

Bernadette crouched—ugh, she was sore from squats this morning. She pushed her long brown hair out of her face but looked at the docent and furrowed her brow.

"I'm serious," the docent insisted.

Tentatively, Bernadette reached out a hand.

The chapel was relatively warm for a snowy winter day in March—but as soon as Bernadette's hand hit the air above the stone, she felt the chill.

"The Winterstone," the docent said. "It's colder there than anywhere else in the chapel. It was like that in London, too, though not until Anne Askew was martyred."

"Right," Bernadette said. That hadn't been in the materials. "And that's where you discovered the body. Stretched out like Anne Askew on the rack." She took her phone out of her purse and snapped a picture of the Winterstone.

"Makes me think that someone was drawing a parallel between Mr. Thompson and Anne Askew," the woman said, a dreamlike tone to her voice. She turned to the altar and gestured to the two stained-glass windows, each about three feet tall, in the back wall. "In the fifteenth century, when this chapel was originally built, the two windows were much smaller. And"—the woman's voice lilted with tour-guide precision—"of course back then the stained glass didn't have an image of Anne Askew."

Bernadette's phone gave a buzz in her hand. Oh—maybe that was Dr. Woodhead calling her back. Finally. She looked at the screen—it was just a reminder. 2:45 P.M. *Call Sophie.* Right—she'd be home from school now. It would have to wait, as much as that pained her. She put the phone back in her purse.

"You'll notice the archway above the altar is a segmented three-pointed arch," the docent began, and launched into a speech that sounded lovingly rehearsed. Bernadette followed the docent's eyes and hands as she talked. The chapel was dark and cramped, not at all like the European cathedrals Bernadette had seen; the walls felt too close despite the high ceiling. The putty-colored stone arch—the segmented three-pointed arch, as the docent called it—separated the altar from the dozen wooden pews, six on each side of the aisle where the Winterstone lay. The simpler windows on the side of the building did little to let in the gray afternoon light.

"This building was transported stone by stone from London in the 1870s. The Winterstone was the first piece of cargo to cross the Milwaukee River Bridge."

Bernadette, sensing the end of the visitors' script, nodded. "This is truly a fascinating building."

"It is, isn't it?" The docent gazed happily at the archway above the altar. "Some people think this building is eerie, but I don't. I love it." Her face darkened. "And to think that someone used this gorgeous chapel to..." Her voice trailed off.

Bernadette hesitated, then reached out and put a hand on the docent's shoulder. "I'm sorry." It felt right—not *I'm sorry for your loss,* but almost. It's like the loss was of the sanctity of the building, sullied with the victim's body.

Assuming, of course, that it was murder.

Bernadette took her hand gently from the woman's shoulder. "I'm afraid I have to ask you a few more questions."

The docent nodded.

"What time did you check on the chapel last night?"

"It must have been around eleven-thirty. I had a council meeting that ran long, and I went home first before I remembered I hadn't prepared the chapel properly." She closed her eyes. "If I'd set the incense up before the council meeting..."

Then she would have found the body this morning instead of last night. Bernadette smiled with a touch of sadness and as much sympathy as she could muster. The docent was used to a gentle life, Bernadette decided. Eggshell sweater, graying hair pulled back into a messy bun, cat's-eye glasses. Bernadette's files said she'd been the chapel docent for thirteen years.

"Did you enter through the front door?"

The woman's head snapped up. "Oh—uh, yes. The front door."

"And did you see the body as soon as you entered?"

"No, it was still dark. I walked behind the pews to turn the lights on. This is a fifteenth-century building. There was no light switch installed next to the door when it was constructed." Her eyes lost focus. "I turned the lights on—the switch is back there, behind the curtain—and when I turned around, I noticed Mr. Thompson, lying there on the Winterstone."

"Did you touch the body at all?"

The woman recoiled. "Why would I do that?"

Bernadette gathered her hair, as if putting it in a ponytail, then draped it over the front of her left shoulder. "Check for a pulse. Administer CPR. Anything like that?"

The docent shook her head. "I saw him lying there, and I knew he was dead."

"Why?"

"I—I don't know. I just felt it. No soul in the vessel."

"You saw a syringe next to the body?"

"Yes. Resting on the floor near Mr. Thompson's right arm."

"Did you touch it?"

"No."

"Did you hear anything? See anything?"

"A kind of a blue-green residue in the syringe. I thought that was a little strange."

So did the M.E. That's why she called us. Bernadette looked up from her folder. "What about on your way from the parking lot to the chapel? Did anyone appear to be coming from the church?"

The docent shook her head. "The campus was pretty deserted. At 11:30 on a Monday night, especially when it's this cold, no one's out."

"Did you know Mr. Thompson?"

"I knew who he was, but not much more than a wave of the hand as we passed each other. I knew he was active in Agios Delphi. I was the one who gave him the key to the chapel."

"Ah," Bernadette said. "Agios Delphi holds services here."

"Well, with Anne Askew so central to their religion, of course they do." The woman's gaze returned to the stained-glass window.

Bernadette opened the file folder she was carrying, past the photos of the young man on the stone floor, lying on his back, his arms stretched awkwardly above his head. She had to be careful with the phrasing. "In my research," she said, "I assumed that Agios Delphi was—well, a little outside the requirements of the kind of religious organization that would be allowed to have services here."

The woman shook her head. "The Anne Askew Chapel is administered by Kilbourn Technical University," she said. "As we get our budget from public funds, we're not allowed to discriminate." She put her hands on her hips. "Who did you say you were with?"

"CSAB."

The woman's eyes went wide. "Hang on—*see-sab*." She repeated it exactly as Bernadette pronounced it, but with confusion in her voice.

"The Controlled Substance Analysis Bureau."

The docent's face relaxed. "Oh—See Ess Ay Bee." She paused. "Didn't I read that Dr. Kep Woodhead came to work with you after his TV show finished?"

"He's an investigative consultant." Bernadette smiled widely. *And he won't return my calls.*

"What does that mean?"

"He lends his skills and knowledge to the team, but he doesn't have a badge. He's paired with a case analyst who's a law enforcement officer." *Lucky me.*

"I bet he's great at that," the docent gushed. "I loved him on *Cases That Won't Die.* Such a shame he was only on for the first two seasons. The new guy who replaced him is so bland." She sighed, seeming to forget, for the first time in the interview, that she was standing in the middle of a murder scene. "Of course, it would be hard to get another investigator with a— well, *superpower.*" She tittered.

"So," Bernadette said carefully, "I have some good news and some bad news."

The docent blinked. "Don't tell me—he's working on this case?"

"He is," Bernadette said, nodding firmly, but keeping a serious look on her face.

"Oh, that's wonderful!" The docent took a breath. "Do you —do you think it would be possible to meet him?"

"Well," Bernadette said, "do you remember the episode in Jacksonville? At the barbecue restaurant?"

The docent laughed. "How could I forget? All the smells of the pork, and the ovens, and that sauce, and those spicy peppers, yet Dr. Woodhead yelled at the cashier for wearing strong cologne and tainting the evidence collection!" She chuckled, a hand over her mouth—this time in modesty—then her laughter abruptly stopped. "Wait—you said bad news?"

"I'm afraid it's your perfume," Bernadette said. Then hastened to add, "It's a lovely scent. And it's perfect on you. But —well, this is a crime scene." Bernadette tapped her nose. "You know, his, uh, *superpower.*"

"Oh," the woman said, realization dawning on her face.

"I don't want him to treat you like that cashier in Jacksonville," Bernadette said quickly. "I know you'd love to meet him, but while he's working, it would be best if you left the chapel."

"I'm the caretaker of this building," she said, a note of indignation in her voice.

Bernadette nodded. "If you'd like to discuss the matter with my boss, Lieutenant Stevenson is in the campus security office coordinating plans with the local police."

The woman stared at Bernadette, unblinking, then dropped her shoulders. "No, that won't be necessary." She stepped around the flags, and walked slowly toward the front door, stopping to pick up her coat from the back bench. She put on the coat, looking wistfully at the altar, then turned and pulled the door open.

The docent almost ran into another woman in a black police uniform and a Milwaukee Police wool cap who was standing next to the front door, talking on her cell phone. It was police detective Kerrigan Dunn, her cheeks flushed light pink from the cold. She ended the call and took a step into the chapel as the docent walked away into the snowy afternoon.

"The IT guy is coming in a few minutes," Dunn said.

"You mean Curtis?"

"What—the skinny guy in the leather jacket? No—not *your* tech guy. The one who works for the university." Dunn consulted her notebook. "Nick LaSalle. He should be able to get us some cell service inside the chapel."

"Good." Bernadette wondered if she had time to step outside and talk to Sophie before Dr. Woodhead arrived. But she looked around the chapel. Was everything arranged the way it should be? Were there any scents that would put him off? She didn't have the sensitive nose he did, but she slowly paced around the chapel once more, searching for anything that would distract him from his job.

She remembered the letter she'd received—a handwritten letter, of all things—when she first was assigned to Dr. Woodhead. It was from the previous case analyst.

Bernadette—

You drew the short straw, I see. I don't have much advice, except if you let him get under your skin, that'll be the beginning of the end. Figure out how to get the best out of him. He'll try to run off, so keep him close.

Why did I leave? Let's just say he never insulted me enough that I could make a formal complaint, but always enough that I felt it. And he disappeared on me once too often.

If you can survive Woodhead, getting back to being a field agent will be a piece of cake. Go thrust him out at gates, and let him smell his way to Dover.

Best of luck,

Martin

She'd been puzzling over the letter for a few weeks now, especially that last line. Martin had always been a fan of the sports page, not Shakespeare, but when Bernadette had looked up that last line, it turned out to be a quote from *King Lear*. A particularly nasty passage of the play, at that. The letter did not soothe her anxiety about her demotion.

The front door opened again, and a tall white man peered inside. He was in his fifties and wore black slacks with a sportscoat, a white oxford shirt, and a blue-and-yellow striped tie. He had a folder under one arm and a determined gaze in his intense brown eyes.

In the photo in Bernadette's folder, still out in the car, he'd looked younger, with a full head of dark brown hair and a clean-shaven face. This man's hair and beard were salt-and-pepper—a similar look to the gray houndstooth design of his sportscoat. His silver-rimmed glasses sat down too far on his nose.

There was no doubt. He was her new assignment: Dr. Kep Woodhead.

Chapter Two

HE DUCKED THROUGH THE DOORWAY, PUSHED HIS GLASSES UP, then raised his nose and sniffed.

"Dr. Woodhead, it's a pleasure to meet you." Bernadette stuck out her hand in greeting.

He closed his eyes and held up an index finger. Bernadette lowered her hand. Detective Dunn looked over her shoulder at Bernadette, who gave a slight shrug.

Bernadette could almost hear the seconds tick by in her head.

Finally, Dr. Woodhead opened his eyes and pointed to the table on the altar holding a brass censer, a sphere resting on a stand with notches in the top half and an ornate cross on the lid. "Did the CSI team say how long ago that incense was burned?"

The detective followed his gaze. "No. Not since the body was found, anyway. I don't think." She hesitated, then spoke quickly. "And I'm Detective Kerrigan Dunn, Milwaukee Police." She didn't offer her hand.

"Most of the incense had already been burned, judging from the smell. Benzoin was used." Woodhead sniffed again, ignoring

Dunn. "I'm getting other styrax scents as well; perhaps a touch of frankincense. Is incense used in the services? *Are* there even services held here?"

Kerrigan Dunn nodded. "The Anglicans have their service Sunday mornings, of course." Detective Dunn took out her notebook and consulted it. "We've got a group of Seventh-Day Adventists Saturdays, and a small Presbyterian group Sunday evenings. Tuesdays, of course, it's the Agios Delphi people."

"I only found out a little about them," Bernadette said. "It's an odd name for a church. Delphi was the name of the oracle from *Oedipus Rex*. Is it Greek Orthodox?"

The detective scoffed. "It's no kind of orthodox. More like a pyramid scheme dressed in religious clothing."

"I know it's not a mainstream denomination," Bernadette said.

"If I recall correctly, our victim was a member." Dr. Woodhead opened his folder. "Yes, here it is: 'Mr. Thompson was a member of a local church called Agios Delphi.'" He turned a page. "Agios Delphi of Greater Milwaukee. Kymer Thompson was an elder." Woodhead glanced up at the detective. "Twenty-five and an elder. That's humorous." He did not smile.

Woodhead had a point: he was young to have such an elevated position in the church. "Detective," Bernadette said, "the Agios Delphi group meets here on Tuesdays, correct? But last night was Monday."

"Right," Dunn affirmed.

"So why was Mr. Thompson inside the chapel yesterday?"

"Perhaps he was trying to, I don't know, cleanse the bad juju from the chapel for tonight's service. Maybe that's one of the things the elders have to do for the, uh, church." Dunn landed on the last word harder than necessary.

"Detective Dunn," Dr. Woodhead said absently, reading the report from the folder, "are you able to maintain impartiality, or will your opinion of the victim's religion color your investigation?"

Dunn formed her hands into a steeple. "I haven't said anything that isn't relevant to the investigation, Dr. Woodhead. This organization is known to use methods to separate their congregation from their money. I have a thick folder back at the District 5 station full of fraud allegations. Widens the net we need to cast for suspects."

Woodhead raised his head, a smile touching the corners of his mouth—the smile looked friendly, but his eyes flashed behind his glasses. "You haven't answered my question. Will your dislike of Agios Delphi affect your ability to investigate this crime?"

"I believe I'm more familiar with Agios Delphi than you are." Dunn crossed her arms. "And like I said, I haven't mentioned anything irrelevant."

"CSAB was called," Bernadette broke in, "because your M.E. strongly suspects that ibogaine caused Mr. Thompson's death. That requires investigation—ibogaine is a class 1 controlled substance. We need to work together." But she couldn't catch Woodhead's eye when she said it.

Dunn pressed her lips together and was silent.

Woodhead looked up at the vaulted ceiling. "So Agios Delphi uses this space for their services on Tuesday nights?"

"Yes," Dunn answered.

"How did Mr. Thompson gain access to the chapel?"

"According to the docent, he was one of the two people from the Delphi group who had a key. He was an elder in the organization, and he lived in university-owned housing, so he was close."

"Who's the other member with a key?" Woodhead asked.

"Vivian Roundhouse."

Bernadette remembered the name from her conversation with the docent. "Ms. Roundhouse is the Agios Delphi priest."

Woodhead flipped back a page. "Ah. Yes." He turned to face the back wall, stepping closer until his nose was only an inch or two from the stones. Pushing his glasses up again, he took a long whiff and kept sniffing.

After the third sniff, the muscles around Woodhead's eyes tightened.

Uh oh. That wasn't a good sign.

He opened his eyes and looked at Detective Dunn.

"Is something wrong?" the detective said.

And then Bernadette caught the faintest whiff of it—perfume. And not the same scent the docent wore.

"You—" Woodhead began.

Then Bernadette caught his eye. She set her mouth in a line. He had already upset Detective Dunn by questioning her ability to stay neutral. They needed Dunn on their side—and if he insulted her again, she might not be cooperative. "I tried to reach you several times, Dr. Woodhead."

"Yes, I know."

That wasn't a response she'd expected. "I'd hoped you would give me some direction on clearing the crime scene for you so this kind of thing wouldn't happen."

Woodhead looked at Bernadette impassively. "It wouldn't have helped. You wouldn't have been able to prepare it to my satisfaction."

Oof. Martin's letter was prescient.

"Does someone want to tell me what's going on?" Dunn asked.

Woodhead turned to face her. "You're contaminating the crime scene."

Dunn narrowed her eyes. "Excuse me? I haven't touched anything."

"It's not—"

Bernadette steeled herself and interrupted. "Dr. Woodhead, as I'm sure you saw on TV, has a gift for identifying subtle scents. It's what makes his expertise in poisoning cases such as this so invaluable. But"—she gave Woodhead a questioning look, then spoke haltingly—"perfumes, strong deodorant soaps—those can mask the scents he's trying to find at crime scenes."

"Oh," Detective Dunn said.

"*Theme Music*," Woodhead muttered. "Obviously."

"What?" Bernadette said. "Did you say *Theme Music*?"

Dunn glanced at Bernadette. "He's right. The name of my perfume—*Theme Music*."

"That's correct," Woodhead said tersely. "Would you step outside?"

"Outside the crime scene?"

"Yes." Woodhead lifted a hand, palm in, fingers down, and made a shooing motion.

Bernadette winced.

Dunn scoffed. "Sure. Wouldn't want to disturb the famous TV star with my overpowering stench." She walked out, not quite stomping, into the snowy day, but left the front door open.

"We haven't been properly introduced, Dr. Woodhead," Bernadette said, keeping her hands down. "I'm your new case analyst, Bernadette Becker."

"Salmon will mask scents too," Woodhead said.

Bernadette cocked her head.

"What?"

"Salmon. You must have had some earlier."

"Not since last night, and I showered and brushed my teeth twice since then. Surely I don't—"

"You smell like urine."

Bernadette took a step back.

"The trimethylamine oxide in the salmon breaks down into ammonia. Very similar scent profile to urea. It's extremely distracting."

Bernadette shook her head and followed the detective out the front door.

"He's a real charmer," Dunn said under her breath.

Bernadette grunted. "Yeah. We're getting along like a house on fire."

Chapter Three

BERNADETTE STRODE PAST DUNN, WHO WATCHED DR. KEP Woodhead through the open chapel door, and took out her cell phone. It took a moment, but the *No service* warning disappeared, replaced by four bars. She tapped the screen.

It went right to Sophie's voicemail. Probably on the phone with her dad or a friend from school. She paused, staring around the frigid quad with its leafless trees, everything gray, brown, and white. Her puffy purple coat was the only pop of color. She ended the call without leaving a message; she didn't want to sound desperate to talk.

She closed her eyes, then walked back, shoes crunching in the snow. She stopped next to Dunn, still watching the scene unfold inside the chapel. "Did I miss anything?"

"He's been standing like that since we left."

Woodhead stood still under the altar archway, eyes closed, like he was expecting the Muse to strike. Perhaps he was waiting for the perfume and the salmon smell to dissipate. Then, in one fluid motion, he stretched himself to full height, and inhaled, eyes wide open.

Bernadette had never seen such a dramatic intake of breath

before.

Dr. Woodhead began to tread carefully around the room, using his hands to waft air in front of his face. He stopped for a long time in front of a table in the apse. Perhaps he was trying to figure out the specific incense in the golden thurible.

She got closer, stopping at the edge of the nave.

Woodhead, not noticing her, stared at the floor as he walked down the center aisle of the nave and came upon the small removable flags that marked where the body had been found. He closed his eyes, crouched, and breathed slowly in.

"It's cold here," he said.

"Part of the magic of the chapel," Dunn said from outside the open door.

He cocked his head, a thoughtful look on his face, pushed his glasses up, and inhaled again.

His eyes opened, and he shook his head. "You're throwing me off, Bernie."

Bernadette tensed at the nickname.

"You and your salmon," Woodhead continued. "I can *still* smell the trimethylamine from your—"

Then he closed his eyes again. A faint sniff.

"Wait," he said softly.

Then he crouched again, sniffed again.

"Definitely trimethylamine."

He stood and inhaled.

"Huh."

"What?"

"It's not you."

Bernadette chuckled. "Great. I don't smell like pee."

He closed his eyes again. "It's the wrong smell. It isn't the oxidation of the fatty acids in salmon, but it's still trimethylamine."

Bernadette rolled her eyes. "Our victim worked at the freshwater science lab at the university. You're probably smelling his job. Not my dinner from last night."

"The Freshie," Dunn offered.

"Oh, yes, the laboratory," Dr. Woodhead said. "I saw that in the report, but I assumed it was your typical university chemistry lab."

"Nope. It's hands-on. One of the best freshwater science labs in the country," Dunn said.

Dr. Woodhead set his folder down on a pew, got on his hands and knees on the stone floor, and stretched his long, lean torso over the area where Kymer Thompson's body had been a few hours earlier.

"It's not any species of fish I'm familiar with. Trout and salmon are common in Lake Michigan. Those are easy distinctions to make."

Bernadette turned to the detective. "Do you know what kind of fish they study at the Freshie?"

Dunn shook her head. "Sorry, I don't. Maybe he didn't even work with fish—he might have been a computer guy or a kelp farmer for all I know."

"Has anyone been to the laboratory?" Woodhead asked.

"You mean have the Milwaukee police started their interviews?" Detective Dunn scratched her temple. "Yeah. We interviewed Professor Lightman."

Woodhead grunted. "Thompson's supervisor?"

"Yeah."

"You didn't think to ask him what Thompson worked on?"

Dunn put her hands on her hips. "I didn't conduct the interview."

"Did you see evidence of a struggle? Had anything been broken? Had any fish been killed under mysterious circumstances?"

"Your nose works great, but your ears need improvement,

Doctor. I told you, I didn't conduct the interview."

Woodhead put his nose an inch from the stone floor and inhaled loudly.

Bernadette and Detective Dunn looked at each other but didn't say anything.

"Has anyone interviewed the protestors?" Woodhead asked. "A simple search on news-related items related to the laboratory revealed several articles reporting protests of their scientific research." Woodhead sighed heavily, as if he were explaining to children why they couldn't draw on the wall. "Have any of the protestors been interviewed?"

Dunn shifted her weight from foot to foot. "We started looking into it."

Woodhead's glasses slipped down his nose again as he looked up at Dunn. "What does that mean?"

Detective Dunn exhaled in a grunt. "Just what I said. We started looking into it."

"I saw two groups mentioned in the articles. Justice for Oceans and the Lake Shore Piscary Association."

Bernadette smirked. "Justice for Oceans? Are they aware that Lake Michigan isn't an ocean?"

"It's a national organization," Dunn said, pursing her lips.

"A save-the-fish group, and a catch-the-fish group," Bernadette mused. "One of them is upset that the lab is hurting the fish, and the other is upset that the lab has dibs on hurting the fish?"

The corners of Detective Dunn's mouth turned up slightly.

Woodhead, still lying down in the aisle, had his nose close to the stone floor. "I assume," he said, "that the medical examiner has attempted to minimize the disturbance to the potential evidence in this building."

Detective Dunn rubbed her chin and nodded.

"I also assume no one has walked through the area where

the body lay." Woodhead turned his face back toward the stone floor, staring and sniffing, occasionally tilting his head to the side. The seconds ticked by. The snow was quiet as it fell, a hush descending inside the chapel. Bernadette leaned against the stone archway at the entrance and shivered.

"We can be fairly certain," Woodhead said finally, "that the body was moved here after Thompson was killed."

Detective Dunn stared at Woodhead. "We already knew that. Look at the position he was in. Someone obviously placed him with his arms up and wrists out."

"Yes," Woodhead said, "but they could have killed him in the chapel and *then* arranged his body."

Dunn narrowed her eyes. "We were never thinking that. Kymer Thompson didn't have a jacket."

Woodhead looked up. "Was that in the report?"

"The photos of the body," Dunn said.

Woodhead harrumphed. "He could have taken his jacket off, draped it over a pew, left it on the floor—I can think of any number of possibilities. It's also conceivable that he came dressed in a jacket to meet his killer here, and the killer absconded with the jacket."

"I thought you said—"

"I *know* that he wasn't killed here. Not enough of his smell was transferred to the stones when his body temperature was above thirty-five degrees."

"Thirty-five degrees?" Dunn had a confused look on her face.

"Celsius," Bernadette said. "I don't know if I agree with the conclusion that no jacket means he wasn't killed here. I've seen football games in the winter where people have their shirts off, wearing green-and-gold body paint. These are Wisconsinites. Don't you all see heavy coats as a sign of moral turpitude?"

Detective Dunn laughed. "Those football fans are jammed

in with fifty thousand of their closest friends—and they're all drunk as skunks anyway." She shook her head. "Nope. You live here, you'll see. People like Kymer Thompson get sober, put on a coat, and complain that they've had enough of the snow. He wouldn't have walked in without a jacket."

"Did you search for Mr. Thompson's coat at the lab?" Bernadette asked.

Dunn sighed. "Is your hearing as bad as his? I didn't do the interviews. I didn't visit the lab. Once my bosses made the call to CSAB, I staked out the chapel and waited for you. I spoke on the phone to your people when they were on their way here." Dunn pulled her notebook out. "Lieutenant Stevenson and your tech specialist—Janek, is it?" Dunn pronounced the beginning of Curtis's last name with a J sound, and not a Y sound.

"*Yann*-ek," Woodhead corrected, getting to his feet.

"Yes, Maura and Curtis briefed me," Bernadette said. "I meant the plural you. Your team."

"Not to my knowledge. I gave Lieutenant Stevenson the names of our forensic investigators. Janek"—Dunn emphasized the Y sound now—"said he wanted to look at the victim's bank accounts and cell phone records. I noticed the two of them didn't seem anxious to stick around."

"They would have contaminated the crime scene," Woodhead said, with a faraway tone in his voice.

Bernadette lifted her chin. "Dr. Woodhead? Is something the matter?"

He stared down at the floor, but his eyes were closed. "My nose doesn't lie," he muttered.

"What?"

"According to the file," Dr. Woodhead said, "Mr. Thompson was killed with an injection of a foreign substance the medical examiner believes to be ibogaine. That's not usually lethal unless Thompson had a sensitivity—or they used a high dose. And I can't detect the scent of any ibogaine in the aisle—which by itself may not be surprising." He pointed to the area behind the pulpit. "But the smell of iboga bark, on the other hand, is quite strong, particularly near that table."

"Iboga bark?" Dunn said, incredulous. "You can tell the difference between ibogaine and iboga bark?"

"That's correct." Woodhead set his mouth in a line.

"Wait," Bernadette said, closing her eyes. "Iboga bark—that's *not* a Schedule 1 narcotic. It's a mild hallucinogen, isn't it? Originated in Central Africa, I think, from the *tabarnanthe iboga* plant. Still used in some religions." She rubbed her forehead.

"But it's not just that. I also detect the smell of iron."

"Iron?" Bernadette said. "Like an iron capsule? The dietary supplement?"

He shook his head adamantly. "No, no—it's not the smell of ferrous sulfate. It may be ferritin."

"Ferritin?" Detective Dunn asked. "What's that?"

"It's a blood protein that contains iron," Bernadette said.

"A blood protein? You're saying someone bled in here, but the killer cleaned it up? I thought you said you were sure the body had been moved."

"No," he said. "This is a specific kind of ferritin. One from —if I'm not mistaken—fish." He frowned. "That must be related to the trimethylamine. But there's something I can't quite identify about the fish. I'm not sure how much the smell overlaps—if the trimethylamine and the ferritin are bound up together. But then, that might not make a difference."

"Why not?" Dunn asked.

"My working theory is that the corpse was moved. If Mr. Thompson worked at the Freshwater Science laboratory, that likely explains the fish smell."

"Why would the body be moved?" Bernadette mused.

"To throw us off the trail," Dunn said, a note of exasperation in her voice.

"Of course, of course," Bernadette said, "but what is it about the chapel specifically? Did the killer want us to view this as a religiously motivated killing?"

"It's possible that it *was* religiously motivated," Dunn said. "After all, Thompson was an elder. And the position of the body was unusual. If you're killed and you go down, your arms and legs spread out. Not Thompson. He was found on his back, with his arms straight up above his head."

"The docent noticed that too," said Bernadette. "It makes sense if they had two people move the body. One grabs the arms, one grabs the feet."

Woodhead shook his head. "Even so—the pictures in the file look like his body wasn't placed there haphazardly. It could have personal or religious significance. Perhaps someone didn't feel that Agios Delphi deserved to share this chapel."

Dunn shot him a look. "What's that supposed to mean?"

Woodhead cocked his head. "You've implied it several times —you view the church as a cult. It seems like that's an opinion shared by many. Someone may have taken it too far."

Bernadette grimaced and turned to Dunn. "He wasn't trying to accuse you of anything." She shot a withering look at Woodhead, but he was walking through the narrow rows of wooden pews, back and forth, like ascending the switchbacks of a mountain trail. His glasses had slipped down his nose again.

She turned her attention back to Dunn. "Has your team identified any suspects?"

"No, but we've been delayed," Dunn admitted. "It took us a while to figure out jurisdiction. This isn't technically on campus, so it's the city's problem. But they use university resources, so coordination took a few hours longer than usual."

Bernadette nodded. "So the body's location created enough

jurisdictional red tape to give the killer some extra time?"

Detective Dunn shook her head. "I hate to burst your bubble, but I think putting the body in the chapel had more to do with making it look like a religious ceremony. I don't think they cared about any jurisdictional issue."

Woodhead stared up at the ceiling. "We'll keep all avenues of inquiry open."

"If many of the avenues of inquiry are pointing back to fish, we should visit the lab," Bernadette said. "Do our own interview of Professor Lightman."

Woodhead turned back to the altar. "I'll work on the incense next." He shook his head. "I wish you had taken pains to make sure no one had burned incense before I arrived."

Bernadette frowned. "No one has burned incense since *I* got here, Dr. Woodhead."

"I prefer to work alone. Perhaps I can meet you and the team back at the university's administration building." Woodhead lifted his arm and gave another shooing motion.

"How soon?"

"Forty-five minutes. Perhaps sixty." Woodhead scrunched up his nose. "Maybe in an hour I'll forget how disappointed I am that you let the detective in the chapel when her perfume was so strong. I thought they would have given you better training than this when dealing with me."

Bernadette crossed her arms, debating. She was supposed to be Woodhead's case analyst: she had the badge for access to crime scenes, interviews, and police resources, while he steered the investigation. She'd been assigned to work with him for anything he needed. And now he needed her to leave.

She could wait for him outside, even in the cold. Bernadette walked over the threshold into the chilly late afternoon, closing the front door behind her.

A tall, lanky figure crossed the quad, coming toward the

chapel. As he came closer, she saw that he was taller than Dr. Woodhead and young—not as young as an undergraduate, but young. The man wore glasses with thick black plastic frames, a bushy light brown beard, a Kilbourn Tech wool hat, and a navy blue jacket. Dunn stepped around Bernadette.

"Are you the IT guy?" Dunn asked.

"Uh—yeah," the man said. "Nick LaSalle. Campus security told me what happened. My boss asked me to come out here and meet with you."

"I'm sorry," Bernadette said, "what's your role here?"

"Oh—I'm in charge of IT for everything outside the main campus."

Bernadette cocked her head. "Is the chapel not on the main campus?"

"Not technically, no."

Dunn nodded. "It's a whole political thing. I'll tell you later."

"So should I get to work?" LaSalle asked.

Bernadette could smell pastrami on his breath, heavy on the spices. Dr. Woodhead would be angry if LaSalle's garlic breath contaminated the scene. Cell service or no, she couldn't let him inside.

"Cell signals are weak inside the chapel," LaSalle continued. "Administration thought I could install signal boosters or a Wi-Fi repeater. Better upload times to your network."

"Thanks, Mr. LaSalle," Dunn said. "Yeah, you can come through."

"Actually—" Bernadette began, shooting Dunn a warning glance.

"Oh," Dunn said, stopping in her tracks. "Maybe that's not what the federal team wants."

A confused look washed over LaSalle's face. "Federal team?"

"They're with CSAB," Dunn said.

"See—what?"

"The Controlled Substance Analysis Bureau," Bernadette said.

"Oh," LaSalle said, "I've heard of you. You think the dead guy died of some weird drug overdose?"

Bernadette smiled. "We're gathering evidence." She turned to Detective Dunn and wrinkled her nose; Dunn gave her a barely perceptible nod.

"I wouldn't be surprised, you know," LaSalle said. "There's a crazy church group that meets here on Tuesdays. I can't remember their name."

"Agios Delphi," Dunn said.

"Right. One of the research scientists at the Freshie—sorry, the College of Freshwater Sciences—he kept inviting me to their services. He was always talking about how the church has a way to get you closer to God. Took me a while before I figured out it was because of some drug—like, a tree root or something that's supposed to give you visions." He shook his head. "I'm not into that."

Interesting. Ibogaine came from iboga bark—maybe that's what LaSalle was referring to.

Bernadette glanced at Dunn. "Mr. LaSalle, we'll need you to make a statement. Anything you might know about this researcher and this hallucinogen he might have had. Or his ties to Agios Delphi."

LaSalle put up his hands in front of him. "I don't know the guy. I don't know anything about it."

"Just some background information," Bernadette said.

LaSalle patted his backpack. "Maybe after I install the Wi-Fi repeater."

"Perhaps in an hour or two," Dunn said, blocking the entry with her body. "After the federal team has a thorough analysis of the crime scene."

"I—" LaSalle began.

"In fact, why don't you come with me to the campus security office?" Bernadette asked. "My colleagues are already there."

LaSalle frowned. "I just came from the admin building. It's literally next door to campus security. You had me walk all the way out here in the snow?"

"I'm sorry for the inconvenience," Bernadette said, "but we're talking about a dead body in the chapel. I'm afraid this is more important."

LaSalle slumped his shoulders. "Sure."

Bernadette pulled Dunn aside. "You can stay with Woodhead?"

"Uh—sure. You don't want *me* to walk him to the security office?"

"I want to talk with him on the way."

Dunn gave Bernadette a wistful smile. "You're the feds in charge of the investigation. Do what you need to."

Bernadette turned to LaSalle. "All right, let's head over there."

LaSalle grumbled as he turned and walked with Bernadette.

Bernadette had walked from the security office to the chapel but wasn't entirely confident in the path to get back. Still, she watched LaSalle out of the corner of her eye. "Do you remember who that researcher was?"

LaSalle bit his lip.

"No one is looking to get him in trouble," Bernadette said gently.

"It's not that. I—I can't remember his name. I know he was about my age."

"Which is?"

"Twenty-six. I think he's a grad student or something. Everyone called him 'Tommy,' but that wasn't his name."

Bernadette pursed her lips. "Kymer Thompson?"

LaSalle's eyes brightened. "That's it."

"When did you first meet him?"

LaSalle pointed to the right. "The security office is this way."

"Sure," Bernadette said. "Sorry. First time on campus. Do you remember when Thompson first made the offer to you?"

"What—to join him at his church? I don't know. Probably after the school year started."

"How about the first time he told you about the hallucinogens?"

"Um, I'm not sure."

Bernadette stopped and cocked her head. "I told you, he won't get in trouble."

LaSalle frowned.

"And neither will you," she quickly added.

LaSalle kept walking. "Am I under arrest?"

"For what?" Bernadette said. "You haven't done anything, have you?" A large brick building loomed in front of them. A door to the left had lettering stenciled on the window: *Security Office.*

"I'm not comfortable with this," LaSalle said.

"What's uncomfortable about it? I'm asking you a few questions about your relationship with Kymer Thompson." As soon as the words were out of her mouth, she regretted them. *A few questions about Kymer Thompson—not about "your relationship" with Kymer Thompson. That sounds like he's a suspect.*

Sure enough, LaSalle cocked his head and turned toward the administration building. "I'm free to go, right?"

Bernadette sighed, kicking herself mentally. "Yes. I'm sorry. That was a poor choice of words. You're not a suspect. We're trying to get the full picture of what happened."

"How about you try some of the other people in the

church?" LaSalle said as he backed away. "Or his co-workers? I'm just the guy who set up his work PC." He turned, then looked over his shoulder. "He offered *me* drugs, not the other way around. I don't appreciate being treated like a criminal."

Great. The first afternoon working a case in her new role and Bernadette couldn't even get a simple statement. She hoped LaSalle wasn't the person to go to for records of Kymer Thompson's computer use.

She paused at the door to the security office, then took her phone out of her purse. Bernadette tapped the screen.

This time, Sophie picked up on the first ring. "Hi, Mom."

"Hi, Sophie. Did Dad pick you up from school?"

"He called me and said you'd gotten called out of town." Sophie paused, and Bernadette heard the unspoken, accusatory *again* at the end of the sentence. "Olivia's mom picked me up. I'm studying at her house."

"Oh, okay." Bernadette cleared her throat. Olivia wasn't a good student. "Dad agreed that you'd stay with him until I get back."

"He told me. He'll pick me up when he gets off work. I thought I was staying with you all week."

"This is new for both of us, Sophie. We're trying to figure it out."

Through the window of the security office, she could see a faint reflection of herself: her eyes, far apart but always a little squinty; dark eyebrows close to her browline; a strong, Roman nose; a large mouth with lips that she thought were too thin; a jaw that had her father's squareness. Her puffy purple winter coat didn't do her any favors: she was strong, with big, muscular arms, but she looked boxy and awkward in winter clothes. Under the faint reflection through the window, her co-workers, Maura Stevenson and Curtis Janek, were visible, in the middle of a conversation with each other. Maura, elegant in her earth tones, her dress and jacket flawlessly tailored, was talking with her hands. Curtis turned to her, his fair freckled face serious, in his signature dark brown leather jacket, his attention completely on her.

That used to be Bernadette bonding with Maura during the early days of a case. Even after Maura's promotion to lieutenant.

There was silence on the phone, and Bernadette realized Sophie was waiting for her response. "Sorry, Sophie. What did you say?"

"I asked when you were coming home."

"Hopefully in just a few days. But this is my first case in my new job. It might be a little longer."

A sigh. "Fine. I have enough stuff at Dad's to get me through the weekend."

"Thank you, Soph. I know this is sudden."

"I'm used to it." Sophie's voice was icy.

Bernadette licked her lips, thinking of how to stay calm. "I know. And it wasn't as big of a deal when Dad and I were together. But it'll get easier. I promise."

Silence.

"Anyway," Bernadette said, "I love you. I'll call you later." She glanced up; Maura and Curtis were still in serious conversation.

"I gotta go," Sophie said. "See you when you get home."

Three fast beeps told Bernadette that Sophie had hung up.

When she was younger—even two or three years ago— Sophie would end long-distance conversations with her mother by saying, "Hope you catch the bad guys." Bernadette supposed the advent of junior high made Sophie too cool to say things like that now.

Sophie was angry about the breakup—although Bernadette wasn't quite sure who Sophie blamed. She took a deep breath and entered the security office to brief Maura and Curtis.

Chapter Four

"Kymer Henry Thompson," Woodhead read, laying the file on the table next to his Bloody Mary. Two slices of bacon and a skewer of pickled vegetables stuck out the top of the mason jar. "Twenty-five."

"Grad student at Kilbourn Tech," Bernadette said, taking a sip of her diet cola and rearranging her puffy purple coat over the back of her chair. "Getting his Ph.D. in biosciences."

The wood-paneled restaurant interior was right out of a hunting magazine, and the chairs were too hard for Bernadette's taste. But the online reviews had been excellent, and the late afternoon happy hour hadn't deterred Dr. Woodhead from ordering a breakfast cocktail. Maura and Curtis had declined Woodhead's invitation.

Woodhead turned the page in the file to an array of four photos. He peered closer. "Do you see the discoloration around this spot on his upper arm? Is that the needle mark?"

"It is." Bernadette sipped her soda.

"At first glance, this appears to be a simple overdose case. Why did CSAB get called in so quickly?" He turned the page. "Ah, yes, that's right. The M.E. recognized the aquamarine color of the remnants of the ibogaine in the syringe." He looked up. "Have they classified it as a homicide?"

"That's their preliminary call. When have you ever seen a drug user stab themselves in the upper arm like that?" Bernadette shook her head. "The M.E. didn't believe it was self-inflicted."

"I have never encountered a situation in which ibogaine was *injected* to obtain a high." Woodhead stroked his beard. "It would be difficult to remove enough ibogaine from iboga bark to kill a full-grown man. The extracted ibogaine would be unlikely to fit in a single syringe." Woodhead held up the photo to the light. "Tell me, Bernie, where did the killer get this?"

"It's 'Bernadette.'" She drummed her fingers on the sides of her glass thoughtfully. "The first place I would look is the church. They use iboga bark."

"Placing the shredded bark under one's tongue is the common method to achieve the feelings of euphoria and the mild hallucinations that are revered in many of these religious ceremonies." He leaned forward and tapped the edge of his glass, once, twice, three times. "Who converted the ibogaine into liquid form, and how did it get into that syringe?"

Bernadette cleared her throat. "Iboga bark may be uncommon in North America, but ibogaine is used for addiction treatment both in the United States and Mexico. There's a clinic in Baja California that uses bark from the *tabernanthe iboga* shrub. They shred it and the patients ingest it."

"Information easily obtained on the internet," Woodhead said dismissively, stirring his drink. "How many murder cases have you investigated?"

Bernadette shifted in her seat. "I spent most of my career working on money laundering cases. This is my first homicide investigation."

Dr. Woodhead's face was impassive. "Interesting. It must be

hard to get good handlers. Murder is certainly *not* money laundering."

Bernadette felt her face grow hot. "I never said it was."

Woodhead straightened up. "I don't know anywhere ibogaine is used for treatment in the U.S."

"Officially, nowhere," Bernadette said. "In practice—that's another matter."

"How might the church procure iboga bark, then?"

Bernadette leaned back and ran her fingers through her hair. "I worked on taking down a string of clinics in Florida a couple of years ago that ran Norco and OxyContin. They distributed other substances, too, including iboga bark. You can order the seeds online for ten bucks, and it's not technically a schedule 1 narcotic until you extract the ibogaine from the bark. The church could have ordered the bark from a clinic like that, or ordered the seeds online to grow in a greenhouse here. And it would all be above board."

Woodhead plucked a piece of bacon out of his Bloody Mary. "An interesting line of inquiry. We'll tell Curtis to track the church's finances. We can examine property records to ascertain if any church members have greenhouses on their land." He bit a piece off the bacon. "Of course," he said with his mouth full, "you and I shall interrogate the Agios Delphi priest."

Bernadette hoped the interview wouldn't be another opportunity for Woodhead to insult her. She pulled her phone out of her purse and tapped on her email. "Oh—the M.E.'s email came through while we were in the chapel." She tapped and scrolled, then nodded. "Here we go. Cause of death: sudden cardiac event. Not a heart attack." She scrolled and grunted. "And nothing congenital."

"I seem to recall case reports where ibogaine resulted in cardiac arrest."

"It's not common, but patients have reported serious heart problems with ibogaine."

Dr. Woodhead nodded. "But surely the person who prepared this couldn't be aware of the effect it would have on the victim. It affects such a low percentage of people—"

Bernadette drew in her breath through her teeth.

"What is it?"

"It says here the remaining ibogaine in the syringe was at fifty times the usual concentration." She frowned. "That would be enough to kill our victim. It would be enough to kill anyone."

"What is the report referring to with the term 'the usual concentration'?"

"I think it means the ibogaine strength of shredded iboga bark. The kind I saw at the Florida clinic." She scrolled again. "Yes, that's the baseline—just under two percent. Wow. That syringe was full of almost pure ibogaine."

He cocked his head. "What reason would anyone have to create ibogaine that concentrated?"

Bernadette put her phone back in her purse. "I don't know. I think a church would use the bark in its natural form. They wouldn't try to extract ibogaine from the iboga bark at all."

Woodhead took a drink of the Bloody Mary, set it down on the table, stared at it for a moment, then pulled a sweet pickle off the skewer. "An ugly pickle if I've ever seen one," he murmured.

"Most pickles are ugly," Bernadette said. "Okay, for that concentration of ib—"

"You are a pickle of a particularly grotesque countenance," Dr. Woodhead interrupted, holding the pickle in front of his face. "Thou art a boil, a plague sore, an embossed carbuncle."

Another *King Lear* reference. The letter from Martin was

instructive, that was certain. "People are eating, Dr. Woodhead."

He bit half the pickle off and dropped the rest of it into his drink, then raised his eyes to Bernadette. "There must be another source for the ibogaine," Woodhead said.

"Then let's find it." Bernadette leafed through the file. "Okay—Thompson left a message with the campus police the night before he died."

"Yes." Woodhead blinked. "I read that. He said he suspected that a theft would occur in the lab."

Bernadette nodded. "But he didn't specify when, and the recording was cut short." She continued to read. "It doesn't say whether or not he mentioned it at work the next day."

"If he feared for his life, surely we would have heard about it."

"That's a recording I'd like to listen to." Bernadette turned the page. "I don't have any interview notes with people from the lab."

"We'll ask Detective Dunn for them tomorrow." Woodhead opened the folder again and stared at the photo, a blowup of the discoloration of Kymer Thompson's arm. He muttered to himself.

"I missed that, Doctor."

"I said, I need to further research Agios Delphi. See if the religion advocates the use of ibogaine in addition to iboga bark —or for that matter, the use of any injected hallucinogens. Detective Dunn seems convinced of their deceit and trickery." He shook his head. "It's not a common belief system. I'd be surprised if much academic documentation exists on Agios Delphi at all, never mind their use of ibogaine."

Bernadette sipped her soda. "I'd never heard of the religion before."

Woodhead took his phone out of his pocket and tapped a

few times, then handed the phone across the table. "This is all I was able to find."

Bernadette read the article stub.

Agios Delphi is a religion of unknown but probably North American origin, first appearing in records in the late 1990s. It is characterized by belief in God, delivered through the testimony and teachings of the Protestant martyr Anne Askew. The concept of spiritual enlightenment, known as the Anchor of Delphi, can be achieved through an "enhanced meditation process." Some members use substances to attempt to enhance their meditation, though those substances vary greatly from church to church, with some locations eschewing hallucinogens and some going without enhancement altogether.

Practitioners of the religion call themselves and each other *Delphinians*.

The highest concentration of Delphinians is in Baja California, Mexico; and in Minnesota and New Mexico, United States. Social anthropologists estimate roughly 10,000 practitioners worldwide, with about 75% of those residing in the United States.

"Only ten thousand practitioners, yet we come across one of the dead ones." Woodhead stirred his Bloody Mary with the skewer of pickled vegetables then took three noisy, large gulps.

Bernadette frowned as Woodhead set his drink down. "It's almost five, Doctor. We've still got a full day's work ahead of us. We should go."

Woodhead winked. "It's fine, Bernie. Three grams of protein in the bacon, and a full two servings of vegetables—four with the tomato juice."

"*Bernadette*," Bernadette said. She took another sip of her soda to stop herself from commenting on his drinking during the workday. Instead: "Should we go see the professor?"

Woodhead took the vegetable skewer out of his Bloody Mary, a chunk of jicama on the end. He grabbed it between his teeth and pulled it off, then chewed it with his mouth open. He pointed the skewer at Bernadette. "We must take the time to gather our wits about us. A few moments of respite can freshen the mind."

"We have a murder to solve." She turned the soda glass around and around. "I know there aren't cameras in the chapel," she said, "but we should see if there are cameras at the Freshie."

"Your demeanor surprises me." Woodhead returned the skewer to his drink. "Usually, my handlers try to establish a rapport with me."

"I'd rather see if we can get footage from ATMs or any CCTV recordings from businesses in the ten blocks between the Freshie and the chapel from Monday night."

Woodhead waved his hand over the table. "For example, previous handlers would use social situations like this to inform me how important trust is between us."

"First of all," Bernadette said, "I'm an—" She bit her tongue; she almost said *agent*. "A case analyst, not a handler. Second of all, trust might be important between us, but you need to know that I'm committed to solving this case and that I have your back. Discussing ways to find the killer will build a better relationship than making small talk over cocktails."

"Ah—I see where you're going with this. Next you'll tell me I'm a valuable part of the CSAB team."

"You don't need me to tell you that."

There was silence between them for a moment.

Woodhead took a long drink and set the empty glass down. "So," Woodhead finally said, "what do you want to talk about next? My TV show? My reputation for burning through handlers?"

Bernadette weighed her options. She wanted to interview the people from Thompson's life, but Woodhead obviously had a point he wanted to make first. "You *have* been through quite a few case analysts in the last five years."

Woodhead put his elbows on the table. "My solve rate is high. I'm sure it's easy for my handlers to get promoted once they've worked a few cases with me." He nodded. "Take Marty, for example. To what position did he get promoted?"

"Martin quit CSAB. Walked into Maura's office after your last assignment together and resigned on the spot." In fact, Martin had given Maura Stevenson an ultimatum: either fire Woodhead or accept Martin's resignation. But she wouldn't tell Woodhead that.

"I'm sorry to hear it," Woodhead said, sitting back. "I can, admittedly, be demanding, but these cases are unusual, and therefore I have high expectations of my handlers." He clicked his tongue. "Though I must say, I'd told Lieutenant Stevenson that I prefer not to work with women."

Bernadette blinked. "You told Maura *what*?"

"You might as well know now. I find women—distracting."

She bristled. "Listen, *Doctor*, I don't know what year you think this is—"

Woodhead pointed to his nose. "Distracting. Your perfume is Grace de Champagne, though why the Delicéuse Perfumery named it that, I have no idea. It's clearly got stronger hints of vanilla and oak than of good champagne—it should smell like limestone and freshly-baked bread, or even pears or apples."

"I'm not wearing perfume today." Bernadette was flummoxed; Grace de Champagne was her usual scent.

Woodhead waved his hand dismissively. "The residual oils have embedded into your clothing. Besides, that Kebble Proust

Coconut Moisturizer you apply to your face has a strong cocoa butter scent, which conflicts with the oak. Further, the Dark Sun liquid soap you used this morning is all citrus and clove, which combats the other scents."

"Are you finished?"

"Dark Sun, by the way, has the same chemical makeup and almost the exact scent profile as Barker's Fresh Spring, which is ten dollars cheaper per bottle. It's lighter on the clove, too, which won't browbeat your perfume."

"Maybe I like the clove."

The doctor sniffed. "You can't *tell* the difference. The soap I can forgive, especially if you're traveling, but you should never pair a perfume like Grace de Champagne with that moisturizer to begin with. The patchouli alcohol and the alpha-bulnesene in the—"

Bernadette held up her hands. "Men can use cologne and aftershave and deodorant soap and hair products. I bet many of them are equally... *distracting*."

"Some men," Dr. Woodhead said. "But not the ones who have been my handlers. And when I've told them to leave off their cologne or aftershave, they're happy to comply. My nose is, after all, why CSAB values me as highly as they do."

This was it. They'd been working together less than half a day, and already he was pushing her buttons, insulting women, insulting her. Staying just close enough to the line for her to think maybe pushing back wouldn't be worth it. "Duly noted," Bernadette said evenly.

She took another sip of her soda and had to force it down. No. This wouldn't do. She had to push back, or at least draw a line in the sand. "Dr. Woodhead?"

"Yes?"

"Have you asked the women who disrupt your olfactory senses to leave off their perfume?"

"I have. It insults them."

Bernadette leaned forward. "It's possible that your tone and your attitude are the problem, not what you're asking them to do."

Woodhead scowled. "My attitude?"

"You've already made it very clear to me that you think I'll be confrontational if you ask me to stop using scented items in my morning routine."

"I haven't said anything of the sort."

"You've made the comment about women in general. You're assuming I'll be insulted."

"You won't be?"

She sat back and crossed her arms, mirroring him.

"You have to ask me nicely. Not condescendingly. And use my name correctly."

Woodhead's brow wrinkled.

"You know exactly what I mean. My name is Bernadette. You haven't called me that once."

"I prefer calling you 'Bernie.'"

"'Bernie' is a corpse from a terrible 1980s buddy comedy," said Bernadette. "I had to go through that humiliation in school. I don't want to hear any quotes from that movie under anyone's breath when investigating cases."

Woodhead's upper lip curled slightly. "I had a horrific ex-girlfriend at university named Bernadette. *I* don't wish to remember her every time I speak your name."

"Then call me 'Becker.' I don't call you 'Kep' and I *certainly* don't call you 'Woody.'"

Dr. Woodhead winced.

"We can keep this investigation professional," Bernadette continued. "Professional and unscented. Otherwise, I'll be making a lot of *Toy Story* jokes at your expense."

Woodhead shifted in his seat. "Ms. Becker," he said, as if

chewing the words, "I'd greatly appreciate it if you would elimi-nate scented soaps, skin care products, and perfumes when we are working together."

Bernadette stared at him. The seconds ticked by.

"Please," Woodhead finished.

"As long as I can expense unscented items, I'm fine with making changes during our investigations."

Woodhead's jaw dropped open, then snapped shut as he reached for his Bloody Mary. "Marty never gave me problems like this." He brought the drink to his lips before he realized it was empty.

He should have. He could have avoided a nervous breakdown.

Bernadette's phone rang in her purse. The screen said *Barlow Finnegan*. She rolled her eyes. "It's my ex. I've got to take this. Be right back."

Bernadette rose from the table, answering the call as she walked out of the restaurant onto the frigid sidewalk. "Hi, Barlow."

"Hi, Bernadette. Sophie needed me to pick up her purple pullover and her—uh, Dominic Mannequin flats. I'm in her bedroom, and I have no idea where they are."

"The pullover is on the top shelf of her closet with her other sweaters. And it's Dominic *Milano*. Those are the gray two-tone shoes that look a little like the ballet flats she wore last year." Bernadette gathered her long hair and draped it over the front of her left shoulder; the ends were cold. "I'd suggest trying her shoe rack, but she doesn't put them away."

The sound of rustling. "Okay, I've got the pullover. And—" The soft *thump* of a closet door ending its slide against the closet jamb. "Well, well, Ms. Becker, you don't know your daughter as well as you think."

"What's that supposed to mean?"

"The Dominic Milano shoes are in the shoe rack. She put them away."

Bernadette said nothing.

Barlow's voice was gentle. "I'm not attacking you, Bernadette."

She snorted. "You're certainly—" The words caught in her throat. She was angry. She had every right to be angry. The CSAB training instructor—*her* trainer for the last year—was now Barlow's new girlfriend. The worst of it was, Bernadette was stronger and more fit; she could take Lisa in a fight.

But sometimes youthful exuberance matters a lot more. And, she supposed, giving him the attention that she hadn't. Not for a while.

The silence stretched between them, Bernadette on the defensive as if Barlow was daring her to finish the sentence.

"I'm sorry." Bernadette cleared her throat. "It's five o'clock. When are you picking up Sophie?"

"It's six o'clock."

Right. Time zones.

"And Sophie's having dinner over at Olivia's."

"Give you and Lisa a chance to have a romantic evening." The words were out of her mouth before Bernadette could stop them.

"I talked to Olivia's mother," Barlow said, as if Bernadette hadn't said anything. "Picking her up at seven thirty tonight. And I can drop her at school, no problem."

"You don't have an early class?"

"Not this semester." The sound of a zipper—a tote bag or small suitcase, maybe. "Thanks for helping me find those things. I'll have Sophie call you before bed."

Bernadette blinked. "Uh—thanks."

Barlow ended the call. She stared at her phone for a moment, then looked up, getting her bearings—

And saw the IT person—the one who she'd met in front of the chapel—walk quickly down the sidewalk on the other side of the street.

What was his name? Nick something. He carried a large black tote in each hand; they looked heavy.

Maybe he could answer her questions about security cameras at the Freshie—save her some time in the morning. And she could get things back on track with him. Apologize if she had to.

She glanced up and down Ninth Street, then hurried across, glimpsing Nick as he turned the corner onto Highland Avenue. He was more than a block ahead of her.

He was heading toward the river—maybe toward the Freshie? Or was there another off-campus facility he needed to service?

"Nick!" she called, but he quickened his pace.

He crossed Eighth into a sea of parking garages. The basketball arena loomed ahead. Was that where he was headed?

"Nick!" Bernadette considered breaking into a run. She was sure she could catch up with him in a moment or two, but she'd already scared him off earlier.

No response. Nick moved both bags to one hand, then pulled his phone out of his pocket and held it to his ear.

"Nick!" Louder this time.

He was nearly running now, and Bernadette jogged to keep him in her sights. She hadn't taken her puffy coat when she took the call from Barlow, and her fingers were starting to lose feeling. Bernadette glanced up—Nick began to run across Sixth Street as the flashing red hand warned pedestrians not to enter the crosswalk.

"Nick!"

She stopped at the corner at the red light and watched,

heart sinking, as Nick was swallowed up by a mass of people walking by the arena. She craned her neck but couldn't see—

An engine revved hard.

She turned her head—a light blue van bore down on her. Coming fast.

Onto the sidewalk.

She dove out of the way and landed in a slushy pile of snow.

Tires squealed as the van jumped the corner—almost taking out the bus stop sign—right where she'd been standing, then squealed down Highland Avenue.

Chapter Five

Bernadette, heart pounding, scrambled to her feet, the salt on the concrete crackling under her boots.

License plate? Could she see the license plate?

No. Too far away.

She looked around, brushing the snow from her trousers. Other pedestrians stood on the sidewalk, but they'd been at least twenty feet away.

"Did anyone get the plate number?" she shouted.

No answer.

Her breaths came in short, quick bursts. She took a few steps down the sidewalk, back and forth, until she got herself back under control. Another deep breath.

Only four blocks back to the restaurant.

She was aware of everything: her shoes clomping on the ground, her breaths tinny and hollow in the cold early evening air, the people passing, laughing—or hands deep in the pockets of their jackets, their faces wrapped in scarves.

She was sweating lightly when she opened the door to the restaurant and took her seat.

Woodhead took another bite from the vegetable skewer. "That was your ex-husband?"

Bernadette felt the blood rush back into her fingers. "Well—soon-to-be ex-husband, anyway."

"Did you have a fight?"

Bernadette glared at him.

"It's none of my business. You were gone a long time. I thought we were trying to establish a rapport."

"And I thought we were trying to solve a case." She glanced across the table. "I saw the IT guy walking toward the river. He was carrying a couple of tote bags."

"What IT guy? Curtis?"

"No, no, the IT worker from Kilbourn Tech. The one who's in charge of all the facilities that aren't part of the main campus."

Woodhead's eyes showed no recognition.

"Oh, that's right. You were still in the chapel. Anyway, I followed him."

"For what purpose?"

"I thought he could save us some time. Give us some information on the tech situation at the Freshie. Maybe we could get video footage or figure out what physical security systems they have."

"What did he say?"

"Nothing. I lost him." Bernadette opened her mouth to tell Woodhead about the van that almost careened into her, but the words died on her tongue. She cleared her throat. "You're finished?"

He pushed the empty glass away. "I am."

"Good." She picked up her folder. "Who do we interview first? The supervisor at his worldly job, or the leader of his spiritual family?"

"We must prioritize the murder weapon. Let's follow the iboga bark."

"That would be the priest. Vivian Roundhouse." She stood. "Let's go."

⁂

BERNADETTE PILOTED THE BLACK SUV THROUGH THE gentle, dark, snow-covered turns of Lincoln Memorial Highway for fifteen minutes, passing a sign that read *Welcome to Whitefish Bay,* then turned left into a subdivision. Dr. Woodhead looked out of the window at the large two- and three-story homes lining the streets. "The priest lives out here?" he asked.

"It sure looks like it."

"I thought religious leaders were supposed to be less ostentatious."

Bernadette guffawed.

"Does Vivian Roundhouse have some sort of television deal?"

"You had a TV deal, Doctor. Do you live in a house like one of these?"

Woodhead was silent.

"And she's got a Mercedes in her driveway." Bernadette slowed in front of a large three-story house with Roman-style pillars adorning the front porch. "Maybe she has a greenhouse in her backyard, too."

She put the SUV in park and pulled down the visor to check her makeup as Woodhead got out. She hadn't used much that morning, and her large hazel eyes had bags under them—not too surprising after her long day. Her white skin was paler than usual—she hadn't seen the sun most of the winter—and her freckles had even faded. Her dark brown hair was flat from the cold, dry air. She ran her hands through it, trying to get her hair to wake up, then scrunched up her face, pushed up the visor, and got out of the SUV.

Woodhead stepped ankle-deep into a mound of snow at the curb. He shook his boot off and joined Bernadette at the shoveled driveway, where they walked to the large front door between the largest, most elegant of the columns. They stood out of the light yet frigid wind, under the overhang.

Bernadette reached out and rang the doorbell, grabbing her identification out of her purse.

After a moment, the door opened, revealing a woman in her early fifties, about a decade older than Bernadette. The woman had rosy, full cheeks in contrast to her pale skin. She stood about five foot three. Her black hair was pulled back into a casual ponytail, but her tan cashmere sweater and her shiny black trousers looked expensive. She wore light brown sheepskin slippers, and she smiled while her eyes were curious.

"Can I help you?" The woman's eyes drifted to the identification badge Bernadette was holding.

"Vivian Roundhouse?" Bernadette asked.

"Yes?"

"My name is Bernadette Becker from the Controlled Substance Analysis Bureau. This is my colleague, Dr. Kep Woodhead."

A look of confusion darkened Roundhouse's face. "The Controlled Substance—"

"I'm sorry," Bernadette said carefully, "but have you talked to the police in the last twenty-four hours?"

Her smile fell. "I—I, no. Is it Allan? Did something happen to him?"

Apparently Roundhouse hadn't heard of Kymer Thompson's death, and Bernadette hadn't checked with Detective Dunn before coming. She'd never had to tell an interviewee that someone close to them was dead. Yes, it was a member of her church, and not, for example, this Allan person—a husband or son, if she had to guess—but it might still be difficult. For now, though, Bernadette had the advantage: she could question Roundhouse without telling her about Thompson's death. Perhaps the priest would slip and let more out than she wanted.

She opened her mouth and took a deep breath.

"I'm sorry to inform you that one of the members of your church passed away unexpectedly last night," Woodhead said, clasping his hands in front of him.

Bernadette shot a withering gaze at Woodhead, who didn't notice.

He sallied on. "May we come in and ask you some questions?"

"I—" Roundhouse started, then closed her mouth. "No. I'm afraid this isn't a good time. The church has its service tonight, you see—"

"Ah," Woodhead said, "that might be a problem. I'm flummoxed, quite frankly, that no one has informed you. The body was found in the chapel, and I'm afraid it's an active crime scene. You may not be able to hold your service this evening."

"What?" Roundhouse raised her voice. "I can't believe this —under whose authority?"

"The Milwaukee Police Department," Bernadette said, cutting in. "They haven't attempted to contact you?"

"I was... out," Roundhouse said. "I took a walk, as I often do, before I have our service. Clear my head, and all that."

"I expect," Dr. Woodhead said, leaning forward on his toes, "that it would have been quite a cold walk."

"I love the cold," Roundhouse said. "Invigorating. Gets the blood going."

"Where did you walk?" Bernadette asked.

"My normal route," Roundhouse said. "I go out to Big Bay

Park then walk along the shore." She cleared her throat. "I went past the high school and then came home."

"You neglected to mention the part where you stopped at Donut Monster," a woman said from the other room, followed by the clicking of heels on tile. "Where are your manners, Viv? Invite the agents in from the cold."

"Well, I—"

The other woman came into view behind Roundhouse. About five feet tall and Asian, with a wide face and kind, glittering eyes, she pulled the front door open more and motioned for them to enter the house. "I've put the kettle on."

A hot drink might pop the bad attitude out of him. Bernadette entered first, in front of Dr. Woodhead, and the shorter woman turned and led them through an open foyer and into the kitchen.

"I'm Suzanne Thao, by the way."

"Bernadette Becker. Do you live here?"

Thao chuckled. "Heavens no. Viv and I are friends. I stopped by after Viv finished her afternoon walk." She smiled.

The kitchen was light and airy, with granite countertops and stainless-steel appliances. On the counter next to the sink, an electric teakettle quietly rumbled.

"We're a small congregation," Roundhouse said. "I shudder to think who might have died."

Bernadette pounced. "Actually, I wondered if you could tell us where you w—"

"Kymer Thompson," Woodhead said.

"Kymer Thompson what?" Roundhouse asked.

"He was the body found in the chapel."

Roundhouse gasped and grabbed the counter for support. "No—Tommy?" The shorter woman hurried around the kitchen island and placed a concerned hand on Roundhouse's back.

Woodhead stared at the large stainless-steel range behind

the priest. "We understand he was fairly high up in your church."

"He was," Thao said, rubbing Roundhouse's back gently. "Very devout."

Woodhead leaned forward. "When was the last time you saw Mr. Thompson?"

"Oh—last week." Roundhouse's voice trembled.

"Last week?"

"Yes." The priest swallowed hard and let go of the counter. "He came to the service last Tuesday, but I haven't seen him since. He's quite busy at work and with his graduate classes."

"I see." Bernadette turned to look at Dr. Woodhead, who was in the breakfast nook, taking large inhalations through his nose.

"He was committed to the church," Roundhouse said. "He often helped set up the service. Brought some of the incense from time to time."

"Was there—" Bernadette stopped herself. No—it wasn't time to go right into the ibogaine yet. "Is there some significance to Anne Askew?"

"To Delphinians, you mean? Or to Tommy in particular?"

"To Tommy in particular," Bernadette said, then looked around. "You're all the way up here in Whitefish Bay, leading one of the few religious—uh—organizations that use the Askew chapel. Did Tommy have a particular affinity for her?"

"Agios Delphi considers Anne Askew to be a prophet," Roundhouse said, a touch of defiance in her voice. "She sacrificed herself and went through a living hell for what she believed in. The king had her tortured on the rack, which destroyed her body so badly, she couldn't even sit in a chair. My members *all* have a particular affinity for her."

Bernadette rubbed her forehead. If Thompson's body in the rack position was somehow uniquely significant to

Tommy, she would have a hard time getting it out of Roundhouse.

Roundhouse continued, "So strong was her belief in the power of the individual to experience the divine without—"

"Yes—yes, I've read the literature," Woodhead interrupted. "The rack is significant, then? As significant as, say, the cross is in mainstream Christian denominations?"

Roundhouse bristled. "No one wears a miniature rack on a chain around their neck if that's what you mean. If you insist on insult—"

"I'm sorry," Bernadette said, holding up her hands. "I assure you—it's out of ignorance, not malice. Any religious symbolism surrounding Mr. Thompson's death might help us figure out what happened."

Roundhouse covered her face with her hands and her shoulders began to shake. Thao draped an arm around her shoulders and the priest turned toward Thao, hiding her face.

Bernadette stood awkwardly for a moment.

Roundhouse sniffled and broke from Thao. "My apologies."

"I understand."

"Tommy was a rock," she said. "He was the connection who brought younger people into the church. We aren't a large group, but he was the one who found the rule allowing us to have services in the chapel to begin with." She took a breath and shuddered. "I—I'm not sure what we'll do without him." She wiped her eyes with the back of her hand. "Look, I don't know what religious significance there could possibly be to Tommy's death."

Bernadette chose her words carefully. "Do you perform any ceremonies in the chapel?"

"Certainly."

"What do those entail?"

Roundhouse sighed. "We have several. One where members

join and dedicate themselves to God. A blessing ceremony. We believe Anne Askew liked ritual."

"Does Agios Delphi perform a death ritual?" Woodhead asked.

Roundhouse put her hands on her hips. "A ceremony not unlike a wake or a memorial service. We call it an anchor ceremony. Calling it a death ritual sounds pagan."

"What makes Anne Askew such an important prophet?" Bernadette asked.

"She viewed the world as if it were at war with the spirit." Roundhouse glowered. "Have you not read that Askew had visions of the future?"

"I guess not."

"Her vision encompassed all the senses. Not merely seeing the future, but getting sounds, smells, tastes as well."

"Smells?" Bernadette shot a furtive glance at Woodhead, but he was back to wandering the large open kitchen, sniffing.

"That's correct," Roundhouse said. "She once smelled burning flesh, thus prophesying her own death when she was burned at the stake."

"And your group tries to duplicate her visions," Woodhead said from the kitchen. "Iboga bark, if I'm not mistaken."

Bernadette shook her head. In money laundering cases, she always let the interviewee take the lead. Not reveal what she already knew or what the evidence was. But Woodhead—a much more experienced investigator of homicides—had ignored all that. Immediately put the cards on the table. Iboga bark. Now Roundhouse knew that CSAB realized drugs were involved.

Suzanne Thao and Vivian Roundhouse stared at each other, then Thao nodded. "Yes. We believe that during her lifetime, divine spirits placed the sacred iboga bark in Askew's mouth, allowing the visions to come to fruition."

Roundhouse drew herself to her full height. "*I saw a royal throne where Justice should have sit, but in her stead was one of moody cruel wit.*"

Bernadette looked Roundhouse in the eyes. "Was that written by Anne Askew?"

"Her ballad, written in prison. We use many parts of her poems and songs in our ceremonies."

"And you believe that these visions—like Justice on this royal throne—uh, came to fruition due to Askew's use of iboga bark?"

Woodhead nodded. "Akin to a reverse eucharist, but with hallucinogens."

"That's reductive," Roundhouse said, her nostrils flaring. "And a little insulting. The iboga bark isn't magic. Askew had a family in her congregation from West Africa. They brought the sacred iboga bark and Askew used it to grow closer to God."

Bernadette nodded.

"I'd like to show you some pictures from the crime scene," Woodhead said.

Bernadette's head snapped up. "Doctor—that's not—"

He looked over the top of his glasses at her. "Who better than the Delphinian priest to tell us what the photos might mean?"

"It's not—" Bernadette started.

"I apologize if these are difficult for you to view," Woodhead continued, "but the positioning of Mr. Thompson's body— especially now that we know how Anne Askew was tortured— seems to be symbolic."

"I can't let you show Viv those pictures." Suzanne Thao stepped around the kitchen island between Dr. Woodhead and Vivian Roundhouse. "She's been through enough as it is."

"No, no, Suzanne," Roundhouse said, "if Kymer Thompson's

body was found in the Askew chapel and it has anything to do with Agios Delphi, we need to know. *I* need to know."

Dr. Woodhead walked toward the kitchen island, placing the open folder on it. He turned a few sheets, then came upon a paper with a photo array. He looked up grimly at Vivian Roundhouse, nodded almost imperceptibly, then stepped back next to Bernadette.

Roundhouse's face paled as she turned toward the island. Palms flat on either side of the folder, she leaned forward, her shoulders tense.

"Photos 3A through 3N," Dr. Woodhead said.

Bernadette nodded—a young man on his back, wrists together above his head, ankles together, straight below his torso.

"That's the position of the rack," Roundhouse mumbled.

"The same position in which Anne Askew was tortured," Woodhead said. "What does it mean?"

"What does it mean?" Roundhouse repeated.

"Forgive me for being crude, but sometimes bodies are found with their tongues cut out because they've given the names of their higher-ups to the authorities, for example. Perhaps the position of the rack has similar import."

Roundhouse closed the folder, looked up at Woodhead, and blinked. "I don't understand what you're implying."

"Have other Delphinians died like this? Or been buried in this position?"

Roundhouse shook her head. "It's not a position for burial."

"But," Woodhead pressed, "whoever did this knew how significant Anne Askew is for Agios Delphi. This cannot be coincidence."

Suzanne Thao stepped to the island and opened the folder to the photos.

After a moment, she shook her head. "I don't know who

would do this. We discuss the torture that Anne Askew went through in our services, but we don't put anyone in that position in life *or* death."

"Is it possible," Bernadette mused, "that the killer was from another religion and was calling Mr. Thompson a heretic?"

Thao and Roundhouse glanced at each other nervously.

"I don't think so," Roundhouse said. "Delphinians find this position worthy of Anne Askew. While I haven't seen it before, I believe this would tell the world that Agios Delphi is true and that this man was a deserving soul. This wouldn't be a mark of heresy."

"Let's turn our attention to the injection site in Mr. Thompson's arm," Woodhead said. "Does this needle spot have significance?"

"We don't do any of that," Thao said icily.

"Someone did," Woodhead said. "Our preliminary reports suggest that the poison that killed him was ibogaine."

Roundhouse wrinkled her brow.

"The hallucinogenic ingredient in iboga bark," Bernadette said. "Quite concentrated, in fact."

"Concentrated?"

"That's right," Woodhead said. "Are you familiar with any type of iboga bark concentrate?"

Roundhouse's eyes went wide. "We—there are some—"

"Stop talking," Suzanne Thao murmured to Roundhouse, then turned to Woodhead. "I don't think Vivian will be answering that question."

"We don't care about the religious uses of—" Bernadette began.

"Planting the seeds of *tabarnanthe iboga* is legal," Thao said. "Owning and cultivating the plants are legal. But the legal gray area comes from extracting ibogaine from the bark. Ibogaine is an illegal drug."

"That's correct," Bernadette said.

"Chewing on the bark isn't against the law," Thao said, "at least according to the way we interpret *Gilman v. Minnesota.* Technically, there's never a time where any illegal drug is in our possession."

Bernadette nodded. That's how CSAB interpreted the *Gilman* decision too. "You know your law on iboga bark."

"Which means I also know that extracted ibogaine has no waivers for religious use." Thao laid a hand on Roundhouse's shoulder. "Vivian believes strongly in getting closer to God, but she hasn't used anything illegal in our religious ceremonies."

Roundhouse scowled.

"I realize that you both are from the Controlled Substance Analysis Bureau." Thao emphasized the words *Controlled Substance* and squeezed Roundhouse's shoulder when she did so. "And these substances are most certainly what you're interested in."

"We're investigating a homicide," Bernadette said.

"Vivian and I can both assure you that we had nothing to do with his murder."

"Surely," Dr. Woodhead said, "you must have some iboga bark—"

"Again, that's not illegal, and unless you have a warrant, we won't confirm or deny anything."

Bernadette nodded. She was willing to bet money that her original assessment when she pulled up was correct: there was a greenhouse in the backyard full of *tabarnanthe iboga* plants.

"This news has come as a great shock to Vivian," Thao continued. "Mr. Thompson was a valued elder, and now Vivian is emotional and fatigued. I think it's time we concluded this interview."

Roundhouse turned her face to Thao, who nodded. "Right,"

she said, "it's hit me hard. I need to pray for Mr. Thompson, and I respectfully ask that you—uh…"

"Leave," Thao finished.

"Thank you for your time," Bernadette said, walking to the island and picking up the folder.

"One more thing," Woodhead piped up. "Where were you last night between midnight and three A.M.?"

"Here," Thao said evenly, as she crossed her arms.

"I was directing my question to Reverend Roundhouse."

"I was with her," Thao said. "All night."

Woodhead looked from Thao's determined face to Roundhouse's resigned eyes. "Have a good evening, ladies."

Bernadette nudged him with her shoulder, and they walked out the door.

Chapter Six

BERNADETTE SLID BEHIND THE WHEEL OF THE SUV, AND Woodhead got in on the passenger's side. They both kicked the snow off their boots, closed their doors, and stared into space.

Bernadette glanced at him. "Is everything all right?"

"Organizing my thoughts," Woodhead mumbled.

"Do you think the priest did it?"

"I'm withholding judgment until I have more facts." Woodhead put his seat belt on. "I suspect the reverend and her companion wish to avoid the police confiscating their stores of ceremonial iboga bark. Beyond that, I haven't formed an opinion."

"Were you able to, uh, find any clues in the house?"

Woodhead folded his arms and was silent.

Bernadette rolled her eyes as she started the engine. "Smells. Did anything smell strange?"

"I didn't smell the unusual freshwater fish smell that I recognized in the chapel, if that's what you're referring to."

"What about iboga bark?"

"Yes. But faintly—like the smell of marijuana when someone

returns from a concert, not from when someone is growing the plant in the next room."

"I think she's got a greenhouse in the back."

"It's possible. I didn't smell *tabarnanthe iboga* at the front of the house or inside, but it's possible." Woodhead shifted in his seat. "If she had killed Thompson, I'm confident I would have detected trimethylamine oxide in the entryway."

"The fish smell?"

He set his mouth in a line. "In layman's terms, yes."

"And you didn't?"

"No."

Bernadette drove out of the parking spot. "Suzanne Thao said she was with her. But what if they were at Thao's place and not Roundhouse's? She could have cleaned up and changed clothes there. That might have gotten rid of the smell."

Woodhead nodded. "Perhaps." He sank down into his seat and rubbed his chin, his eyes focused on the road.

Bernadette glanced at him, then turned her attention to the road as they drove back toward downtown. The minutes ticked by; the evening had turned dark, and the sky threatened snow. "Anything jumping out at you yet?"

"Why move Thompson's body to the chapel and arrange it in that fashion?"

"There must be significance to the body placement." Bernadette rested her hand on the gearshift. "We need to look at both of those women—Roundhouse and Thao. They're each other's alibi, and they know enough about Anne Askew and the church to put Thompson's body in that position."

"You're making a bold assumption that they're lying," Woodhead said. "You're also focused on a single issue at the murder scene, ignoring others."

"Like what?"

"The murder weapon placed next to Mr. Thompson, for

example. A syringe wouldn't stay in his arm. Why not leave it where he was killed, or better yet, dispose of it? Why place it next to the body?"

Of course. "Because the killer wanted the ibogaine to be found."

Woodhead nodded. "There's no other explanation that makes sense so far. It occurs to me that the killer may be throwing the blame onto someone else."

"Or maybe they're trying to send a message to Agios Delphi," Bernadette said. "After all, the M.E. found traces of ibogaine in the hub and barrel. Since that's technically the same ingredient that causes hallucinations in iboga root, it could be a warning."

"Like what?"

"Like... I don't know. Stay out of our iboga bark supply chain, maybe."

"Iboga bark supply chain? Are you suggesting the existence of an organized ibogaine distribution organization powerful enough to kill someone—yet so small as to be threatened by a fifty-member church in Milwaukee?"

Bernadette was silent.

"Ridiculous," Woodhead said. "Besides, didn't you say that Roundhouse likely had a greenhouse to grow the *tabarnanthe iboga* herself?"

Bernadette pressed her lips together and tightened her grip on the steering wheel. "It's one possibility."

"Turn back toward the river," Woodhead said. "Mr. Thompson spent much of his time at the laboratory. We should visit there again. This time, we may be able to search Mr. Thompson's desk."

"We can go to the Freshie tomorrow."

"I believe we would gain an advantage by going this evening."

"This evening? It's after seven, and I haven't had dinner yet."

"You heard Detective Dunn. The police haven't yet cordoned off the laboratory. If anyone there has evidence to conceal, don't you think they'd be working late or erasing files?"

Bernadette hesitated, then nodded.

The Freshie was off campus, directly to the east on the bank of the Milwaukee River. The SUV turned onto Highland Avenue. The street was nearly deserted, and snow began to fall.

"Looks beautiful," Bernadette said.

Woodhead grunted. "The beauty is only temporary. Within a fortnight, the snow will melt, then freeze again. Then some sodden-witted fool will be late to meet their compatriots for a night of debauchery; he shall tumble to the sidewalk and break a limb, then litigate against the city for two million dollars."

Bernadette rolled her eyes.

"This scenario is not hyperbole." Woodhead folded his arms. "It's happened before. Why do you suppose all the medium-sized American cities are going bankrupt?"

"Do you believe the moon landing was faked, too?"

"My scenario is not a conspiracy theory. It's a loophole in American law designed to fleece the American taxpayer."

Bernadette turned left on Old World Third Street, next to a large brick building with the Kilbourn Tech Freshwater Sciences logo. She pulled into the parking lot, with only a few cars parked at the edges, and a black sedan parked close to the entrance.

Dr. Woodhead got out of the SUV and stared at the sedan, snow piled on the hood and roof. "This car hasn't moved in a while; I'd wager it's been in this very spot all day. I believe it belongs to Professor Jude Lightman."

Bernadette nodded. Thompson's boss was on their interview list, and Woodhead's intuition might very well save them time. She turned her back on the building and looked across

Old World Third. *The Wurst of Milwaukee,* with a neon sign of an anthropomorphic bratwurst, beckoned to her. Her stomach grumbled; she hadn't eaten anything since lunch. She looked up; light streamed from all the Freshie's second-floor windows.

They walked to the building entrance. The sign next to the double glass doors gave no clue as to what was done on each floor. Bernadette pulled with an ungloved hand; the metal door handle was freezing to the touch, but the door didn't budge.

"Closed," Woodhead said.

"We could get Lightman's number from the university directory," Bernadette said. "Maybe he'd let us upstairs."

"I obtained the professor's contact information while we were en route," said Woodhead. He pulled his phone out of his pocket, tapped the screen, and held it to his ear.

"Yes, Professor Lightman, good evening. This is Dr. Kep Woodhead, a special investigator with the Controlled Substances Analysis Bureau." His tone, unlike his dealings with the detective or with Bernadette, was jocular, friendly, fun—as if he were asking Lightman to go out for a beer rather than interview him for a murder that had been committed the night before.

He paused, listening.

"Ah, yes, I'm aware that you've already spoken to the Milwaukee Major Crimes Unit, but we're now leading the investigation. We'd like to talk with you, but it appears the downstairs door is locked."

Another pause.

"I realize it's late." Another pause. "Certainly. We can come to campus tomorrow during one of your classes." A beat or two. "I understand. We'll meet you here, tomorrow afternoon, in front of your co-workers. They'll see you've been visited by two law enforcement groups on two separate occasions, but I'll explain it to them so they won't get the wrong idea."

A short hesitation.

"Of course. Uh huh. Thanks. Yes, the front entrance. See you shortly."

He ended the call and put his phone back in his pocket, and immediately his smile fell away from his face.

"That was—" Bernadette struggled to find the right word. *Masterful* sprang to mind, but given the cautious state of affairs between the two of them, she didn't want to use anything that would sound like she was mocking him. "Very effective," she finished weakly.

He nodded curtly and put his hands in his coat pockets. "I left my scarf in my suitcase in the hotel," he grumbled. "Don't let me forget it tomorrow."

"Oh—uh, sure. Will do."

They stood there in silence, the snow floating down on them. It was getting late in D.C. and Bernadette wondered if Sophie had done all her homework, or if Olivia had been a bad influence. Sophia was supposed to call before bedtime, too.

It felt strange. This was supposed to be Bernadette's week with her daughter.

Bernadette stared at the fading trails of footprints between the front door and the parking lot, and the two fresh tracks she and Woodhead had made. A faint humming from inside the building might have been the elevator. Then from inside the hallway, a man emerged, tall and slender, but with somewhat broad shoulders. Late thirties—a little younger than Bernadette. He had olive skin, as well as curly black hair, ruffled and artfully unkempt, as if he couldn't be bothered to get a haircut.

Ah, one of those. He tries too hard to look like he doesn't try too hard.

As they introduced themselves, Lightman's eyes raked over Bernadette from her boots to her face. He wore thin wire-rimmed glasses, his pullover half-zipped over an Oxford shirt. His khakis weren't pressed, but neither were they unbearably wrinkled.

The whole package: handsome, intelligent. And from the way he carried himself and smiled coyly at Bernadette, he was aware of what his package could offer.

He pushed the door open with one hand. "I don't know where the time went," he said. "I called my wife and said I would be home by six o'clock, and here it is, past seven, and I'm still working."

Dr. Woodhead gave the professor a wide, fake smile. "If you love what you do, you'll never work a day in your life—am I right?" As the two men shook hands, Woodhead clapped Lightman solidly on the left shoulder, as if they were old friends.

"That's the truth," Lightman said, nodding.

"Shall we go up to your lab?"

"Oh—well, it's not exactly in a great state for you to see it."

"I'm sure," Woodhead said, "with all the work you do, getting it cleaned up for company isn't at the top of the list. But I'm afraid we'll need to see Kymer Thompson's work area."

"I don't know," Lightman stuttered. "I'm not sure the university would be okay with that."

"Our lieutenant has coordinated everything with the campus police," Bernadette said. She wondered if Maura had, in fact, okayed this visit, but Lightman seemed like he was stalling.

Woodhead's grin broadened. "Again, we can come back tomorrow—with a proper warrant. Your staff can stay out of the way while we search, can't they?"

Lightman hesitated. "I'll be happy to talk with you down here."

"We're looking into the death of your grad student, Mr.

Lightman," Bernadette said. "Dr. Woodhead might be too polite to say this, but I don't want to wake up a judge."

"Give me a second." Lightman turned and pulled his phone out of his pocket. After speaking on the phone in hushed tones, he turned back around. "I suppose we can do this without a warrant."

"There you go." Woodhead clapped Lightman on the shoulder again. "That's my preference, too; I hate disrupting people's workdays. It's much easier when we can be ourselves around each other, am I right?"

"Are you the only one in the lab tonight, Professor?" Bernadette asked.

Lightman turned, a touch of uncertainty in his gait, and pushed the button for the elevator. "The boss always has to be the last employee to go home, right?" The elevator doors opened, and the three of them stepped inside.

The professor leaned over and pushed "2," and the doors slid closed. The elevator crackled to life, jerking, then whined as the elevator lifted them to the second floor.

"Holy mackerel," Woodhead said. "This elevator sounds like it'll drop us all into the fiery pits of hell." He laughed loudly and turned to Lightman. "Is it always this noisy?"

"Yeah," Lightman said, "this is the way it's always been. I admit, I noticed it too at first, but I guess I'm used to it."

"I tell ya, it sounds like something out of a horror movie." The elevator stopped, the "2" illuminating. The doors opened.

Woodhead screamed at the top of his lungs.

Lightman jumped sideways and banged into the elevator wall.

There was nothing outside the elevator.

Woodhead erupted into peals of laughter.

"Aw man, I'm sorry," Woodhead said, wiping his eyes and catching his breath as his laughter devolved into chuckles, "but the way that elevator creaked and moaned, I would've sworn there'd be an axe murderer standing at the door when it opened."

Lightman stared at Woodhead, unsure how to proceed. Woodhead looked at Bernadette, angling his head toward Lightman.

So this was a game. Had the blunt, forward questioning of Vivian Roundhouse been a game, too? Bernadette felt a headache coming on.

But she could play too.

"What the hell is wrong with you, Dr. Woodhead?" Bernadette shouted, smacking him on the arm. "I've been up since four this morning, and you have been a pain in my ass since the moment we met. This man opened the office up late at night for us, and now you repay his kindness by giving him a heart attack?" She flinched. "Oh—shit—sorry, that's too soon, I know it is, mentioning a heart attack—Mr. Thompson died of heart failure. I apologize for my choice of words."

"It's fine," Lightman muttered.

"You," Bernadette said, pointing in Woodhead's face, "get to do the grunt work for that little escapade. Let's have you start with going through Kymer Thompson's desk. Once you assess any—"

"Hang on, hang on," Lightman said, "Tommy worked with some proprietary material. I'll need to make sure anything confidential is properly secured before you go through his desk."

"Oh," Dr. Woodhead said, hanging his head, "I understand. I'll wait out here, then, while Ms. Becker asks her questions." Woodhead's eyes darted between Bernadette and the professor, and suddenly, Bernadette got it. Lightman didn't want to talk to Woodhead—he wanted to talk to *Bernadette*. Her black suit and puffy coat weren't exactly va-va-voom material, but maybe

Lightman liked his women fit and muscular even under layers of winter clothes.

"Professor," she said brightly, "is there somewhere we can put our jackets?"

"Oh, the coat rack—" Lightman began, then stopped.

"Something wrong?" Bernadette paused, half out of her puffy purple coat.

"It's fine," Lightman said. "I'll take them and hang them on the rack in my office."

"We can do it ourselves."

"Nonsense. I insist."

Lightman took both their coats and opened the door to his office, walked in, and a moment later returned, leaving his door open.

"Thanks, Professor. Is there a conference room where we could talk?"

He turned his head to a darkened room with the blinds pulled. "I, um, don't really see the reason for that. There's no one else in the building. We can talk right here."

"Or in your office, if you prefer."

"Not necessary. This won't take very long, will it?"

Out of the corner of her eye, Bernadette saw Woodhead nod slightly, and then she noticed his chest expanding—he was taking a deep breath, getting a good sample of all the smells of the lab.

"Let's see how these first few questions go," she said. "What was Mr. Thompson working on?"

Lightman smiled sadly. "We all called him Tommy, Ms. Becker."

"Sorry. What was Tommy working on?"

Lightman nodded. "Six years ago, we got funding to research the effects of different freshwater-based organic matter on a variety of cancer cells. The specific target was lung cancer, though it's been expanded to cover breast and bone cancer too."

"God's work," Woodhead cut in, smiling broadly, without a trace of irony.

Lightman tapped his chin thoughtfully. "Yes, I suppose that's how he saw it. You know, he was quite committed to his church. Maybe he felt that the work he was doing here was saving people's bodies and the work he was doing in the church was saving their souls."

"Are you a member of Tommy's church?" Bernadette asked.

"Me?" Lightman scoffed. "I'm afraid I'm too grounded in reality for faith-based systems to hold much sway over the way I look at the world, Ms. Becker."

"But you didn't object to Tommy's religion?"

"On the contrary," Lightman said. "He was one of the few authentic people I knew. Lived what he preached—and that's uncommon. His worldview made him a better scientist."

"How so?"

"He made our big breakthrough."

"He did?"

"One particular combination of organic matter and an existing medication showed promise. It was a combination that Tommy discovered—it's absolutely brilliant, I must say, although the idea of combining organic matter and existing drugs had been proposed before."

"How did Tommy discover the combination? Was he running experiments in a lab?"

"No, no," Lightman said. "He was in charge of maximizing the organic matter."

"'Maximizing the organic matter'?" Woodhead asked. "I'm not familiar with that term. Can you elaborate?"

"I can't reveal the details of the research," Lightman protested. "I'm sorry, but if this got out, the grant money would disappear. We've been working too hard on this, and we're closer than we've ever been to starting a clinical study."

"Oh, I see," Woodhead said. "Your funding came from a pharmaceutical company."

"I'm not at liberty to—"

"Come now, Professor Lightman, I wasn't born yesterday. If funding had been provided by a public agency or a nonprofit, they'd be willing to share this information with law enforcement. Only a pharmaceutical company would be so—"

"I still can't reveal the source."

Bernadette thought for a moment, then reached out and gently touched Jude Lightman's elbow. "What if we sign an NDA? We have a murder to solve. We're not interested in disclosing intellectual property."

"Even if I wanted to," Lightman said, "I couldn't. Not without a subpoena."

Woodhead grunted. "This murder affects you, Professor. If one of your other grad students or employees killed him, you want to know. If Tommy sold your intellectual property to a competitor or on the black market, you want to know. If your research is compromised, you want to know. I suggest you think of ways you can help us move our investigation forward. If you lose your funding because you hid valuable information, you'll have only yourself to blame."

Lightman's head swiveled from Woodhead to Bernadette and back, and finally he sighed. "I can show you some aspects of our research. If anyone asks, I didn't allow this. Follow me."

Lightman strode toward a dark hallway. The overhead lights turned on as he walked through, Bernadette on his heels, Dr. Woodhead behind her a few steps. Bernadette found herself at the top of a metal staircase, and walked down the narrow steps behind the professor, her boots clanking on the steel.

At the bottom of the stairs, Lightman turned to a metal

door, unmarked, punched in a code on the keypad next to the doorframe, and the light turned from red to green. He opened the door, letting Bernadette through first.

Inside the room, eight clear acrylic tanks, each roughly five feet wide, came into view. The tanks lined a single wall, and low blue lights were the only illumination in the room. Bernadette stepped closer; the tanks were half-full of silt or mud. No fish were visible in the tanks.

"Clear tanks? Aren't industrial tanks usually opaque plastic?"

"For breeding and fish farming, yes. But we need to view the ammocoetes."

"The what?"

"Sorry—the scientific name for the larvae. They're in the mud."

Bernadette stepped closer and peered through the acrylic. She thought she saw movement in the silt, like wriggling worms, and a chill went down her spine.

"There they are," Lightman said. "Do you know anything about lampreys?"

Bernadette shook her head. "Only that they're a kind of fish."

"I should have known," Woodhead mumbled. "Lampreys."

"A primitive fish," Lightman replied. "They've been around for millions of years. Before fish evolved jaws."

"Native to the area?"

"These kind are. Silver lampreys. Not the sea lampreys you might have heard about."

"They're parasites," Woodhead said.

"As adults," Lightman quickly added. "Yes, they latch onto other fish and derive nutrients from their blood. But not the ammocoetes. They're fed a special diet of sargassum and gracilaripsis, along with salmon and trout parts."

Bernadette stepped closer to the tank, trying to see the larvae. "You said sargassum and—"

"Gracilaripsis. Types of spirulina algae," Woodhead said. "Those are two types of exceptionally iron-rich algae, if I'm not mistaken. Why the high iron concentration?"

Lightman hesitated. "Well—we, uh, harvest the adult lamprey livers because of the high amino acid content."

Woodhead nodded enthusiastically. "Ferritin."

"Oh—you're familiar with ferritin," Lightman said, his face brightening. "This is a different type of ferritin, though. Tommy discovered it." Lightman began to talk with his hands, his eyes sparkling and animated. "And the livers from this type of lamprey produces more of this type of ferritin than—well, anything else in existence. Feed the ammocoetes an iron-rich diet and we can double the ferritin."

Bernadette rubbed the side of her nose. "Why do you need this specific kind of ferritin?"

"Excellent question." Lightman beamed, in full professor mode. "This particular molecular structure interacts with the— uh, other medication, resulting in a compound that destroys cancer cells without triggering an immune system overreaction."

"Wait—you're saying that you've cured cancer?" Bernadette asked.

"That's a vast oversimplification," Woodhead said.

"Well, not by *that* much," Lightman said. "The test results have exceeded our expectations."

"How soon will it be available?" Bernadette asked.

"It takes a few years for ammocoetes to mature," Lightman said, his face more serious, "and we can't harvest their livers until they become adults. The first batches of ammocoetes are maturing now. With any luck, we'll be in clinical trials in six months, and if the human trials are promising, we could go to market in three years. I expect enormous demand—this could potentially treat the two most common cancers in the world."

"Will there be enough lampreys to meet demand?"

"We think so," Lightman said. "Adult lampreys don't do well in captivity, but there's a coastal section of Lake Michigan north of Port Washington which is ideal for silver lamprey nests. The adults that don't get harvested are released there—and we're stocking the fish they feed on, too."

Bernadette put her hands on her hips. "I thought the Freshwater Science department didn't tinker with ecological systems."

Lightman nodded. "That's why our study is limited to a two-square mile area of the watershed."

"That must cover quite a bit of coastline," Woodhead said.

Lightman crossed his arms. "What's your point?"

"There must have been groups who didn't like what you were doing. Justice for Oceans, for one."

"They were quite vocal at first," Lightman admitted. "They don't like us altering what they say is the natural population of the rivers and streams."

"Any specific threats?" Bernadette asked.

"Not to my knowledge, no. Some obnoxious signs and chanting with a bullhorn a few months ago. But it's toned down over the last few weeks."

Woodhead pressed on. "There's a fishing union protesting as well."

"Yeah, the local one based in Milwaukee. Can't remember the name."

"Lake Shore Piscary Association," Bernadette offered. "Any threats from them?"

"They're losing the public relations war. We're killing an ugly, parasitic fish to make a life-saving medicine. The fishermen are the ones destroying the ecology of all the lakes and rivers here."

"Sounds like a great sound bite for social media," Woodhead said.

"All's fair in love and war," Lightman replied. "Justice for Oceans has one huge disadvantage: lampreys aren't cuddly or cute. Many people find them disgusting. When the public sees pictures of the silver lamprey's open mouth and circular teeth, grotesquely bigger than the rest of its head, or sees one latched onto the side of a river trout or a Chinook salmon, suddenly donations dry up."

"Sounds like the university's PR people trained you well," Woodhead said.

"This area of study—the lamprey livers, the high-iron amino acids—that was all Kymer Thompson's idea?" Bernadette asked.

"The whole team contributed, but yes, Tommy first had the idea of combining the amino acids with ibogaine to create—"

"With *what*?" she interrupted as her ears perked up.

Lightman closed his eyes and swore under his breath.

"*Ibogaine?*"

"Forget I said anything. That's one of the pieces of intellectual property—"

"Ibogaine is what killed Tommy, Professor," Bernadette said. "Intellectual property or not, we need to know about the murder weapon. Do you keep ibogaine here on site?"

Lightman's eyes darted back and forth between Woodhead and Bernadette, and he finally slumped his shoulders in defeat. "Yes. We have ibogaine here. We based our grant application on a study from the University of Montreal a few years ago about how animal proteins change the properties of benzos."

"Benzos?" Bernadette said. "You were experimenting with medications like Valium?"

"Valium is in the class of benzodiazepines, yes. We didn't use that medication specifically."

"How did Kymer Thompson come up with the idea to use ibogaine?"

Lightman shifted his feet.

Bernadette took a step closer. "We know he's a member of the Agios Delphi church, which uses iboga bark in their rituals. Did Thompson bring iboga bark one day to try it out?"

"I—" The professor straightened up. "He didn't explain why he suggested it but adding ibogaine to the study didn't add much to the cost. We tried different combinations. Benzos—and ibogaine—applied to various organic freshwater assets."

"Assets? You mean fish livers."

"There were many other organisms in our original experiments," Lightman said.

"How often are people down in the aquarium?" Woodhead asked.

"The tank rooms? Quite often. We take water samples. We feed the ammocoetes four times a day. We try to mimic the sun as if they were still in the lake, and of course there's a continuous wash of plankton and algae, so we space it out."

"And what about the ibogaine?"

"The ibogaine?"

"It's been illegal for purchase or distribution in the United States for decades, Professor. How did you get ahold of it?"

"Illegal?" He cocked his head. "No. What we have isn't illegal."

"I assure you, it is." Bernadette paused. "Schedule 1 controlled substances have strict physical control requirements, Professor. Vaults or safes. Alarm systems. Surely you know all this." She leaned forward. "You must have signed off on it. You're responsible for making sure that any ibogaine is carefully audited."

"Ah," Professor Lightman said. "I see where the miscommunication is." He laced his fingers behind his head. "Technically, what we have isn't ibogaine."

Bernadette folded her arms.

"Ibogaine is narrowly defined by the government," Lightman continued. "Our substance is synthetically modified from a different iboga alkaloid than the ones listed in the official definition of ibogaine. It's got almost the same molecular structure, but not the same family tree—quite literally."

"You've found a loophole."

"We've found a way to keep our research legal and save the university hundreds of thousands of dollars in storage and compliance costs. Plus, we might save millions of lives." Lightman locked eyes with Bernadette. "Come on, Agent Becker. Some bureaucrat convinced Richard Nixon half a century ago that ibogaine was as dangerous as cocaine and ecstasy. Anyone who reads the studies knows that's not true—it can successfully treat alcoholism and heroin addiction. Trust me, no one is breaking into our stash of chemically altered ibogaine to get high."

Bernadette tilted her head. "Except that's what killed Kymer Thompson."

Lightman screwed up his face. "If Tommy had been killed with drain cleaner, would the feds show up at my door asking how I unclog my kitchen sink?"

"The fact is," Bernadette said, "someone injected ibogaine—the kind that's heavily concentrated, like your synthetic loophole ibogaine—into Kymer Thompson and murdered him. We'll need the names of everyone who had access to your ibogaine supply, vault or no."

Lightman wrinkled his nose. "I believe that crosses the line. We'll need a subpoena for that."

Woodhead was staring at the ammocoetes in the tank. "Professor Lightman," he said, "let's get back to who could have motive to kill your top graduate student in this program."

Lightman nodded.

"You said Justice for Oceans hadn't attempted intimidation tactics. But you failed to provide an answer to whether the Piscary Association issued threats."

Lightman looked down at the floor. The pale blue lights above the tanks shone through the water, making shadows of waves on the concrete.

Finally, Lightman sighed. "I've got some friends in that group, and I know what fishing means to this community. I wouldn't have authorized using that area as a spawning zone for silver lampreys if I'd thought we'd disrupt the local fishing industry."

"But some members of the group disagree."

Lightman nodded. "The president of the organization made a speech at the last meeting about how we can't do this to their livelihoods, and he said we'd be sorry if we continued."

Bernadette frowned. "You'd be sorry?"

"Well—I think his exact words were, 'No one can mess around with our fishing lanes.' They'd made up these T-shirts —*Go for the gold, say no to silver,* with a picture of the lamprey and a big X through it. But that doesn't sound like inciting violence to me."

"The president of the Piscary Association said that?"

"I don't think he meant—"

"That's Douglas Rheinstaller, correct?"

Lightman exhaled, long and slow. "Correct."

Bernadette pressed on. "What about Tommy's personal life? Did he have a lot of friends?"

"He was active in that church. His girlfriend went there, too."

She frowned; her notes didn't mention a girlfriend. "Her name?"

"Annika Nakrivo. An undergrad transfer student here. She's an intern—helps out in the lab."

Ah—she'd been listed as a co-worker in the file. "Great." She stepped closer to Woodhead. "Maybe we need to do a wellness check on her, too."

"Okay," Lightman said, fidgeting. "Anything else you need down here?"

Bernadette looked at Woodhead; his eyes were closed and he was breathing in and out slowly.

"Dr. Woodhead?" she asked.

"Oh—sorry. The smell of cleaning products distracted me. I detect bleach in particular. Isn't that a dangerous chemical to use close to the tanks?"

"The janitors wash the floors almost every night," Lightman said.

"Have they been in tonight?"

"Uh—no, I believe they get here around eleven."

"So why is this floor freshly mopped?"

"It hasn't been cleaned since yesterday."

Woodhead shook his head. "No. The bleach smell hasn't dissipated enough for that to be twenty-four hours old. With a regular strength bleach-based floor cleaner, I'd estimate that the cleaning was done this morning—not at midnight."

Lightman scoffed. "You can tell by the smell?"

"I can."

"Perhaps the janitors have already been in. I don't schedule when the floor gets cleaned." Lightman turned to Bernadette. "If you follow me upstairs, I'll get Tommy's girlfriend's contact information."

"Sure."

Lightman let Bernadette go first, then stepped in front of

Woodhead, who brought up the rear. Bernadette was on the last step from the top.

An alarm sounded, loud and echoing in the stairwell, and Bernadette clamped her hands over her ears.

"What the hell?" she said, spinning her head around. Lightman's eyes opened wide, and his face was taut. Bernadette opened the door at the top of the stairs—and saw a short figure run by wearing an olive sutro jacket.

"Hey!" Bernadette yelled, and the woman turned her face slightly—a small nose, pale skin, large eyes—then turned and ran down a corridor.

Bernadette sprinted after her. The corridor was narrow, and the sound of a door opening echoed in the hallway. "Stop! Federal investigator!" Bernadette yelled, but the door slammed. Twenty feet farther and Bernadette pushed the door open quickly and had to grab the handrail to keep from falling down the stairs.

Another door opening, this one at the bottom of the steps. The woman was lengthening her lead.

Maybe in the open snow, Bernadette's boots would serve her well enough to catch up to the woman. The door slammed shut below.

She raced down the stairs, pushed the door open, and kept running—

Her feet slid out from under her.

She hit the icy concrete sidewalk hard on her left hip, the shock reverberating up her side and down her left leg. It was so painful she barely heard the car door close. She tried pushing herself up, but her feet slipped again, until finally she pulled herself forward and got to her hands and knees. She reached inside her jacket—her holster and gun were still there.

A Subaru WRX across the parking lot turned on its lights and its engine roared to life. Bernadette scrambled to her feet, pulled her badge from her pocket, and sprinted across the lot, her hip shooting sparks of pain down her leg.

The Subaru backed out of the space, wheels kicking up ice and snow.

Bernadette sprinted to the car and launched herself onto the hood. She landed facing the windshield, her head toward the passenger seat. Pamphlets—was that a picture of a blue whale?

The woman in the driver's seat was visible out of the corner of Bernadette's eye. Blonde. A round face.

Bernadette felt the transmission shift. She banged the badge three times against the frigid windshield.

"Federal investigator!" she yelled.

The engine hummed, and the indecision hung palpably in the cold night air.

"You want to drive out of here with a federal cop hanging onto your hood? Not a good idea."

Bernadette pushed herself back from the windshield and got a good look at the driver. Scared. Determined. A button nose and a cleft chin; large, wide-set gray eyes.

"Get out of the car!" Bernadette barked. *If she accelerates, I'll be thrown off.* She hopped to the ground. "You have three seconds to get out!"

The engine turned off and the door opened. "I'm sorry, I'm sorry." The woman's voice was high and warbly. "I—I panicked. I'm sorry."

"Out of the car."

The woman stood, wearing the sutro jacket. About five-two. She held her hands halfway above her head.

"Turn and put your hands on top of the car."

"I'm sorry," the woman said, complying. "So sorry. I don't know what I was thinking."

Bernadette stepped forward and patted her down. No weapons. "What's your name?"

"Cecilia."

"You have a last name?"

"Carter. Cecilia Carter."

"What were you doing in the building?"

"I—I—"

"It's not a hard question, Cecilia. Do you work in the building?"

"Uh—no."

"Why were you there?"

"I—I'd rather not say."

"We're investigating a murder, Cecilia. Do you want to rethink your response?"

Cecilia Carter bowed her head. Her breaths were coming short and quick. She hadn't taken her hands down.

"I work—"

Silence.

"You'll need to give me more than that," Bernadette said.

"I work for Justice for Oceans."

Chapter Seven

BERNADETTE GRIMACED AS SHE AND DR. WOODHEAD STOOD in front of the Freshie and watched the taillights of Cecilia Carter's Subaru disappear down the street. After calling campus security and having them turn off the alarm, Lightman had declined to press criminal trespassing charges, then locked up the building and left in his car a few moments later.

"Thanks for having my back, Dr. Woodhead." She hoped he'd catch the sarcasm dripping from her voice.

He glanced at her. "My contract specifies that I'm not eligible for hazardous duty. I am untrained in the usage of firearms. I would clearly be inept at situational conflict. I fear I'd be a liability, possibly compounding your problems by requiring rescue if I attempted to insert myself into any situation where physical conflict occurs."

"You're doing me a favor, is what you're saying," Bernadette said. This was why Barlow wouldn't ever load the dishwasher: because he said he couldn't do it the way she wanted it done. Sure, buddy.

"I don't like it any more than you do."

Again: sure, buddy.

They both got into the SUV and closed their doors, and Bernadette started the engine as Woodhead turned to her.

"I still had to retrieve the information about Kymer Thompson's girlfriend, remember?" He took a paper out of a folder and handed it to Bernadette. "Annika Nakrivo."

Bernadette turned the overhead light on and studied the picture. The printout read that she was nineteen years old. She looked young in the photo, too, but her bright, ice-blue eyes were world-weary. Maybe *hurt* was a better word. She had a shoulder-length bob and light brown hair. A dark black beauty mark, perfectly circular, above her upper lip on the left side was her most distinguishing feature. She had thin lips and a square jaw. She wasn't classically beautiful—not the way Barlow's new girlfriend was—but her features were arresting.

"Do we know anything else about her?"

"I've sent her name and information to Curtis. He's performing a search for Miss Nakrivo's background and address."

Bernadette nodded. "Do you want to go talk to her tonight?"

"I believe that would be a wise use of our time." Woodhead glanced at Bernadette. "Did you figure something out?"

"Maybe I'll tell you over dinner." As if to punctuate the sentiment, Bernadette's stomach growled.

"You've been staring at the bratwurst restaurant on the other side of the avenue. We may dine at that establishment if you wish."

Bernadette looked at her watch. "Ten minutes to nine. I hope their kitchen is still open."

They walked across the street and pulled open the door to the bar and grill. The restaurant was empty but for a few patrons.

The bartender looked at them sideways when they asked if

the kitchen was still open. "Just in time. Decide fast." The bartender handed them laminated menus as they took their seats on the tall stools in front of the wooden bar.

"Bratwurst, kraut, mustard, side of fries," she said. "And a Spotted Cow."

"Lady knows what she's looking for," the bartender said. "What can I get you, man?"

Woodhead blinked and looked from one side of the bar to the other then looked past the end of the bar. Bernadette followed his gaze. *The Wurst of Milwaukee* was long and narrow, dartboards in the back, with long tables the length of the building. A chalkboard above the bar said *Specials* but whatever had been there was erased with a smudge of white chalk.

"The same," he said. "Also, do you offer Milwaukee old fashioneds here?"

"*Wisconsin* Old Fashioned," the bartender said. "Sour or sweet?"

"Uh—I don't know."

"Sweet," Bernadette piped up. "And let's get some cheese curds for an appetizer. Since we're going for the whole Milwaukee experience."

The bartender nodded. "You from Wisconsin?"

"No, but my boss went to school here," she said. "She gave me some recommendations."

The bartender clacked the edges of the menus on the bar twice and went back into the kitchen.

"Do Wisconsin Old Fashioneds taste good when they're sweet?"

Bernadette chuckled. "No. Maura says they're terrible, but apparently they're better than the sour."

"Why did you let me order it?"

"Maura said everyone has to try it once."

"You didn't order one."

"Nope." Bernadette grinned. "Taste it. If it's offensive to your taste buds, order a Spotted Cow after."

"What kind of beer is Spotted Cow?"

"I don't really know. It's delicious, though." She looked at Woodhead out of the corner of her eye. "But I like salmon, so take my beer recommendations with a grain of salt." She turned toward the front and tapped her fingers on the bar.

The bartender set the drinks in front of them. A maraschino cherry bobbed in Woodhead's drink. The golden-hued beer in front of Bernadette had a layer of thick foam on top.

Bernadette caught the look in Woodhead's eyes. "Want a taste?"

"Well—yes. Thank you."

She pushed the beer in front of him, and he bent his face down to sniff.

"Oh," he said. "Slightly sweet. Malty. Bananas and cream."

"Sure, we'll go with that."

He took a tentative taste. "Interesting. Nice and crisp. Not a lot of hops either."

"You like hops?"

"No." Woodhead licked his lips. "A bit of a corn taste in the back there. But I didn't smell the corn. Interesting." He pushed the glass back toward her.

"Now you've had the most famous beer in Wisconsin."

"Something to mark off my list." He placed his hands palms down on the bar. "And now for the Milwaukee old fashioned."

"The *Wisconsin* Old Fashioned."

Woodhead raised the glass to his mouth and then pulled the glass away. "What—what the hell is that?"

"What do you mean?"

"You ordered it sweet—but I didn't expect it to be so—so cloying. My pancreas is pained just from the smell."

"You know what's in a classic old fashioned, right?"

"Bourbon, simple syrup, a splash of soda, orange peel, cherry. There's an ongoing debate whether the orange peel and cherry should be muddled with the simple syrup."

"So in the Wisconsin Old Fashioned: instead of bourbon, this has brandy, and instead of soda water, this has Sprite."

He set the drink down on the bar. "You must be joking."

"I'm not."

He furrowed his brow. "You were aware of the ingredients, yet still encouraged me to order it?"

"You wanted to try it." Bernadette smiled.

Woodhead pushed the drink back on the bar as his glasses slipped down his nose. "Out of my sight! Thou dost infect my eyes."

Bernadette tried to stop from rolling her eyes and failed.

Woodhead turned to her. "In the parking lot, you appeared to draw a conclusion. Do you wish to share?"

"Professor Lightman is hiding something, much like the Agios Delphi priest." Bernadette reached over and pulled the Wisconsin Old Fashioned in front of her.

"What?"

"I think he's cheating on his wife." She picked the drink up and sipped. "Oh, wow, that *is* sweet. I can feel my teeth rotting out of my skull."

"Cheating?"

"Yes." Bernadette nodded emphatically. "If I'm right, it's with Cecilia Carter."

"The Justice for Oceans woman who was arrested for trespassing?"

"Yes. She didn't want to say what she was doing there."

"And you didn't ask her point-blank?"

"I did. She wouldn't say. And it didn't click for me until you told me she'd been arrested before. I assumed she was nervous because she didn't want to get arrested, but that's not right. She was nervous because she was at the Freshie and didn't want it made public."

Woodhead scratched his beard. "Surely she was there to cause some sort of trouble."

Bernadette shook her head. "She had time alone in the office to damage computers, steal research, all kinds of things. I don't think Justice for Oceans knows she was there, otherwise she would have done something in the office. And as far as we know, she didn't." She sipped the Wisconsin Old Fashioned again and made a face.

"So you leap to the conclusion that she and Professor Lightman are engaged in a clandestine relationship?"

"Think about how Lightman reacted. How he didn't want us to come up to the office."

Woodhead took his drink back, then spun his glass in a circle. "Did you notice the conference room?"

"I noticed the door was closed."

"And the blinds were drawn." He picked the old fashioned up, sniffed it again, then put it back down. "And Lightman didn't want you going in there."

"I know he was reluctant to offer it as a place to meet."

Woodhead nodded thoughtfully. "No one opened the conference room door before we all went downstairs to the fish tanks."

"No." Bernadette thought for a moment. "And this obviously wasn't their first time. Cecilia knew about the ice at the bottom of the stairwell and jumped over it."

"After you chased her out, I went back upstairs and discovered the conference room door was wide open. It's possible she was hiding in there."

Bernadette took a sip from her pint glass. "If Lightman and Carter were hooking up, why would they do it on a day that his grad student had been killed? Are men really that horny all the time?"

Woodhead nodded. "Many are, yes. Most of them can tamp down their urges at inopportune times, but all it takes for some men to act on those urges is a willing partner."

Bernadette rolled her eyes.

"That's not hyperbole, Bernie—"

She shoved a finger in front of Woodhead's nose. "You start calling me 'Bernadette' or I'm dumping that cocktail over your head. I mean it. I hate being called 'Bernie,' and I know you've got a problem with your ex-girlfriend, but we've been having a tenable working relationship up to this point. Stop calling me 'Bernie' or it will soon be *un*tenable."

Woodhead blinked. "You're too sensitive."

"And you're not sensitive enough."

The bartender came with their bratwursts and fries, setting one down in front of each of them. "Can I get you anything else?"

"Can I get a side of spicy mustard?" Bernadette asked.

"Comin' right up."

Woodhead exhaled loudly as the bartender scooted off into the kitchen again.

"Now what is it?"

He picked up his bratwurst and bit into it. "Nothing," he said, through a mouthful of sausage and kraut.

"It's not nothing."

Woodhead swallowed. "Heavily spiced foods reduce your sensitivity to smell."

"What are you talking about?"

"The spicy mustard."

Bernadette turned and looked at him. "You know, when we first found out about this case, Maura asked *me* to be the poison expert and the super smeller. But no—I told her that I wanted to eat some salmon and spicy mustard on this trip, so she'd have to find someone else."

"You're making fun of me again." He took another bite.

"You insult people who can't smell as well as you. And yes, I'm making fun of you. Your sense of smell is a gift. A wonder of nature. A convergence of fortuitous DNA."

Woodhead stared down at his plate. "It's not a gift, believe me. Do you have any idea what it's like to go on a date and smell *everything*? Not only your date's perfume or her sweat or whether she washed her underwear, but also the slightly rancid cheese at a table across the restaurant, the bubble gum stuck under a movie theater seat, the cocaine snorted in the hotel room by a previous guest. It's not a recipe for getting along with people."

Bernadette chewed thoughtfully.

Woodhead shook his head. "People expect to have normal conversations with me, and all I can think of is the smell of hard-boiled eggs or propane or the number of ants in someone's backyard."

"Ants have a smell?"

Woodhead nodded. "You know how a certain percentage of the population thinks cilantro tastes like soap? Well, it's the same thing with ants."

Bernadette turned quickly to Woodhead and stared at him wide-eyed. "You think ants taste like soap?"

"No, no—oh, you're joking. Ha ha. This is serious. A small percentage of the population can identify the smell of ants."

"I think I understand." Bernadette swallowed her bratwurst bite. "My daughter has misophonia. She can't tolerate the sound of other people eating."

Woodhead hesitated, then said, "That is a common way that misophonia expresses itself, yes."

"She also hates the sound of a cat cleaning itself with its

tongue. Coughing. Sneezing. People drinking." Bernadette took a sip of her beer. "Getting through a meal with her is tough. Whatever you want to talk about, serious or not, all she can hear is the lip smacking and chewing and swallowing." She set the beer down. "Is that what it's like for you, too?"

"I suppose so. I've learned to compartmentalize it the last few years."

"How do you do it?"

"It's easier when I have something to focus on. For example, this bratwurst. I'm focusing on eating it, so I don't concentrate on the spilled margarita on the floor that's at least two days old."

"I didn't even notice that."

"If I have a case to focus on," Woodhead continued, "it's much easier. A case provides a reason to shut out the distracting smells."

"Did you do that today?"

"Yes, many times. For instance, at the lab, I was compartmentalizing the old cottage cheese in the trash in the aquarium room so I could focus on the smell of the lamprey ammocoetes."

"Is that the fishy smell you recognized in the chapel? And blamed on my breath?"

"I believe so." He wiped his hands on the napkin and laced his fingers together, elbows on the bar. "My theory is that Mr. Thompson spilled some of the water from the lamprey tank on himself at work. Perhaps a lamprey had even touched him— jumped out of the tank, or what have you. I suppose that could have happened if he was transferring some lampreys to other tanks, or if he was removing sick ammocoetes so they wouldn't infect others."

Bernadette picked up her bratwurst and took another bite. "How can that help us find the killer?"

"I don't have enough information to answer that. However, if Cecilia Carter and Professor Lightman are covering up a sexual relationship, neither will be helpful to the investigation." He took his last bite. "One genuine Wisconsin bratwurst eaten. It is accomplished."

"You need to have at least one sip of the old fashioned, Dr. Woodhead. I did."

Woodhead shook his head. "Not a chance."

The bartender appeared. "Everything good?" His eyes dipped to the untouched Wisconsin Old Fashioned. "The drink isn't your speed, huh?"

"He was expecting something a little closer to a classic old fashioned," Bernadette said.

"Not the first time I've heard that." The bartender chortled. "Oh—you never got your curds. I'll see if—"

"It's okay," Bernadette said. "I think we're done—those brats are pretty big."

"I'll get your bill."

Bernadette turned. "Was the bratwurst worth it, Dr. Woodhead?"

"Since our short-term plan is to work closely together, would you consider referring to me as 'Kep' instead of being so formal? 'Dr. Woodhead' was my mother."

Bernadette smiled. The bartender set the bill down between them.

Kep eyed the bill as he took out his phone. "I just received a text with Annika Nakrivo's address from Curtis. She lives in the university's dormitories."

"You want to interview her next?"

"Or we could divide and conquer."

"What? You mean split up? One of us interview Nakrivo, one of us interview Carter?"

"Two interviews, two of us."

"As your case analyst—and as an *official* federal investigator —I need to be with you during questioning at all times."

"I believe you will find that to be a guideline and not a rule."

"You have a reputation for taking advantage of that particular guideline, Kep. For our first case together, let's make sure to color inside the lines."

Chapter Eight

THE FOUR-STORY DORMITORY, JUNEAU HALL, HAD BEEN converted from the Old Juneau Hotel in the 1980s. The dorm rooms were not only larger than average but had private bathrooms. The greeting area was a converted lobby, the restaurant now a dining commons. Everything around Juneau Hall was dated but large, cushy, and comfortable. The carpet was a shade of beige that leaned strongly into gold, and the walls were painted a deep burgundy, giving the whole lobby a collegiate sports team feel.

Bernadette entered through the automatic doors in front of Kep and strode to the converted concierge desk, CSAB badge out. "Federal investigator," she said to the young woman in the gray-and-gold Kilbourn Tech sweatshirt. "Can you direct me to the room of Miss Annika Nakrivo, please?"

"It's late," the young woman stammered.

"Be that as it may, we still need to speak with her."

"Is—is she in trouble?"

"Can you direct us to her room, please?"

The young woman scrambled under the desk and came out with a set of card keys. "I'll need to look her up on the computer." She typed for a few moments on the keyboard. "Room 327A —oh, one of our singles. I'll need to escort you there because of the elevator security."

"By all means."

"Follow me." The woman walked purposefully down a wide hall and turned left into a bank of elevators. Several students were getting out of one of the elevators, and the woman skillfully wove past them. Kep and Bernadette squeezed past the students and into the carriage as the doors started to close.

Kep hummed tunelessly and bounced on the balls of his feet.

Bernadette began to sweat under her puffy purple coat. That was the problem in extreme temperatures. In Milwaukee in the winter, it would be ten degrees outside, appropriate for down jackets, wool hats, and multiple layers, and then inside it would be like a sauna. In Phoenix in the summer, it would be one hundred twenty degrees, hot enough to make the soles of tennis shoes stick to asphalt, and yet indoors icicles would be forming from the tops of doorways.

"Not many singles in this dorm?" Bernadette asked.

"Only a few," the woman said. "A quirky space or two that weren't full hotel rooms. They have shared bathrooms in the hall. Even though they're singles, they don't get taken very quickly."

"Because they're quirky?"

"Some of them were linen closets. They had to do some creative interior space management to make sure those rooms had windows. The room Miss Nakrivo is in—well, that used to be a storage area for luggage carts. The space is narrow. It's usually the last room to be booked every year."

"How did she get it?"

"My guess is she was a late add. It's an unusual room, but it suits a certain kind of personality."

The elevator doors opened, and the woman led them down a hallway where the color scheme was reversed from the lobby: burgundy carpet and beige walls. A nameplate reading *327A* was next to a door that was narrower than the others in the hallway.

"Here it is." The woman knocked. "Annika? Annika, this is the Security Desk. There are a couple of police officers here to see you."

Bernadette didn't bother to correct *police officer* to *federal investigator*.

The door creaked open, and Bernadette could see inside. It was an odd space, perhaps twenty-five feet long but only about six feet wide. All the furniture was against one wall: a dresser, a wardrobe, a desk. There was a loft area above the door; boards were attached to the wall in a kind of makeshift ladder. Bernadette assumed the bed was in the loft.

The young woman holding the door open stood about five and a half feet tall and looked similar to her picture. Her face was luminous, with smooth, pale skin, and the printout photo had failed to capture how striking she was.

"Annika Nakrivo?" She took out her badge. "My name is Bernadette Becker. I'm investigating Tommy's death."

"You want to talk to me, right?" Annika had an American accent, not southern, not midwestern, but generically American.

Bernadette nodded, putting her badge back in the inner pocket of her puffy purple coat, then taking out a notebook. "I understand that Kymer Thompson was your boyfriend."

Annika nodded, dry-eyed. "We've been dating since January."

"And when did you arrive on campus? You transferred, right?"

"Yes. I—I got here after the new year. I met him when I went on a tour of the Freshwater Sciences building. The transfer students can sign up for that if they have one of the approved majors."

"And you do?"

Annika nodded again. "Chemistry."

"Where were you on Monday night?"

"I was here. Studying."

Bernadette scribbled in her notebook. "Can anyone confirm?"

"Well—not really. I didn't leave my room after coming back from the dining commons."

"And—you and Tommy go to the same church?"

Annika smiled sadly. "Yes. I was excited to come to Kilbourn Tech because there was a Church of Agios Delphi here."

"You were a, uh, Delphinian before you came?"

"Yes. I'd only been to a few services. It's nice to be more involved here."

"Where are you from?"

"All over. I moved around a lot as a kid."

"Why Kilbourn Tech?" Bernadette asked.

"The College of Freshwater Sciences. It's one of the best in the nation."

"Then why are you a chemistry major?"

"I'm on the waiting list for Freshwater Sciences. They give priority to enrolled students."

Bernadette nodded, and Kep walked into the room.

"When was the last time you saw Tommy?"

"Sunday. We studied, then he took me out to eat. We saw a movie, too."

"Annika," Kep called, "are you certain Tommy didn't come visit yesterday?"

"I'm sure."

"Did you travel to the laboratory yesterday? I understand you work as an intern there."

"Yes, I work there, but no, I didn't go to the lab." Annika looked down at the floor.

Bernadette tried to catch her eyes. "One thing that interests me is that your church uses iboga bark in its services, and your work uses ibogaine in its research."

Annika nodded. "Yes. That was because of Tommy."

Bernadette nodded.

"He told me that when he began work on the project," Annika continued, "he went through the sacraments of initiation with Agios Delphi, and when he took the iboga bark, he had a vision of using the bark to save the world. He was very excited about it—at least, that's what he told me."

"We didn't hear that from his supervisor."

"Professor Lightman?" Annika snickered. "Do you think he'd have listened to a grad student who said he had a vision after taking drugs that they should use that very same drug in their research? Lightman would have laughed him out of the program."

"I see."

Annika rubbed the back of her neck. "Tommy believed he was a conduit for the divine."

Bernadette stepped into the dorm room.

"Uh—sorry, you said you're the police?"

"Federal investigators," Bernadette said. "We deal with suspicious deaths from controlled substances."

Kep was looking closely at the top of Annika's dresser. Bernadette turned to the woman from the security desk, waiting a few feet away from the door, looking awkward.

"We can check out at the front desk when we leave if you like," Bernadette said.

"Yeah, okay," the woman said, shutting the door.

Although the hall hadn't been noisy, the muffled silence of the dorm room was stifling. One person might have been reasonably comfortable in this long, narrow, oddly-shaped room. Three was pushing it.

Bernadette looked around. "It's an unusual room."

"It's good enough. It's cheap. And it's private."

"Do you enjoy your work at the lab?"

Annika screwed up her mouth. "I enjoy being part of something potentially life-saving. But the work itself? It's feeding algae and fish parts to lamprey larvae. It's mindless and smelly."

"Putting in your time so you get accepted into the Freshwater Sciences program?"

"That's right."

Bernadette looked around the narrow room. Three framed photos on her desk and dresser. She looked closer; two were snapshots of Annika and Tommy together, the third picture showed two teenaged girls embracing and smiling at the camera in front of a nondescript house. "Do you know anyone who'd want to hurt Tommy?"

Annika scratched her nose. "Well—he would have probably said he didn't have any enemies."

"But?"

"There was—a little tension in the church."

Kep rotated a quarter-turn, listening.

"Another elder?"

Annika looked down at the ground.

Bernadette clicked her tongue. "Was it Reverend Roundhouse?"

"I shouldn't say anything. I wasn't there—I don't really know."

"Your boyfriend is dead," Kep said from across the room. "Anything that will help us find the person responsible will be greatly appreciated."

Annika put her hands over her face, her breaths shaky.

"I'm sorry," Bernadette said gently, "but it's true."

"Tommy said they argued last week." Annika's voice cracked.

"What about?"

"The project uses a lot of ibogaine. When the reverend found out he was using ibogaine for something other than religious purposes, they argued."

Bernadette cocked her head. "I was under the impression the reverend didn't know Tommy's work used ibogaine."

"I know that Tommy and Reverend Vivian had a big fight. At least, Tommy was real upset about it." Annika wiped her eyes with her hand.

Bernadette looked at Annika carefully. There was something she wasn't being forthcoming about. She waited a beat, then another.

"She was here Monday night," Annika said.

"The reverend? Here—in your dorm room?"

"Yes."

"How did she get past the front desk?"

"I don't know. She's a priest. Maybe they let her come up."

"You're saying she came to your door?"

"Yes."

"Did you answer?"

"She's my priest. Of course I answered."

"And did she come in?"

Annika looked at the floor again. "You know what? Forget I mentioned anything. She'll deny coming here."

"Did the two of you fight, Annika?"

"She didn't—" Annika closed her eyes. "She was looking for Tommy, okay?"

"What time was this?"

"About nine."

"And you didn't tell anybody—"

Annika looked up at Bernadette. "Who would I tell? The security desk? 'Hey, don't let my priest in'? Please."

"Maybe we can take a look at the security footage."

Annika snickered. "The security footage? Ha. See if you can find it. It always mysteriously disappears when someone isn't doing their job."

Kep grunted. "You've lived here no more than three months, and you're already acting like a jaded soul."

Bernadette shot Kep a withering look.

Annika crossed her arms. "You only need to have footage vanish once or twice before you realize the security team is here to protect Kilbourn Tech, not the students."

Bernadette nodded. "Okay." She glanced at Kep—whatever he was doing, he didn't seem finished. "How about work? Did Tommy have any conflicts there?"

Annika nodded. "Eddie Taysatch. He was another grad student. Tommy got most of the credit and the glory for the project. I think Eddie was pissed off about it."

"What makes you say that?"

"Oh—uh, he would say some stuff under his breath. Especially when Tommy was credited for something Eddie did."

"Eddie still works at the lab?"

"Yes."

"Do you know," Kep said, walking over to the two women, "who underwrites your research?"

"I don't think I'm supposed to say."

"A large multinational corporation has invested millions in this project, correct?"

"Like I said, I'm not supposed to tell anyone."

"Are there any other companies who would benefit if this project failed? Like, say, if one of the important researchers died?"

Annika shifted her weight from foot to foot. "I don't understand what you mean."

"You know, a competitor. This medication could make millions, right?"

"*This* medication? I don't know. We're still running tests on mice. I think Professor Lightman sees himself getting rich off this project, but it's way too early to tell. I think you're looking in the wrong place."

Bernadette nodded and sighed. Maybe the professor was a little too enthusiastic about the project. She nodded at Kep. "Are we ready? Got everything you need?"

"When are you scheduled to work in the lab next, Miss Nakrivo?" Kep asked.

"Tomorrow."

"We may come by. See if the lab jogs your memory anymore."

"Uh—no, I remember everything quite well."

Kep nodded. "Sometimes a good night's sleep can alter one's perspective. I'm sorry for your loss. Have a good evening."

"If you think of anything," Bernadette said, "give me a call." She pulled a business card from her purse and handed it to Annika.

They left the narrow dorm room.

"Thoughts?" Bernadette said.

Kep crinkled his nose as they stopped at the elevators. "I smelled the lampreys in there as well. She works in the lab, so I would expect a certain amount of trimethylamine. I'm afraid that doesn't provide additional information." The elevator arrived and they got on. Kep scratched his beard. "Annika seemed quite broken up about Tommy's death, didn't she?"

"For a moment. She was more unsettled about Roundhouse visiting, though."

"Surely you're unconcerned about a visit from Annika's spiritual advisor."

Bernadette set her mouth in a line. "Are you kidding? That was a red flag. Annika says Roundhouse showed up, then told us not to mention it and that Roundhouse would deny being there." She glanced at Kep. "Why would she do that?"

"You suggested the reverend was looking for Tommy. Do you believe that Roundhouse intimidated Annika during her visit?"

"I don't know, but something doesn't add up." The doors opened and they stepped out into the lobby. "And Roundhouse didn't include a visit to the dorm in her version of events."

"We can press the reverend on her whereabouts in our next interview with her."

"Or we can get answers now." Bernadette strode to the front desk.

The woman behind the counter, glanced up at them. "Signing out?"

"Not quite," Bernadette said. "We'll need to view your security footage from Monday night. We'd like to see if Annika had a visitor."

"A visitor?"

"Her priest from the Anne Askew Chapel."

The woman hesitated. "No, I don't think so. That would be highly unusual."

Bernadette nodded. "That's why we'd like to view the recording."

"I'll—uh—have to see if we can do that," the woman said, picking up the phone. "Give me a second."

Bernadette and Kep took a few steps back from the podium.

"Anything else concern you?"

"As I said earlier, she appeared to grieve Mr. Thompson's death," Kep said, "and yet I didn't smell Annika's tears."

"You—you can normally smell people's tears?"

"Of course," Kep said. "I can smell the salt, of course. There are trace amounts of hormones in tears as well. The male tears of many mammals have a protein called ESP1."

"Like—like 'extrasensory perception'?"

"'Exocrine secreting peptide,'" Kep said. "It stimulates vomeronasal sensory neurons in female mice, and the hypothesis is that the peptides operate similarly for humans."

"Well, that clears it up, Doctor," Bernadette said. "You can smell this—this ESP1?"

Kep nodded. "It's faint, but yes."

"And women's tears? They have an equivalent?"

"I'm sure the research journals will catch up," Kep said. "For now, they've studied the reactions of men to women's tears. They haven't isolated any of the proteins or hormones yet."

"But you can tell."

"Yes. I can tell, and I couldn't smell her tears. I don't believe she was crying."

Bernadette shrugged. "Well, so what? Maybe she was dating him because she thought he'd be rich one day. Maybe she liked what he could do in bed. And maybe she thought we wanted to see an emotional reaction so she tried to will herself to cry in front of us. It wouldn't be the first time that someone has faked grief yet not been responsible for the person's death."

"No," Kep said, "but it may mean that we shouldn't trust everything she says."

"I *don't* trust everything she says."

Kep narrowed his eyes. "Are you quite certain about that?"

"What's that supposed to mean?"

"It means," Kep said evenly, "that you wanted to believe her.

That you wanted to believe there's a conspiracy against her telling the truth."

Bernadette snorted a laugh.

"You do *want* to believe her," Kep said softly.

She crossed her arms. "That doesn't mean I won't do my due diligence. The fact that I'm sympathetic makes it more likely that victims and suspects will open themselves up to me." She pointed at his chest. "A fact that you have already taken advantage of during this investigation."

"What are you talking about?"

"Lightman wanted to talk to me, not you."

"That has nothing to do with your sympathetic nature and everything to do with Lightman wanting to bed every woman he meets."

Bernadette glanced at the woman at the security desk. She was off the phone.

"We can continue this later," Bernadette said, turning and striding to the counter. Kep followed. "Any update?"

"Um," the woman said, "I'm not sure how to tell you this, but it appears that the security footage from Monday night is—well—it's missing."

Chapter Nine

The Outsider Hotel was a little too modern in its design for Bernadette's taste, and she had to ask for a room with a tub—it was a forty-dollar upgrade.

And while the wood, granite, and leather in the hotel room was stark and sterile, the claw-foot tub was heavenly. She felt all her muscles, tense from dealing with Dr. Woodhead, loosen and relax. It was too late to call Sophie, so she found a playlist on the audio system, and soothing spa-like sounds of synthesizers and nature washed over her. She exhaled thoroughly, the release starting at the top of her scalp and skittering through her body to her toes.

After her bath, she wrapped herself in a robe, brushed her teeth and collapsed on the bed, immediately falling into a heavy slumber.

She woke as the sun peeked through the opening in the curtains. She grabbed her phone. Not quite six thirty. Her alarm wasn't about to go off yet, and she could still call Sophie—it was only an hour later in D.C.

"Mom?" Background noise—Sophie was probably in the car.

"Hi, Soph. Everything okay?"

"Yeah. On our way to school. Sorry I didn't call last night."

"No problem." Bernadette's voice was light, breezy. "Any tests today?"

"I have a quiz in math."

"Did you study?"

"Over at Olivia's."

Bernadette took a deep breath to stop herself from saying anything negative. "Okay. Tell Dad hi."

"Oh—uh, Lisa's driving me."

Oof. Did Bernadette gasp?

"Is that okay? Dad had an early staff meeting."

He promised that he'd take you to school. "No, no, that's fine."

Sophie lowered her voice. "Lisa's pretty cool, Mom. You really need to give her a chance."

Ugh. Like a knife twisting in her gut. "I know, honey. It's complicated. Listen—I'll give you a call tonight. Good luck on your quiz."

"Thanks."

And then she was off the call—no *I love you*, no *hope you catch the bad guys,* nothing. Sophie had spent most of the afternoon with a C student, had eaten dinner over at her house, then was being driven to school by Barlow's new girlfriend.

Bernadette sprang out of bed and threw on her sweats. Grabbing her card key, her phone, and her earbuds, she went to the workout room on the second floor.

Ugh. Two elliptical machines, already taken by two middle-aged men who were chatting about marketing strategy, and a treadmill that looked at least a decade old. Some sad-looking free weights. Still, better than nothing.

Bernadette felt the men's eyes on her as she got onto the treadmill, heard their conversation falter, but then she cranked up the speed and increased the volume of her workout mix, and soon saw nothing but the red LED display in front of her, the digits moving up steadily.

Each step on the treadmill shot pain down her leg. She hadn't looked at her hip, but she was sure the bruise was ugly. The pain reminded her of the futility of chasing Cecilia Carter. She hadn't gotten answers to any of her questions, either. Despite resulting in an earlier-than-expected bubble bath, the whole situation bothered Bernadette.

The men, still talking business, left halfway through her run, and she did fifteen minutes of weights with only the buzz of the fluorescent lights keeping her company.

She chose the stairs instead of the elevator and bounded up the steps two at a time. Back in her room, her legs were restless. She didn't feel like a shower yet. Bernadette grabbed her debit card and went down in the elevator, out the revolving door of The Outsider Hotel, and ran through the shoveled sidewalks and the bracing morning chill toward the drugstore on Water Street.

The store was small, and its selection of unscented soap, deodorant, shampoo, and moisturizer was wanting, but Bernadette found one of each, bought them at one of the self-checkout kiosks, pocketed the receipt, and returned to her room. The short run in the cold—and without a jacket—had woken her up, and she got herself ready with the unscented products.

The restaurant on the ground floor of The Outsider was an overpriced Italian-inspired bistro with a coffee bar in front. Bernadette entered past a sleepy barista operating an espresso machine, with four people already in line in front of a harried-looking cashier. She looked at the menu but felt uninspired.

Her phone rang in her purse; she took it out; it was Maura. "Good morning, Lieu."

"Sorry I didn't return your call last night." Maura said. "I was exhausted when I got back to the hotel. Anything to report?"

"You'll have the write-up later this morning. We were busy." Bernadette bit her lip. Part of her wanted to mention following the IT guy with the black tote bags and her near-miss with the van, but acting alone and leaving Woodhead at the restaurant might get her in trouble. She walked to an empty corner by the front of the restaurant and lowered her voice. "We visited the priest from Thompson's church. Then we visited the lab where Kymer Thompson worked—"

"Where you detained Cecilia Carter," Maura said.

"—and then interviewed Thompson's girlfriend at her dorm."

"Anything forming in your mind?"

"It's early yet, but the priest is emerging as a suspect."

"A priest?"

"Don't worry about the PR blowback, Maura. It's the Agios Delphi priest. Most people here think it's a cult. The priest has an alibi from a woman who I think is involved with her romantically. Statement from Thompson's girlfriend that they were arguing over the drug that killed him. Nothing concrete yet. We'll keep digging."

"I'll get Curtis to run the priest's financials and phone records."

"Sure." Bernadette paused. "I'd like to interview Cecilia Carter."

"Give me the rundown on what happened last night."

After Bernadette explained, Maura clicked her tongue.

"Oh," Bernadette said, "you don't think she's worth pursuing?"

"I didn't say that."

"Yeah, but you're clicking your tongue."

Maura chuckled. "Is that why you always beat me at poker?"

"Come on, Lieu—a lady never reveals her secrets."

"Since you phrased it so delicately, Bernadette, no, I don't think this will be a fruitful avenue of inquiry. But if we don't follow up, we won't have done due diligence. And I can't tell you not to go based on my gut. So—prioritize other avenues first, would you?"

"Sure."

"You coming into the office?"

"As soon as Dr. Woodhead gets here." Bernadette pulled the phone away from her face to look at the time. Ten minutes after eight. Kep was late. "You haven't seen him this morning, have you? We were supposed to meet ten minutes ago."

Maura tutted. "Watch out you don't give Dr. Woodhead too much leeway. He'll take it and ditch you. That's one of the reasons Martin couldn't handle being his case analyst." Maura paused.

The pause was heavy—Bernadette could feel Maura weighing whether to tell her to watch herself, too.

Bernadette closed her eyes—she didn't need reminding that she wouldn't be getting another chance, that she'd run out of warnings. Her next misstep would be the end of her CSAB career—and she'd never be an agent again. She pictured herself begging for a job with her father's insurance agency back in Denver. The thought made her stomach turn.

Maura's voice snapped Bernadette back to the present. "Everything else okay with Dr. Woodhead?"

Bernadette felt her cheeks grow hot. "He keeps insisting on calling me 'Bernie.'"

Maura sighed. "I know you think that being assigned to Woodhead was some sort of punishment—"

"It's fine, Maura." Bernadette managed a smile. "I know it was my own fault, and I know it could have been worse."

"Well, yes, but you have the right skill set for dealing with

Dr. Woodhead." Maura paused. "I've been trying to get you assigned to this role for the last year, Bernadette."

Bernadette blanched.

A slight rustling on the other end of the phone. "This morning I got a call from him complaining about you."

"Oh, shit, really? I didn't think—"

"In all the time Dr. Woodhead has been with CSAB, we've gotten complaints after his new case analyst's first day every time."

Bernadette walked over to an empty bar table and leaned her elbow on it. "It's comforting that I'm not the only one he's complained about."

Maura laughed. "You're actually the only one *he's* complained about. It's always been the case analyst making the complaint. You really admonished him in front of a suspect?"

"Yes. Professor Lightman—but it was for show. It was Kep's idea."

"No, no," Maura said, "Dr. Woodhead referred to your visit with the priest."

"Oh. Well, yeah. He was angering her. We needed her cooperation."

"See," Maura said, "this is what I mean by your unique skill set."

"You mean—it's okay that he complained about me? But Dr. Woodhead has solved almost every murder case put in front of him. Aren't you worried that I'll throw him off his game?"

"No one's given Dr. Woodhead boundaries before."

"He calls me 'Bernie.'"

"He called Martin 'Marty,' and Martin never said anything until he resigned." Maura paused. "Are you okay with him?"

"I'm not going to pretend Dr. Woodhead is easy to work with."

"You won't dump a bottle of red wine over his head, will you?"

Ugh. It had only been three months since the incident with Barlow at the holiday party, and Bernadette could already tell that would follow her the rest of her career. She attempted a laugh. "It's not like he left our marriage to shack up with the CSAB training instructor."

Maura clicked her tongue. "Don't bring Lisa into this."

An awkward grimace crossed Bernadette's face. "You know that was a one-time thing, and I've gone through enough in the last few months."

"We have to hold ourselves to a higher standard," Maura said evenly. "But I have every confidence you'll get back to your former level of effectiveness."

Bernadette pulled her hair over her left shoulder with her free hand and tried to change the subject. "So what do you and Curtis have going on today?"

"What?" Maura said.

"While Dr. Woodhead and I are conducting more interviews? What suspects are you two looking into?"

"Oh—right. Curtis is already down at District 5 getting started. We've got Kymer Thompson's laptop from his apartment, and we need to go onsite to review his desktop machine. University policy—and I don't have the time to do the paperwork dance."

Bernadette exhaled. "Let's hope one of his emails or texts sheds some light on why he was killed."

"You know," Maura said, "you don't seem at all concerned about what Dr. Woodhead said about you."

I must be doing a better job of hiding my nerves than I thought. "Should I be?"

"No."

Bernadette hesitated. "Will you let me know if that

changes?"

"Yes. Boundaries are a good thing, Bernadette. I'll see you when you get in."

"Thanks, Lieu." Bernadette ended the call, then turned to face the bistro's window. The Third Ward was both beautiful and dirty this morning: the snowbanks white and pristine contrasting with the weathered buildings and the sounds of the elevated freeway. The sidewalks were clear; the valets in woolen hats and overcoats were in constant motion to stay warm even though no cars were in sight.

She walked from the entrance of the restaurant through the lobby, around the fireplace, and out the revolving door. She had only her suit on and nothing to cover her head, and the chill seeped through her trousers to her calves and thighs. The tips of her ears began to tingle.

To her left, she saw all the way down Chicago Street, past a sushi restaurant, past the parking lot, to the Summerfest grounds. Lake Michigan was on the other side of that, and the elevated freeway hundreds of feet above the frontage road pushed the sound up and made the rush hour seem miles away.

From around the corner, holding a bag with *The Elegant Doughnut* printed on the side, came Kep Woodhead. He wore a knit cap pulled low over his ears, a blue track suit, and running shoes. He stared down at the sidewalk, as if making sure he wouldn't slip.

"Fancy meeting you here," she called to him, and he jerked his head up.

"Good," he said, "you're awake."

"Awake? I'm ready to go. We were supposed to be in the car fifteen minutes ago." She motioned to the bag of donuts. "Did hearing that Vivian Roundhouse stopped at that donut shop inspire you?"

"Yes, most definitely."

"All right—well, look, you need a shower, right?"

"I certainly can't show up at the police district station in my current state of cleanliness," Kep said, handing her the bag of pastries. "The hotel restaurant didn't open until seven, so I went for a run. I happened upon the gourmet donut place around the corner while I was cooling down."

"There's a treadmill in the hotel gym."

Kep shuddered. "Do you honestly believe my nose can tolerate hotel gyms?"

Bernadette was silent. She needed to get to the police station, but Kep was nowhere near ready to go.

Kep pointed up Chicago Street away from the lake. "I followed this street to the Milwaukee River. There's a wooden walkway right beside the water. The river is frozen, and it's beautiful. I followed the walkway to the confluence, where it separates two buildings of million-dollar condos from a small marina. When the wooden walkway ended, I found myself at the edge of Lake Shore Park. It's a great run. I almost slipped and fell a few times because of the icy footpaths, but when I arrived at the art museum, I turned back toward the hotel and walked right past the gourmet donut shop."

It was the most talkative she'd seen Kep this trip—besides when he was trying to keep Professor Lightman off kilter. She would welcome it if they hadn't been running late. She tilted her head. Maybe Kep was one of those horrible morning people.

Speaking of which. "Let's go inside. I'll grab you some coffee while you run up and get ready." Bernadette turned toward the revolving door.

"Oh, I think I'd like a hot tea before I go up." He pointed to the bag. "I do not partake of gourmet donuts often."

"What did you get?"

"I was intrigued by their maple bacon donut," Kep continued, "but bacon gets soggy in icing. Left out in the open, it begins to break down from the sugars and the oxygen in the air. The maple bacon donut they had didn't smell very good, so I didn't purchase any."

Wow, when he gets going, he can't stop. "We're running late, Kep."

"Eventually, a few other unusual flavor combinations won me over. The three donuts I purchased smelled the best. I think I will like these."

She looked out of the corner of her eye at him. "You don't think I will like them?"

"I don't have solid footing from which to make a decent recommendation. You like salmon and spicy mustard, after all."

She smiled and then realized he wasn't joking.

Bernadette walked in through the revolving door, Kep on her heels, and turned toward the restaurant. The line had dwindled to two people.

Kep stood behind her—a little too close. She could smell his sweat. Surely he was aware of how his post-run odor was affecting the air around him.

He must have noticed her face. "Shall I sit at a table on the other side of the lobby?"

"Sure."

"Do they have tea?"

"It's a full-service espresso bar, Kep. So yes, I'm certain they do. What kind do you want? You kind of strike me as a Lipton tea fan." She smirked.

Kep took the bag of donuts from Bernadette and turned up his nose. "I prefer English Breakfast. If they have none, Earl Grey will suffice." He walked away.

After she gave the cashier their orders, the barista brought her a pot of hot water and tea bags—they had plenty of English Breakfast—with a side of milk. She hurried across the lobby, balancing it all, to the seating area with sofas and low tables. Kep was at a small table next to the window, and he was staring out at the street, the snow lightly falling, nearly in slow motion. He didn't even turn to her as she set the teapot, tea bags, and milk on the table in front of him.

She walked back across the lobby, hoping the barista wouldn't take too long to make her cappuccino.

After she claimed her scalding-hot drink, she returned to the table only to find it empty.

"I didn't even get a donut," she muttered.

Chapter Ten

BERNADETTE FINISHED HER CAPPUCCINO, THEN FILLED HER cup with coffee from the heated urns three times. She scrolled through her phone, checking on Sophie's grades on the school's online system. Her English grade was down to a B-. Her math score had slipped several points, too.

Well, what did you expect? You've upended the girl's life.

She got up from her chair for another refill and found the urns had vanished. She checked the clock on her phone: 9:06.

Over an hour late. Great.

She looked around the lobby. Dr. Woodhead was still nowhere to be seen.

"Maura'll kill me if I show up without him," she muttered. She took out her phone and texted Woodhead.

> *I'm ready to go. We were supposed to be at District 5 an*
> *hour ago*

Bernadette walked to the hall leading to the elevator, but found no one. For a moment, she considered ordering another cappuccino, but when she looked back at the espresso bar, the line stretched into the lobby.

She stepped up to the registration desk.

"Hi, there," Bernadette said. "Can you ring Kep Woodhead's room? We were supposed to meet down here an hour ago."

"Certainly." The woman behind the desk tapped on her computer, then picked up the phone. After a moment, she set it back in its cradle. "I'm afraid there's no answer."

Bernadette looked at her phone. No reply to her last text. She hesitated, then heard Maura's words: *your unique skill set.*

I'm leaving in 2 minutes with or without you

"No worries," she said brightly. "If you see him, tell him to take a cab."

BERNADETTE PARKED ON VEL R. PHILLIPS AVENUE IN FRONT of a pale yellow house with brown trim, the snow piled up a couple of feet high on the parking strip. She looked out of the driver's-side window across the street to the flat-roofed one-story brick building. The lettering on the brick column under the eaves read *Milwaukee Police District 5.* This was the correct location, all right, but Bernadette had expected a larger building, perhaps three or four stories, and not in a residential neighborhood. It could have been mistaken for an elementary school or a dentist office. Maybe that was the point.

Taking a deep breath, Bernadette opened the door and hurried across the street. The sky had clouded over, threatening to snow. For now, the weather held off.

She went in through the front doors and to the front desk, where she stepped up to the officer on duty.

"Good morning," he said, and smiled at her. It felt like the first friendly smile she'd seen in days. She looked at his badge —*Chesapeake*. Then back into his eyes: dark brown and kind. He seemed to be around Bernadette's age—and she realized she'd been staring.

"Morning." Bernadette took off her puffy purple jacket and draped it over her arm. Her black pantsuit wasn't tailored as well as one of Maura's outfits, but at least it flattered her shape more than the boxy coat. "I'm one of the CSAB people, here for the next few days. Or weeks. Depending on how quickly we solve the Kymer Thompson case." She pulled the identification out of her purse and opened the badge holder.

Chesapeake handed her a visitor's badge—no rings on his left hand. "Nice to meet you, CSAB person. What's your name and phone number?"

Bernadette felt her cheeks redden. "I—I'm sorry?"

He pulled the log sheet on the counter toward him. "For the log sheet. We need your name and cell phone number."

"Of course," Bernadette said. The tips of her ears burned. She lowered her head to look through her purse. She pulled a business card out. "Here you go—all my information."

"Thank you," he said, eyes dancing. "Still need to sign in, though."

Once upon a time, before she'd married Barlow Finnegan, she might have flirted with the police officer—but she'd forgotten how. "There should be another of us coming along shortly," she said. "Kep Woodhead."

Officer Chesapeake nodded. "Your boss has him on the list. He's not in yet. You can go back to the detectives' station. Through the double doors, down the hall, then on your right."

She checked her phone—9:38—as she walked through the double doors and down the hall.

Curtis Janek, still wearing his soft dark brown leather jacket he'd had on the day before, sat in front of two computer monitors that sat on a large conference table. Maura and Detective Kerrigan Dunn stood behind him, watching over his shoulder.

Maura glanced up and waved Bernadette over. Maura stood two inches taller than Bernadette's five-five, with long hair in tight curls and wide-set, inquisitive dark eyes. Her brown skin, a shade lighter than Chesapeake's, was flawless and perfect; her camel-colored peacoat and cream scarf appeared elegant yet effortless. Bernadette quickly walked over and stood behind the two women. Lines of code flew by on both screens.

"What are we looking at?" Bernadette whispered to Maura.

"We found a keylogger on Thompson's personal machine," Maura murmured back. "Curtis is running a check now to see if it matches the profile of any known malware."

"I'll have to run additional tests to be one hundred percent sure," Curtis said, "but from the installation logs, I'd be shocked if the keylogger didn't come from the work machine."

"What makes you say that?" Bernadette asked.

"The dates of the transmission logs," Detective Dunn said. "The keylogger became active in late August. But the logs on the personal machine don't show any transmissions until right after Labor Day."

"A long weekend when Kymer Thompson might have brought some files home," Maura suggested.

Curtis nodded. "Right. A USB drive was the likely source of the infection."

"Do you really think this is relevant?" Bernadette asked. "Malware gets onto PCs all the time."

"Curtis doesn't think this is normal malware," Maura said.

"I didn't say that," Curtis said. "It's a customized version of Fogability."

"Fogability?"

"Yes. That's a popular keylogging program I've seen before—there's nothing new about the malware itself."

"Good work, Curtis." Maura moved her hand to his shoulder and clapped it twice. "Do you think you can find out who this program belongs to? Where the logs went?"

"Possibly. Give me another three or four hours."

"A call to the university IT department might save us all some time," Maura said. "If they put on the keylogger at the request of a third party—or of the administration—we can eliminate this as an avenue of inquiry."

"The IT specialist showed up yesterday in front of the chapel," Bernadette said. "Nick LaSalle. He'd met Kymer Thompson before—he said Thompson had tried to get him to come to church. And he mentioned the hallucinogens."

"Why didn't he give a statement?"

"I, uh, scared him off, I guess," Bernadette said. "He was a little jumpy anyway, and I started asking him softball questions on the way over. Only I guess they weren't softball enough."

Maura tapped her foot. "We may need to talk with him about this program. Maybe he'll reconsider."

Bernadette grimaced. It was time to come clean. "I saw him afterward. After we left campus. He was walking toward the river down Highland Avenue. I followed him. He crossed at a light in front of me, and I lost him in the crowd."

Curtis frowned. "What were you following him for?"

"I thought I'd see if I could put things right," Bernadette said. "Ask about security cameras at the Freshie, keep it professional. But then maybe I scared him off."

Maura nodded. "So we need to talk to Nick LaSalle for multiple reasons, and he's avoided you twice."

Bernadette changed the subject. "Speaking of the keylogger, have we looked into Kymer Thompson's financials? Anyone steal money from his online bank account? Tried to open a credit card in his name?"

"Not that we've found," Curtis replied.

"And—if this *is* related to the murder," Bernadette said, "why leave the malware on the PC?"

Maura pursed her lips. "It's possible the killer didn't have time, or couldn't log in. It could have been installed by one person and Kymer Thompson killed by a different person."

"I suppose that's true." Bernadette paused. The sound of Curtis's fingers flying over the keys was distracting. "Is the keylogger still on Thompson's work PC? Do we know if there are keyloggers on any of the other computers?"

"Not yet. We can check when we go back."

"Why not let them know now?"

"Because," Maura said, "it's possible that people in the IT department did it. Maybe our friend Nick—or someone who works with him. Perhaps they were bribed or otherwise compromised. It does us no good to tell them."

"What if someone from IT deletes the malware before we can get to it?"

Detective Dunn took a step back. "Excellent point. Maybe we should go there now."

"Bring the cybersecurity team to them," Curtis said, typing on his laptop. "They might complain that the computers regulate the fish water or something. Don't give them an opportunity to make excuses."

"This isn't our first rodeo," Detective Dunn said, her nostrils flaring.

"Not ours either," Curtis replied.

"Okay—we're all on the same team here," Maura said, putting her hands in front of her, palms out, as if she were a soccer player who'd tripped an opponent. "Let's make sure we move as quickly as we can to gather the right evidence."

Detective Dunn nodded and walked out of the room.

Curtis turned to the screen, which had spit out search results.

Bernadette leaned forward. "What does it say?"

"It looks like the keylogger on the home PC was activated in early September," Curtis said. "When it was installed, it started transmitting data to an IP address registered to a company in the Maritime Antilles on September 7."

"And you said the work PC infected the home PC?"

"That's my theory."

"But isn't that unusual?"

"Yes," Curtis agreed. "Usually home PCs are the ones infected first, because workplaces are usually more stringent about security than home users."

"But not in this case?"

"No. Thompson copied four spreadsheets onto a USB thumb drive on September 4—I assume it was at work, because the spreadsheets contain information regarding the lampreys, and the author name of the spreadsheet matches one of Thompson's co-workers. The USB drive we found has the keylogger on it too, and I think that's how it hitched a ride home."

"Have you found anything in the transmission logs?"

"All of the spreadsheet data, information about the fish and the lampreys, some details about the, uh, harvesting of the iron-rich amino acids—it's all there."

"Something for everyone," Maura mused. "Information for the eco-terrorists, the fishing Mafia, the pharmaceutical competitors."

"And that's just the work stuff," Curtis said.

"What else did it transmit?"

"Schedule of the Agios Delphi services. Personal email. Online banking passwords. Social media account information."

"Anything interesting in social media?"

"I was going through that," Curtis said. He clicked on a line of code on the screen and the monitor filled with a dozen photos of an attractive young woman with light brown hair, large ice-blue eyes, and a beauty mark on her cheek.

Bernadette blinked. "Huh. Lots of pictures of his girlfriend."

"What?" Curtis asked.

"His girlfriend. Annika Nakrivo."

"That's not Thompson's girlfriend." Curtis clicked on one of the pictures and it enlarged, showing the woman next to a man in a tuxedo with an award in his hand. "That's the actress Mariska Sikmo."

"Mariska who?"

"Sikmo. She's in a bunch of indie films. Period pieces, stuff like that." Curtis looked at Bernadette. "The beauty mark is kind of her thing."

"Oh," Bernadette said. "And Annika's beauty mark is above her lip, not on her cheek." She stepped closer. "Annika's got more of a square face, too."

"Hang on," Maura said, peering over Curtis's shoulder. "I've seen her somewhere."

"Any one of a dozen movies," Curtis said.

"No, that's not it." Maura's eyes lost focus, then snapped back. "She was in that TV series—*Six Wives*. I knew I remembered her."

"*Six Wives?*"

"Historical drama about Henry VIII." She looked in triumph at Curtis. "She played Anne Askew."

Curtis's mouth fell open. "And—and Annika Nakrivo looks exactly like her?"

Bernadette scratched her temple. "I wonder," she mumbled.

"What?"

"Well—when Kep and I talked with her yesterday, she said

she'd been a member of the church for a while. I wonder if she saw that TV series, realized how much she looked like Anne Askew, and then found this religion. Maybe she felt like it was too big a coincidence—that it was divine interference."

"Divine interference?"

"Not all tinfoil hats are, uh, made of tinfoil." Bernadette exhaled loudly. "Okay, that's not an elegant analogy, but you get what I mean."

Maura raised an eyebrow.

Curtis scrolled down. "You said Thompson was devout?"

Bernadette nodded. "That's what his priest said."

"I believe it. All these photos of Mariska Sikmo and not one shot of her nude or even from that lingerie scene she did—" Curtis snapped his mouth shut and started typing again.

Maura leaned forward, ignoring him. "When were those images downloaded?"

"I've got evidence from the first night the keylogger was on here." Curtis scrolled. "Tapered off a little around January, though. Still visits these sites every so often, but not with the frequency he used to."

"Why would he need to?" Maura said, rubbing her chin thoughtfully. "Thompson had his very own Mariska Sikmo—or his very own Anne Askew, if you want to look at it like that."

"Do we know if she started dating him after she got the job in the lab?" Curtis said.

"They started dating in January," Bernadette said. "Less than a month after she got to Kilbourn Tech."

"So why is the keylogger on this machine?" Curtis sat back. "The key logs have to have a purpose. Hackers don't put these on systems and then not do anything with the information they transmit."

"What usually happens?" Maura asked.

"They can harvest credit card numbers and login information to online financial institutions," Bernadette responded. "Usually, the hackers buy as much stuff as they can and transfer as much money as they can and then get out of Dodge. It doesn't look like any of that happened, though."

"It's only been two months," Curtis pointed out.

Bernadette leaned over and tapped the screen. "The keylogger's been on since Labor Day. That's six months."

"Thompson would have been informed by now if his financial information was taken, right?" Maura said.

"Not necessarily," Curtis said. "Some of these hackers harvest the financial information and sell it over the dark web to the highest bidder. It could take six months or longer before the fraud gets out in the open."

Bernadette nodded.

Detective Dunn re-entered the room. "Okay," she said, "we've got two people from our cybercrimes unit on their way down to the lab right now. I've asked them to give us any information they find."

Maura looked around the room. "Where's Dr. Woodhead?"

"Met me in the lobby at eight," Bernadette said. "He wasn't ready—he'd just gotten back from a run. He went up the elevator and haven't seen him since. I texted him twice, no response."

Maura clicked her tongue. "You showed up here without the consultant for whom you're responsible?"

"I did. You asked me to come into the District 5 office, and I followed your directions. Dr. Woodhead is an adult, and he knows how to prioritize his work. As well as take a taxi."

Maura stood unblinking at Bernadette for a few seconds, then nodded.

The officer from the front desk—Chesapeake, that was his name—came around the corner. "Agent Becker?"

Bernadette looked up at him and his kind brown eyes, and

she didn't bother to correct him. "Hello, officer. Do you need something?"

"I just received a call from Dr. Woodhead. He says he'll meet up with you later."

Bernadette pulled her phone out. No response to her messages. And she had four bars of signal. "He has all our cell phone numbers. Why in the world..." She raised her head. "Did he have any other information for us?"

"No, that was the whole message."

"Did he at least say he was sorry for eating all the donuts?"

Chesapeake smiled. "He failed to mention anything about donuts."

Bernadette nodded with a quick glance at Maura. "Thanks, Officer Chesapeake."

He nodded. "You're more than welcome. And if you need some lunch recommendations, let me know. This neighborhood is residential, so you have to know where you're going if you want something decent." He smiled easily, and Bernadette couldn't help but smile back.

"Thank you."

Maura shook her head as Chesapeake went back toward the front desk. "All right, Curtis. I'll see if anyone from IT can meet us at the Freshie to go through the work computer."

Curtis looked up from his screen and grinned. "Oh— speaking of the Freshie, I got some video from the gym across the street from the lab. It's from Monday night, right around the time of the murder. Can't see the back door or the parking lot, though."

"Anything of note?" Maura asked.

"See for yourself." Curtis casually turned the monitor so Maura could view it. "A few people here and there until about ten. Then nothing until a few minutes past one A.M., when a homeless woman pushing a shopping cart comes down Riverwalk and out of the camera view. But then comes back a few minutes later, like she missed her turn. Then she turns toward the university."

"Could that be our killer?"

Curtis shook his head. "Not nearly enough time to go in, inject Kymer Thompson, wait for him to die, load him up in her shopping cart, and head out."

Dunn nodded. "I know her. She's a homeless woman who's always on the Riverwalk. I only know her as Rhonda. She's always there with her cart every night about this time."

"Okay," Maura said. "Let's keep searching." She turned to Bernadette. "While we get an address for Cecilia Carter and jump through whatever legal hoops Justice for Oceans has for us, you should interview Eddie Taysatch. He's a grad student who worked with Thompson on the lampreys. He called in sick today."

"Oh—Annika mentioned him," Bernadette said. "He and Thompson didn't get along. He called in sick, huh?"

"Yes. He lives in the university apartments over on Juneau and Eighteenth." Maura pulled her phone out and tapped the screen; Bernadette's phone buzzed in her purse. "There's the address. See if he's really sick or if there's something else going on."

Bernadette turned her head toward the hallway. "Should I wait for Dr. Woodhead?"

Maura bobbed her head at Detective Dunn. "Kerrigan? Feel like doing a local-federal partnership interview? Inter-agency goodwill and all that?"

Dunn stepped forward. "Sure. I'd be happy to join you."

"And I," Maura said, "will do what I can to locate the wayward Dr. Woodhead."

Chapter Eleven

BERNADETTE RODE IN A POLICE CRUISER WITH DETECTIVE Dunn, who drove. They turned out of the parking lot onto Vel R. Phillips, then after a couple of turns, merged onto Interstate 43.

She looked at Kerrigan Dunn, who stared intently through the windshield. "How long have you been a detective?"

"Two years." Dunn looked over her shoulder and changed lanes. "Not what I thought it would be."

"Really?"

"Yeah, it's a lot of paperwork. I worked my ass off to get promoted to detective, and I get assigned all the bad shifts."

"Oh. I'm sorry."

Dunn turned off her signal. "Not your fault. I'm only on this case because none of the other detectives want to work with the Feds."

"So much for inter-agency goodwill."

The detective gave the windshield a half-smile. "Me, I'm here for the cases. And I gotta say, this is the most interesting case I've had since joining District 5."

"You don't get interesting cases?"

"Some. There were fifteen or twenty homicides in the district last year. Mostly territory shit. A couple of drug deals gone wrong. The occasional domestic dispute that turned deadly. But this! A body found in the Anne Askew Chapel on the Kilbourn Tech campus? That's some crazy stuff. I got interviewed by Channel 58 for the first time yesterday. They never care about any of our other cases, but a white kid killed with a weird poison? They're all over it." She barked a laugh. "When the media finds out about the cult, that'll be good for another week of coverage."

"Yeah." Bernadette exhaled long and slow. "It's an interesting case, though. I mean, the cult is based around Anne Askew, and the victim's girlfriend looks like that actress who played her on TV. That'll get a couple extra days of attention."

Detective Dunn chuckled. "I can almost see the interview in my head. People have been copying their looks after movie stars for decades, haven't they? The girlfriend gets some hair dye, a pair of tinted contacts, a little makeup, and she looks like the cult's female messiah." She glanced at Bernadette. "I'm telling you, that religion is odd."

They exited the freeway at Highland Avenue, and a few minutes later pulled into a parking spot on Eighteenth Street between Highland and Juneau. The snowbank on the right side of the car wasn't too high—Bernadette estimated she could open the door without much trouble.

Detective Dunn turned the car off and stared wistfully at the set of three-story university apartment buildings. "When I worked this neighborhood as a beat cop, the most I ever had to do around here was bust some kids for growing pot plants, maybe a little possession. Now that it's decriminalized, I don't even have to do that."

Bernadette's foot slid as she was coming around the corner of the car, but she righted herself. The two of them walked across Eighteenth Street. She pulled her phone out of her purse and tapped her rapidly freezing finger on the message from Maura.

"Building two, apartment 348."

"It's a walk-up," Detective Dunn said.

"Okay."

A few minutes later, after ascending two flights of stairs, they were standing in front of apartment 348. Detective Dunn pushed the small black doorbell button. A buzz sounded inside.

A man with black curly hair and dark brown skin answered the door. He wore a Henley long-sleeved shirt and blue jeans. His handsome face was marred by swelling and discoloration around his eye. "Hey," he said. "Can I help you?"

"Eddie Taysatch?" Detective Dunn said, flashing her badge.

"Yes, that's me."

"You're not at the lab?"

"Oh." A crease appeared between his eyebrows. "Uh—no. I called in sick."

"You don't look that sick to me."

"I'm—I don't have the flu, if that's what you mean. One of my co-workers died on Monday, and—well, things are weird there. I need some time to process it."

"That's why we're here, Mr. Taysatch."

"Because I'm taking a mental health day?"

"No—because of Kymer Thompson's murder."

Eddie's eyes widened. "You're calling it a murder? Lightman didn't tell me that."

Detective Dunn nodded. "Mind if we come in? It's cold out here—and you're letting all the heat out."

"Uh—sure."

Behind the door, a kitchen table was shoved under a window, with two lonely-looking wooden chairs pushed haphazardly underneath. The kitchen itself was spare: two burners and a small oven that would have barely fit a baking pan. A small refrigerator and a stainless-steel sink with an old-looking chrome faucet completed the kitchen—not very much cabinet space, and from what Bernadette could tell, no dishwasher.

Looking to her right, the small living room had wall-to-wall burnt orange carpeting, a small blue sofa, and a single chair with an odd, concave shape.

Eddie shut the door behind them. "What can I do for you?"

"I'm Detective Kerrigan Dunn. This is Agent Bernadette Becker of the CSAB." Dunn gestured to Eddie's face. "Nasty black eye you've got there."

"Yeah," Eddie said. "I don't get paid enough for this."

"What do you mean?"

"Got sucker-punched coming into work Sunday afternoon," Eddie said. "The guy from the fishing collective, or whatever they call themselves."

"Piscary Association," Bernadette offered.

"Right. I opened the front door and the guy turned and punched me as hard as he could. I fell down—almost hit my head on the sidewalk, and he walks away."

"You didn't call the police?"

Eddie laughed. "Sure. Me, a twenty-five-year-old Black guy, filing an assault charge against a fifty-year-old white guy who probably lives in the suburbs, whose wife belongs to the Junior League. How do you think that would go for me, Officer?"

"Detective," Dunn said absentmindedly. "And, yes, I can understand your reluctance to contact us."

Eddie looked at Bernadette. "Who did you say you were with?"

"The Controlled Substance Analysis Bureau," Bernadette replied.

"What are the Feds doing here?" Eddie leaned against the wall.

"Investigating the death of your co-worker," Dunn said.

"I mean, sure, homicide is serious, but why the Feds?"

Bernadette took a deep breath. "CSAB protects communities from dangerous substances. Kymer Thompson was killed by one of those dangerous substances. That makes it federal business."

Eddie nodded, fascinated. "Cool."

Detective Dunn arched an eyebrow. "Cool?"

Eddie blanched. "Well—no, I mean, the fact that Tommy's dead isn't cool."

Detective Dunn took out her notebook. "Let's start with something easy. Where were you on Monday night between ten o'clock and one in the morning?"

"In the Byron Library on campus. Grading papers for Dr. Obermeyer's organic bio class," he said, sitting in the concave chair and motioning to the sofa. "Well, until about midnight—then I bundled up and left."

"Can anyone vouch for you being in the library?"

Taysatch turned his eyes toward the ceiling. "I don't know. There were a lot of other people there. Midterms and all. Maybe one or two of them would recognize me."

"But you didn't talk to anyone?"

"No."

Detective Dunn nodded. "How did you get along with Kymer Thompson?"

Taysatch pressed his lips together. "We were work colleagues."

Dunn tilted her head. "That doesn't answer my question."

"I suppose it doesn't." Taysatch leaned back in the chair and sighed. "I suppose you'll find out anyway. He and I didn't get along."

Dunn nodded. "And why was that?"

"He had an annoying tendency to take credit for work I'd done."

Dunn tilted her head sympathetically. "And that made you— what? Angry?"

"Annoyed," Eddie said evenly.

"What did he take credit for that you'd done?" Bernadette asked.

"We altered the larval diet to enrich the ferritin in the silver lampreys' livers. It was my idea, but Thompson took the credit."

Detective Dunn nodded. "And did that make you angry?"

"I didn't say I was angry. I said I was annoyed."

"I know you said you were annoyed," Dunn said, raising her eyebrow. "I'm asking you if you were angry, too."

"Fine, I was angry," Eddie said. "But now that he's dead, I have *no* chance to prove that I'm the one who suggested it first."

"Really?"

"How do you think it will look to the media and the public —not to mention any future employer? I'll tell you how it will look—it'll look like I'm trying to steal glory from a dead guy." He shook his head. "That wasn't the first idea of mine he took credit for, either, but now that he's gone, we'll probably name the damn medicine after him."

"TommyContin," Bernadette suggested.

A smile played at the corner of Eddie's mouth. "Yeah. Heh." He leaned forward in the weird chair. "If I wanted to claim what were rightfully my ideas, I needed that asshole alive."

Bernadette scooted forward on the sofa. "Did you do anything to try to get proof?"

Eddie frowned. "Like what?"

"Maybe recording a conversation?" Bernadette glanced over at Detective Dunn. "Or getting information off his computer?"

Both women watched Eddie carefully as he closed his eyes and bowed his head. "I tried to get him to admit it. I recorded a couple of our conversations on my phone."

Bernadette looked over at Dunn again. "I believe Wisconsin's a one-party consent-to-record state," she said, and Dunn gave a slight nod. "There's nothing illegal in what you did. Do you still have the recordings?"

"Uh—I guess so. There's nothing useful on there. He was paranoid."

"Paranoid?"

"Yeah. Kept saying he knew what they were up to."

Dunn raised her eyebrow. "What *who* were up to?"

Eddie stood and started pacing. "He didn't tell me. Hell, I didn't care who he was talking about. I wanted him to talk about the idea for altering the larval diet, but he kept talking about the lampreys. He walked out of the room. It was like he wasn't even listening to me."

"Would you be able to send us those recordings?"

"What—like over email?"

"Yes."

"I guess so."

"Is there anyone who might have wanted to hurt Tommy?" Bernadette asked.

"Hurt? Yes. Killed? No."

"Who'd want to hurt him?"

Eddie paused. "I wanted him to admit what he did, for sure. I can't deny it—I complained about him all the time. But I didn't kill him. I'm sure there are cameras around the library. I know people saw me." Eddie sat on a straight-backed chair across from Bernadette. "I should have taken that job at Parr Medical instead."

"A job? Instead of grad school?"

"I could have left after last year," Eddie said. "Parr offered me a lot of money. But I'd come this far—I thought finishing my degree was more important." He sighed. "But sometimes finishing what you started isn't the right move."

Dunn nodded. "It's a nice story, Eddie, but I know it's not always easy to keep your anger in check. Even if it's the smart, sensible thing to do. Kymer Thompson's been stealing from you. Kymer Thompson's been getting busy with a cute girl who looks like a movie star. You've got nothing to show for your hard work."

"I'll still get my degree in June."

"Still," Dunn said, "I bet you've thought about how great it would be to punch him in the face. Just once."

Bernadette watched Eddie's face as his eyes lost focus, and he stared at the wall. Yes, he was picturing it.

"And," Dunn continued, "maybe the two of you were working late on Monday night. Maybe he was down there in the aquarium area, shuttling his precious lampreys from one tank to another. And maybe something snapped. Maybe you're not the one who got the first punch in." She tapped her eye. "That's quite the shiner there, Eddie. You sure it was the guy from the Piscary Association?"

"Positive," Eddie said through clenched teeth. "I even filled a form out with HR. It didn't have anything to do with Kymer Thompson."

"Okay, Eddie," Detective Dunn said. "What did you do after you left the library at midnight?"

Eddie bristled. "You have some nerve accusing me. Just because I'm—"

Dunn folded her arms. "Just because you're what?"

"Never mind," Eddie muttered. "I grabbed a late dinner. There's a new all-night Thai place on Second and Wells."

"What did you have?"

"Yellow curry with tofu and eggplant." He paused. "I might still have the receipt."

"You pay with a credit card?"

"Uh—no. Cash."

"Tofu and eggplant? That sounds healthy."

"I'm a vegetarian."

"A vegetarian?" Bernadette arched an eyebrow. "And yet you kill fish and pull their livers out to cure cancer?"

"I'm a walking paradox." Eddie's upper lip curled slightly. "After I ate, I walked straight home. I got back around twelve-thirty, maybe twelve forty-five. My roommate had fallen asleep in front of the TV. I woke him up when I came in."

"He can confirm your whereabouts?"

"I guess so. He was pretty out of it and went straight to bed. Maybe he remembers."

"Is he a grad student too?"

"Yes. Philosophy."

"Philosophy?"

Eddie rocked the chair back on two legs. "He's dying to wear a tweed blazer with elbow patches."

"Is he home?"

"No. In class until four."

"You have a phone number for him?"

Eddie eyed them, then grunted and got up. He walked into the kitchen and came back with a sticky note and a pen. He wrote on it and handed it to Detective Dunn as she stood.

He took out his wallet and leafed through the bills, then withdrew a receipt. "There. That's for the Thai place Monday night. Now, if you don't mind," he said, "I'm on call tonight. I've got some errands to run."

"Actually," Bernadette cut in, "one more thing. How hard is it to take a syringe full of ibogaine without anyone knowing?"

"It's under lock and key on the third floor in a temperature-controlled cabinet."

"That didn't answer the question. Who has access?"

"We need to inject it into the fish livers, Agent Becker."

"Even though ibogaine is a Schedule 1 controlled substance?"

Eddie cocked his head. "Not our version of ibogaine. At least, our paperwork says it's not. The extractions are from a different source and don't meet the legal definition—"

Bernadette nodded. "I see you know about the loophole, too."

"Just because our ibogaine is classified differently doesn't mean it's a loophole. It still meets our research needs without requiring the controls and the oversight."

"So—what, you just take the ibogaine whenever you want?"

"It's not just me. Tommy had access, Professor Lightman does too." Eddie rubbed his temples. "We have controls in place. Anyone who takes it needs management approval, and there's a sign-out process. But it's not that expensive, and the combination of ibogaine and ferritin has presented the most promising results so far."

"Does the Freshie enforce the sign-out process?"

"Of course. I always sign it."

"Be honest with us, Eddie," Dunn said. "If someone wanted to take some ibogaine without signing it out, how hard would that be?"

"Well, I—" Eddie stopped, then screwed up his mouth. "I guess it would be pretty easy. You could sign out with someone else's name. Or..."

"Or what?"

"The security personnel aren't always there."

"Doesn't sound like you have oversight," Bernadette said. "Anyone with access to the building can take it."

"They'd need a key to the cabinet."

"Which everyone has." Bernadette sighed. "Anyone tried to get high off it?"

"In that concentration? Not likely."

Bernadette shook her head vigorously. "It'd be easy to dilute. Get a teaspoon and a gallon of vinegar and you'd have enough ibogaine to get a whole dorm high."

"Or a whole congregation," Dunn murmured.

Bernadette stood and stared at Eddie. "Where's the accountability? Where's the audit trail?"

Eddie looked at Bernadette blankly. "We're not doing anything illegal. Besides, I'm a grad student researcher. I don't have any input into the Freshie's policies."

Bernadette's phone buzzed in her purse, but she ignored it and let it go to voicemail. "Who's responsible for the security procedures?"

"Uh—I don't know. Professor Lightman, maybe? Or—the IT department runs the computer systems that control the key cards, the alarm systems, that kind of thing. They're the ones we requisitioned the cabinet from."

"Not campus security? Isn't that unusual?"

Eddie shrugged. "I don't make the rules."

So many loopholes for what ought to be a Schedule 1 substance. Great.

"I need to run those errands before my on-call time starts," Eddie said. "I think we're done here. I'll walk you out," Eddie said, pulling on a green overcoat and a gray knit cap.

All three of them walked down the stairs, Bernadette pulling her phone from her purse. Maura had left a voice message.

"Bernadette, it's Maura. I received the campus security recording of Kymer Thompson. I'm forwarding it to you—it's not a lot to work with, but it does sound like he knew his life was in danger. I'm sending this to Dr. Woodhead too—maybe it will get him back to the station."

Bernadette stopped at the ground floor landing and turned the speakerphone on as Eddie walked ahead of them and out the door.

"What are we listening to?" Dunn asked.

"The message Kymer Thompson left with campus security the night he died."

The recording started: the voice a nasal tenor with a midwestern lilt. "Hi—uh, this is Kymer Thompson, Graduate School of Freshwater Sciences. I believe the Freshie—uh, the Freshwater Science Lab Building—will get broken into tonight, yeah. I don't know who, but I think they might cause some damage. Uh, I guess I mean a lot of damage. I'd like a couple of security officers over here. I have some evidence they're going to kill—"

The recording cut off.

"Nice of the campus security office to cut off the recordings at thirty seconds," Dunn muttered.

"Did Kymer Thompson think his life was in danger?" Bernadette asked.

"I don't know. He certainly thought *someone's* life was in danger."

"Or he could be talking about the lampreys."

Dunn nodded. "But no one tried to kill the lampreys. They killed *him* instead." She motioned her head back toward the apartment building. "You think it was Eddie? He was angry enough to kill Thompson, right?"

They walked out the front door, and Bernadette caught an idling blue van out of the corner of her eyes at the curb.

It looked familiar.

She glanced to her left, away from the van. Eddie walked down the sidewalk, purposefully. With a start, Bernadette realized it was the same shade of blue as the van that tried to run her over.

Bang.

A pinging sound next to Bernadette's ear.

Eddie crumpled to the sidewalk.

Chapter Twelve

A SCREECHING OF TIRES.

Detective Dunn yelled.

Bernadette ran down the sidewalk toward Eddie. He was lying on his back, shaking. Bernadette crouched next to him. A red stain in the shoulder of his overcoat was spreading.

"I—I—" Eddie sputtered, eyes wide. "What happened?"

Lots of blood. The bullet might have hit an artery. Faintly, Bernadette heard Dunn's shouts fading. She was going after the shooter. Maybe the shot came from the blue van.

"I'm calling for help, Eddie," Bernadette said. She'd been at CSAB a long time, but no one had ever gotten shot in front of her before.

Call the paramedics. Apply pressure. Bernadette fumbled with her phone and dialed.

"Nine-one-one, what's your emer—"

"I need an ambulance," Bernadette said as calmly as she could, but she heard the note of panic in her voice as she put the phone on speaker and set it on the ground next to Eddie. "Eighteenth and Juneau. A man's been shot. He's still conscious. I'm with him."

Bernadette unwound her scarf, catching it on her earring in her haste. She pulled the scarf free and put it on top of Eddie's wound, under his open overcoat, and leaned on the wound with both hands.

Eddie gave a strangled cry and swore loudly.

Her heart pounded in her ears as she gave the dispatcher her name and federal ID number.

"Sending an ambulance now," the dispatcher said.

"How long?"

"I'll get an ETA in a moment."

"There's a lot of blood," Bernadette said. She could feel the blood soak through the scarf.

Ugh. Sophie gave her this scarf last Christmas. It was her favorite.

No. No thinking about that now.

"Less than five minutes, ma'am," the dispatcher said.

"You're gonna be okay, Eddie," Bernadette said, leaning forward to put more weight on the wound. "The ambulance will be here any minute."

"I got shot?"

"There was a light blue van in front of your apartment building," Bernadette said.

"Is that who shot me?"

"Maybe." *Was that the same light blue van that almost ran me over?* Bernadette shifted her weight, the cold sidewalk digging into her knees. "Do you know someone with a blue van?"

Eddie gave a laugh and then winced. "That bastard."

"Who? Who do you mean?"

"Only person I know who drives a light blue van." He wheezed.

No blood in the airway. That was a good sign. "Who, Eddie? Who is it?"

Eddie giggled. He was going into shock.

"Who, Eddie?" A siren around the corner, getting closer.

"Tommy," Eddie said. "Tommy drives a blue van."

❧

DETECTIVE KERRIGAN DUNN PLUNKED HERSELF IN THE CHAIR next to Bernadette in the hospital waiting room. "Some morning," she muttered to Bernadette, tapping on her phone.

Bernadette blinked. How long had she been sitting there?

She'd ridden in the ambulance with Eddie, but he couldn't answer any of her questions. Who'd want to hurt him? Why would anyone target him? The oxygen mask went on and then Bernadette was useless, only getting in the way as the paramedics had tried to stabilize him.

It was a handful of blocks to Aurora Sinai, and after the ambulance pulled in, two men rushed Eddie through double doors. Bernadette wasn't permitted to follow. A health care worker had escorted her to the waiting room.

She looked at the phone. Four missed calls from Maura. One from Dunn.

"I missed your call," she said.

Dunn drummed her fingers on the arm of the chair. "You had a lot on your plate."

Bernadette shut her eyes. "Eddie told me that Kymer Thompson drives a blue van. He thought Tommy was trying to kill him from beyond the grave."

"Yeah." Dunn leaned back in her chair. "Tommy didn't have a car, though. I've already put in a request to see if the Freshie had a blue van."

"I almost got run over last night by a light blue van," Bernadette said quietly.

"What?"

Bernadette told Dunn about following Nick LaSalle, then losing him at the arena and the van coming up on the sidewalk.

"You need to put that in your report."

"Of course." Bernadette had to get her head in the game. She'd known when she accepted the demotion—and really, what other choice did she have?—that she'd be working homicides, and it could be more dangerous than money laundering. In the last fifteen years, she could count on one hand the number of times she'd drawn her gun—and she'd only fired it at the range. That *ping*—that was the bullet whizzing right by her ear. Another couple of inches and she'd be dead. If she'd been much taller, it would have hit *her* shoulder, not Eddie's. And if she hadn't jumped out of the way, she'd have been hit by the van— maybe the same van—the night before. "You didn't get a license plate, did you?"

"Partial," Dunn said. "Wisconsin plates." Her phone rang and she answered immediately. "Dunn." A pause. "Right, I should have thought of that. Anyone in particular?" Another pause. "No, that's everything I need for now, thanks." She ended the call and turned to Bernadette. "Guess who the van belongs to."

"If you say Kymer Thompson—"

"Maybe I should say, 'Guess *what* the van belongs to.'"

Bernadette squinted at Dunn. Not the Freshie—she would have said. Then it hit her, and she felt stupid for not thinking of it sooner. "Agios Delphi."

"Yes. I'd say there's a lady priest we need to start putting the screws to." Dunn stood.

"Are they putting an APB out on the van?"

"Yes. You ready to go?"

"All the way out to Whitefish Bay?"

"Maybe. We'll check the Anne Askew Chapel first. Agios

Delphi was supposed to have their weekly service there last night. Maybe Reverend Roundhouse is there cleaning up."

"I thought their service was cancelled."

"You'd rather drive all the way to Whitefish Bay and realize she's back here?"

Bernadette closed her eyes. Only a couple of hours ago, she'd been inches away from leaving Sophie without a mother.

"Bathroom," Bernadette said, and got to her feet without looking Dunn in the eye. She saw the sign for the ladies room and thirty seconds later she was looking at herself in the mirror above the sink.

I am a badass, she thought, and breathed out, but the air caught in her throat. Even though she wore a dark suit, it wasn't hard to tell that she was stronger than the average forty-year-old—hell, than the average twenty-year-old. She regularly benched one-sixty-five. She could have lifted Eddie Taysatch into the ambulance by herself if she had to. *I am strong. I am strong enough to take this on.* She found a hair tie in her purse and put her hair back into a ponytail.

She could take Vivian Roundhouse. She could take both Vivian and her girlfriend if she had to. She closed her eyes and envisioned the last round of training shots she'd taken. It was the most accurate she'd ever been—her instructor said she was in the ninety-fifth percentile of agents.

But accuracy on the shooting range didn't always translate in practice. She'd read the articles—accuracy dropped to thirty percent in real-world scenarios. And whoever the shooter was *had* been accurate. There must have been thirty feet between the car and Eddie Taysatch.

Unless the shooter had intended to hit Bernadette instead—

Bernadette opened her eyes, and the room spun for a moment before snapping into place. This wasn't helping. It wasn't doing any good to think about it here. She'd go see Vivian Roundhouse, she'd get answers or she'd kick some ass.

Why get rid of Eddie Taysatch? Did he know something? Did he see something?

She looked in the mirror and straightened her blazer, took a deep breath, and walked out the door.

❧

DUNN DROVE THE CRUISER, BERNADETTE IN THE PASSENGER seat, turning onto Twelfth Street from Highland Avenue.

"There was an open spot back there," Bernadette said.

"Let's drive around the campus. The chapel's up here on the left—let's see what we can find."

"What we can find?"

"Any light blue vans that might be parked on the street."

Bernadette shook her head. "You put out an APB on the van. Do you really think someone shot Eddie Taysatch and left it parked on the street?"

"Stranger things have happened." They turned into the campus. The snow let up until only a few flakes fluttered to the earth. "Did Eddie say anything else?"

Bernadette turned away from the street—no sign of the van yet. "What?"

"You rode with him to the hospital. Did Eddie say anything else?"

"No. He was going into shock."

"You didn't see the driver, did you?"

"Nope."

Dunn rubbed her neck, then put her hand back on the steering wheel. "Even after we talk with Vivian Roundhouse again, we've got a bunch of people to interview. There's the head of the Piscary Association, Douglas Rheinstaller. We can lean on him—he's the one who punched Eddie, after all."

"How hard do you want to push?"

"We can bring him into the station and charge him with assault if we need to."

"Maybe he's got a light blue van, too. Or maybe someone else at the Piscary Association."

"I checked. He doesn't have a van, but we'll check out the other members of the board, maybe a few of his friends. It's a common make and model."

"Where do we interview him?"

"He lives out near the airport. Works as an electrician. Gets home about three. I vote for heading over there after we talk with the reverend."

Bernadette looked out the window again. Still no blue van.

Dunn braked for a stop sign. "You think your sniffy colleague will turn up any time soon?"

Bernadette tapped the armrest thoughtfully. "Who knows? He has a history of going AWOL on cases."

"Then why keep him around?"

"He's impossible to replace."

Dunn tapped the steering wheel thoughtfully. "Can he really smell when this ibogaine stuff has been in a room?"

"I think so. Obviously, my bosses think so, too."

Dunn turned a corner and Bernadette recognized the street. They'd made a loop all the way around campus. "I don't think we'll find the van."

"Me neither." Dunn pulled in front of a parking meter at the curb, and they got out, the passenger door gently scraping a mound of snow.

"What exactly is your plan, Detective?" Bernadette asked.

"Let's ask the reverend about the van," Dunn said. "See

where that leads us. Maybe she can ask her bestest buddy Anne Askew if she can see the van from the sky."

Bernadette shot Dunn a look. "You don't need to be disrespectful."

Dunn ignored her and quickened her pace to the quad.

Bernadette ran to keep up. "What do you think happened? You have a motive in mind?"

"I have some possible scenarios."

"Such as?"

"Here's one possibility. Kymer Thompson was stealing ibogaine from the Freshie to get it for the church's rituals. Maybe he started blackmailing her."

"We'll need to check the logs at the Freshie."

"Logs can be forged."

"So how do you think we can prove—"

"I said it's a possible scenario, Becker. I don't have the answers. This is all speculation." Dunn thrust her hands into the pockets of her coat. "Besides, you're the one who asked."

"Right. Sorry."

"If my wild guess is right," Dunn mused, "Kymer Thompson sees the priest's nice expensive home, her Mercedes, he figures he's taking the risk of getting kicked out of the program if he's found out. Then he ups the price. Maybe negotiations get out of hand."

"And how does that explain the syringe?"

Dunn shook her head. "I don't know yet."

"And how does Eddie Taysatch play into this?"

"He notices the missing ibogaine. He threatens to go to the cops."

"Does he threaten to blackmail her too?"

"It's one possibility. I bet after we talk to Roundhouse, we'll have a better idea where to focus our resources."

"I shouldn't have asked," Bernadette said. "We both need to go into this with an open mind."

Dunn scoffed. "Now you sound like you're advocating the use of iboga bark. If I put a little pinch between my cheek and gum, it'll open my mind, is that it?"

Bernadette barked a laugh. "That's exactly it, Detective. Me, an investigator with the Controlled Substances Analysis Bureau, encouraging a police detective to get high on a schedule 1 narcotic."

Dunn grunted.

They found themselves at the front door of the chapel. A sign hung on the door reading *No Tours Today*. Dunn reached out and knocked.

The chapel docent—the one Bernadette had interviewed—opened the door a crack. "Sorry, ladies," she said, "we're not offering any tours—" Then she saw their faces. "Oh. It's you again."

Dunn held up her badge. "We'd like to speak with Vivian Roundhouse. Is she in?"

The docent stepped back and pulled the door open.

Chapter Thirteen

THEY WALKED INTO THE CHAPEL, DUNN LEADING THE WAY. Bernadette removed her knit cap and, as she stepped into the aisle, a shiver ran down her back. It was hard to tell if the chill in the Winterstone was real—or if it was a product of the cold March day and the open chapel door.

Vivian Roundhouse knelt beside a wooden table in the apse, taking tall red candles off the table and placing them in a long, squat box on the floor.

"Good afternoon, Reverend Roundhouse," Bernadette said.

Roundhouse glanced up but continued with her work. "You were at my house yesterday. You're the federal agent."

"Investigator," Bernadette corrected. Oof, she sounded so pedantic. "This is Detective Kerrigan Dunn from the Milwaukee Police Department."

"I hope these candles aren't a problem for you," the reverend said. "I'd hate for there to be some controlled substance in the wax."

"We have a few more questions."

Roundhouse cackled. "I didn't think you came here to get on the guest list for Tommy's anchor ceremony."

Bernadette cocked her head. "Anchor ceremony?"

"His memorial service," Dunn said to Bernadette.

"*I am not she that list my anchor to let fall,*" Roundhouse recited. "Anne Askew believed her journey through this life was as a ship crossing the sea. Our Tommy has crossed."

"When is the ceremony?" Bernadette said.

"Friday evening."

"Is it all right if we pay our respects?"

Roundhouse looked into Bernadette's eyes. "Are you serious?"

"If it's not appropriate—"

"No, it's fine," Roundhouse said. "We'd be happy to have you."

Roundhouse set down the two candles in her hand, grabbed the edge of the table, and pulled herself to her feet. "But that's not why you're here."

"No." Bernadette cleared her throat. "Were you looking for Tommy on Monday night?"

Roundhouse knit her eyebrows. "Monday night? No."

"You didn't visit Tommy's girlfriend looking for him?"

"Of course not. Why would I have done that?"

"We have a witness who puts you at Annika Nakrivo's door shortly before the murder."

Roundhouse shook her head firmly. "I was nowhere near the campus that evening. You heard Suzanne—I was with her all evening."

"Yes," Bernadette said, "and since I received conflicting information, I'm trying to clarify where you were. You didn't go to campus first and then come back to your house?"

"No. I worked on my sermon in my study all afternoon. Suzanne arrived about six o'clock."

"Where's your study?"

"It's one of the spare bedrooms in my house."

"So you didn't leave the house after midday?" Dunn asked.

"No." Roundhouse glared at the two of them. "Is that all?"

"One more thing," Bernadette said. "Does Agios Delphi own a light blue van?"

Roundhouse pursed her lips. "May I ask what this is about?"

"Can you answer the question, Reverend?" Dunn said, a touch of menace in her voice.

Roundhouse paused. "The church does have a van, yes."

"Where is it now?"

"One of our members has offered to garage it for us."

"Garage it for you?"

"That's right. You may have noticed that there's no room for our church materials at the Anne Askew Chapel," Roundhouse said. "Many of the items we need for our services can go in boxes in my trunk, but the van—when we need it—can't be kept here."

"Who's storing the van?"

"I told you—a member of the church."

"Which member?"

Roundhouse looked from Bernadette's face to Dunn's and crossed her arms. "I don't believe I'm obligated to provide that information to you."

"Listen, *rev*—" Dunn began.

Bernadette interrupted. "That van was involved in a shooting earlier today, Reverend."

A pause. Roundhouse blinked rapidly. "Is—is Suzanne okay?"

"Suzanne?" Bernadette said. "That's Suzanne Thao, who I met at your house yesterday?"

"Is she okay?"

"No one in the van was shot, Reverend," Bernadette said. "We believe someone shot a gun from the van and injured a co-worker of Kymer Thompson."

The Agios Delphi priest reached for the edge of the table and leaned against it. "But Suzanne's okay?"

"We don't know who was there," Dunn said. "I didn't get a good look at the driver. You're saying that Suzanne Thao stores the van at her residence?"

Roundhouse shook her head. "Not at her residence. She owns a commercial property in Walker's Point. We keep the van there."

"Does she rent out the property?" Dunn asked.

"Not yet. She bought it cheap after Superior Salt & Feed went out of business. But it's been sitting empty for a while. She plans on renovating the property before she offers it for lease again."

"And she lets the church keep its van there?"

"Yes, and we've put some items in storage in the warehouse. She's working on retrofitting part of the building for a conference room so our elder board can meet."

"Do you know where Ms. Thao is?"

Roundhouse scowled. "No."

Bernadette stepped forward. "Your church is listed as the registered owner of that van, Reverend, so we have to ask. Where were you at ten thirty this morning?"

"On my way to the chapel."

"Were you in the van?"

"We keep the van at the warehouse. I was in my own car."

Bernadette turned to Dunn. "All right," Bernadette said, "let me confer with my colleague."

"Ask anyone," Roundhouse said. "I got here at ten forty-five. Walked straight in."

Bernadette nodded and she and Dunn walked together into a corner, behind the pews. "What do you think?"

"The apartments are only a few blocks away," Dunn said.

"She could have shot him and gotten dropped off here. An accomplice could be getting rid of the van right now."

"Maybe we need to go to the salt warehouse. See if the van's there."

Dunn shook her head. "I don't think it is. The way the shooter's probably thinking, we could have officers there before the van could get back."

"You think if the shooter is Vivian Roundhouse and the driver is Suzanne Thao, they're actually taking all of that into account? Maybe they didn't think anyone would see them, and that Suzanne would get back to the warehouse without any problems."

Dunn shook her head again, more adamantly this time. "No. I don't buy it."

"But it's enough for a search warrant for her property, isn't it?"

"Roundhouse's property? No. It's probably enough for the warehouse, but not where Roundhouse lives." Dunn flexed the fingers of her right hand. "You have anything else you want to ask her?"

"Not right now." Bernadette frowned. "But if it's not Round-house or Thao, why use this van?"

"Could be someone else at the church." Dunn squinted. "Maybe someone's trying to put the blame on the church. Or one of the members."

"Roundhouse has to be our prime suspect. She doesn't have a good alibi. She's the head of the nonprofit that owns the van."

"It's all circumstantial. Besides, you saw her react when she heard there was a shooting involving the van. She wanted to know if Thao was okay."

"Right," Bernadette said, "but even so, given the evidence, and having Eddie Taysatch in the hospital, with his life still in danger, we can't let her go."

"If we bring her in, the clock starts ticking on when we can formally charge her," Dunn said. "I'm not confident we can build a case against her in forty-eight hours."

Bernadette was silent.

"We could get a couple of uniforms to watch her after we check out the salt factory," Dunn said. "Can't be a big priority—we're already getting slammed by the chief for all the overtime this month—but it's better than nothing."

"We can't let Roundhouse leave, though, can we?" Bernadette asked. "I mean, she might have shot Eddie this morning."

Dunn shook her head. "If we can't place her with her van, we can't place her at the scene of the shooting."

"I don't like it."

Dunn clenched her jaw. "Unless you want to get her on some fake federal domestic terrorism charge, we can't bring her in. We could ask her to come down to the station with us, but what exactly would we ask her there that we didn't ask her here?"

❧

BERNADETTE STARED OUT THE PASSENGER WINDOW OF Dunn's cruiser on the drive back to the District 5 station. The snow had lightened into occasional flurries.

She couldn't get Eddie's pleading eyes out of her mind, the incredulity that he'd been shot. She closed her eyes for a moment. Eddie would be all right, wouldn't he?

She figured, when she'd gotten demoted to case analyst, that her days of excitement in the field were over. Then a flash of Sophie's face—only a *what if*—but she saw Sophie's face crumple when in her mind she was told that her mother had been shot in the head and wasn't coming back to Virginia.

Bernadette's phone rang, and her head snapped up as her eyes popped open. She hit *Answer* and put the speakerphone on.

"Becker."

"Hi, Bernadette. It's Maura."

"Oh, hi, Maura. You're on speaker—I've got Detective Dunn here with me. Any word from Dr. Woodhead?"

"Not since he said he'd meet up with you and Dunn later." Maura paused. "How are you two doing?"

"We believe the shot came from the Agios Delphi van. But we're not able to connect Vivian Roundhouse to the vehicle. It wasn't stored near Roundhouse's residence or the Anne Askew Chapel."

"I asked some of my officers to go to the warehouse where the van was stored," Dunn piped up. "It's the old Superior Salt & Feed in Walker's Point. Out of business for a few years. Roundhouse's girlfriend keeps it there."

Maura was silent.

Bernadette glanced at Dunn, but her eyes were on the road. "What is it, Maura?"

"Didn't Annika Nakrivo say that Vivian Roundhouse had visited her on Monday night?" Maura responded. "The night of the murder?"

"That's right."

"Roundhouse drives a Mercedes."

"Right," Dunn said. "Neighbor across the street took her dog outside about nine forty-five. Swore the Mercedes was in the driveway." A note of uncertainty hung in her voice.

"What is it?" Maura asked.

"Probably nothing—but most of the people in that neighborhood are well off."

"So?"

"It's winter. If they can, they put their vehicles in their garages."

"There are many good reasons not to have a car in a garage," Bernadette said. "Even in winter. Even if you're rich. And you don't have to be a murderer for any of them."

"No," Dunn said carefully, "but you've met women like Vivian Roundhouse before. You saw how meticulous her house is. She's a control freak."

"Maybe the garage is where she lets it all hang out," Bernadette said, a smile touching the corner of her mouth. "Maybe it's crammed to the brim with old magazines and broken file cabinets and trash she refuses to throw away."

"Or maybe," Dunn said, "she parked it outside in the driveway specifically so people passing would think she was home."

"Hang on," Bernadette said. "Didn't she say she was over at Suzanne's?"

"No. Suzanne was at her house. Not the other way around."

"She still could have been at Annika Nakrivo's dorm," Maura said. "She could have gone in Suzanne's car. Or in the van, for that matter. Maybe she parked it near campus Monday night. Then she took it to shoot Eddie Taysatch this morning."

"It's all speculation," Bernadette said. "No real motive, no sign that she was at any of those places."

"I'm telling you this so you don't rule her out," Maura said.

Dunn snickered. "Oh, there's no chance of that." Her phone rang and she answered it, holding it to her ear with one hand as she drove with the other. "Dunn." A pause. "Okay. Let's keep the APB. Widen the search area to neighboring counties." She pulled the phone away from her face. "Officers arrived at the old salt warehouse. Gate's open. No sign of the van."

"Any cameras in the area?" Maura said.

"We're checking, but the warehouse didn't have cameras,

and there aren't any businesses near that area—not near enough to get a good look at the property."

"Still, maybe we can see the van drive by at some point."

"It's a long shot," Bernadette said.

"Better than the shot we have now," Maura said. "Where are you heading?"

"Back to District 5," Dunn said.

"Did you get a statement from Douglas Rheinstaller?"

Dunn hesitated.

"Oh," Bernadette said. "The guy who punched Eddie Taysatch a couple of days ago."

"I know." Dunn glanced at Bernadette. "Send his address."

"He lives in Bay View," Maura said. "I'm texting the address to Bernadette. Bring him in to the district office. If he won't come voluntarily, arrest him on suspicion of assault. It'll give us some leverage."

"We're heading through Bay View right now." Dunn cleared her throat. "I did some background on Rheinstaller yesterday. This guy's been a commercial fisherman twenty or thirty years. Do you think holding him on suspicion of assault will make him talk? He's used to being on a boat, confined in a tiny space, for days on end."

Bernadette's phone dinged; it was the address.

"Being in open water is a lot different than being confined in a cell," Maura said.

"True." Dunn sighed. "I want him off the streets too. He punched a scientist who was trying to do his job, and now that scientist has been shot. But I want you to know—I don't expect him to talk."

"Of course, Detective Dunn," Maura said. "We'll support your decision."

"Thank you," Dunn mumbled.

Bernadette gave Dunn the address and Dunn nodded.

"If you do bring Rheinstaller down to the station, try to do it in the next hour. We're talking to the IT worker responsible for the lab—Nick LaSalle. He'll speak with Curtis about the keylogger programs found on Kymer Thompson's machine. Bernadette—you may want to sit in."

"Are we talking to the LaSalle at the Freshie?"

"We're still negotiating the location."

"Are you going to call Dr. Woodhead again?"

"As soon as I hang up with you," Maura said.

The cruiser turned onto a residential street with small, one-story homes set back from the street. About a hundred yards away on the right side of the street, a man in a parka, a Boston Bruins winter hat, and a light blue scarf covering his face stood stoically on a shoveled driveway.

"Never mind," Bernadette said. "We found him."

⁂

"It's about time you got here," Kep Woodhead said. "I was losing confidence that you'd arrive at this address."

"What are you talking about?" Bernadette said, closing the patrol car door behind her. "You're the one who's gone AWOL for the last few hours." Her boots crunched on the snow.

"Douglas Rheinstaller has been the subject of five complaints in the last six months from three different people at the lab—one of whom was Kymer Thompson. I also discovered the assault on Eddie Taysatch. Witness statements make fascinating reading sometimes. It was obvious you'd want to talk with Rheinstaller. I'd have thought he'd be first on your list after the girlfriend."

"How long have you been here?"

"About two hours."

"Standing out here in weather like this?"

"Don't be silly. There's an excellent taphouse on the main thoroughfare. I had a delightful midday meal, and a wonderful beer."

"Pinky's Taphouse?" Dunn asked, coming around the front of the cruiser.

"That's the one."

"They've got a great selection of IPAs."

Kep chortled. "I have found there's no such thing."

Bernadette rolled her eyes and turned to Dunn. "The over-hopped IPAs are, uh, offensive to those with a, uh—"

"Superschnozz. Yeah, I got it." Dunn shook her head.

Bernadette grabbed Kep's elbow and pulled him to the side. "I waited in the hotel lobby for over an hour for you to show up."

Kep pulled himself out of Bernadette's grip. "I was able to get further in the case without your assistance."

"You wasted hours of my time, Kep," Bernadette hissed. "Maura's been trying to reach you, too."

Kep looked sideways at Bernadette. "I know you're my handler—"

"Case analyst."

"—but I have an investigative process."

"You can't disappear like that."

Dunn cleared her throat. "So—all three of us are going up there?"

Bernadette took a step away from Kep. "Looks like it."

"All right," Dunn said, "you show your federal IDs, and see if he'll come voluntarily. We'll even say he can drive his own car to the station."

"Sure," Bernadette said, pulling out her identification.

"Perhaps we can ask to enter his domicile first," Kep said.

"Why?" Dunn asked.

Bernadette blinked. Her eyes were dry from the cold. "So he can smell."

Dunn looked at Kep, who nodded.

"You've gotta be crazy," Dunn said. "This guy's been a commercial fisherman for decades. His house probably smells like low tide. You think you'll recognize the smell from Thompson's corpse?"

"The lamprey has a distinct odor from the trout and salmon that Rheinstaller is paid to catch," Kep said. "I'll recognize it."

Dunn shook her head. "He's got the odor of a zillion trout and a zillion and a half salmon. And you think you'll stick your nose into his house and with one whiff be able to tell if he was in the lamprey aquarium for five minutes?"

"You don't have to believe me," Kep said. "CSAB believes me, and I've got certifications that say I'm an expert with my—how did you put it?—superschnozz."

Bernadette chuckled.

"Shall we get started?" Kep turned and walked up the path to the front door. The porch was small—miniscule compared to Vivian Roundhouse's residence. Dunn reached out and rang the doorbell. No dogs barked.

Bernadette heard rustling inside, then the deadbolt turning, and finally the door creaking open. A tall man, at least six-four or six-five, stood in the doorway, dressed in a red-checked flannel shirt and a pair of dirty blue jeans. His feet were clad in thick gray wool socks.

"Douglas Rheinstaller?" Bernadette said. She tried to keep her voice even, but it sounded high in her ears.

"Aw, shit," Rheinstaller said. "What did I do now? One of those science geeks say I scared 'em off with my ugly mug?"

"We do want to have a word with you," Bernadette held up her identification.

"CSAB? Why does a drug agency want to talk to me? I ain't even smoked pot for twenty years."

"We need to establish your whereabouts late Monday night," Bernadette said. "And we have a complaint for assault that we need to discuss."

"Oh, please," Rheinstaller said. "One of those pissy little lab rats, right? He can take away *my* livelihood, but I can't defend myself?"

"Perhaps we should come in, sir," Kep said. "It's rather cold out here and—"

"The hell you are. I know my rights. You aren't setting foot in this house."

"Really," Kep said, "I think you'll find that we'd like to eliminate you as a suspect—"

"No. Nice try."

"Mr. Rheinstaller," Bernadette said, "we'd rather have a productive conversation, not—"

"If you're not arresting me," Rheinstaller said, "you can get the hell off my property."

"Okay, we'll do it your way," Dunn said, taking her handcuffs off her belt. "Douglas Rheinstaller, you are under arrest for assault and—"

The front door slammed in their faces.

Bernadette saw red.

She launched herself past Dr. Woodhead's side, planting her left foot, then punching her right leg forward.

The heel of her boot made a satisfying low *thwack* as it made contact below the doorknob—followed by the sound of splintering wood.

The door swung open hard and connected with Douglas Rheinstaller's hip—he hadn't even had time to turn the deadbolt. He stumbled backward, his heel catching the edge of the tile, and fell, sprawling into the tiny living room in front of a worn tan couch.

Bernadette pounced on top of him, landing on the small of his back. He was a big man, but he gave a whine as all the wind escaped his lungs. She grabbed his left wrist and twisted his arm behind his back. "Douglas Rheinstaller," she repeated, "you are under arrest for assault."

"And resisting arrest," Dunn said, appearing at Bernadette's side, pulling the other arm behind his back, and cuffing his wrists together. "You have the right to remain silent…"

While Dunn was reading Rheinstaller his Miranda rights, Bernadette stood up. She caught a bemused grin on Woodhead's face and glared at him. "Aren't you stepping inside to get that whiff of lamprey you were hoping for, Doctor?"

"Right," Kep said, "I appreciate the reminder. Your crime-fighting technique vied for my attention for a moment."

"The key is to drive the heel of your foot into the weakest part of the door," Bernadette mumbled.

"You didn't even jump-kick."

"Come on," Bernadette said, rolling her eyes. "That's a Hollywood move. You've gotta have a solid plant foot. Otherwise, you lose power."

Kep knelt next to Rheinstaller and inhaled deeply, then rose, stepped into the living room between the coffee table and the television, and inhaled again. Then he shook his head.

"We won't find any crime here except punching Eddie Taysatch in the face," Kep said.

Bernadette helped Detective Dunn get Rheinstaller to his feet. "How did you know about that?"

Kep pointed at Rheinstaller's cuffed hands. "Swollen knuckles here. Mr. Taysatch had a black eye when he went for his morning run. I take it you also paid a visit to Mr. Taysatch?"

Bernadette nodded. "And after our interview, a light blue

van drove up, and someone in there shot Taysatch right in front of us."

Kep's face fell.

Rheinstaller groaned. "I don't know nothing about that. I didn't shoot anybody."

"Do you own a gun, Mr. Rheinstaller?"

"I'm not saying nothing."

"How about a light blue van? Maybe the Piscary Association has one."

Rheinstaller was silent.

Kep blinked and steadied himself against the door frame.

"You okay, Kep?" asked Bernadette.

Kep looked up into Bernadette's eyes. "He was shot in front of you?"

"That's right." Bernadette felt the tug on her insides, the phantom look on her daughter's face.

Kep glared at Rheinstaller on the ground. "I don't know where he was this morning," Kep said. "The smell of the lampreys is absent both in this house and on Mr. Rheinstaller's clothes. I also smell no ibogaine here." He turned to the hand-cuffed man whose eyes shot daggers at Bernadette. Kep bent down and sniffed.

"What the hell are you doing?" Rheinstaller spat.

"I don't smell nitroglycerin," Kep said.

"Nitroglycerin?"

"Modern ammunition is primarily wood pulp soaked in nitroglycerin. A little mercury fulminate in the primer for that nice little metallic zap that sets my teeth on edge. But I smell none of that on Mr. Rheinstaller. If he had shot Eddie Taysatch this morning, I would smell it."

"You'd be able to smell that over the fish?" Bernadette asked.

"Correct."

Bernadette put her hands on her hips as the detective pulled Rheinstaller to his feet and led him outside in cuffs. "Mr. Rheinstaller gets the back seat all to himself, but that means only one of us can ride back to the district station with Dunn."

"I don't want to go back to the district station. I'd like to talk with Annika Nakrivo again."

"The girlfriend? You may want to talk with you, but I doubt she'll agree to another interview." Bernadette held the broken front door open for Kep, then followed him out to the driveway, watching Dunn as she opened the back door of her cruiser for Rheinstaller. "I think we need to speak with a couple of the suspects in the first round. Besides—Curtis is interviewing the IT specialist who was responsible for the software on the lab's computers. I want to make sure we sit in on that."

"That task requires no scent identification. Curtis should have it covered—after all, he's the technology expert, isn't he?"

"Still," Bernadette said, "let's not get ahead of ourselves."

Dunn closed the rear door after putting Rheinstaller inside. "You're saying you want me to leave you here?"

"How far away is the Kilbourn Tech campus, Detective?" Kep asked.

"Too far to walk, that's for sure," Dunn said. "Three, maybe four miles, and you don't want to do it when the sidewalks are icy."

"We'll order an Uber," Kep said. "Come on, Bernie, let's catch our killer."

She glared at him. "Bernadette."

Dunn laughed. "With a woman who can kick like that, you *better* get her name right." She opened the driver's door. "Maybe I'll see you at the station later." She disappeared inside the car, pulled into the street, and a moment later she turned the corner and was gone.

Bernadette glared at Kep, who had pulled his phone out of

his pocket and was requesting an Uber. "You sure you want to talk to Annika Nakrivo again? Curtis may know his tech, but he doesn't know what questions to ask in an interrogation."

Kep lowered the phone from in front of his face. "Six minutes," he said. "And I have to ask—when have you interrogated *anyone*? Aren't you a handler—sorry, *case analyst?*"

"You assume I've always been a case analyst, Kep. It is entirely possible I have more interrogation experience than our good Detective Dunn."

Kep's eyes glittered with amusement. "Be that as it may," Kep continued, "my nose won't do the case any good at the station. My olfactory talents will be put to much better use interviewing Miss Nakrivo again."

"Even better if you go back to the lab, if that'll be your argument," Bernadette pointed out. "There will be a full contingent of employees and interns there—you can sniff them to your heart's content, and I can even ask a question or two."

Kep snapped his fingers. "Interns—of course. Miss Nakrivo is scheduled to be at the laboratory today. She won't be at Juneau Hall." He brought his phone back up in front of his face and tapped the Uber app.

"See?" Bernadette said. "There's a reason you need a case analyst babysitting you and your supershnozz. So don't go disappearing again."

Chapter Fourteen

IN THE BACK OF A NEON GREEN KIA SOUL—ONE OF THE messiest Uber cars she'd ever seen—Bernadette looked over at Kep. Why had he disappeared that morning? Where had he gone, and why hadn't he allowed his case analyst to go with him? She wanted to discuss strategy once the two of them got to the lab, but Kep's eyes were closed as he leaned back in the seat, his glasses almost halfway down his nose. Clearly, he didn't want to talk.

They arrived at the Freshie a little before three o'clock, and Kep exited quickly, then breathed in dramatic fashion.

"What's the plan here?" Bernadette asked. "Usually, I talk strategy on the way so I know what I'm getting myself into."

"I apologize," Kep said. "That car was rank. Fusarium—Cladosporium—the smells were so bad I couldn't think. I was in no condition to review tactics." The Kia drove off, and Kep turned to it. "Would thou wert clean enough to spit upon."

Bernadette sighed. "Okay, we haven't gone in yet. Do you want to seek out Annika first, or do you want to have another conversation with Lightman and ask him where he was this morning? See if he knows anything about Eddie Taysatch getting shot?"

Kep blinked. "Do you have any reason to suspect the professor?"

"No. But the question will surprise him. It might make him more likely to tell the truth about things he might otherwise keep hidden. Affairs. Skimming off the top. Stuff like that." Bernadette folded her arms. "We could divide and conquer, but personally—despite the fact that you clearly hate working with me—I think you and I have enough complementary skill sets that it makes sense to be together when we question Lightman and Nakrivo."

Kep pulled his winter hat further down on his head. "I suppose you're right."

"Who do you want to start with?"

"My preference is to interview Miss Nakrivo first. I would like to get more information about her visit from the reverend Monday night."

"Which she doesn't want to talk about."

"I'd like to press her on her reticence. Perhaps the work environment will force her to reveal more information to try to end the interview in haste."

"It's possible." Bernadette pressed her lips together. "But someone who doesn't even cry about her boyfriend dying might be too smart for that."

Kep stared at the ground.

"What is it, Kep?"

"I suspect Miss Nakrivo is lying about the nature of her relationship with Thompson."

"You don't think they were really boyfriend and girlfriend?"

"I'm not sure," Kep muttered.

"But something smells rotten in Denmark?"

Kep glanced at Bernadette, who grinned melodramatically and raised and lowered her eyebrows quickly. He chuckled.

They walked in through the lab's front entrance, entered the elevator, and pushed the "2" button. The loud grinding of the elevator's mechanisms echoed the grinding of the gears in Bernadette's head. Something was still missing. There were plenty of suspects, plenty of lies, plenty of misdirection. But all the lies and misdirection might not add up to murder. Means, motive, and opportunity—Professor Lightman, Nakrivo, Taysatch, and the reverend too. Kep's nose had for the moment ruled out Rheinstaller, but Bernadette wasn't so sure he wasn't somehow involved.

The elevator doors slid open to reveal the large, open bullpen. Off to the side of the main floor, sitting at Kymer Thompson's old desk, sat Curtis Janek in his leather jacket and Nick LaSalle, who wiped his brow with his flannel shirt sleeve.

"I did not expect your technology specialist to be onsite," Kep hissed, getting out of the elevator with Bernadette.

"They must have negotiated meeting here instead of the District 5 station," Bernadette whispered back. "That's what we wanted to begin with, remember?"

"We must chart a new course." Kep pointed to the back hall that led to the stairs. "Perhaps I'll investigate the aquarium again. It might be unlocked during business hours."

Bernadette nodded. "And I'll talk to Curtis. Maybe ask the IT guy where he was going last night with two big tote bags."

A plan flashed through Bernadette's head—she wasn't sure she could pull it off, and the thought of it made her palms sweat, but she had to try. "Come with me," she said in a low voice. "Stand behind me, like you're questioning the IT guy too, then you can slip down the hall."

Kep pursed his lips and followed Bernadette.

"Curtis," Bernadette said loudly, stopping in front of

Thompson's desk. "I thought you were going to talk to IT down at the station."

"It makes more sense to see the keylogger in action," Curtis said, confusion washing over his pale face.

Kep walked around the desk, taking a position behind the seated Curtis.

Bernadette turned to Nick LaSalle. "You're the IT guy we met at the chapel."

LaSalle looked up at Bernadette and blinked. "That's right."

"Nick LaSalle, isn't it? You're in charge of all the IT that isn't on the main campus, if I remember correctly?"

Curtis cleared his throat. "I'm running some diagnostics to see when the keylogger was installed and where the commands originated."

"Like I told Mr. Janek," LaSalle said, "I don't have any idea about that. I'm a Windows guy. I set up the PCs, I do the password rules, I put the antimalware on the images—"

Bernadette took a deep breath and tried to channel Sophie in a bad mood. "Sounds like you didn't do a very good job."

LaSalle's head snapped up. "I do my job *fine*. The university doesn't have the budget to spring for some of the more sophisticated security packages—and besides, most of our PCs are too old to run them anyway."

In the corner of Bernadette's eye, Kep stepped back, sinking into the shadows as he disappeared down the hall.

"I know what I see," Bernadette snapped. "Someone who's too incompetent to protect their own network."

LaSalle scowled. "There's only so much I can do," he said.

"Serves the university right," Bernadette said, "hiring IT people without real degrees. You probably got your certificate from Fly-By-Night Technical Institute."

"I got my degree in computer science from Kilbourn Tech,"

LaSalle spat. "Graduated with honors. Blame the university budget, not the messenger."

"Who's your manager?" Bernadette demanded.

"*Hey!*" Curtis stood up and put his body between Bernadette and LaSalle. "No more of this." He put a finger in Bernadette's face. "Mr. LaSalle is being cooperative."

"I *was* being cooperative," LaSalle said. "If I keep getting accused of doing things I clearly didn't do, you all can do your own work."

"Maybe it would be better if we *did* do our own work. At least we'd know it wasn't screwed up on purpose." Bernadette put her hands on her hips. "And you might be cooperative now, but you sure weren't yesterday when I saw you walking down Highland Avenue carrying two big tote bags."

"I don't know what you're talking about." LaSalle averted his eyes but made no move to leave.

"Is everything all right out here?" The voice behind Bernadette made her jump slightly. Professor Lightman stood behind her, his mouth turning down at the corners.

Bernadette looked around the bullpen area. A half-dozen employees were all seated at their desks; some looking at her, some trying pointedly to ignore the kerfuffle. Good—she'd made enough of a scene to put Lightman on his heels. "I think we should speak in your office."

"I told you I didn't have anything to do with installing the keyloggers!" LaSalle whined.

"We can speak out here," Lightman said sternly.

"I don't think we can," Bernadette said, "unless you want personnel matters to be heard by everyone on this floor." At that, another two heads popped above their computer monitors at the desks around the bullpen.

Lightman glared at her, then turned and strode into his office. Bernadette followed him, closing the door behind her.

"Listen," Lightman began, sitting down in his chair, "I like you, Agent Becker, and the IT guy doesn't report to me, but I can't have you getting hysterical in here."

Bernadette felt her lip curl and took a deep breath, letting it out slowly.

"I was on the phone with the people in charge of our grant," Lightman continued. "There are rumblings that they want to delay. We're competing to get to market before another medication, and a delay could mean project cancellation. Poof, there goes my funding—there goes *everyone's* job. I'm lucky I hung up before you started yelling. It's not conducive to a stable work environment."

"Neither are murdered employees, Professor."

Lightman gritted his teeth.

"Where were you at ten thirty this morning?" Bernadette demanded.

Lightman blinked. "This morning? I—why do you want to know?"

"Because one of your *other* grad student researchers was shot in front of his apartment building."

The color drained from Lightman's face.

Bernadette took a step forward. "Considering ibogaine was what killed Kymer Thompson, and considering Eddie Taysatch was shot this morning, the lab is looking more and more like a common element."

Lightman opened his mouth, then closed it. "Is Eddie—is he okay?"

"The last I heard, he was going into surgery," Bernadette said. "I haven't gotten a phone call to let me know the shooting is a murder investigation yet." She cocked her head. "Who else knows the details of what you're working on here?"

"Well—Tommy and Eddie, of course." He blinked and

looked balefully up at Bernadette. His eyes were wide, and his breaths were short and quick. "And me."

Bernadette shook her head. He was scared. Maybe he was scared of getting caught, but Lightman was acting more like he was scared for his life.

"What sort of information would Tommy and Eddie have that someone would want to kill for, Professor?"

"I don't know," he said, his voice small.

"Tell me where you were on Monday night, Professor. Give me someone who can corroborate whatever story it is you're planning to tell. Tell me where I can find Cecilia Carter. Show me that the ibogaine you have here isn't the same concentrated version injected into Kymer Thompson's arm. Give me something to eliminate you as a suspect. Show me that I can trust you."

Lightman shifted uncomfortably in his seat. "Am I under arrest?"

Bernadette hesitated. While Lightman had been cagey, he was likely trying to hide his affair with Cecilia Carter. Even if she'd wanted to bluff an arrest, she didn't carry handcuffs. A gun for protection, yes, but no cuffs. That was Maura's department —and Bernadette and Kep were supposed to keep the lieutenent apprised of the investigation, especially when they were close to arrest. She wished Detective Dunn was still with them.

"That really depends on what you have to say for yourself," she said.

But her hesitation gave away her weakness. She saw it in Lightman's eyes, through the fear for his personal safety covering the rest of his face.

"I'll say nothing more without a lawyer present," Lightman said.

"Not even about Cecilia Carter?"

Lightman leaned back and clamped his mouth shut, glaring at Bernadette.

The professor was looking more and more like a dead end. He wasn't acting guilty—he was acting like he was afraid of being next on the list.

Something wasn't quite right with the IT guy, though. She closed her eyes and ran through the conversation with Nick LaSalle. She'd accused him of being incompetent. He'd pushed back.

And then once she'd purposely ratcheted up the accusations, he snapped.

If I keep getting accused of doing things I clearly didn't do, you all can do your own work.

What had she accused him of?

Of *not* doing his job. Of *not* putting adequate security on the systems. Of *not* doing things. She'd never accused him of actually *doing* anything.

So why did he deny installing the keyloggers?

It's possible that he was flustered. But it was also possible that Nick LaSalle *had* installed the keyloggers. And that even a whiff of an accusation was enough to trigger his defenses.

"Well?" Lightman stared at her.

Ugh. She'd gotten lost in thought.

Lightman knew he wouldn't be answering any more of Bernadette's questions. She sighed. This was not the way to claw her way back to full agent status.

"No," she said, "no, I won't arrest you. But you don't have an alibi for Monday night."

Lightman scoffed. "I had no reason to kill anyone. Removing Tommy and Eddie isn't good for the project *or* for me. It's the best way to make sure the funding gets pulled. If that happens, we're all not only out of our jobs, but the students will have to scramble to get into another lab program to fulfill their degree requirements."

"Not the undergrad interns."

"Are you kidding? Without this program, most of them wouldn't have even applied to Kilbourn Tech. Some of them have these internships in exchange for lower tuition. There's literally no one in this lab who'd be better off with Kymer Thompson dead. A murder *in* the program is the murder *of* the program."

"Sometimes in the heat of the moment, the rational decision isn't always made."

Lightman glared at her.

Bernadette turned and left Lightman's office.

The door closed behind her, and she gazed across the bullpen. Other employees surely could be interviewed. She wouldn't get anywhere with Nick LaSalle—not after attacking him verbally in front of everyone. And besides, Curtis was with him.

Annika Nakrivo might be with the lampreys in the aquarium room where Kep could interview her. But if not, maybe she was at her desk. But Bernadette didn't want to hyperfocus—that's how things went sideways.

The work area had six other desks besides Thompson's. As LaSalle and Curtis worked at the victim's computer, Bernadette began to question the other employees.

Half an hour later, she'd talked with five of them. No one liked Tommy—he was not only arrogant but constantly proselytizing. Everyone she spoke with said they avoided him. One of the researchers, Letitia, postulated that Annika had lost some sort of bet in which she had to pretend to be Tommy's girlfriend for a year. Letitia thought it was creepy that Annika looked so much like Mariska Sikmo. The other employees and interns did not know who Sikmo was but agreed that Annika and Tommy mismatched.

Bernadette sat in the guest chair in front of the last intern's desk.

"So you're the federal agent investigating Tommy's murder." The tall Black woman looked at Bernadette out of the corner of her eye as she typed, then leaned back and appraised her through browline-style spectacles.

"That's me. Bernadette Becker."

"Zadie Michaels. Nice to meet you." She leaned forward. "You've been asking about Annika and Tommy, huh?"

"How would you characterize their relationship?"

"Weird," said Zadie. "It would be one thing if they had similar interests. All they seem to have in common is this place."

"And Agios Delphi," Bernadette added, handing Zadie a business card.

"Oh—is that the church that Tommy's always talking about?"

"Probably. Annika's a member too."

"Oh," Zadie nodded emphatically, "that makes sense. They're a tiny church, aren't they? If they're the same religion, that explains it. Probably the only two people the same age in all of Milwaukee who are in that crazy cult."

"What do you think of the Anne Askew Chapel?"

"Me? Well—I think it's crazy that someone decided to ship it all the way from London to Milwaukee, stone by stone. It's pretty cool, though. A fifteenth-century chapel right here on campus. I wish more people had heard of Anne Askew. I tell my friends from high school about it, and they think she's a new pop singer."

"Did you know Anne Askew is a central figure in the religion that Tommy and Annika belong to?"

"No."

"And did you know Agios Delphi uses ibogaine in their ceremonies?"

"What? You mean the same stuff that we inject in the fish livers here?"

"They chew up the plant bark, and it's a lot less concentrated, but yeah."

Zadie shook her head. "I heard ibogaine can cause hallucinations. Not much more than that, though. I didn't know it had religious significance."

Bernadette smiled. "It's a relief to finally talk to someone who knows about the medication you're making."

"I don't know about that," Zadie said. "Sometimes I don't have enough to do to fill up my day here, so I read the literature from the studies. At least I don't have to gut the lampreys. They're nasty. Like something from a horror movie."

The employee at the desk next to Zadie stood up, stretched, and walked toward the elevator. Zadie glanced at him out of the corner of her eye, and when he pushed the down button, she leaned closer to Bernadette. "I shouldn't be telling you this, but Tommy and Eddie were the brains behind all the breakthroughs."

"I thought Professor Lightman was behind most of it."

Zadie shook her head. "He's been skating by on the work of his grad students for years now. With Tommy gone and Eddie in the hospital, I hope this last formulation works. Otherwise, we'll all be rearranging deck chairs."

Bernadette rubbed her neck; it was starting to hurt. "Lightman's got a reputation for being brilliant."

"Not at all earned, I promise you. And we all know it."

"Why doesn't anyone say anything?"

"Because he's got the financial connections. Without him,

we'd have no research to work on." Zadie's eyes twinkled. "Do you want to see something crazy?"

Bernadette tried not to let her surprise show, and she nodded. "Sure."

"This is because you called that asshole IT guy out," she said. "Ordinarily I'd keep this under wraps." She clicked her mouse, and a web browser came up on her screen. She typed hurriedly and a curvy, scantily clad brunette appeared.

"This is what you wanted to show me?" The brunette looked familiar, but Bernadette couldn't quite place her.

"You don't recognize her, do you?" Zadie grinned conspiratorially. "Lighten the hair a few shades, give her a haircut, put her on a diet to lose ten pounds, who do you see?"

Bernadette squinted.

Zadie rolled her eyes. "And get a Sharpie to put a big dot on her upper lip. Come on, white people don't look *that* much alike."

"Oh," Bernadette said, eyes widening.

Zadie pointed to the woman's face on screen. "You do see it, right? Annika Nakrivo, straight up."

Bernadette nodded. "But—that's not what this page says." There was something else, too—she'd seen this woman somewhere before, and it wasn't with the beauty mark or the collagen.

"Nope. *Verity Vivacious.* I don't know about you, but I don't think that's her real name." Zadie laughed.

Bernadette blinked as the hot pink text on the black background jumped out at her. "Is this an escort site?"

"It sure ain't a church choir."

Bernadette cocked her head. "It says she's based in Miami—is that right?"

"That's what it says."

"I know some women work their way through college by

stripping or by, you know, escorting. So maybe that's what she did. Now she's at the top university of her choice, about to get into a great science program."

"Except," Zadie said, "she's auditing all her classes."

"What?"

"Yep. She and I have lunch sometimes. I was stressing out about my midterms, and I asked her why she wasn't stressed—and she said she's paying for her classes, but not taking them for credit."

"They let her do that and stay in the dorms?"

Zadie waved her hand. "Some loophole. You know the type of people who always find cheat codes for everything. I think she's one of those."

"But why? If this is the college of her choice, why isn't she taking the classes for credit?"

"No idea. None of my business."

"Is she in today?"

"She is, but I think she's headed out early." She pointed to a door. "That opens into another hallway and into another bullpen like this one. She's the third desk on the left." Zadie put her elbows on the desk. "Her boyfriend was killed, so Lightman told her to go home."

Bernadette glanced up. Curtis was still working on Thompson's computer, and she caught LaSalle giving her a nasty look.

I told you I didn't have anything to do with installing the keyloggers.

Oh—that was what was bothering her. They'd only found a keylogger program on one computer—Thompson's. But he'd used the plural: *keyloggers.*

Maybe he knew about Thompson's home PC too.

What else did Nick LaSalle know?

Chapter Fifteen

AFTER TALKING WITH ZADIE, BERNADETTE FOLLOWED THE hallway behind the door to Annika's desk. She hoped Annika hadn't left yet—and found the young intern behind the desk, computer screen on. Kep stood on the other side of the desk, trying to appear relaxed but failing.

"I'm unsure why you're not as concerned about the security footage disappearing as we are," Kep said. "Even if she's the reverend from your church, it's not appropriate for her to be in your dorm room if she's not invited."

"It's not that I'm unconcerned," Annika said. "I'm resigned to the fact that someone stole the footage."

"You're resigned?"

Annika rolled her eyes. "There are *so* many girls on my floor who do drugs. Not weed. I mean cocaine, X, molly. Last week they had their dealer come up to the third floor with them. He didn't want to be caught on camera."

Kep nodded. "Are you implying that the drug dealer stole the security footage?"

"It's the most likely explanation." She sniffed. "Listen,

Professor Lightman is insisting I take the rest of the day off. Am I free to go?"

"Not quite," Bernadette replied. "I wondered how much work you do with the ibogaine—and if you've got access to the locked cabinet upstairs."

Annika shrugged. "My job is dealing with the fish enzymes."

"Are you saying you don't have access to the ibogaine?" Bernadette asked.

"Not that I know of."

"Even though it's used by your church?"

"I don't know how the church gets its ibogaine."

"Have you taken ibogaine at any Agios Delphi meeting?"

Annika folded her arms. "I don't believe I'm going to answer that."

Kep nodded. "But Tommy was an elder there, wasn't he? Did you ever see him take any ibogaine for the church?"

"No," Annika said, "and if you're going to throw wild accusations at my dead boyfriend, you can do it when I'm not here." She grabbed her pack, her parka, and her purse, and stomped off around the corner.

"Congratulations," Bernadette said. "You've pissed off another witness."

"Pissed her off enough to make her forget her notebook," Kep said, already leafing through the spiral-bound pages Annika had left on top of the desk.

Bernadette leaned forward. "Last year, Annika Nakrivo was working as an escort in Miami."

Kep put a hand to his chest and rolled his eyes. "Oh my stars. A young lady who chooses to work her way through school. I haven't clutched my pearls this tightly since I saw a 1987 Afterschool Special on the dangers of marijuana."

Bernadette elbowed Kep. "Cut it out. If that was the only thing that raised suspicion, it'd be one thing. She faked crying when her boyfriend is dead, which again, by itself doesn't mean much. But now I found out she's auditing all her classes this semester."

"She's—what?"

"Weird, right? She had to work for an escort service to pay for college, but then she pays tuition for a semester and doesn't even take her classes for credit? That doesn't make any sense."

Kep slowly shook his head. "No."

"Do you have something else on your mind?"

Kep nodded. "There's a second room down on the aquarium level."

"Did you break in?"

"It was unnecessary. The second room is behind another metal door marked *Research Room 12*. Inside, I discovered additional tanks with more ammocoetes."

"Did you find anything besides baby lampreys?"

"I found evidence strongly suggesting Research Room 12 is the murder scene."

Bernadette shuffled back a step. "The murder scene?"

"I detected a faint odor of bleach last night. Today, I arranged myself on the floor to better ascertain where the scent was strongest."

"And?"

"There was an area on the floor in front of Tank 15, about two meters long by one meter wide, where I detected bleach more strongly than anywhere else."

"I imagine they have lamprey accidents once in a while. Fish blood everywhere."

Kep nodded. "Yes, and I smelled bleach in a few other places in the room, but those spots were older—at least a couple of weeks if not longer. This one, though, is only one or two days old—and there's a slight undercurrent of ibogaine."

Bernadette pursed her lips. "This is a facility with a *lot* of ibogaine. Supposedly under lock and key, but still."

"No ibogaine is stored in the aquarium rooms." He set down the notebook. "There are other explanations why someone may have carried a small measure of ibogaine into the aquarium rooms."

"Right. But even so, we need to get CSI to check the room out *now*. If there's physical evidence of the murder, the team needs to find it."

"Hence, we should call our friends in forensics and immediately secure the scene."

They passed Lightman's office, crossed the bullpen area, and reached the top of the stairwell.

A door opened behind them, and Bernadette turned to see Lightman sprinting across the office toward them.

"Where do you think you're going?" he shouted, his face turning red.

"We believe that Kymer Thompson was killed in your second aquarium on the first floor—"

"Absolutely not," he said, seething. "We're not risking our research—"

"This is a murder investigation," Bernadette said evenly, "and Research Room 12 is a possible murder scene." She turned away.

"How dare you go down there without a warrant," Lightman said. "We've given you access to Tommy's PC, and this is how you repay our cooperation?"

Kep took out his phone, dialing. "I'm confident the facts will show that the burden of probable cause has been met."

"I strongly disagree. Maybe it's time to get our lawyers involved." Lightman puffed out his chest as he pulled his own phone out.

Kep was silent as he held the phone to his ear. The gears in

Bernadette's head were turning, but she couldn't come up with anything to say to stop Lightman from calling his attorney.

Lightman dialed. "Jude Lightman for Wanda Salesi," Lightman said into the phone. "It's urgent." He paused.

"Good afternoon, Lieutenant," Kep said into the phone. "I believe we've discovered the location where Kymer Thompson was killed. We'd like a CSI team to come out right away."

"Ms. Salesi, hello. I'm sorry to inform you that federal agents are attempting to shut down one of our research labs. That could jeopardize the entire project."

"Research Room 12 on the first floor of the Kilbourn Tech Freshwater Sciences lab building," Kep said.

"I think we'll need an injunction as soon as possible," Lightman said. "No, I don't know what their evidence is." He looked at Bernadette. "Would you care to tell me why you believe Kymer Thompson was killed in Research Room 12?"

Bernadette breathed in through her teeth. "Evidence suggests the presence of blood, the murder weapon, and attempts at cleanup."

"Did you hear that, Ms. Salesi?" He paused again. "The murder weapon being—what? A knife? A gun?"

Bernadette wanted to punch the smug look off his face—it was the same look Barlow had after he'd told her about his late-night work conference. But she stretched her fingers instead and said, "A syringe full of ibogaine."

"A syringe full of ibogaine," Lightman said. "Like the kind we inject into literally dozens of iron-rich lamprey livers every day. In a research lab. In an aquarium room where lamprey blood gets on the floor frequently. A room which we clean top to bottom several times a week. If there's been a particularly rowdy bunch of lampreys, even more often." He paused again. "No, Ms. Salesi, it doesn't sound to me like they have much of a case either."

"Thank you, Lieutenant. Contact me when we can expect the CSI team's arrival." He hung up. "We were obligated to call this in," Kep said to Lightman. "I suspect a man was killed in that room. It's my duty to report that."

"Good luck," Lightman said. "We'll have the injunction signed before your boss hangs up with CSI."

Bernadette stepped forward. "We'll wait for CSI to get here. Or the injunction."

Lightman, phone still against his face, stomped back into his office and slammed the door.

She turned to Kep. "What now?"

"Now we wait."

"I don't understand why he's so upset," Bernadette said in a low voice. "If you're sure that the murder happened here, Lightman might as well be off our list of suspects. It's much less likely that he was here when Thompson was killed." She folded her arms.

"It's not about his guilt or innocence of Thompson's murder," Kep said. "He's upset about the funding for the research project. That sizeable grant is obviously from a pharmaceutical company, and the more the laboratory is involved with the murder investigation, the higher the chance that the funding will get pulled."

"Ah. Follow the money."

"Exactly," Kep said. "The concentrated ibogaine and the maturity of those silver lampreys are the most important two things in this lab. Both might be worth killing over."

"With Kymer Thompson murdered and Eddie Taysatch shot, I believe Lightman fears for his life." *Although it's hilarious that his employees think he's incompetent.* "Think we should put a protective detail on him?"

"At the very least, an officer should be stationed at his

house. Perhaps we can ask Detective Dunn if the police have implemented additional precautions."

"Right." Bernadette motioned toward Thompson's desk with her head. "Come on. Let's see if Curtis is done playing hacker for the day."

Curtis was finished when they arrived at Thompson's old desk. Nick LaSalle refused to meet Bernadette's eyes and mumbled something about getting back to the university. Curtis shook his head as LaSalle headed for the elevator.

"Sorry for all the drama with the IT guy," Bernadette said in a low voice. "I was trying to catch him off guard. He's not being candid about where he was last night—and I don't think he's being honest about the keylogger program, either."

Curtis nodded. "Yeah, well, he got really nervous after you yelled at him. Didn't know which way was up."

The elevator arrived, LaSalle got on, and the doors shut behind him. A weight lifted from Bernadette's shoulders, though she wasn't sure why. She cleared her throat. "He answered a couple of questions strangely. I think he's involved."

"Do you believe he was instrumental in installing the keylogging program onto the victim's PC?" Kep asked. "Or are you suggesting he was involved in Mr. Thompson's murder?"

"I mean—" Bernadette stopped, then put her chin in her hand.

"What?" Curtis asked.

"I meant with the keylogging program. But after seeing him avoid me last night and deny it today, maybe he was *more* involved than that."

"What—you think he's a suspect?" Curtis knit his brow. "That's a stretch. There's nothing suggesting that LaSalle and Thompson were more than passing acquaintances."

"But he's responsible for security on the PCs," Bernadette pointed out. "And if the keylogger ended up on Thompson's machine—and on his home machine too—that would suggest that LaSalle is at least a suspect for installing the malware."

Curtis shook his head. "LaSalle set all the machines up at the beginning of the school year—at least for the grad students and the interns. There were a couple who started in June, but most started in August."

"And there was only one machine here at the lab with the keylogger? Not Jude Lightman's? Not Eddie Taysatch's?"

"No, only Thompson's PC. And I was right: it was infected in August, as soon as Thompson started here. It infected a USB drive the Friday before Labor Day. Someone targeted Kymer Thompson."

"What was the attacker looking for?"

Curtis squinted and shook his head slightly. "I'd be guessing. Thompson had access to almost all the research in the lab. And he had more access to the lampreys than anyone else."

"But the murderer killed *him*. The lampreys weren't touched."

Kep's phone buzzed. He looked at his screen, then shook his head. "Maura hasn't even put the request into CSI yet, and the judge signed the injunction. Now they have to set a date for a hearing, They have successfully blocked our access to Research Room 12."

Bernadette tapped her foot. "Did they give you any idea when the hearing will be?"

"The clerk gave me the impression it could be later today. However, I suspect she was being overly optimistic, as it's already quite late. Personally, I'm hopeful we can access the room first thing tomorrow. However, the scene could be even more contaminated at that point, and we run the risk that nothing we find would hold up in court."

Curtis hoisted his laptop bag up to his shoulder, pulling the collar of his leather jacket flat underneath the strap. "So you're done here as well? You two need a ride back to the station?"

"Yes." Bernadette shot a look at Kep, who nodded. "And let's get out of here before Lightman has a chance to gloat."

The three of them were silent in the elevator on the way down to the ground floor. Kep climbed into the back seat of Maura's rented black SUV, lost in thought. Bernadette took the front passenger seat as Curtis started the engine.

Curtis snapped his fingers. "Oh—I got some information on that priest. The one who lives out in Whitefish Bay."

"Vivian Roundhouse? Great."

"Divorced. Her ex-husband is the CEO of Jefferson Systems. Lives up in Mequon in an equally nice house."

"Is his name Allan?"

"No—that's her son. He's a civil rights attorney in Chicago."

Bernadette tapped her foot. "What about her van? What about her whereabouts on Monday night?" She shook her head. "Background's nice, but we need confirmation of her movements."

"She's a priest," Curtis said. "Ugh. I hate the optics on that."

"If we're lucky," Bernadette responded, "the media will treat her like the head of a cult, not like a priest."

"She's not our only suspect," Kep said from the back seat. "Let's not forget your suspicion of Nick LaSalle."

"Nor yours of Annika Nakrivo, who won't even cry."

Kep gave her a tight smile. "We haven't talked to Cecilia Carter yet."

"The woman whose car you jumped on at the Freshie last night?" Curtis asked.

Bernadette grunted.

"Maura and I wanted to bring her in, but her address is in California," Curtis said. "She's apparently in Milwaukee on a long-term assignment, but we haven't discovered where she's staying yet."

Bernadette set her mouth in a line. "Cellphone records? Financials? Credit card payments?"

"I'll put that at the top of my list."

They arrived at the District 5 station five minutes later. The handsome Officer Chesapeake had been replaced by an older policeman with a scowl evident in spite of his walrus-like mustache.

They walked into the warm, stuffy back room. Detective Dunn was on the phone talking animatedly.

Maura was standing at the printer as it spit out a stack of pages. She glanced up at them. "Oh, good, you're all back. Any luck at the Freshie?"

"We confirmed how the keylogger got onto Thompson's machine," Curtis said. "Remotely installed at work using an anonymized IP address. Then Thompson brought home a USB stick and infected his home PC."

"Any idea who installed it?"

Curtis glanced at Bernadette. "Go ahead."

Bernadette nodded. "Nick LaSalle oversees the computers at the Freshie. He's acting overly defensive."

"Overly defensive? How?"

"Some odd statements. I called him incompetent to see his reaction."

"Which was?"

"Instead of telling me how well he did his job, he denied that he'd installed the keyloggers on purpose. I never accused him of wrongdoing."

Maura rubbed her chin thoughtfully. "Not necessarily indicative of anything."

"The other thing is that we only found a keylogger on Thompson's work machine. But LaSalle said 'keyloggers'—

plural. I think he knows that it was installed on his home machine, too."

Maura clicked her tongue. "Anyone who works in computer security would assume that a piece of malware found its way onto multiple machines. Or it could just be a slip of the tongue."

Bernadette was silent.

Maura sighed. "But we can dig deeper." She turned to Curtis. "Any chance of getting past the anonymizer?"

"I'm on it." Curtis said, as Dunn hung up the phone and looked up at them.

"In the meantime," Maura said, "let's get a forensic accountant to look at Nick LaSalle's bank accounts. Any big payments, expenditures, deposits."

Dunn stood up. "I'll ask Lesley to help out. She's the best forensic accountant we've got." She paused. "And one more thing. We got a hit on the van."

"The Agios Delphi van?" Bernadette asked.

"On camera Monday at 5:37 P.M. going into the Galena Street Garage."

Right after trying to mow me over on Sixth Street. "Where's the Galena Street Garage?"

"About three blocks north of the Anne Askew Chapel."

"And when did it leave?"

"Tuesday morning, ten fifteen."

"Payment?"

"Kymer Thompson's credit card at the exit gate. The camera got a great shot of the driver's-side door."

"So," Maura said, "whoever drove the van may have killed Kymer Thompson and taken his credit card. Did we look at the robbery angle?"

Dunn shook her head. "Wallet was still on him. Forty dollars in cash. No indication that anyone took anything."

"So who drove the van?" Bernadette said. "You had uniforms go to the old salt warehouse?"

"Nothing," Dunn said. "Gate was open. No vehicles. No sign of forced entry, but no tire tracks either—but it's been snowing. And no cameras in the area. We have no way of knowing if that van was ever there, never mind figuring out who drove it."

Maura smacked the table with her hand. "I want your forensic accountant to look at Agios Delphi as well. Something's not right here. The reverend had opportunity for both the Thompson murder and the Eddie Taysatch shooting. She's got shaky alibis for both. And she's the main person with access to the van."

"Motive?" Bernadette asked.

Maura screwed up her mouth before she spoke. "Both Thompson and Taysatch had access to enough ibogaine to keep her congregation high for the next decade. Let's push on the ibogaine angle and hope something shakes loose."

Dunn shook her head. "I'm sorry, folks. I know it's technically possible that Reverend Roundhouse could have left her van at the Galena Street Garage and killed Thompson back at the lab, but it was twenty degrees below freezing that night. I don't see how anyone could drag a body ten city blocks—from the river to the chapel—without arousing suspicion."

"Maybe she *Weekend at Bernie*'d it," Kep said, casting a quick glance at Bernadette, who gritted her teeth.

"She did what?" Curtis asked.

"Oh, you poor child, *Weekend at Bernie's* was before your time," Kep said, chuckling. "It's a piece of cinematic drivel from the late 1980s about a murdered CEO and the two entry-level employees who pretend he isn't dead. The two of them carry the corpse around and pose him like he's still alive. Several slapstick moments are considered classic by those who appreciate the medium."

"And the garage doesn't have the van leaving until Tuesday morning?" Bernadette asked, ignoring the second knowing glance from Kep.

"That's right," Dunn said. "Of course, if she had an accomplice, maybe they took the accomplice's car to move the body."

"Is there anything else they could have used?" Bernadette said. "It's a fairly straight shot from campus to the Freshie. Is there—I don't know, a bicycle, or some sort of rickshaw, or maybe a free streetcar that could have gotten them from Point A to Point B?"

"The streetcar is on the other side of the river, and it doesn't go close to the chapel. You'd have better luck with a shopping cart." Dunn chuckled. "Two winters ago, someone pushed a shopping cart off the roof of the shopping center next to the Freshie, and it landed in the ice in the river. Sort of got half-submerged, and it stayed there until spring. The YouTube video went viral."

"Hmm," Curtis said. "Is it easy to filch a shopping cart from a local grocery store or from the shopping center?"

"I was joking about the shopping cart. Mostly homeless people who have them—like Rhonda. We saw her on one of the security cameras the night of Thompson's murder. She walks with her shopping cart down the Riverwalk every night."

Curtis's phone dinged, and he read the screen. "Oh—wow."

"What?"

He looked up at Dunn. "Two weeks ago, Douglas Rheinstaller bought a hundred pounds of TFM from Wildlife Specialties up in Fond du Lac."

"TFM? The fish poison?" Bernadette asked.

"Used to control the lamprey population," Kep said. "It's particularly poisonous to their ammocoetes."

"Their what?" Maura asked.

"Their larvae." Dunn nodded. "I had to do a report on TFM

in seventh-grade science. We used to have a real problem in the 1950s with sea lampreys killing the fish in Lake Michigan."

Kep looked down at his laptop screen. "3-trifluoromethyl-4-nitrophenol. Considered a toxic respiratory irritant."

"But doesn't kill trout or salmon," Dunn said. "Only the lampreys."

"So it's the perfect substance to have on hand," she continued, "if one were planning to poison an aquarium full of them."

"Right," Dunn said. "You usually see those types of orders from the Department of Fish and Game. They apply the TFM to the tributaries where the larvae are most common. Fishermen who are out on the lake wouldn't use it—Rheinstaller wouldn't have any need for it."

"But Rheinstaller was the president of the Piscary Association," Bernadette pointed out. "He wasn't a regular fisherman. Maybe he had a reason to purchase the TFM."

"With the spring thaw coming," Dunn said thoughtfully, "there's a possibility that he didn't think Fish and Game was moving fast enough. Something else to ask him."

"Any word on Cecilia Carter?"

Curtis nodded. "I put in a request with her wireless provider. We'll see where she is soon enough."

Bernadette thought for a moment. "Detective, with what's happened to Thompson and Taysatch, do you think there's any merit in putting a protective detail on Jude Lightman?"

Dunn nodded. "Probably. We should station an officer at the Freshie too. The bosses will hate the overtime, but they'll approve it. I can get that started."

"Call Lightman first. See if he'll even agree to it." Bernadette scrunched up her face in thought.

"What is it?" Maura asked.

"Annika Nakrivo," Bernadette said. "She's made an accusation about Reverend Roundhouse, who's one of our main suspects. If Kymer Thompson told his girlfriend about his research, maybe Annika needs protection, too. Especially if the cameras at her dorm can't be relied on."

"I'm headed over there next," Curtis said. "I might be able to salvage some footage—or at least figure out how they deleted the recordings. It might give us a clue on who did it."

"Annika seems to think it was drug dealers," Kep said.

"Or campus security not wanting to do their job," Bernadette interjected.

Maura shook her head. "She's taking wild guesses. Curtis, you get over there, and if Annika's in her dorm room, tell her we'll be adding her to our protective detail." She turned to Dunn. "How long will it take to get protection in place for them?"

"The request has to go through channels. It'll take an hour, maybe two—more if there's any delay about approving overtime."

"Okay, Curtis," Maura said, "stay with Annika until the uniform gets there. I don't know if the reverend will show up, but this has the potential of turning messy pretty fast."

"What about the camera footage?" Curtis said.

"It can wait until after you've confirmed she's safe."

He typed a short message on his laptop, hit the enter key with a flourish, then turned to Bernadette. "I got the wireless carrier information for Cecilia Carter, and I forwarded it to you."

"Thanks."

Curtis grabbed his leather jacket off the back of the chair and turned to Maura. "Can I take your SUV?"

Maura nodded. "You call us the moment you see she's safe," she said. "If we have another incident on our hands, we need to know as soon as possible."

Curtis gave the team a thumbs-up as he left the office.

Chapter Sixteen

BERNADETTE OPENED THE EMAIL FORWARDED FROM CURTIS. Ten spreadsheets. She double-clicked the first one and was greeted with tiny text in dozens of columns and what appeared to be hundreds of rows.

"You okay?" Dunn asked.

"I need an Excel-to-English translator."

Dunn smiled, then got up. "I'm going to stretch my legs. See what Lesley's uncovered."

"Lesley?"

"Lesley Gill. Our forensic accountant, remember?"

"Right, right."

"We'll be here a while. I'll order some dinner. You have anything in mind?"

"Definitely no Wisconsin Old Fashioneds for me. Other than that, I don't know. Something good."

Dunn smiled and turned to Kep to ask him about dinner.

Bernadette focused her attention on the laptop screen and began to dig into the cell phone records. The whole month was in the report, not just the last few days. There was an insane amount of detail—the second spreadsheet contained all the SSIDs of the Wi-Fi networks she'd connected to; the third, triangulation coordinates. She discovered she could enter the coordinates into her Maps program, and it would give her a reasonable two- or three-block radius of the location of her phone. A single set of coordinates took almost five minutes to complete on the map. She scrolled down—there were thousands of coordinate entries. Bernadette shook her head; Curtis loved the whirrs and clicks and beeps of stuff like this.

She clicked the tab for the day of the Kymer Thompson murder and scrolled down to the late evening. After a few coordinate searches, Bernadette zeroed in on an apartment building downtown, not too far from Veterans Memorial Park on Lake Michigan. That must be where Cecilia Carter was staying. Rental? Lease? Maybe an apartment paid for by Justice for Oceans?

She sent an email to Curtis asking him to look at the lease agreements for the building. Maybe a name would pop out.

Then she clicked back on the SSID spreadsheet. Maybe Carter had connected to a router in her apartment that day— and maybe the internet service provider would be able to link to it.

So much information—the dates started three weeks previously. Bernadette began to scroll.

Hold on.

She stopped and clicked back one screen.

Wildlife-FdL.

Hadn't Rheinstaller purchased TFM from Wildlife Specialties in Fond du Lac two weeks before?

She went back to her email, and a message from Dunn was there with a copy of the receipt.

Yes. Douglas Rheinstaller. Wildlife Specialties, Fond du Lac, Wisconsin. Timestamped 4:17 p.m. Wow—almost five thousand dollars for a hundred pounds of TFM. That would leave a mark on his credit card bill.

Bernadette clicked back on Cecilia Carter's SSID spreadsheet. *Wildlife-FdL*. Connection made 16:06; connection dropped 16:18.

Douglas Rheinstaller and Cecilia Carter were there at the same time. While he was buying TFM—and her Wi-Fi connection dropped a minute after his transaction was complete.

❦

"It's a big coincidence, and I don't like it," Maura said. "But it's not a smoking gun. It's not illegal to buy TFM, and it's not illegal for them to be together when he purchased it."

"Maybe not," Bernadette conceded, "but we can ask him about it, can't we?"

"For what purpose?" Maura said. "Thompson wasn't poisoned with TFM. Eddie Taysatch wasn't shot with TFM. So the guy has a hundred pounds of the stuff in his garage—where's the crime?"

"Politics make strange bedfellows," Bernadette said. "Normally, the two of them would be at each other's throats. But they have a common enemy." She took a deep breath. "What if their plan is to kill all the lampreys, but they had to get Thompson and Taysatch out of the way first?"

Maura shook her head. "Pure speculation at this point. Not saying you're wrong, but you've got to get more than innuendo and a Wi-Fi report. There are plenty of reasons they could be together that don't involve conspiracy for murder. And with Cecilia Carter's lawyers? You better be sure that you're accusing her of something real."

"You're saying no fishing expeditions." A lilt in Bernadette's voice.

Maura closed her eyes, a smile touching the corner of her mouth.

"Sorry."

Chuckling, Maura sat back in her chair before clearing her throat and putting a serious look on her face. "Also, the forensic accountant sent the reports back. She couldn't find unusual activity on Nick LaSalle's accounts."

Something pinged in Bernadette's gut. "Really? Can I see that?"

"I'll print it out if you want, but you really think you can catch something that the forensic accountant didn't?"

"Uh—I don't know. I guess I need to see it for myself."

"Fair enough." Maura tapped the computer, and the printer roared to life.

Bernadette stood up. She'd been sitting too long. She needed to get her blood pumping. Maybe a weight session at the hotel gym, or a run in the cold weather.

She walked over to the printer. The transactions started six months prior—no one could accuse the forensic accountant of not being thorough. She looked through the list: paychecks every other Friday. A rash of payments on the first of the month: rent, utilities, insurance, college loan. A small car payment.

The next month, it was the same: rent, utilities, insurance. LaSalle ate out a lot, at mostly fast food or cheap restaurants. There was the Bratwurst House. Groceries. Car payment, college loan. Then the next month: mechanic. Oof, over two thousand dollars—and the car wasn't even paid off yet. This was Christmas, and there were a few big purchases: mostly from online stores and from the shopping center next to the Freshie. Rent, utilities, insurance, car, college loan. Fewer restaurants, though. Christmas was pricey for somebody at their first job out of college.

January. A nice restaurant. Maybe he'd gotten a gift card—oh, wait, no, this was the debit card. She looked back. Yes, a cash deposit of a few hundred dollars. Maybe from grandparents for Christmas. Rent, utilities, groceries. Insurance and a car payment.

February. Rent, utilities, groceries, insurance, car payment.

Bernadette blinked.

She looked at January and February again.

Nick LaSalle had gotten his bachelor's in computer science at Kilbourn Tech. It was an expensive school. He'd had to get college loans and he'd been out of school—what? Three or four years, tops. He'd paid his college loans in October, November, and December.

So why did he stop paying them in January?

"Lieu," she said, hurrying over to her boss, "I found something. LaSalle stopped paying his college loans."

Maura knitted her brow. "He stopped paying his loans? Maybe he had a rich uncle die."

"If he had," Bernadette said, "we'd see a big lump-sum payment."

"Maybe his *mom* had a rich uncle die."

"Maybe," Bernadette said. "But we should look into this."

Maura took the statement from Bernadette's hand and opened another window on her machine. "This might take a minute." She frowned. "You know, Curtis would be able to do this faster."

"When did he get to Annika's dorm?"

Maura took her phone out of her purse. "I must have missed his call." She tapped her phone app and scrolled. "Uh—no. Nothing from Curtis yet."

"Maybe she wasn't there, and he went looking for her."

"Don't you think he would have called if he'd done that?"

Bernadette ran her hands through her hair and scratched her scalp, grimacing. "I'll try to track him down. Maybe something happened when he arrived, and he got distracted." She dropped her hands, then tapped the statement on the desk next to Maura's laptop. "Let's figure out what happened to this loan."

Bernadette walked into the small windowless office where she'd looked at DMV photos and took her phone out, tapping *Curtis Janek* in her phone.

Ring. Ring. Ring.

Curtis's voice. "Curtis Janek." Then a computerized female voice. "Is not available. To leave—"

Bernadette hung up and called again.

Still no answer.

Maybe he has his phone on vibrate. A brief, flitting thought: Maybe something had happened to Curtis—and maybe something had happened to Annika too.

Curtis struck Bernadette as responsible and level-headed. He wasn't the type to go rogue. She tried to think of a reasonable explanation for his disappearance, but she kept coming back to a car accident or a medical emergency.

Bernadette called a third time. No answer.

The nagging voice in her head grew louder: something had happened. Someone tried to hurt Annika, and Curtis had gotten in the way. He could be in the hospital—or worse.

She dropped her hand to her side, still holding the phone.

Kep looked up. "What is it?"

"Curtis isn't answering his phone."

"He's what?"

"He's not answering."

"Well." Kep leaned forward and rested his chin in his hand. "Perhaps his battery is dead, or maybe he left his phone in the car and thought it was more important to protect Miss Nakrivo than go back and get his phone."

"Or he's hurt. Car accident or..." Bernadette trailed off.

Maura looked up. "I'll ask for a patrol to be sent to the dorm right away." She stood and began walking toward the front desk.

"Should we go too?" Bernadette asked.

"I don't know yet." Maura turned the corner.

Bernadette glanced up at Kep from across the table. "So," she said, "now what do we do?"

"This would be an excellent time to find a restaurant and eat dinner. I don't want to wait for Detective Dunn."

"How can you think about food?"

"I think there's a perfectly reasonable explanation for his disappearance."

"You do?"

"Yes." He nodded. "As I said, it's much more probable that he has a dead cell phone battery than anything else."

"He would find a land line or borrow a cell phone. He's responsible."

"He's twenty-five. Young people don't always think things through."

Of course Kep would say that. He vanishes for hours at a time and ignores his phone. I bet he thinks that it's no big deal—and maybe I'm overreacting because I'm worried about Sophie. She looked at the clock on her phone—she still had an hour or so to call Sophie and say good night. Bernadette looked at Kep out of the corner of her eye. "So you don't think we have anything to worry about?"

"I don't. So why don't you try to get something done before Lieutenant Stevenson returns?"

She stared at Kep for a moment. "Yeah. Keep my mind off

all the horrible unrealistic scenarios swimming around in my head."

"Precisely."

"Maybe I'll work on the questions I can ask Douglas Rheinstaller."

"I already told you he isn't our murderer."

Bernadette chuckled. "Yeah, I know you didn't smell lampreys, but I discovered that he and Carter were possibly together when he bought the TFM. Maybe he wasn't the one who pulled the trigger or pushed the plunger, but I bet he knows something that's relevant." She typed his name into the county's system and waited for the data to appear. "So—are you working on Annika Nakrivo?"

"Correct." Kep tapped his keyboard. "Lesley emailed us an address for Miss Nakrivo in Miami, and her appearance is quite different. According to her rental agreement, she vacated her apartment on October 31."

"And we know she arrived in Milwaukee in early January," Bernadette said thoughtfully.

He tapped again. "Lesley hasn't discovered Miss Nakrivo's whereabouts for November or December."

"Maybe she went to spend the holidays with family. Or if she knew she'd be in Milwaukee in January, she could have couch-surfed for two months. There are a lot of possible explanations."

Kep took his glasses off and rubbed his eyes. "Yes, probably. I wish I could find definitively where she had been. She has a certain appearance in Miami in October, and then reappears ten weeks later with a slightly altered face and a beauty mark, three thousand kilometers away. It's odd."

"But she might not have left a trail."

"I find it hard to believe that she would be able to cover her digital footprint completely," Kep said. "She'd find it difficult to delete records of credit card receipts, airplane tickets, storage unit agreements—"

"Storage unit agreements," Bernadette interjected, glancing back at her screen.

"What is it?"

She pointed to the laptop monitor. "Three days ago, Rheinstaller reported that his backyard storage shed had been broken into."

"He did?"

Bernadette nodded. "Patrol went out to investigate. Shed's lock was broken, and the shed was empty. But Rheinstaller wouldn't say what had been taken. He refused to make a report to the police."

Kep frowned. "He refused?"

"Right."

"Are you suggesting," Kep said, "that someone stole the forty-five kilograms of TFM from his shed?"

"Maura would tell me I'm speculating." Bernadette paused. "But I can't think of another explanation for why he wouldn't tell the police what was stolen."

"I can think of several: illicit drugs, pornography, or perhaps defalcation."

"You're saying he could've been skimming from the Lake Shore Piscary Association?"

"I'm saying it's a possibility."

"Speaking of the Piscary Association..." Bernadette clicked her keyboard and pointed to the screen. "Okay—the Association has their meeting minutes online." She paused as she read.

After a moment, Kep leaned forward. "Do you see anything of note?"

"Not yet. Unless you care that the trout population is slated to be down this year."

Bernadette continued to read, then clicked to the previous month. "Oh."

"What?"

"It looks like Kilbourn Tech asked Wisconsin Fish and Game to significantly reduce their application of TFM in the tributaries and streams that feed into Lake Michigan." Bernadette scrolled down. "Well, look at this. The argument got quite heated."

"Really?"

"Rheinstaller said that cutting the TFM application in half will put another twenty thousand sea lampreys into Lake Michigan."

"Not silver lampreys?"

Bernadette kept scrolling. "Silver lampreys are native to the area, but sea lampreys are an invasive species. Remember Dunn's seventh-grade science report? Sea lampreys almost put fishermen out of business before TFM came along. And if the TFM is reduced, the Piscary Association says the sea lampreys will destroy the trout and salmon population. The president said the season will be hard enough with the lower trout numbers, and now there will be even fewer trout if the sea lampreys survive to adulthood. The university countered that the cancer treatment is one of the exceptions to the economic rules. Someone else points out that this is an argument that should be made at the city level, not to the Piscary Association." She looked up. "That could explain why Rheinstaller ordered the TFM."

Kep nodded. "If he was thinking of acting on his own and applying the TFM in areas where the Department of Fish and Game wouldn't..."

"He didn't file the police report because he wouldn't want to call attention to his plans to illegally kill all those lampreys."

"Or," Kep mused, "sometime between when Rheinstaller

called the cops and when they asked him to finish the report, he realized who had taken the TFM and no longer wanted to report it."

Bernadette wrinkled her nose. "If you're right, who did he suspect had taken the TFM?"

Kep scratched his head and sighed. "You've asked an awfully good question. And one I believe we must answer."

Chapter Seventeen

Bernadette and Kep walked around the side of Rheinstaller's house, opening the half-height gate in the low chain-link fence that led into the backyard.

An aluminum shed, about ten feet wide by five feet deep, abutted the wall of the detached garage.

"If the TFM would attract thieves, it seems weird to have it out in the yard," Bernadette muttered.

"Yes, but TFM is volatile," Kep said. "It won't explode if one sneezes too loudly, but the product is flammable and can cause respiratory irritation. I wouldn't want it around the house while I'm preparing breakfast."

They stood in front of the shed door; it had no lock.

Kep swung the shed door open. It was empty.

"You are as a candle," he muttered to the empty space, "the better part burnt out." He stepped inside.

Bernadette could smell something: a little like fertilizer, a little like rat poison. Not very strong—maybe she wouldn't have even noticed it if she weren't specifically searching out an odd smell.

"The scent is definitive," Kep said. "Rheinstaller stored the TFM in this shed, and it's obvious that it's no longer here."

"Why didn't you smell it in the house or on his clothes?"

"One of the reasons Fish and Game uses TFM is because it breaks down quickly," Kep said. "So when it's applied directly to areas where there is a high population of ammocoetes, it kills most of them, then dissipates to levels safe for other fish."

"And how come you can smell it?"

"A much higher amount of TFM was stored in here," Kep said, "and this is a closed shed in sub-freezing temperatures. It doesn't break down as rapidly when it's dry."

Bernadette nodded. "So do you think he planned to kill the lampreys in the lab?"

Kep stepped out of the shed. "It's hard to say. Surely he would have known this could be traced to him."

"Right," Bernadette said. Her phone rang in her purse. *Barlow Finnegan*. Again. She exhaled loudly.

"That sounds like an ex-husband sigh," Kep said.

"It's definitely a none-of-your-business sigh." She answered the phone, walking toward the house, out of Kep's earshot. She was glad his hearing wasn't as keen as his nose.

"Hello, Barlow."

"Listen," he said, "I know you're probably busy, but your daughter is very concerned about you. You usually call by now."

"I'm sorry. I'm working on a case."

"She saw a story online about a shooting today in Milwaukee, and she was worried it was you. I told her she had nothing to worry about, and that you probably weren't anywhere near the shooting. But she seems to think she was rude to you when she last spoke to you, and she's beside herself."

Bernadette was quiet.

"Bernadette?"

She shut her eyes and flinched at the memory of the bullet whizzing past her ear.

"You've got to be kidding," he said softly. "You were there? Are you okay?"

"I'm fine," she said. "I wasn't—I didn't—"

"You're not supposed to be in danger," Barlow said. "You told me this assignment would mean less time in the field."

"It does. This is the first trip I've gone on in months. It was a fluke."

Barlow sighed. "What if I have to tell our daughter—"

"I could get into a car accident or get electrocuted in the kitchen," Bernadette said. "I'm not quitting. Besides—"

A pause. "Besides, what?"

Besides, I don't know how to do anything else. "I was going to say I'd be home soon. But I don't know if I will."

"Well, at least talk to Sophie. She'll put on a brave face, but talk to her."

"Right. Yes. Put her on."

Small talk. Sophie, instead of her usual monosyllabic responses, spoke a few sentences about her day. She didn't mention anything about the shooting in Milwaukee, and Bernadette didn't offer anything, either.

A moment of awkward silence. No questions about the bad guys. Not even a glimmer of interest.

"Okay, Mom," Sophie said. "I should get back to my homework."

"Okay," Bernadette said. "Thanks for being understanding. I don't think this will happen more than a few times a year now. Not like when I was an agent."

"Love you," Sophie said, and ended the call before Bernadette had a chance to say it back.

Bernadette rubbed her forehead. The cold made her lungs hurt a little, and it made her breathe more slowly. That helped.

She straightened her parka, put her phone in her purse, and walked back to the shed, where Kep stood outside it, looking thoughtful.

"Let's go grab a coffee," Bernadette said. "Maybe we do a little work at the café and get more information on Mr. Rheinstaller."

"Use our laptops to connect to an insecure Wi-Fi network when we've got a suspect installing malicious keylogging software? No, I don't think so. At any rate," Kep said, "we both have a few questions for Rheinstaller."

"You want to talk to him without Maura's approval?"

Kep's glasses slipped down his nose. "Maura doesn't have to approve my questions."

KEP AND BERNADETTE SAT AT THE METAL TABLE IN THE windowless room in front of a one-way mirror. Even though it was late, the guards had allowed the interview after Bernadette flashed her ID.

Kep scrolled on his phone while they waited for the guards to bring Rheinstaller, and Bernadette kept glancing over to him.

"Any word from Maura?" Bernadette asked.

"About what?"

Bernadette furrowed her brow. "About Curtis. Has she heard from him?"

"No, I haven't had any communications with the lieutenant." Kep looked up. "I'm searching the location data of a wireless network provider," he said.

"For this case?"

"Yes."

"Will you share your thoughts with the whole class?"

The door opened suddenly, and a guard came in with

Douglas Rheinstaller—dressed in a WDC orange jumpsuit—and handcuffed him to the table. The guard nodded to Kep, then he stood in the corner of the room. Rheinstaller glared at the guard, then turned to face Kep.

"I'm not saying anything without my lawyer," Rheinstaller growled. "I should make bail in the next day or two. And I'll beat this. I doubt anyone will want to press charges."

"You can listen," Bernadette said.

Kep sat back and folded his arms.

Rheinstaller's eyes fell on Bernadette's face, and narrowed into slits. "You're the one who'll pay for my new front door."

Bernadette lifted her chin and stared back at Rheinstaller. "On Saturday—two days before the murder of Kymer Thompson—you reported a theft on your property. Your back shed. You called the police but decided against reporting the crime."

"Neighborhood kids," Rheinstaller said.

Bernadette was dying to remind him that he said he wouldn't talk without a lawyer present, but she held her tongue. "We have chemical evidence that the shed contained a piscicide, commonly called TFM, that's used to eliminate the lamprey population in the Great Lakes."

"Yeah, well, I happen to be the president of the Piscary Association," Rheinstaller retorted. "I've got a seat on the council that deals with controlling the lamprey population every year. There's a reason I have that stuff."

"Is there a reason neighborhood kids would steal it?" Too late, she realized she'd asked a question.

But Kep leaned forward and spoke quickly. "That chemical can kill silver lampreys as easily as sea lampreys," he said, "and you had a heated disagreement with Kilbourn Tech over their management of the lamprey population."

"In the lab, they can do whatever they want," Rheinstaller

said. "I got no beef with them. What happens in the lab stays in the lab." He grinned at his weak joke. "But"—and his face fell into a frown—"I'm much less forgiving when the sea lamprey population spikes. It means I can't put food on the table. I represent men and women with families. They struggle to keep their heads above water during a good season. And when these elitists come in with their test tubes and Bunsen burners, and they look down their noses at us—like our families don't matter, like they don't care if we starve. That's when I start getting angry."

"Fortunately," Bernadette said, carefully choosing her words, "you can't be arrested for *wanting* to commit a crime. And someone prevented you from dumping all the TFM into the aquariums at the Freshie."

Rheinstaller laughed. "I told you, I don't care about their lab. I wouldn't set foot in the Freshie if you paid me a million dollars. It's my trout and salmon I care about."

"But you didn't get to defend them," Bernadette said quietly, "and now all the families you represent will lose out because the sea lampreys will live."

Rheinstaller opened his mouth, and then a look of realization came over his face. He clamped his jaw shut, leaned back in his chair, and looked at the floor.

"Maybe there's a way for the assault charge to get knocked down to a misdemeanor," Kep said to Bernadette.

"How?"

"I wager the district attorney would look kindly on someone who assisted federal investigators with a murder case."

Bernadette nodded. "Of course. DAs *do* look kindly on that kind of thing."

"My theory is thus," Kep said. "Whoever stole the TFM from you planned to poison the lampreys in the laboratory. This scuttled your plan to coordinate a sizable TFM rollout to fishermen near and far. I assume your plan was to utilize an amount of TFM in the streams and rivers equal to what Fish and Game used last year." Kep smiled. "You're a smart man despite your best efforts to conceal your intelligence, Mr. Rheinstaller, so I'm confident you were aware your plan was illegal. You calculated the risks: not only could you go to jail, but you knew you might even lose your fishing license permanently. It was a gamble you were willing to take."

Rheinstaller stared at Kep, unblinking.

"When a thief stole the TFM from your shed, you became angry and let your emotions take control. You called the police because you thought only of retribution. After you calmed down, however, you recognized the gift you'd been given. Perhaps the realization came when the officer was at your house, or perhaps you noticed something in the shed. Whatever it was, it struck you that the person who'd stolen the TFM would kill the lampreys not in the rivers but in the laboratory." Kep pressed his palms together. "While this wasn't the action you planned to take, it was more than good enough to achieve your ends. With the lampreys in the lab dead, the project would be finished, and Fish and Game would lift their restrictions on the TFM. You'd get everything you wanted, and you wouldn't have to commit a crime or risk getting caught." Kep shook his head. "Your name might not even have come up in the investigation if you hadn't assaulted Eddie Taysatch."

Bernadette hadn't heard—or even thought of—Kep's theory before, but she had to admit it made sense.

"Are we on the right track, Dougie?" Kep asked.

"Douglas," Rheinstaller said automatically.

Kep nodded. "I bet the thief's plan would have gone forward without complication as well. Unfortunately, Kymer Thompson came into Research Room 12 unexpectedly and interrupted the perpetrator, who panicked and improvised.

Suddenly, there's a problem: a dead body without dead lampreys. By the time the killer disposed of the corpse, it was too late to finish the job."

"It could have been a dry run," Bernadette noted. "Or they could have been taking computer files or ibogaine." She took her phone out and began searching for information on TFM.

"I don't know anything about any dead bodies," Rheinstaller said, meeting Kep's eyes. "I don't know who killed Kymer Thompson, I don't know why they moved his body." He looked back down at the floor. "And I don't know who stole the—" He bit his lip. "I don't know anything about any TFM."

"We have the receipts in our possession, Dougie," Kep said. "You purchased forty-five kilograms of TFM."

"What?"

"A hundred pounds," Bernadette said.

Kep nodded. "That amount is enough TFM to kill the lampreys in the project's spawning zone, isn't it?"

Rheinstaller set his mouth in a line.

"I wouldn't be surprised if the Piscary Association coordinated efforts around the state," Kep said.

"Or maybe," Bernadette said, "you were planning it with another organization. A group you don't want anyone to know you're working with."

Rheinstaller shifted uncomfortably.

"I don't know what Cecilia Carter was doing with you when you bought that TFM in Fond du Lac," Bernadette said, "but I bet the other board members of the Piscary Association wouldn't be too pleased to find out."

"I believe the colloquialism is 'sleeping with the enemy,' although perhaps you left the literal meaning to Professor Lightman." Kep's face remained serious as he took out a paper from the folder—Rheinstaller's credit card statement. "Forty-six hundred dollars on your credit card. To me, that seems like a reasonable investment to make for your continued livelihood. It could be an expense reimbursed by the Piscary Association. Perhaps a hundred or so members are contributing fifty dollars apiece." Kep put the credit card statement back in the folder. "However, I can't imagine they'd be so amenable to reimbursement if they became aware of your arrangement with Justice for Oceans."

Rheinstaller scraped his shoes against the cement floor.

"Maybe it was Cecilia Carter who stole all that TFM from you," Bernadette suggested. "After all, she was with you when you bought it. Perhaps she was the only person who knew you had it."

Rheinstaller's eyes were focused on the table.

"We're close to the truth," Kep said to Bernadette. "In another forty-eight hours, I'm confident we'll uncover all the information we need to capture the murderer. Then we won't need Dougie to assist us anymore."

"Drop the assault charges," Rheinstaller said.

Kep frowned. "No, we can't drop the assault charges completely. I could be persuaded to recommend lowering the charge to a misdemeanor."

"Suspended sentence, maybe," Bernadette said. "No jail time if we can work our magic. Maybe a fine."

Rheinstaller shook his head. "Drop the charges completely."

Kep looked at Bernadette. "What are your thoughts on Dougie's suggestion?"

"He *does* seem like he'd probably fight Eddie Taysatch again. Maybe he'd even shoot him."

"I propose we allow Dougie to return to his cell," Kep said. "It's possible he may make bail after he's arraigned."

"He won't have to spend the weekend here, will he?"

"It's already Wednesday," Kep said. "I'm not familiar with the procedures of the Milwaukee police department, but in my home city, if the police fail to process the bail bond by 4:00 on Friday afternoon, the prisoner isn't released until Monday morning."

Rheinstaller glared at Bernadette, saying nothing.

"All right." Bernadette got up and nodded to the guard. "We're done here."

Kep followed her out of the room.

❧

IN THE PARKING LOT, BERNADETTE STARTED THE ENGINE OF the SUV and turned the heater on full blast. Kep closed his eyes.

"You okay?" *Maybe he's finally worried about Curtis.*

"I fear I'm missing a connection," he said. "We have numerous suspects, and they all have motive. Some motives appear more compelling than others, but we've eliminated precious few. After we arrested Rheinstaller, I thought we had eliminated him. Unfortunately for him, his involvement in this case is undeniable, even if he isn't guilty of murder."

Bernadette's phone buzzed, and she took it out of her purse. "What is it?"

She tapped the screen. "Maura's texting me."

"Ah, has our young hacker friend returned to the nest?"

Bernadette shook her head. "But she found Nick LaSalle's money trail."

Chapter Eighteen

"Thanks for calling me back," Maura said. "Can you all hear me?"

"Loud and clear, Lieu," Bernadette said. "You're on speaker."

"We discovered why Nick LaSalle stopped paying his college loans."

"Excellent," Kep said. "What are your findings?"

"Back in January, he was awarded a scholarship—the Midwestern Regional Scholarship for Computer Science."

"Nice generic name," Bernadette said, then cocked her head. "He got the scholarship *after* he graduated?"

"Unusual, to say the least," Maura said. "Some of these large tech corporations that are sitting on trillions of dollars are paying off the college loans for some of their employees in exchange for staying at the company for a certain number of years. Decreases turnover and the loss of—uh, what do they call it—institutional knowledge."

"But Nick LaSalle works for the university who educated him," Bernadette said. "Is there anything at all that would be considered 'institutional knowledge' for an IT manager at Kilbourn Tech?"

"That's another unusual thing—it wasn't a scholarship given by the university. It was a third party."

"Who?"

"I'm working on that right now."

"Look at the tax ID," Bernadette said. "Even if the scholarship was given anonymously, the payor has to be registered for a tax write-off."

"Okay—let me check." The sound of typing on Maura's end. "Hmm. 'Anonymous Donation.' No tax ID."

"Check the location. That can be obfuscated, too, but maybe whoever set up that scholarship overlooked it."

"Cleveland, Ohio." Maura paused. "Sure would be a lot faster with Curtis here. He'd know how to speed this up."

Bernadette looked at Kep, but he was staring at his phone, lost in concentration. She cleared her throat. "You still haven't heard from him?"

"The uniforms visited the dorms," Maura said, "but there was no sign of him."

"How about the SUV?"

"We have a BOLO issued. And nothing in the local hospitals."

"Maybe no news is good news."

"Maybe," Maura said distantly. "Aha—there's an EIN. It looks like it's associated with an umbrella corporation. Mid-America Medical Holdings, Inc."

An itch in Bernadette's brain.

Kep typed on his phone. "I'm performing a web search. It takes a Herculean effort to obfuscate the name of a company like this. Perhaps they left a footprint behind."

"I bet they own Parr Medical," Bernadette said.

"Parr Medical?" Kep continued to click on his screen.

"That's right. The company that offered Eddie Taysatch a job. They're based in Cleveland, right?"

Kep looked quizzically at Bernadette.

"Oh, of course. You were off following your *own* leads this morning." She exhaled loudly. "Parr Medical offered Eddie Taysatch a job to jump ship before the school year. Eddie didn't do it because he wanted to see this research through."

Kep rubbed his chin. "Is it possible Eddie Taysatch discovered something about the scholarship?"

"Like what?"

"Perhaps he found out that it wasn't awarded in good faith," Kep said. "It could be why he was targeted."

Bernadette's brow creased. "You're saying it was a bribe."

"I'm raising the possibility," Kep said, clicking on his phone screen. "Perhaps this is all tied into corporate espionage."

"Hang on," Maura said, keys clicking in the background. "Parr Medical. I've come across their name before."

Kep's eyes widened. "You're right—the holding company is owned by a different subsidiary of Parr Medical."

"That's where I saw it," Maura said. "Parr Medical is a competitor to Eponymous Pharmaceutical."

"Who?"

"Eponymous Pharmaceutical. They're the company whose grant is funding the cancer project at Kilbourn Tech."

"You knew who was funding the Freshie project?" Bernadette said. "We've been trying to get it out of Lightman since we got here."

"Curtis ran an inquiry with the FDA. The results just came back an hour ago." She typed on her keyboard and hit the enter key, then Bernadette's PC dinged. "There you go."

"No matter who they are, they're working on a cure for cancer," Kep said. "Is stopping the Eponymous research so important that Parr Medical would kill one of their competitors' employees?"

"It might be," Maura said. "If they were developing a

competing medication and if their release schedule was significantly behind Eponymous." She exhaled. "Eddie Taysatch got out of surgery half an hour ago. He lost a lot of blood. It's touch and go."

"What do we do next?" Bernadette asked.

"I'll keep digging," Maura said. "If I can get Lesley to research this too, we may get some good leads."

"Have you heard anything about when the warrant hearing might be?" Kep asked. "We need CSI in that room."

"I've talked to the U.S. Attorney," Maura said, "but it might not be enough to approve the warrant. Dr. Woodhead might have to get on the stand and talk about his unique talent."

"My supershnozz," he said brightly.

"Your what?"

"Never mind," Bernadette said quickly.

"I don't expect to get an update until tomorrow morning," Maura said. "Although if I keep pressing, the judge may conduct a hearing this evening. But I wouldn't hold my breath—Judge Baldwin isn't a fan of federal government overreach."

"That's probably why he's dragging his feet."

"It's certainly possible," Maura admitted. "Are the two of you conducting more interviews tonight?"

Kep and Bernadette looked at each other.

"I think we should keep going," Kep said.

"Who do you want to talk with?"

"Have you procured an address for Cecilia Carter yet?"

"I've narrowed down the address to an apartment building. We need the unit number. We might have it soon."

"Then while we're waiting, let's talk to Professor Lightman."

"Again?"

"Yes," Kep said. "He needs to tell us exactly what the endgame of this project is. Now that we know Eponymous Pharmaceutical is bankrolling the research, he won't have to break his confidentiality agreement—and he might be more forthcoming."

"True. Especially if he's afraid his life is in danger."

"At least he should be aware that someone paid Nick LaSalle to install spyware on an employee's machine."

"Should we talk to LaSalle too?"

"Let's see what Lightman has to say first."

"Dunn put a protective detail on him," Maura said. "He's still at the Freshie."

"Is Curtis back?"

"No, and he hasn't checked in yet," she said, a note of worry creeping into her voice. "The officer I sent down there reported that nothing was amiss at the dorm, and Annika Nakrivo didn't answer her door."

"He'll turn up soon enough," Bernadette said, hoping it was true. "We'll be on our way to the lab."

Bernadette ended the call, turned the heat up, and sighed.

Kep glanced over at her. "Are you all right?"

"I'm concerned about Curtis. He's been out of touch for hours."

"You heard Maura—there's a BOLO on the SUV. Curtis will turn up with a perfectly reasonable explanation behind his absence."

Bernadette paused for a moment, then shook her head. "Actually—no. As much as I'd like to say that I'm most concerned about my missing co-worker, Curtis's disappearance isn't what's bothering me. I'm annoyed because you ditched me this morning. I looked like an idiot in front of Maura."

"You don't need to worry about me."

"I'm your case analyst, Kep," she said. "Worrying about you is pretty much the entirety of my job description."

Kep crossed his arms. "I don't like being kept on a leash. Maura knows it. You won't get in trouble."

Bernadette snorted in exasperation. "If you haven't noticed, Kep, I'm your sixth case analyst in the last two years. You ditching me isn't good for our working relationship, and it's not good for my continued employment at CSAB. You want to tell me why you gave me the slip?"

Kep dropped his arms to his sides and gave Bernadette an exasperated look. "May I remind you we have a suspect to interview?"

"May I remind you that we could have used your super-schnozz this morning? May I remind you that a bullet passed within inches of my head?"

Kep was quiet for a moment, then he ran his hand over his face. "A little over three years ago—after New Year's—my son was murdered."

Bernadette inhaled sharply.

"I gave a lecture at a forensics conference in town," he said, "but I was still a suspect. My son and I were not on good terms. He'd been employed at a website that defined 'news' loosely. His job title was 'Journalist,' but the site is the equivalent of a gossip magazine. The company was unstable; my wife and I had to send him money more than once when his paycheck was 'delayed.'" He sighed. "He and I had argued, quite vehemently, earlier that day. He had the byline on an article on my TV show."

"*Cases That Won't Die?*" Bernadette asked.

"That's the one. He had printed some of the complaints about the show I'd said at home. I had some unkind words about the directors, about one of the other experts on the show, and about the viewers. The producers had little choice but to let me go." He looked down at his hands. "I suppose I only have myself to blame that the police went through my financials with such a fine-toothed comb. I was forced to take a leave of absence in my research position too, and six months later, when the investigators finally declared I was no longer a suspect, they also declared it to be a cold case. My son had been murdered, and there was no justice for him."

"Oh—Kep, I'm so sorry."

"My marriage didn't survive, either. My wife blamed me. She didn't trust me anymore. I threw myself into my work. I expanded my consulting business and started with CSAB. I started making enough money to hire a private investigator."

Questions zoomed in Bernadette's head. How did Kep's son die? Where was he killed? Did he get to smell the murder scene? But she kept her mouth shut.

"If you are wondering where I was this morning, I received a call from my private investigator."

Bernadette was silent.

"It seems we have a lead for the first time in a few months." Kep rubbed his eyes with both hands. "I didn't tell you about this because I didn't want to cause a lot of drama. And I hate getting questions about it. I took the call, and then I walked around outside to calm myself down, and then I didn't want to be around anyone. I did a little investigating on my own. By the time I caught up with you and Detective Dunn, I was myself again."

Bernadette nodded.

"I won't lie to you—this might happen every so often. I might get a call from the private investigator. There's a new detective assigned to the cold case who wants to make a name for herself, so I'm trying to convince her to look at some new evidence that my investigator is digging up. I wish I could say that the case I'm working will always take top priority, but it won't."

"Did your other case analysts know about this?"

"Many of them were aware to varying degrees. Two of the handlers knew nothing and were probably the most frustrated by my confounding disappearances. I told Marty everything, and he was quite angry with me, because he didn't feel like he could tell Lieutenant Stevenson."

"Maura doesn't know?"

"She is aware my son was murdered. She knows I occasionally disappear for a few hours. I suspect she thinks I'm partaking in mind-altering drugs, or perhaps drowning my sorrows in a bottle of top-shelf liquor. Or it's possible she has a better opinion of me: that I'm simply a man who desires solitude and does not particularly care for the company of others." Kep gave Bernadette a wistful smile. "I suppose that's not far off from the truth."

Bernadette started the engine.

THEY PULLED INTO THE PARKING LOT OF THE FRESHIE at eight thirty. Kep closed the passenger door, and they walked across the lot. As they approached the double glass doors, the elevator opened inside and Zadie Michaels walked out. Kep rushed forward as Zadie pushed the door open.

Zadie gave a start, then relaxed when she saw Bernadette's face. "Oh—good evening, officers—uh, agents. Whatever. You're back?"

"We have a few more questions for Professor Lightman," Kep said.

"All right. You need me to take you up?"

"We know the way."

"What are you doing here so late, Zadie?" Bernadette asked.

"An intern's work is never done." Zadie sighed. "I'm trying to find the latest research data that Tommy compiled. He should have backed it up from his machine to the network on

Monday afternoon. And now with Eddie out too..." She trailed off.

"Right." Bernadette looked at the ground as Kep held the door open.

"So you weren't able to find the data?" Kep said.

"No. Not on the hard drive, not on the network."

"Do you think someone erased it?"

Zadie snickered. "As Professor Lightman says, I don't get paid to offer suggestions; I get paid to find the information."

Bernadette smiled. "I'm starting to see what you mean about Professor Lightman."

"Seriously," Zadie said.

"Thanks for letting us in," Bernadette said. "Have a good night."

Zadie walked out to the parking lot, and Bernadette and Kep entered the small lobby, pushing the elevator button. It opened immediately and the two of them got in and pushed "2." Bernadette took her federal identification out of her purse.

"I bet Professor Lightman is sick of talking to us," Bernadette said as the doors closed. "I didn't exactly leave things on good terms this afternoon."

"When we share that his competitors may have the laboratory's proprietary information, his attitude toward us may not improve." Kep scratched his nose and pushed his glasses up. "However, if he knows the keylogger was installed, and if he hasn't taken steps to correct it, you and I may be adding another suspect to the list."

"Then we should slow-play it," Bernadette said. "See how he reacts to our questions about the data going to a competitor."

"Agreed."

A uniformed officer stood in front of Lightman's office and nodded as Bernadette showed him her identification. Lightman saw them through the office window and leaped up from his desk.

"You two need to get out of here or I'm suing your whole agency for harassment."

Bernadette folded her arms. "Is that the thanks I get for protecting your life?"

"What—you mean the officer following me around like I'm a criminal?"

Kep cut in. "A Kilbourn Tech employee was paid by another medical company—one of Eponymous Pharmaceutical's competitors—to put that spyware on Kymer Thompson's machine."

Jude Lightman's face paled. "What?"

"You heard me. We've tracked the payment."

Bernadette shot Kep a look. While she suspected the payment to Nick LaSalle might be a bribe, she didn't have the evidence to back up that claim. Still, it was a useful thing to say to get Lightman to calm down. And Kep didn't have the same job requirements to follow as Bernadette.

"You've tracked—what?"

"The payment, Professor. Tens of thousands of dollars to an employee to install the keylogger."

"One of the interns?"

"We're not at liberty to say," Bernadette interrupted. "But you should know the project has been compromised."

Lightman's neck muscles tightened.

"Leaked information from Kymer Thompson's PC is being sent to one of Eponymous Pharmaceutical's competitors."

"The keylogger?" Lightman's nostrils flared. "And—how did you know our project was being funded by Eponymous? We've got agreements in place. The employees don't even know."

"CSAB is a federal agency, Professor. We've got ways to get

sensitive information. Especially when it's relevant to a murder investigation."

Lightman sat on the corner of his desk then covered his face with his hands. "I can still save this," he said. "The results of the early tests were promising. We were toying with the dosage. We've applied for clinical trials."

"I know you're disappointed—"

"Disappointed!" Lightman roared. "The five-year survival rate of lung cancer is less than twenty percent. This could have made that *eighty* percent—maybe even ninety with the right dosage. Hundreds of thousands of lives saved over the next decade." He slapped the desk with an open hand. "But those lives represent over a billion dollars in profit. Parr Medical is behind this, aren't they? They're working on their own treatments, but they aren't nearly as close as we are. There's no way they're going into clinical trials for another three years—maybe longer." He rubbed his forehead. "They're willing to let hundreds of thousands of people die so *they* can make profit instead of Eponymous." He looked from Kep's face to Bernadette's. "What happened? Why was Tommy killed? Why was Eddie shot?"

"We're following the evidence where it leads," Kep said. "We'd like the CSI team to analyze the aquarium room. including Research Room 12."

"Look—I don't want to be an ass," Lightman said.

Bernadette grunted.

"But if you get a bunch of CSI techs in that room, we won't be able to control the environment for the ammocoetes. I don't know what chemicals they'll spray, or what they'll do to the water."

"You think the CSI team will harm the lampreys?"

"It's a delicate balance. Diet. Water conditions. Environmental nutrients. When they grow to adults, their livers must have enough of the right amino acids. It's not something you can undo on a computer screen."

Bernadette rolled her eyes. "You don't even have an overnight staff, Professor."

"We have alarms if something goes wrong."

She blinked. "Alarms?"

"Yes."

"Like sirens and lights?"

"Yes. And two of our employees are immediately called. If something gets out of sync with the water pH or the temperature goes haywire, the on-call staff can be here in ten minutes."

"On-call staff?" Bernadette remembered Eddie's admonitions to end the interview—running errands before he went on call. "Who exactly is scheduled to be on call tonight?"

"It changes twice a week," Lightman said. "The schedule is set up in advance."

"Who's on call right now?"

"This week? I'd have to check."

Bernadette nodded. "Can you check now?"

Lightman sighed dramatically but stepped behind his desk. He moved his mouse, clicked around, then harrumphed.

"What is it?"

"Tommy was on call all this week, starting on Sunday. Annika's shift ended yesterday, and Eddie started his on-call week tonight."

Kep and Bernadette shot each other worried looks.

"So—Eddie and Tommy were supposed to be on-call tonight?"

Lightman rubbed his chin with the back of his hand. "Yes—but only in case the alarms go off. And I've been here all evening."

"Has anyone been down to see the lampreys today?" Kep asked.

"Of course," Lightman answered. "The ammocoetes need their feeding. Usually between five and six."

"So no one's been down there since six o'clock?"

"I don't know."

"Let's go check," Bernadette said.

"What—so you can get your team in without my permission?"

"Humor us, please," Bernadette said. "If something's wrong with the aquarium rooms, no one is receiving those emergency calls."

Lightman shook his head. "The alarms would be impossible to ignore. I can get down there in thirty seconds. It would have been a big problem if I'd left, but I can call a couple of the interns and have them on call within the hour."

"Please, Professor—"

"Okay, fine," Lightman snapped. "If it will get you out of my hair." He shuffled out of his office, past Kymer Thompson's desk, and ran his hand over his face. Kep and Bernadette followed closely. He turned down the hall and took the staircase down to the ground floor.

At the bottom of the stairs, he turned to the unmarked metal door and paused.

"That's strange," he mumbled.

"What's strange?" Bernadette asked.

"There's normally a red light..." His voice faded as he punched in numbers, but there was no soft beeping when Lightman pushed the buttons, and no green light when he was done. He grimaced and tried the door.

It swung open.

The room was dark and quiet.

"What the hell," Lightman mumbled. "This room isn't supposed to be—"

Then the smell hit Bernadette's nostrils. Fish—a hundred times stronger than the last time she'd been down here.

Where was the sound of the pumps in the aquarium?

Why wasn't the alarm going off?

A light. Bright, sharp.

Kep had turned the light of his phone on, and he shined it in the clear acrylic tanks.

At first, Bernadette saw nothing but water—a little dirty, but she could still see through it. She'd expected to see the lamprey larvae darting around, or searching the rocks for the detritus and algae that made up their diet.

Instead the tanks looked empty.

Then Kep moved his light up to the top of the water of the center tank.

Hundreds, maybe even thousands, of lamprey ammocoetes, floating on top. Most were one or two inches in length—like worms. Bernadette felt sick.

And there was a dead body floating in the tank among the larvae, face down.

She recognized the leather jacket right away.

Curtis.

Chapter Nineteen

BERNADETTE SAT ON THE COLD SIDEWALK, THE SNOW MELTING onto the lower part of her winter coat pulled taut under her thighs. The temperature was in the teens and the slight but persistent breeze off Lake Michigan made it feel even colder. At least she was no longer in the aquarium with the thousands of dead lamprey larvae and one dead CSAB investigator.

She shut her eyes and let the air numb the tip of her nose and freeze the tears that didn't even make it to her cheek.

Curtis had only been with the group for about eighteen months. It was his first job out of college, and he'd taken to it with zeal. Maura had seen something in him too. He'd already gotten a pay and title bump.

She pulled herself to her feet, and, looking at the ground to avoid patches of ice, walked carefully to the river.

The Riverwalk passed here, a wooden sidewalk at the river's edge, in some places, like it was here, suspended above the river.

She looked up and down the Riverwalk, half-expecting to see Rhonda with her shopping cart, but the wooden walkway was empty. She lifted her chin and gazed out over the ice—the river was a solid sheet. Snow piled on sections of the frozen river, the wind forming drifts, like miniature hills over a landscape. It looked surreal, almost like a snowglobe had broken and its contents spread out.

Bernadette shivered. The icy sidewalk had leached its chill into her body. She wanted to get into a hot shower.

A shadow fell over her from the bright lights of the lab building. She turned; it was Kep.

"How are you feeling?"

Bernadette looked back across the river. "Like shit."

He was silent and shuffled his feet on the planks.

"Is this another poisoning?" Bernadette asked. "Or was he shot, like Eddie?"

Kep rubbed his hands together, a cloud of breath in front of his face. "CSI hasn't said yet. The team removed him from the tank. I wasn't able to see a wound—bullet or otherwise. I strongly suspect another syringe full of ibogaine."

"You smell it?"

"Yes."

"Even with all those dead lamprey larvae?"

"Yes."

Bernadette was quiet. She could hear late dinner patrons straggling out of a restaurant across the river. She cleared her throat. "Do you think the killer took the rented SUV Curtis was driving?"

Kep shook his head. "We found it in the lot on the other side from where we parked."

Bernadette nodded, staring at the lights from the restaurant. "I should have seen that."

"Lightman didn't do it," Kep said. "I'm sure of it."

"No smell on him, right?"

"Correct. But I'm at a loss for a motive, also. *All* of the lamprey ammocoetes are dead." He sighed. "The aquarium tanks are where the stolen TFM ended up. Most, if not all, of those forty-five kilograms were dumped in."

"You sure it was TFM?"

Kep pointed to his nose.

Bernadette nodded. "Even though it dissipates?"

"It dissipates quickly in a running river, not in a fish tank with the filter turned off."

"But you don't suspect Lightman."

Kep shook his head. "I'm aware that Lightman is no saint. He can speak of nothing but Eponymous Pharma putting an end to their funding and eliminating his position. He hasn't once asked about Curtis."

She looked down at her feet. "At least his lawyer won't give us any grief about the CSI team now." She craned her neck to look at the lab building. "They find anything interesting yet?"

"No," Kep said. "I'm hopeful they'll soon discover a syringe. I have noted that whoever killed the ammocoetes was able to get forty-five kilograms of TFM into the aquariums. That's quite a bit of heavy lifting. It would require upper-body strength."

"But—aren't there ten fish tanks? That's only ten pounds in each."

Kep screwed up his mouth. "Yes, you're right. Four-and-a-half kilograms is more than enough to kill them all." He held up a finger. "However, all forty-five kilograms would need to arrive at the same time. That presents a transportation issue."

"The blue van." Bernadette closed her eyes and saw herself chasing after Nick LaSalle, who had been carrying two large totes down Highland Avenue. "Or someone strong enough to carry the TFM a few blocks."

Harsh light and shadows washed over them. Bernadette looked up; a small black sedan turned into the parking lot.

"Is that a Subaru WRX?"

Kep squinted. "I believe it is."

"We'll finally get to interview her." Bernadette took a few steps, but the ice on the ground made the going slippery. Cecilia Carter got out of the car, a worried look on her face, and rushed into the entrance. "I better see if I can stop her before she says too much to Lightman. He probably called her all upset, and she's offering him a shoulder to cry on."

"I'll provide distraction for the professor. Come on." Kep stepped up from the wooden planks onto the asphalt of the parking lot and reached a hand over to help Bernadette.

"I got it," she said, and took a step up.

The lights of the Milwaukee CSI van gave the far side of the building a surreal, ghostly look. Detective Kerrigan Dunn, in a Milwaukee Police wool hat and a long wool overcoat, stood halfway between the van and the propped-open side door which led to the aquarium rooms. She raised her hand in greeting as Kep and Bernadette got closer.

"This is what they get for not authorizing appropriate overtime." Dunn's voice carried across the parking lot and seemed to bounce off the frozen river. "One officer on protective duty. He can't be on two floors at once."

"Do you have a suspect in mind?" Kep asked.

Dunn laughed derisively. "No. That's why we called in the Feds and their fancy consultant with the supersonic sense of smell."

"I'm appalled by your use of catachresis," Kep said.

"My what?" Dunn asked.

"Ignore him." Bernadette stepped closer. "You got a look at the aquarium rooms, though, right, Detective?"

"Yep. Those dead lamprey babies look like gross little worms."

"And more than that," Bernadette said, "they're worthless. Lamprey larvae grow for four or five years before they become adults, and now that these will never get to their adult stage, the scientists won't be able to harvest their livers and inject the ibogaine into them. Literally millions of dollars in investment gone." *And thousands of dead cancer patients.*

"So why wasn't the room hooked up to an alarm?" Dunn asked.

Bernadette crossed her arms. "It was. Nothing went off."

"How can that be?"

Kep shrugged. "We don't know the answer yet. CSI has theories; I suspect someone tampered with the system." He nodded toward the open door. "The room had no lights, and all the systems were off—filtration, pumps. We'll know more when CSI examines the wiring."

From inside, the sound of yelling—a woman's voice and Lightman.

"So much for getting to Cecilia before she talks to the professor," muttered Bernadette.

The three of them hurried into the open side door. There was a second door inside, also open, which led to the stairwell where Lightman had taken Kep and Bernadette earlier. Dunn took the stairs two at a time; Bernadette followed.

Lightman and Cecilia Carter were arguing in the area in front of Kymer Thompson's desk.

"You *wanted* this to happen!" Lightman stuck a finger in Carter's face.

"I did not!"

"Oh, don't lie to me, Cecilia. You've hated that my work harvests the livers from—"

"Listen to yourself, Jude!" Cecilia yelled. "Don't say *harvest,* like the fish are potatoes. They're alive. They're living, breathing—"

"Well, they're neither living or breathing now. And it's your—"

"Do you really think I'd want to save all the lampreys by *killing* all the lampreys?" Cecilia shrieked, turned and began to stomp off—but ran straight into Kep.

"The lady has a point, professor," Kep said.

"I'm not talking about this," Lightman said. "And I'm not talking to *you*." He pointed at Kep. "Or you." He shot Bernadette an angry look.

"You're one of the few people in the building when our colleague was murdered," Bernadette said. "A federal employee was murdered while he was investigating a crime. We don't take that lightly. And we won't let a lover's quarrel get in the way of finding out who did it."

"You think I had anything to do with this?" Lightman said, voice raised. "Those dead lampreys represent years of research and millions of dollars down the drain. We'll be lucky if we don't lose our grant. Next week, I might be out of a job."

"Well, I certainly didn't do it," Cecilia said. "I've fought for the last ten years to keep marine life viable in Lake Michigan. I wouldn't have done that by killing thousands of lamprey larvae."

"Ammocoetes," said Lightman, under his breath.

"What?"

"Look, you say you love them so much, and you keep saying you and I are over because of what I do—the least you could do is call them by their correct name."

"They're larvae."

"They're ammocoetes," Lightman hissed.

Bernadette stepped between them. "Maybe we should interview you in separate rooms down at the station. Come with me, Ms. Carter."

Bernadette took Cecilia Carter by the upper arm, gently but firmly, and began to steer her into the empty conference room.

"Get your hands off me," Cecilia snapped.

"We can do this at the police station," Bernadette said. "Or maybe you'd rather talk to the U.S. Attorney."

It was a bluff, but an effective one. Cecilia stopped protesting and sat down at the conference table.

"Good," Bernadette said, closing the door. She sat at the head of the table, about five feet away from Cecilia.

"I'm not saying anything without my lawyer."

"I've heard that from Douglas Rheinstaller, too," Bernadette said. "Of course, that makes sense when we can put you both at the Wildlife Specialties in Fond du Lac buying a hundred pounds of TFM."

Cecilia's face fell for a split second before her expression changed to dignified shock. "What? I wasn't anywhere near—"

"Your cell phone certainly was," Bernadette said, "and I suspect when we get the camera footage from the store, we'll see the two of you together."

Cecilia was silent.

"You did a great job, acting like you don't want to see those precious lampreys die," Bernadette continued. "But raising them in the lab and releasing them into the wild is sure to screw up the ecosystem, right?"

Cecilia crossed her arms.

"You and Rheinstaller had a common enemy," Bernadette continued. "Those lamprey ammocoetes had to be killed. So you started an affair with Professor Lightman to get information out of him. Maybe to find the weaknesses in the alarm system. Maybe to find out who was on call if something happened."

Cecilia pressed her lips together and turned her body slightly away from Bernadette.

Bernadette stared at Cecilia's face for a moment and saw a slight tremble in her lip.

"Hmm," Bernadette murmured.

Cecilia glanced quickly at Bernadette, eyes defiant, before dropping her gaze to the table in front of her.

"You had a plan to kill the lampreys," Bernadette said slowly, tapping her fingers on the table. "But the TFM disappeared before you could do anything about it."

Cecilia flinched. "I'm not answering anything without my lawyer present."

"I thought you'd stolen the TFM. After all, you were the one person who knew that Douglas Rheinstaller bought it. You might have even helped him put it in the shed." Bernadette leaned forward, resting her elbows on the table. "But you didn't even know it was missing, did you?"

"I told you, I'm not answering any questions without my lawyer."

Bernadette stood. "Wait here."

She left the room and walked to Lightman's closed office door. Through the window, she saw Kep across from the professor, whose eyebrows were knitted, a frown on his face. Bernadette opened the door.

"I don't have time for this," Lightman snapped. "I have to report this incident."

"I think the university is aware of what's going on, Professor," Kep said.

Lightman glared. "I'm not talking about reporting it to Kilbourn Tech—I'm talking about reporting it to the people who are bankrolling this research. We'll be in enough trouble if they have to postpone the clinical trials. If we cancel, my career is over."

"You can't tell Eponymous now," Bernadette said. "It's after hours. They won't be able to do anything until tomorrow morning."

"A moment?" Kep asked.

Bernadette turned her head. Kep motioned toward the corner of the room, and she followed.

"Lightman clearly has no motive," Kep said. "Cecilia, on the other hand—"

"Right. We know she was with Rheinstaller, buying the TFM."

"And who else would know that he kept it in his shed?"

"I don't know that *she* knew it. The two of them were conspiring to kill all those larvae, but... well, the way she's acting? I don't think she had a clue the TFM was stolen."

"How sure are you of that?"

Bernadette screwed up her mouth before answering. "I've seen it before in my money laundering cases. When people realize their trust was misplaced. I don't think she committed the burglary."

Kep screwed up his mouth.

"You don't believe me."

"I said nothing of the kind. We need more data points."

"Fine," Bernadette said. "Go and smell her."

Kep raised his eyebrows.

"If," Bernadette continued, "you can smell TFM or ibogaine or anything else that makes you suspect she had a role in the murders, we'll take her to the station and book her."

"On what charge?"

"We'll figure something out. Go and smell her first."

He slowly shook his head, then walked across the bullpen and into the conference room, closing the door behind him.

The seconds dragged by, and after what seemed like far too long, the door opened again, and Kep came out.

"No," he said. "Cecilia Carter wasn't in the aquarium room today. No TFM. No ibogaine. She's nervous about something— I could smell the cortisol pouring off her—but it's not murder."

"Okay," she said. "We'll let them go. Dunn can take their statements."

Kep nodded. "And you know who we need to find?"

She nodded. "Annika Nakrivo."

"That's correct," Kep said. "If she isn't answering her door, she could be in danger. I hope she isn't floating dead in one of the other tanks."

"Are we still thinking the reverend is a suspect?"

"Yes—although..." Kep trailed off.

"What?"

"Would she be able to lift Curtis into the lamprey tank?"

"Curtis wasn't a linebacker or anything. I'm not even sure he weighed as much as his jacket. I could lift Curtis and dump him in the tank. With that aquarium ladder, I could do it with one arm."

Kep blinked slowly. "Yes," he said, "but you work out frequently. You lift weights."

"We don't know that the reverend doesn't. And besides, adrenaline does strange things to people's physical capabilities."

"The reverend is nowhere near as strong as you."

"All I mean is, don't count her out. She could be the wiry, strong type. Maybe Curtis was on a ladder looking at all the dead larvae, and he fell in when he was killed."

"I understand your point," Kep said. "You should get to work."

Bernadette cocked her head. "Me? What about you?"

"You have to track down Annika Nakrivo."

"You're not coming?"

Kep shook his head. "I can accomplish more here by identifying smells and working with the CSI team. In fact, I should return to the aquarium rooms immediately."

Bernadette put her hands on her hips. "I think you're planning to disappear on me again."

Kep blinked quickly, then pushed his glasses back up on his nose. "I promise you," he said, his steely gaze boring into Bernadette, "my nose at a murder scene is the most valuable asset we have." His voice cracked on the last word. "But someone needs to find Annika."

"Yeah." Bernadette cleared her throat. "Yeah, that makes sense."

And she turned and walked toward the elevators.

Chapter Twenty

BERNADETTE STOOD NEXT TO THE STUDENT FLOOR supervisor in the hallway in front of Annika Nakrivo's dorm room. The woman, a tall blonde with glasses, shoulder-length hair, and a Kilbourn Tech sweatshirt, shifted her weight nervously and cast furtive glances up and down the hall.

Bernadette knocked for the third time.

Still no answer.

"You okay?" Bernadette said to the woman next to her.

"Fine."

"Am I making you nervous?"

"You woke me up in the middle of the night to do a wellness check on the weird transfer student. Wouldn't you be nervous too?"

"Look, you just have to give me the key. You don't have to look in the room if you don't want to." The weight of the gun in the holster under her jacket comforted her.

"What? Oh no—what do you think happened? Did someone attack her?"

"Whoa, whoa, whoa," Bernadette said. "You're way ahead of me. She's not answering her phone or the door. That's it."

The floor supervisor thrust the key into Bernadette's hand and hurried twenty feet down the hall.

Bernadette turned the key in the lock, took a deep breath, and opened the door.

The room looked like it had been ransacked. The mattress was on the floor and all the drawers were open, clothes scattered everywhere. A smear of red on the wall next to the door. Was that blood?

Bernadette stepped inside. No more blood appeared in the rest of the room. The television was on its face but didn't seem broken. She stepped around the room carefully, not touching anything. No shattered glass. A huge mess, though.

She squinted. What were the ransackers looking for? A communication device for the alarm system? A USB stick with proof of who had infected Kymer Thompson's machine? A piece of information on who had stolen the TFM?

Bernadette thought about the notebook on Annika Nakri-vo's desk at work. Nothing spectacular about that. Maybe she took work home with her—a USB drive, maybe like the one Thompson took home that infected his home computer.

She crouched down and stared at the mess surrounding her. Everything had been pulled out of the drawers, and the furniture was turned over. Papers scattered all over—receipts, take-out menus, even a few Justice for Oceans brochures. No mattresses cut open; no broken picture frames. Maybe the intruders found what they were looking for.

Or maybe they took Annika.

Annika might have surprised them when she got to her dorm room. She thought back to Parr Medical's attempts to woo Eddie Taysatch away from the Freshie. Then the van that barely missed her, the bullet whizzing by her ear—

She chewed her lip. Nick LaSalle. He was the prime suspect for the installation of the keyloggers on Thompson's computers.

If he hadn't found what Parr Medical needed, maybe he'd found it on Nakrivo's PC. Had LaSalle kidnapped her?

LaSalle also would be big enough and strong enough to empty a hundred pounds of TFM into the aquarium tanks—and still have enough strength left to kill Curtis Janek and dump him in the tank, too, even without the help of a ladder.

She took out her phone and called Detective Dunn.

The detective answered on the first ring. "Dunn."

"We'll need another CSI team over at Juneau Hall. Annika Nakrivo's dorm room has been ransacked."

"What? Ransacked?"

"It's a mess. No sign of Annika, though."

"Do you think she's been kidnapped?"

"I don't know. She left work early today." Bernadette tilted her head as close to ninety degrees as she could and looked under the plywood bookcase. "I'd like the room fingerprinted." She paused. "The university would have Nick LaSalle's prints on file from when he applied for a job, right?"

"Probably. You suspect that he's the kidnapper?"

"It's a gut feeling. He got that huge scholarship from the shell company owned by Parr Medical. And he's the main suspect for putting the keyloggers on our victim's PCs."

Dunn exhaled loudly. "Didn't Reverend Roundhouse go up there Monday night? You don't suspect her?"

Bernadette glanced around the room. "Could be her. The place is a mess, but nothing looks broken. Might be the politest ransacking I've ever seen. I could see the Reverend hurriedly searching for something but not wanting to damage property."

"I'll contact our missing persons unit."

"Good." Bernadette started to rise to her feet when a yellow sticky note on the carpet caught her eye. It lay face up, and a message in block letters:

. . .

Meet at Superior S&F

BERNADETTE REACHED FOR IT BEFORE SHE REMEMBERED SHE had no gloves on. Instead, she took her phone out and snapped a picture of it.

The sticky note looked recent, as if it had been written earlier that day. Could it have fallen out of a book from the bookcase? A church study group? No—that didn't make any sense. The ink appeared fresh, the yellow of the sticky note bright, not faded.

"Bernadette? You still there?"

"Detective," Bernadette said, "I just found a note that says, 'Meet at Superior S&F.' That's the warehouse where Agios Delphi keeps the light blue van, right? Suzanne Thao owns it?"

"You found a note? And it says, 'Meet at Superior S&F'?"

"Yes."

"Do you think it was meant for you?"

Bernadette hesitated. "I don't know. Maybe whoever took Annika meant to meet someone else there, and dropped the note while they were ransacking the room."

"Or," Dunn said, "maybe it was meant for us to find. Maybe Superior Feed is where we'll get a ransom demand." She sucked in a breath. "Are there any other indications about where Annika might be?"

"Not that I see," Bernadette said. "I might have missed something. But this note is the only thing in plain sight."

"Could be a trap," Dunn suggested.

"So far, it's the only clue we have. I think we have to at least follow where this goes."

"Okay," Dunn said with determination in her voice, "I'll have a team meet you over there. It's at the end of Bay Street. Want me to call Lieutenant Stevenson?"

"Yes." Bernadette put the phone on speaker and pulled up directions in her mobile map. "If there's a chance the kidnapper is still there—"

"Right, you need backup. Wait for the officers to show up. Don't go in by yourself."

"Of course—but we don't know when she was taken. It could have been an hour ago, or it could have been as soon as she walked out of the Freshie. I don't know what we're up against."

"There's been no request for ransom," Dunn pointed out.

"You don't know that," Bernadette said quickly. "People sometimes don't get the cops involved."

"We're involved now," Dunn said. "I'll get a team to Superior Salt & Feed right away."

⌘

BERNADETTE TURNED LEFT ONTO EAST BAY STREET AND HIT a pothole, which rocked the entire SUV. Her phone rang. An unfamiliar 414 number. Her finger almost slipped off the answer button because of the bumpy road.

"Becker."

"Hi, Agent Becker, this is Lesley Gill. I'm a researcher with the Milwaukee Police—I work mostly on identity theft cases, but I heard you needed some extra help with this investigation."

"Hi, Lesley. Yes, my boss told me you're the forensic accountant assigned to this case."

"Good. I heard you and Dr. Woodhead had some questions about Annika Nakrivo?"

"Considering I'm about to invade an abandoned salt warehouse with several officers to try to locate her, yes, we've got some questions." Bernadette crossed under the elevated freeway. While she knew Lake Michigan was directly in front of her, the view was blocked by the huge warehouses and a trio of grain elevators towering over her SUV. A white Toyota Camry with a Kilbourn Tech logo on the side was parked in front of the warehouse closest to Bay Avenue.

A Kilbourn Tech car. Someone from the Freshie? Or maybe it was Nick LaSalle.

About a hundred yards long and seventy yards wide, the building was roughly twenty feet high on the sides with a roof that rose slightly in the middle. Bernadette smelled manure and decay, and she hit the recirculation button on the climate control. "Oof. No one told me it would stink out here."

"That must be the fertilizer factory," Lesley said. "And the sewage treatment plant. It's pretty bad over there when the wind is blowing the wrong direction."

"Okay, Lesley, make it quick. As soon as the cavalry gets here, we're all headed in."

"Sure. Your team pointed out a gap in Miss Nakrivo's whereabouts between October and January. We located a booking in her name on a plane from Miami to Cleveland on October seventh."

"How did we miss that? We checked the airlines."

"But not the charters. Those are in a different system. And she didn't go through the regular TSA checkpoints. That's why we missed her the first time."

Bernadette shook her head. "Let me guess. The plane was chartered by Parr Medical."

"Sorry, Agent Becker, I don't have that information yet."

Bernadette chewed her lip. "Uh—Lesley, I'm not an agent."

"You're not?"

"No." She closed her eyes and swallowed hard. "I'm a case analyst."

"Case Analyst Becker is kinda difficult to say."

She pushed down the negative thoughts. "Then call me Bernadette." She heard sirens behind her get closer, then go silent. "Okay, they're almost here. Anything else?"

"It can wait."

"Are you in the fifth division?"

"Nope. I'm in the police administration building on State Street."

"Working late?"

"As long as you need me. Give me a call at this number when you're done."

"Thanks, Lesley." Bernadette ended the call. For a moment she considered calling Sophie, but it was too late. And Sophie would panic. She blinked hard.

Get it together, Becker.

Two police cruisers arrived, sirens silent and switching their red-and-blue lights off as soon as they pulled into the lot. The night wasn't as dark as Bernadette expected; the sky was clear and the moon three-quarters full, its light shimmering off the snow piled up on the sides of the parking lot.

Both cruisers parked behind Bernadette's SUV. Bernadette opened the door and was hit in the face with a wave of fertilizer stench. She gagged but pulled out her identification and forced herself to walk to the first cruiser like nothing was wrong.

She stood next to the cruiser door as the driver rolled down his window.

"Officer," she said, holding out her CSAB identification and nodding to the policeman behind the wheel. Oh, it was the same officer who'd been at the front desk two days before. And she was standing in front of him in her boxy puffy purple coat. Good thing it was dark—though even in the darkness, she could tell his eyes were tired. "Good evening, Officer Chesapeake. Nice to see you again. Is there a plan?"

"Hello again." Chesapeake nodded and smiled. "In situations like this, the protocol is for at least two officers to make a sweep of the outside of the building while others watch the exits. But we're providing support to a federal operation, so you give the guidance."

Bernadette shook her head. "I won't contradict your protocol, but this might be nothing. I found a sticky note on the floor in Annika Nakrivo's dorm room. We might be knocking on the door of an empty building and then we'll all go home."

"We still check out false alarms." Chesapeake motioned to his passenger, a thirtyish, stocky, pale-skinned officer with a crew cut. "A few years ago, dispatch thought a prank call came into nine-one-one, but Schroeter here broke up a home invasion in process."

Schroeter stared straight ahead.

Bernadette leaned down so she could see into the car better. "Good evening, Officer Schroeter. I'm Case Analyst Bernadette Becker."

Chesapeake motioned with his head to the white Camry. "That vehicle is from Kilbourn Tech. Is it the only one here?"

"Seems like it."

Chesapeake craned his neck to look in his sideview mirror. "We'll call the university. See who might have checked that vehicle out. We'll want to know who we're dealing with."

Schroeter pulled the laptop, mounted on an arm between the seats, in front of him. The screen lit his pale face from underneath as he began to type. "On it."

"I think it might be Nick LaSalle," Bernadette said. "He oversaw the computers at the Kilbourn Tech facilities outside of campus. I assume he has a work vehicle to get from worksite to worksite."

"Why do you think he checked out that car?"

Bernadette paused. "There's a chance Annika Nakrivo was kidnapped, and Nick is the most likely Kilbourn Tech employee to be involved." Bernadette looked down at the asphalt and tapped her foot. "He received a large payment recently. We believe the money was in exchange for installing a keylogger program on our murder victim's computer." She cleared her throat and blinked, Curtis's face flashing in her mind. "I mean, our *first* murder victim."

"Good to know," Chesapeake said. He shifted in his seat.

Bernadette hesitated, then spoke, trying to conceal the nervousness in her voice as she locked eyes with Chesapeake. "So your nameplates give me your last names. I don't think I know your first name. Names."

Chesapeake smiled easily. "Officer Lamar Chesapeake. This" —he motioned to the officer working on the laptop beside him —"is Lance Schroeter. We've got a couple officers from the second district behind us."

Bernadette stood and raised her hand in greeting to the cruiser behind Chesapeake's. "And the other two will guard the back door?"

"That's the idea." He tilted his head at Bernadette. "This is our protocol without confirmation of a hostage situation. Right now, we've got one car at an abandoned warehouse and no threats on anyone's life. If we can get visuals on a hostage, that would be different, but there are no windows in the warehouse."

Bernadette sighed, and the stink of the air made her immediately regret it. Her eyes started to water. She blinked rapidly and cleared her throat, hoping Chesapeake wouldn't notice. "Do you have one of those infrared body-heat detectors?"

Chesapeake shook his head. "You overestimate the Milwaukee police budget. We'll try to establish some visuals, but don't hold your breath."

Bernadette looked at the warehouse. "Okay. There's a front door. Is there a back exit?"

Chesapeake nodded. "If this is a kidnapping and whoever's holding Nakrivo flees, chances are they'll use the rear." He stuck his head out of the window and looked back at the other cruiser. "There are five of us. More on the way if needed."

"You two around the building, those two guarding the back exit, me at the front door?"

"If this does turn into a hostage situation, do you have experience?"

Bernadette remembered: the six-hour standoff in Kansas City. "Yes."

"You have a weapon?"

She nodded.

Schroeter looked up from the laptop screen. "The university's system says the white Camry was checked out by Nick LaSalle on Monday. Hasn't returned it since."

Bernadette nodded. "That just increased the odds of Annika being in that building."

"Okay." Officer Chesapeake opened the door of his cruiser and got out, with Schroeter getting out too. He put on a black wool cap with the Milwaukee Police logo, and Schroeter did the same with a plain gray cap, then handed a radio to her. "Stay in close contact."

Bernadette looked toward the abandoned warehouse. The parking lot was dark, but there were lights from the lakefront and from some of the closer industrial buildings, as well as the elevated freeway. The two hundred feet between the cruisers and the front of the building contained nothing but open asphalt, concrete, and snow. She went to the SUV and got her wool hat, then walked to the passenger's side of the cruiser, waiting to walk up and knock on the front door.

Schroeter conferred with the two officers in the second cruiser then stepped away as the car reversed and drove away. It made a turn around the other buildings and stopped about a hundred feet away from the back of the warehouse. The doors opened and both officers stepped behind the cruiser.

Hands on their holsters, Chesapeake and Schroeter nodded to each other then moved quickly across the moonlit parking lot, their shoes making silent tracks in the snow. Then they both disappeared around the side.

Feeling the chill of the metal passenger door go through her coat, Bernadette shivered. With no cloud cover to keep the heat in, the temperature had plummeted. Bernadette's teeth chattered.

Her radio chirped. "Thirty seconds."

It must be bitterly cold in the warehouse, too. If Annika Nakrivo was in there—and if she'd been in there since the early afternoon—she might be in danger of hypothermia. Bernadette crouched and looked at her watch. She'd need about fifteen seconds to cross the lot and knock on the door.

Twenty seconds.

Nineteen, eighteen—

Bang.

Bernadette jumped. Not a shot. The steel front door had been thrown open and crashed against a concrete pillar.

A strange figure on the ground in the shadows—five legs? Scooting jerkily from the entrance.

The figure moaned. The volume was low, and Bernadette barely made it out.

"Help me, please—someone, help me..."

Annika Nakrivo.

Chapter Twenty-One

Bernadette sprinted toward the figure on the ground: Annika, tied to a four-legged metal chair. Her ankles were duct-taped to the chair's front legs and one of her wrists was still taped to the arm, but she'd gotten her right hand free and was pulling herself along the ground.

Bernadette knelt over her and pulled on the duct tape over Annika's left wrist, but it was too strong for her gloved hands. She fumbled with the radio, then clicked the button. "Nakrivo's out the front door. No sign of others. Repeat, Nakrivo's out the front door."

She kept pulling on the duct tape. Annika had a wool hat, winter coat, and gloves on—fortunate in the sub-freezing temperature. "Is anyone in there?"

The radio in Bernadette's hand crackled acknowledgment. Distantly, car doors closed and distant voices could be heard, urgent, getting closer.

"Thank you," Annika gasped. "Thank you for saving me—"

"Annika!" Bernadette snapped. "Is there anyone else in the warehouse?"

"I—I don't think so. The man left about an hour ago."

"An hour?"

"I don't know. I've been trying to pull free."

"What man?"

"He—" Annika began to sob. "He's the one who fixes the computers at the lab."

"Nick LaSalle?"

"Nick. Yes, that's his name."

Bernadette set her jaw. "Did he bring you here in the university's car?"

"I—" Annika swallowed. "I don't know. I don't remember anything. I was in my dorm room, and then someone knocked on the door. I answered and then—and the next thing I remember is waking up here in the dark, tied up."

"Was anyone with you?"

"Please," Annika said, "please, get me out of this."

Bernadette clicked on the radio again. "She's tied to the chair with duct tape. Bring a knife. And call an ambulance."

"We need to find Nick," Bernadette said. "We need to know where he went. How did he leave?"

Annika sobbed. "No ambulance. Please. No hospital. I want to go home."

"Okay, sweetie," Bernadette said. "We'll get you out of this." In her mind, a clock began ticking. How long had Nick LaSalle been on the run? Was there another payment waiting for him from Parr Medical after the lampreys were all dead?

More sirens.

"You're okay, Annika," Bernadette said. "We've got you. You'll be all right."

Kep Woodhead pushed his glasses up his face as he walked across the frozen parking lot toward the white Toyota Camry, Bernadette beside him.

"You okay?"

Kep smiled grimly. "Curtis's death is hitting me harder than I thought it would. It's been a long day."

"We need your superschnozz for one more thing. Then you can go back to the hotel."

An officer stood beside the Camry, next to a tall, imposing woman with red cheeks, dressed in a parka and a wool Green Bay Packers hat, who was putting several tools into a large metal toolbox. Bernadette assumed she was the locksmith.

"Got it open?"

"Sure," the locksmith said. "If you've got the right tool, these Toyotas open up like a tin of sardines."

"Let's hope this one doesn't smell as bad," Bernadette quipped, looking at Kep out of the corner of her eye. At least the wind had shifted, and the fertilizer stench had dissipated.

"Doors are unlocked, and I left the trunk open half an inch," the locksmith said, continuing to put tools back in the box.

"Thanks." Kep raised the trunk lid and lowered his head into it. "This is it," he said. "I have no question in my mind that someone used this car to transport TFM, probably in these two black tote bags."

Bernadette stuck her head in the trunk. "Those are the same tote bags I saw Nick LaSalle carrying on Tuesday night," she said, fuming. "That's why Nick LaSalle never checked the car back in at the university. He had a hundred pounds of stolen TFM in the trunk."

"That is certainly a theory that makes sense," Kep said, a wavering note in his voice.

Bernadette paused. "What is it?"

"All signs shifted from Vivian Roundhouse, and they now point to Nick LaSalle," Kep said. "The college loan payment, the car he checked out, his keylogger program—it all fits. He had access to the laboratory. I suspect he had access to the computers that control the alarm systems as well."

Bernadette tapped her foot. "No smoking gun, though, right?"

"That isn't the only thing that concerns me."

"Then what?"

"His actions fail to make sense to me. Are we supposed to believe that LaSalle killed Kymer Thompson, shot Eddie Taysatch, and killed Curtis?"

"If you smelled TFM in the trunk, then Nick is the most likely person to kill the lampreys, isn't he?"

Kep took off his glasses and rubbed his eyes. "He's high on the suspect list for killing the ammocoetes, yes."

"And therefore, he's high on the suspect list for killing Thompson and Curtis—and shooting Taysatch too."

"I understand his motive for killing the lampreys—he was paid to do so. However, murder is a different level—one that an IT specialist might be loath to undertake."

Bernadette opened her mouth, then shut it.

"What were you going to say?"

"Thompson and Curtis were killed to stop them from reporting the alarm," Bernadette said. "But you have a point. There must be easier, less homicidal ways to prevent people from reporting alarms. Although the amount of his college loan payoff is more than enough money to buy a hit."

"I suspect LaSalle would try to break into the system and prevent the alarms from being sent in the first place."

"Maybe the system's airgapped."

"Possibly. But there are still quite a few things that don't make sense. What is LaSalle still doing in Milwaukee? Why use the Agios Delphi van to shoot Taysatch? Why kidnap Annika Nakrivo?" Kep rubbed his beard. "Additionally, a large multinational corporation would hire a professional to kill people. Paying an amateur like LaSalle to kill Thompson and Taysatch defies all logic."

Bernadette paused and shuffled her feet. "Maybe LaSalle's work isn't done here. Maybe he wanted to cast the blame on the church so we wouldn't look at him as a suspect. Could be that Annika knew something. Maybe she knew where a vital piece of Thompson's research was."

Kep straightened up. "It's certainly possible."

"What is your gut telling you?"

"My gut doesn't put me on the right path most of the time," Kep said. "That's why I follow my nose." He walked around the side of the car and opened the driver's door, sticking his head in. "Under the smell of Carver's Burgers and Nick LaSalle's pastrami sandwiches," he said, "I can detect Annika Nakrivo's perfume. So it seems she was in this vehicle."

"Fits our theory that LaSalle was the one to kidnap her."

"Correct." He stood up. "I am able to sense the unique scent profile of the lampreys—with the TFM layered beneath."

"So this car is pretty much ground zero for turning the aquarium into a silver lamprey graveyard."

Kep walked around the car, opening each door and sniffing inside. "Can you think of any other scenario that makes sense?"

"You mean, besides Nick LaSalle kidnapping Annika?"

"Yes."

Bernadette nodded. "Sure. We can't rule out the church. This property is owned by Suzanne Thao, the van was owned by the church, the body was found in the church—Vivian Roundhouse might be all over this."

"Suzanne Thao is another possible suspect," Kep said.

"However, I fail to see a motive for either of them to kill the lampreys."

"I know that the supply of ibogaine is a possible motive for Roundhouse to kill Thompson and maybe shoot Eddie," Bernadette said, "but I can't see how those pieces fit together yet to have her kill the fish."

"I agree." Kep paused. "Cecilia Carter. Have we established motive for her?"

"Yes. Motive to kill the lampreys to save the ecosystem, for sure. She has the arrest record, but protesting is a far cry from murder to cover her tracks."

Kep closed the rear driver's-side door. "The time is late, the air is cold, and my energy has waned. Let's head back to the hotel."

Bernadette shook her head. "I'm heading to the State Street district office. A tech down there is sharing some of her financial findings with me."

"At this hour?"

"She's pulling overtime because of the—uh..."

"Because Curtis was killed."

"Yes."

Kep's phone buzzed, and he took it out and looked at the screen.

"Important?"

"A spam text," he said, putting the phone back in his pocket.

"At this hour?"

Kep took a step closer to Bernadette, then lowered his voice. "You know Maura better than I do, but in case she doesn't invite you into her confidences, be—uh—especially careful with what you say about Curtis."

"I know. He was Maura's protégé. So young. So much potential."

Kep blinked, then looked quizzically at Bernadette.

"Did she really not tell you?"

Tell me what?

And then the realization hit her. Maura and Curtis. Kep knew and Bernadette didn't.

"She told you she was having a relationship with Curtis?"

"No."

"Then how—"

Kep tapped his nose.

"Oh, come on," Bernadette said. "You're saying you can identify pheromones or something?"

"Not pheromones. Maura's shampoo in Curtis's hair the last case I worked."

Bernadette shook her head defiantly. "I can't believe that. She wouldn't risk her career for a roll in the sack with a subordinate. No matter how cute he is. Was. I mean—there has to be almost twenty years between them."

Kep took a step back. "I understand that you don't want it to be true. That you believe Maura is worthy of a higher standard. I understand she's a professional, but sometimes the temptation is too great."

"You're wrong."

"Science doesn't lie." Kep sniffed and his glasses slipped down his nose. "We have less control over our choice of mate than you think. Have you heard of the human leukocyte antigen?"

Bernadette felt her blood pressure rise.

"It's a system of proteins that are responsible for the regulation of the immune system. Studies have shown that heterosexual women are more attracted to men whose proteins are dissimilar to their own. That way, their offspring have a better chance of a stronger immune system that can fend off a broader swath of diseases—"

"You're saying," she interrupted, "that Maura risked her

career to sleep with a young subordinate because of the way he *smelled?*"

"Precisely."

Bernadette stamped her feet. "When all you have is a hammer, Kep, every problem looks like a nail."

"What does that mean?"

Bernadette rolled her eyes. "I think you and that hammer in the middle of your face are smart enough to figure it out."

Kep frowned. "Look—this doesn't have any bearing on who murdered Curtis. If we start to get clues that it *was* related to their affair—"

"They weren't having an affair," Bernadette muttered.

"—then I'll bring it up. But Maura's distraught. She's grieving. I advise you to keep your distance on this subject. I can't predict how Maura will react if she thinks we know about her and Curtis."

Bernadette squeezed her eyes shut. "Why tell me at all, Kep?"

"Because," Kep said, "you deserve to know."

She opened her eyes and furrowed her brow. "It won't help us solve the case."

"The truth will out."

Bernadette paused. "What?"

"'Murder cannot be hid long; a man's son may, but at the length, the truth will out.'"

Bernadette glared at him. "For once, could you speak like a normal person?"

Kep pushed his glasses up on his nose. "It's from *The Merchant of Venice*. That's one of the Bard's most well-known plays."

Bernadette gritted her teeth and took a step forward. "Do you even care that our co-worker was murdered?"

"I have solved quite a few more murders than you have," Kep said.

"That's not the only thing that counts."

Kep blinked. "What else could possibly count? The number of times you've been demoted?"

Bernadette felt her heart lurch. She opened her mouth but no sound came out.

"If you don't desire to work with the most successful CSAB investigator of the last two years," Kep said, "you can provide me a ride back to the hotel on your way to State Street."

Bernadette swallowed hard, then found her voice, wavery as it was. "You're done for the night?"

"I am." He pointed to the cruisers. "Perhaps I shall ride with one of the local constabulary."

Bernadette seethed. She should give Kep a ride back—the Outsider Hotel was only a few blocks out of the way—but the thought of spending another second with his smug face and his literary references made her blood boil. She shook her head. "I don't want Lesley to wait any longer for me than she already has."

"I'll bid you goodnight, then." Kep's tone told her he knew her response was bullshit, that she had no desire to be in a car with him even for the ten minutes it would take to drop him off at the hotel. He looked at his watch. "Or good morning." He turned and walked away.

❧

"Nothing else from Nick LaSalle's financials," Lesley Gill said. She looked different from the picture in Bernadette's head: short, spiky auburn hair, several shades lighter than her dark brown skin, and thin gold-rimmed glasses perched on the bridge of her nose. She wore a bright multi-color pullover and black jeans —a far cry from the officers' uniforms, but as she was a civilian employee—and it was the middle of the night—Bernadette understood why she wasn't dressed up. Techies never had to dress up in the office, anyway. At CSAB, if you were one of the few people who knew how the servers worked, you could show up in clown makeup and trousers made from raw bacon and still keep your job.

It was two thirty in the morning, and Bernadette sat in a chair behind Lesley's desk, half-heartedly looking over her shoulder at the database search results on her screen.

"No ATM activity," Lesley continued. "And nothing on his credit cards."

Bernadette crossed her arms. "And he didn't go back to the IT department after leaving the Freshie yesterday?"

"I don't know."

"Can you find out?"

"I can't wake people up in the middle of the night to ask that kind of question, Bernadette," Lesley said. "You'll have to wait till eight o'clock. Maybe even nine."

"I'm sure he's on the run," Bernadette muttered. "We've got to make sure we check the airports, train stations, buses—"

"He had at least an hour's head start on us when you found Annika," Lesley said. "He could be on any of ten different buses, or trains to Winnipeg or Toronto. If he took a charter plane like Annika did, he could already be in Canadian airspace —or, come to think of it, halfway to Mexico."

Bernadette tilted her head back until she was staring at the ceiling, then exhaled.

"At least Annika Nakrivo's okay," Lesley said. "You're the one who found her, right?"

"Yeah."

"Where do you want to start?"

Bernadette pushed herself back into a sitting position.

"Let's begin with Nick LaSalle. Found anything else regarding payments?"

"Nothing but that weird scholarship."

"Did you find the name of any individual behind the payment? Right now, we only have a shell company. A real person could be on the hook for murder-for-hire."

"Even if I found who initiated the scholarship, murder-for-hire would be tough to prove. The payment wasn't made after Kymer Thompson's death—only after the keylogger program was installed." Lesley clicked on the screen again, running her finger under a date that appeared. "And that was back in October. Almost six months ago. Kymer Thompson died earlier this week, but there's been no movement in Nick LaSalle's bank account since then."

Bernadette closed her eyes. She needed some coffee. Or maybe sleep.

"Did you—" Lesley began, then stopped and cleared her throat. "Did you know him very well?"

"Nick LaSalle?"

"No." Lesley shook her head. "Curtis Janek." Unlike Detective Dunn, she pronounced it correctly, with the Y sound at the beginning of his last name. "Had you worked together long?"

Bernadette thought about Maura and Curtis and their hidden relationship, and how Maura would have to fight to keep herself under control because it would mean her job if she couldn't. "Not that long. He's worked for CSAB for a couple of years, but I was reassigned to his team a couple of months ago."

Lesley nodded. "I'm sorry. We lost an officer last year. Hit by a drunk driver during a traffic stop. I—I know how it feels." She stared at her keyboard for a moment. "Do you want to see what I uncovered on Reverend Roundhouse?"

"Yes."

"She's in good financial shape."

"Divorced a CEO, right?"

"Yes. She gets a good chunk of alimony. Church coffers are full—a few big donors, even though the church is small."

"So she'd have no financial motive for killing Thompson," Bernadette said thoughtfully.

"I searched for signs that she was part of the bankroll. You know, for the scholarship. But nothing out of the ordinary for her accounts."

"What about payments for iboga plants?"

Lesley nodded. "Yes, she bought seeds a few times over the last few years. What is it you're looking for?"

"Motive, I guess. It would sure help if we could locate that van." Bernadette stretched her arms above her head. "Anything else?"

"No. I'll start on Annika Nakrivo's finances tomorrow morning. And Eddie Taysatch's too."

"Poor guy. Hasn't woken up yet." Bernadette stood. "I should go back to the hotel and get some sleep. I'm supposed to interview Annika Nakrivo in the hospital tomorrow."

Lesley locked her PC and stood up too. "Yes. I appreciate you coming back here. I know it's late."

"I appreciate you staying so long."

"Are you kidding? It was great. I never get to research this much interesting stuff. I'm usually researching dudebros waving confederate flags who buy souped-up pickup trucks with cash after they get their meth lab up and running." She coughed. "Sorry. I know you lost a colleague—that was, uh, not very professional."

Bernadette's eyes lost focus, remembering Curtis's body in the tank, then blinked and came back to the present. "It's nice to be interested in the work you're doing. Doesn't happen very often."

"How long have you been a case analyst?"

Bernadette snorted. "About three months."

"Oh—I guess I thought you'd been at CSAB a lot longer than that."

"Fifteen years, in fact."

Lesley blinked.

"I was a full-fledged CSAB agent for a decade. Then I had too much to drink at the holiday party, and I dumped a bottle of wine over my husband's head because he was banging the CSAB training instructor. *My* training instructor." Bernadette ran her hand over her mouth. "I vaguely remember making a big, embarrassing scene. In front of my boss. And my boss's boss."

Lesley stifled a laugh. "And you got demoted for that?"

Bernadette hesitated. "I think I'd had it coming for a while, but after the wine incident, Maura couldn't pretend everything was okay."

"You had it coming? What does that mean?"

"Let's just say I'd been off my game for a while."

"Are you saying you lost your mojo?"

Bernadette straightened up and smoothed out her pantsuit. "Sorry. I'm sleep-deprived. Let me know tomorrow if you find anything of note."

Cursing herself for not keeping her mouth shut, Bernadette walked away from Lesley's desk and out the door.

Buzz. Buzz. Buzz.

Bernadette's first thought: *something's happened to Sophie.* She sat bolt upright in bed.

The room was dark—the dream of her backyard in Virginia was fading. She sucked in a breath. Milwaukee. The Outsider

Hotel. She glanced at the clock on the bedside table. 3:48. She'd been asleep less than an hour.

Buzz. Buzz.

Bernadette groaned and looked at the screen.

Kep.

She answered, the growl in her voice overpowering the sleep.

"What the hell do you want?"

Silence for a moment. Was that the wind? Traffic in the background?

"This better not be—"

"I need a ride. Please."

"What?"

"Can you—" Kep swallowed. Was that a break in his voice? "Can you come get me? Please?"

Fifteen minutes later, Bernadette pulled in front of a brick three-story building in Walker's Point. The car hadn't fully warmed up yet, and she put her gloved hands directly over the vent, spitting out tepid air. She glanced at the sidewalk—it appeared to be empty. The only light was a neon sign in the shape of a martini glass ten feet above the street. A man stepped out of the shadows and limped toward the SUV. In the dim light, she could see it was Kep.

"Great," she murmured to herself. "My first assignment as case analyst, and Kep gets injured. Maura's going to take me out behind the woodshed." She pushed the unlock button.

Kep opened the door, and the dome bulb shone its harsh light over his features. Bernadette recoiled—he had a black eye and the left lens of his glasses was cracked.

"Are you okay?"

Kep winced as he sat down. "I don't want to talk about it."

"You don't want to talk about it?"

Kep sank into his seat.

How would she explain this to Maura? Broken glasses? A black eye? A limp? If Kep needed to go to the hospital, she'd find herself on the next plane to D.C., updating her résumé on her laptop.

How badly was Kep hurt?

Bernadette cleared her throat. "Do you need medical attention?"

Silence.

"Kep, do you need—"

"No. I would appreciate a return to the hotel to salvage what little sleep I can get."

Bernadette clenched and unclenched her hands on the steering wheel. "Kep, I swear, I'm not letting you out of my sight for the rest of this trip."

Kep calmly reached up to his face with both hands, took his broken glasses off and placed them on his lap, then covered his face with his hands.

Bernadette turned back to the road—they didn't have very long before they were at the hotel. This was infuriating.

Ugh. Were Kep's shoulders shaking?

Should she be more sympathetic? Kep had obviously had a rough night. But the more she tried to soften her words, the harder her heart felt. Kep had done this on purpose—he'd intentionally made her angry so she would leave him at the crime scene so he could do whatever he pleased. She was lucky he'd just gotten beat up—and not killed.

At the red light turning onto First Street, she glanced over at him. His hands were still over his face.

"What will you do about your glasses?"

After a moment, Kep said quietly, "I have an extra pair."

She sighed and screwed her mouth up. Finally: "Come to my room tomorrow morning before you go downstairs. I can put some makeup on your black eye. It'll keep Maura from asking questions."

He said nothing.

They pulled in front of the Outsider Hotel in the valet area, and Kep opened the door and fled inside.

Bernadette slammed her hand against the steering wheel and swore at the top of her lungs until the word became guttural, grinding in her throat. She stared out the windshield and caught her breath as the smiling valet walked up to the SUV.

Chapter Twenty-Two

Bernadette looked over at Maura, sitting at the conference table in the District 5 office. The lieutenant was staring at her laptop screen, dead-eyed. She'd put her makeup on that morning with a little too much color in her cheeks, her lipstick a little too heavy.

Maura wasn't the only one wearing more makeup than usual. Bernadette glanced at Kep; she'd done a good job hiding his black eye. He cocked his head as if Bernadette hadn't saved his ass the night before—and even shot her a look after an almost imperceptible head tilt toward Maura: *I told you so.*

Unbelievable.

"I spoke to Lesley last night," Bernadette said, turning her head away from Kep. "She ran some checks on Nick LaSalle's financials."

"That's a good idea," Maura said. She sounded far away. "Did she find anything?"

"No activity on his credit or ATM cards. And no payments or deposits into his bank accounts."

"Keep looking," Maura said. "We'll catch this bastard."

Silence at the table.

"Are you satisfied with Nick LaSalle as the prime suspect?" Kep asked.

"Not necessarily," Maura said. "Whoever authorized that scholarship payment from Parr Medical—that will be the key to this case. Paying a hitman to kill a federal investigator has serious consequences."

"Miss Gill was able to get past the anonymizer," Kep said. "We can now prove LaSalle installed the keylogger program on Kymer Thompson's machine. However, we have yet to establish a link between that activity and the murder of Mr. Janek."

Maura shook her head. "I don't want to hear it, Dr. Woodhead. You take care of figuring out how we make the case against Nick LaSalle stronger, and I'll take care of coordinating the effort to find him."

"LaSalle may be in the wind," Dunn offered. "If he had a car, he'd be able to cross the Canadian border. It's been almost twelve hours since we rescued Annika—he could be across the border by now."

"We checked the trains and buses. We've run searches at the airports. No one matching Nick LaSalle's name or description. No cash purchases from anyone even close."

Possibilities of how LaSalle could have eluded them flitted through Bernadette's mind: falsified passports and ID documents. If LaSalle had shaved his face and cut his hair, he'd look like a different person.

"Hey," Dunn said, "did you see that crazy Delphi church is actually going through with their anchor ceremony tonight?"

"I never thought it was off," Bernadette said.

Dunn plowed ahead. "Listen to this: 'Come join Agios Delphi as we celebrate the dropping of the anchor for Kymer Henry Thompson.' Call me crazy, but that sounds weird." Dunn shook her head. "I give my email to those people to get me information about a murder, and they think they can put me on their newsletter list."

"We asked Reverend Roundhouse to invite us to that," Bernadette said. "The last time we interviewed her in the chapel."

"When is the service?" Kep said.

"Six thirty. In the Anne Askew chapel, of course." Dunn practically spat the words.

"I'm off to grab some coffee," Bernadette said, standing and putting on her puffy purple coat.

"Get me a refill, too," Maura said, staring at the screen.

"I'm not getting the coffee here—I'm heading to Colectivo," Bernadette said.

Maura looked up briefly. "Oh—then a large Americano."

"Same," said Dunn.

Bernadette took a deep breath to calm herself, then put on her coat.

"I'll be glad to come with you." Kep jumped to his feet, grabbing his parka. "You could use the extra set of hands."

"I can use a drink carrier. Besides, I need some time to think. Walking is good for that."

"I'll be quiet."

"I won't be very good company."

"That's never stopped me before." He walked ahead of Bernadette toward the front of the building.

They left through the double doors, Kep zipping up his parka as he walked outside. "Do you believe me now about Maura and Curtis?"

"I'm still pissed off at you, if you couldn't tell. You're welcome for the makeup, by the way." The air was cold; Bernadette wished she had her scarf.

"The makeup has a high level of free isocyanates. It smells

like paint, which is quite distracting. Fortunately, much of the scent has dispersed."

Bernadette stomped on an area of the sidewalk where the snow hadn't been swept away. "I don't care if you hate the way it smells."

Kep knitted his brows and glanced at Bernadette quickly before turning his head forward again. "Let's move past it. I'm focused today on the reasons Nick LaSalle would kidnap Annika. Particularly puzzling is—"

"Move past it? No." Bernadette glared at him. "I don't know what you don't understand about our situation. I know you can be serious about this, but you're treating the investigation like a mind game. I understand if you want to take calls from your P.I. about your son's death, but *not* if you want to get drunk and provoke people into beating you up. These games are why case analysts quit rather than work with you. You goad them into making bad decisions." She pointed at his chest without looking at him. "I could have been fired, Kep."

"But you weren't."

"What if the guy who took a swing at you had a knife instead? Or a gun? You think after Maura ID'd you in the morgue, I'd get near an investigation again?"

"You're overreacting."

Bernadette turned on Kep, drawing herself up to her full height. "Did you do your research on me, Kep? I lost a partner in Wichita when the bust we made went sideways. I want to—" She paused. She wanted to get her mojo back, as Lesley had implied. She wanted to have a working relationship where she wasn't being insulted in sixteenth-century verse. "I don't want to lose another partner." She stepped back, breathing heavily. "Even if you are the dumbest asshole I've ever met."

Kep's eyes went wide behind his glasses.

"Oh, you might have book smarts, my friend, but you don't

seem to understand that the ice you're on is just as thin as mine."

Kep stood in front of Bernadette, blinking slowly.

"CSAB puts months of effort and tens of thousands of dollars into training its people," Bernadette said quietly. "Five case analysts, Kep. You've burned through five case analysts in two years. That's at least a quarter-million dollars in training down the toilet." She shook her head. "And sure, your close rate is fantastic. But it won't be long until some bean counter above Maura starts making noise about what a poor investment it is to bring you on as a consultant." She stuck her hands in her pockets. "I bet the only reason you're still employed with CSAB is that they stuck us together to force me to quit."

"Maura wouldn't do that," Kep said.

"Maybe Maura still has faith in me. Maybe. But I'll wager a thousand bucks the higher-ups are using you to get my resignation letter."

Kep was quiet.

Bernadette turned and kept walking, Kep following a step behind. That was a stupid thing to say to him, but until it was out of her mouth, she didn't quite realize how screwed she was. If she stood up to Kep and his random insanity and vanishing acts, she'd drive a wedge between herself and the most successful investigative consultant CSAB had ever had. If she let him use her as a doormat, she'd get blamed for not being able to control him. And she needed to stick around to qualify for her pension—not to mention pay for Sophie's college. She glanced over at him. "Hey, your limp is gone."

"Ice and elevation."

"Ice?"

"There's an ice machine down the hall from my hotel room. And the dry-cleaning bag can be utilized for a satisfactory makeshift ice pack."

He lapsed back into silence.

For a moment, all she heard was the sound of their boots crushing the remnants of the snow on the sidewalk.

"I wanted to be alone," Kep said softly.

"It doesn't matter to me what you do, Kep. Go to a dealer and get some cocaine. Pick up a hooker. Whatever. But I'm responsible for you, and when you disappear, there is no excuse good enough. And I've been an idiot."

"Maura doesn't care."

"It's Maura's ass on the line, too, Kep," Bernadette said as they crossed Locust Street. "You think there won't be an investigation into why Curtis went to Annika's dorm alone? Into why Maura let him take the SUV? Maura's got to be beside herself with worry that someone will uncover their affair. And you think now she'll sweep your cute little disappearances under the rug?"

Kep ran his hand over his beard. "My private investigator essentially fired me as a client." He pushed his glasses back up his nose. "I don't think I'll ever know who killed my son."

Bernadette grunted. "So you decided to get drunk and mouth off to a random guy in a bar?"

He didn't respond. Bernadette felt a pang of guilt—but shook her head. She picked up the pace, and Kep sped up, walking right alongside her.

After a moment, Kep looked up. "Didn't we miss the coffee place?"

"I didn't want coffee. I wanted to get out of the office."

"Why didn't—"

"Shut up for a minute, Kep."

They walked in silence for a moment.

"I'm sorry, Becker."

"No, you're not. You almost got me fired, but you're not sorry. Sorry you got beat up, maybe."

He shook his head. "All right. Well, then, I promise not to disappear again until we solve the case."

Bernadette looked at Kep; he was in profile and the cloud of his breath was visible in front of his face. "The only way we get through this is with each other, Kep. We *must* have each other's backs. We can't afford to work at cross purposes."

"Then let's not." Kep pulled his hat over his ears a bit more. "From my analysis, we have three main suspects."

"I see that too. Reverend Roundhouse, Nick LaSalle, and—well, some combination of Douglas Rheinstaller and Cecilia Carter."

"And we don't have alibis for any of them for the time of Kymer Thompson's murder."

"Suzanne Thao says Roundhouse was with her," Bernadette said. "Although they could be working together."

"But Annika Nakrivo says Roundhouse was in her dorm at the time of the murder," Kep replied. "And for me, two different alibis are as good as none."

"But Thompson's murder doesn't exist in a vacuum—it's related to Eddie Taysatch's shooting and Curtis's murder." She shoved her hands deeper into her pockets. "What could Roundhouse possibly have as a motive to kill all those lampreys?"

"I'll give you one possibility. Now that all the ammocoetes are dead, the reverend doesn't need to be concerned about a potential shortage of ibogaine for the church services. If Eponymous Pharmaceutical shuts down the project, in fact, she could purchase a large quantity of concentrated ibogaine for pennies on the dollar."

"From who?"

"From *whom*, and from the laboratory, of course, once they lose their funding. It would make sense to sell off their assets."

Bernadette wrinkled her nose. "You think a priest committed two murders to get more drugs?"

"It's a reasonable motive."

Bernadette clicked her tongue in thought as she turned left, back toward Colectivo.

"I'd also like to point out the publicity she's getting for holding the anchor ceremony for Kymer Thompson. I'd wager that Agios Delphi brings in thousands, even tens of thousands more during the ceremony than they normally do in donations."

They crossed West Hadley.

"What do you want to do about it?" Bernadette asked.

"You said you got an invitation to the anchor ceremony?"

"Yes."

"I suggest we attend—if for no other reason than to see if Vivian Roundhouse slips up."

"Would your nose be able to tell the difference between ibogaine from say, iboga bark from seeds ordered off the internet, or ibogaine that's been concentrated then diluted?"

Kep shook his head. "I expect everyone will be given a share of crushed iboga bark to place under their tongues. Even if cheap and plentiful ibogaine is the motive, Roundhouse won't use the concentrated ibogaine liquid tonight."

"She would if she's the murderer. The killer had enough ibogaine to inject lethal doses into both Tommy and Curtis."

"I meant that she wouldn't use the liquid as part of the ritual. The chewing of the bark is paramount. What do you propose she'll do—bake the ibogaine into communion wafers?"

"Of course not. I think she'll shred bark from a tree that doesn't cost a few thousand dollars to grow, and she'll soak the bark in the ibogaine."

Kep blinked. "Intriguing theory, Becker. Its validity depends on the reverend's current supply of iboga bark."

"Sure. At some point, we can get a warrant for her backyard and see how much stuff she's growing." She folded her arms. "But there's one more thing that worries me, Kep."

"What's that?"

"We don't yet know *why* both Thompson and Taysatch were targeted. They were the lead researchers on the project. Maybe it was because they would be notified if an alarm went off at the lab. But it could be what they knew. Or it could be some religious motive, if we're suspecting the reverend."

"Oh, I see," Kep said. "Ibogaine is a holy substance and shouldn't have secular usage—something like that?"

"Yep. I could see someone from Agios Delphi taking their religious fervor about Anne Askew and the significance of iboga bark a little too far."

"And that means—"

"Jude Lightman is still in danger. All the lab employees might be in danger."

"Do you think religious fervor has anything to do with Annika's kidnapping?"

Bernadette shut her eyes tight and stopped walking. "Intellectually, yeah. There are a lot of things about a religious motive that make sense." She opened her eyes again. "But somehow it doesn't feel right. Vivian Roundhouse doesn't seem like the kind of deluded cult leader who would inspire followers to kill for her. Or who could convince her congregation that killing Tommy and Curtis was for the greater good."

Kep tilted his head. "Have you any clue how to identify a deluded cult leader?"

Bernadette grunted.

"No. Therefore, I agree we should attend the anchor ceremony tonight." Kep looked into Bernadette's face. "We have a few hours to get more information before the ritual."

Bernadette bit her lip. "I think we should head to the medical center and see Annika Nakrivo."

"Really?"

"Yes. I know she's still there. They kept her overnight for observation. Maybe she remembers something else."

Kep tilted his head to the side.

"And there are a lot of loose ends," Bernadette continued. "I want to hear why she left Miami. Why she changed her look to duplicate Mariska Sikmo. What her plans are if the project gets cancelled. That kind of thing."

"You plan to interrogate a woman who was kidnapped?"

Did Kep honestly want to break out the kid gloves now? "We're trying to solve a murder, Kep."

"It's not unusual for a young woman to earn money for college by becoming an ecdysiast."

"For the love of all that is good and pure, Kep, if I have to start carrying a dictionary around when I'm with you, I'll beat you with it."

Kep grinned sheepishly. "An ecdysiast is someone who takes their clothes off for money."

Bernadette rolled her eyes. "Make sure you use that word around her. That'll get her to really open up."

He paused for a moment. "You know, you did tell Maura and Dunn that you would procure some coffee for them."

Bernadette nodded. "You're right." Bernadette abruptly turned left on Christine Street and Kep almost slipped on a patch of ice trying to follow her. "So—Vivian Roundhouse had means and opportunity. But motive is tricky."

"I disagree. Whether the motive is religion or cheaper drugs, people have killed for less."

They walked in silence until they arrived at Colectivo, where Kep opened the door for Bernadette. She stood in line, Kep behind her, and didn't speak until she gave the coffee order to the cashier.

Bernadette turned, the noise of the espresso machine echoing off the concrete walls of the coffee shop, and took a seat next to the window. Kep took off his wool hat and sat on the stool next to her.

She looked out; the morning commute was starting to fade on King Street. She saw a couple on the opposite sidewalk. They looked to be in their late twenties, holding hands. Maybe walking to work together.

Were she and Barlow ever like that, holding hands, walking down a D.C. sidewalk in the winter? Or did they lose that after Sophie was born, when Bernadette was too wrapped up in her work and Barlow drifted away?

She stared out the window until the couple went around the corner. "This case has been a disaster ever since we got here, Kep."

"I wouldn't call it a disaster."

Bernadette hesitated. She didn't want to lay all her cards on the table, but nothing she had done had worked so far. No wonder Martin had warned her with the letter.

Screw it—who cared if Kep knew everything? "We've made enemies of all the witnesses. We can't track our main suspects. I can't even keep you on task." She put her elbows on the table and leaned forward. "Nothing has worked out in this investigation."

"You haven't been anyone's handler for ten years," Kep said. "It might be similar to riding a bike, but if you haven't done it in a while, you're still wobbly. You can't expect to compete in the Tour de France right away."

Bernadette folded her hands on the table. He'd done his research on her—or maybe Maura spoke to him about the past. Maybe Bernadette had gotten through to him—he might be, for the first time, scared that her resignation would be the end of his CSAB career. This was the first time he'd said *anything* encouraging to her. "If you and I want to turn this case around, Kep, we have work to do. We haven't uncovered the right clues yet. Sure, we can go through the motions of interviewing Annika Nakrivo in the hospital and attending the anchor ceremony tonight, but—"

Bernadette stopped mid-sentence.

"What?"

"Parr Medical paid Nick LaSalle tens of thousands of dollars to put that keylogging software on Thompson's PC."

"Which we can't prove yet."

"Here's what doesn't make sense, Kep. If Vivian Roundhouse is the killer, then the keyloggers don't have anything to do with the murder."

Kep nodded. "I agree, but it doesn't need to. They can be two separate issues."

Bernadette traced an imaginary squiggle on the table with her finger. "Except this result is exactly what Parr Medical wanted. They wanted the lampreys killed. They wanted the research project terminated."

"Are you suggesting that Nick LaSalle is a better suspect than Roundhouse? Do you believe he killed both Kymer Thompson and Curtis Janek acting on his own? That doesn't fit."

"I'm saying," Bernadette said, "that *nothing* fits yet. Rheinstaller and Carter don't fit either. Yeah, we can prove their unholy union to poison the lampreys—but I don't think either of them were in the building the night the fish died. It makes sense for Roundhouse to be involved, up to a point. But then things start to fall apart. Same thing with LaSalle."

"In that case," Kep said, "we must keep pushing."

The barista came around the corner, a drink carrier in his left hand.

Kep took the carrier. "We work the assignment we were given. For most of the investigations on which I consult, I often arrive a minimum of forty-eight hours after the murder was committed. I consider us fortunate that a full day hadn't passed on this adventure. However, I must caution you that we cannot find justice in every case. We cannot capture every criminal. The scholarship payment was unusual; I grant you that. I believe it lulled us into a false sense that we would unlock the secrets of this murder quickly. Yet that payment, by itself, doesn't rise to the level of evidence. I can think of no judge who would approve a warrant based solely on Nick LaSalle's scholarship award."

"Well, then, Kep." She took her coffee. "If Nick LaSalle is innocent, why did he run away?"

Kep stood up and put his wool hat back on. "You seem confident that LaSalle fled. Have you seen evidence of his escape? Have we even checked at the university to see if he was absent from work? Or missing from his domicile?"

"No." Bernadette stood. "But something else is bugging you."

Kep hesitated, then gave a curt nod. "Yes. It has been bothering me all morning, in fact. I can't identify my discomfort, however."

"When did you first start feeling like this?"

"I'm not sure."

"You're sure. You just don't want to tell me."

Kep pushed his glasses up. "The Camry from last evening. There's something odd about the smell."

"Fast food and perfume?"

Kep shook his head as if he were clearing cobwebs. "It's not the scent profile. It's like something doesn't fit."

"Did you smell something your nose recognized but your brain didn't?"

"I don't know." He took his drink from the carrier and sipped. "I was hoping it would come to me with a good night's sleep."

Bernadette laughed, a giggle at first, then a throaty, full laugh. "How'd that good night's sleep work out for you?"

❦

AFTER LEAVING THE COFFEES WITH THE LIEUTENANT AND THE detective, Bernadette and Kep drove toward the hospital.

Kep looked out the window. "Have you heard anything about what the anchor ceremony entails?"

"No."

Kep tapped his fingers on the armrest. "I wonder if there's anything to this whole idea that Anne Askew was tortured on a rack—if that position Kymer Thompson was found in reveals anything about the murderer."

Bernadette gasped.

Kep tilted his head. "Are you all right?"

"Nick LaSalle wasn't a member of Agios Delphi, Kep."

"No, he wasn't."

"So he wouldn't have known to position Kymer Thompson's body in that way."

Kep squinted, thinking. "That's not a reasonable conclusion." He turned toward Bernadette in his seat. "LaSalle's the one who put the keylogger program on Kymer Thompson's machine, correct? Therefore, he could read what Thompson was typing. While most attackers try to steal passwords or credit card information, we believe LaSalle was after more than that. Information, probably about the lampreys and about security at the laboratory. Thompson could have been on some sort of Agios Delphi forum and been arguing over the transubstantiation of iboga bark."

"Or what position Delphinians are placed in when they die. Stuff like that?"

"Correct. It's possible LaSalle read that information—and used it—when he was looking for the lamprey data."

Bernadette nodded. "Is the tech team looking through Nick LaSalle's computer? Maybe his cloud files? Seeing if Kymer Thompson wrote anything that would lead LaSalle to know about the death pose?"

"We should ask Curt——" Kep snapped his mouth shut.

Bernadette shifted in her seat and took a deep breath. "Yes. It's tough to believe he's gone."

"It's tougher for Maura."

"The faster we solve this case, the better for Maura. We can fly back tomorrow or maybe the day after. She can drink a couple of vodka tonics in first class, slip her eye mask on, and not deal with anything or anyone for a few hours. She'll have the weekend to process it."

Kep nodded. "I'll do my best."

"And we can ask Lesley Gill to go over the computer. Assuming her team has access, anyway."

They parked in the hospital lot and stepped out into the bright March morning. It was warming up; Bernadette was sweating in her parka; she took it off and placed it back on the seat. The air was cold with only her blazer protecting her, but the chill nipping at her cheeks and nose was refreshing.

"Do you know what you'll ask Annika?" Bernadette asked.

Kep shook his head. "Maybe you can interrogate her about what she remembers. Try to walk her through it. Take your time; it's possible something will jog her memory."

The hospital lobby was warm, and Bernadette was glad she'd left her parka in the car.

She strode to the front desk, her CSAB identification badge in her hand. "Good morning," she said brightly, although she suspected everyone could tell how fake her enthusiasm was.

"We're federal investigators here to see Annika Nakrivo regarding yesterday's incident."

"Certainly," the woman behind the desk said. She looked to be in her late sixties or early seventies, wearing light blue short-sleeved scrubs and looking down her nose through her glasses at the computer monitor in front of her. "Nakrivo—room 275D. Down the main hall to the elevators, up to the second floor, then turn right. It'll be the nurse's station after the restrooms." She glanced up at Bernadette. "Looks like she's getting discharged this afternoon."

They walked down the hall to the elevators and got in.

"What floor?" Kep asked.

"Weren't you paying attention? Two."

Kep pushed the button, then his face darkened. "Did we station an officer at her door?"

"I don't know. We don't command those resources. Maura probably made the request—she'd be the one liaising with the Milwaukee Police Department."

The lines on Kep's forehead grew.

"What?"

"Maura's not on her game. Curtis was killed. I don't know if they were official, or if they were just a fling, but it's obvious that Maura cared about him. She's not thinking clearly."

The elevator doors opened, and Bernadette stepped out with Kep on her heels. "If you're saying that she can't handle this situation because she's a woman, Kep, I swear to—"

"I'm saying she can't handle it because someone she cares about just died," Kep snapped. "You don't know what a mess I was when my son was killed. Do you have any idea how many errors in judgment I made? How my marriage unraveled because I made bad decisions? It's not because she's a woman, it's because she's *human*." His upper lip curled. "You couldn't even handle a Christmas party when you found out your husband cheated on you. Let's not pretend either one of us is better than Maura."

Bernadette was silent for a moment, with only the sound of their footsteps on the smooth floor keeping them company. Finally, she took a deep breath. "That must have been hard."

"Yes."

The hallway turned to the left, and Bernadette almost tripped over Officer Lamar Chesapeake sitting on a folding chair—in front of room 275D.

"We meet again," Chesapeake said, grinning and standing. "Agent Becker?"

"That's me. Um—Bernadette. Call me Bernadette." She motioned to the door number. "Annika Nakrivo's room, right?"

"That's correct. And you can call me Lamar."

"You've been here since this morning?"

"Since she was admitted." Chesapeake pointed to the chair.

"So I guess CSAB *did* request an officer to be stationed at the door." Bernadette turned to Chesapeake. "How's she doing?"

"She said she was tired after breakfast. I tried questioning her again, but she said she didn't remember much."

"Has her story changed?" Kep asked.

"She hasn't told me anything," Chesapeake said, "so there's nothing to change."

"Why was she kidnapped?" Bernadette mused. "And why isn't she dead with a syringe sticking out of her arm?"

Chesapeake shifted from foot to foot. "That's a good question. I suppose whoever kidnapped her was planning to come back. Maybe to get information out of her, maybe to kill her."

Bernadette nodded and took out her phone. "Let's see if Lesley Gill has any last insights for us before we go into Annika's room."

Lesley picked up on the second ring. "Hi, Bernadette."

"Anything new come up since we last spoke?"

"I should be getting the footage from Wildlife Specialties this morning. We'll hopefully be able to see Cecilia Carter and Douglas Rheinstaller together." Lesley's keyboard taps could be heard on the other end.

"Any luck on the blue van?"

"Not yet. We'll check the long-term lots near Mitchell Airport next."

"Thanks, Lesley."

"No problem. Keep me updated."

Bernadette sighed as she ended the call. "More footage is coming in, but no new information yet."

Kep nodded. "Let's see if we can successfully stimulate Annika's memory."

Chapter Twenty-Three

In her hospital gown, Annika looked surprisingly lithe and strong. Her left arm lay on top of the blanket, her bicep well-defined—almost the size of Bernadette's. Her eyes were closed, but the heart monitor was tracking a strong, steady beat.

"Annika?" Bernadette said gently. Kep walked to a corner of the hospital room and leaned against the wall, standing. He pushed his glasses up on his nose.

"I'm tired," Annika replied.

"I have a few questions."

"I'm too tired to answer questions."

"We need to know who did this to you."

Annika sighed heavily, the corners of her mouth turning down. "I don't remember."

Bernadette pulled the chair next to the bed and sat. "Let's start at the beginning. What time did you get home from work?"

"I'm—I'm not really sure. I left when you were still there."

"How did you get back to the dorm?"

"I walked. Oh—I stopped to get some coffee. I sat inside the coffee shop for a while."

Bernadette sat for a moment, organizing her thoughts. Finally, she took a deep breath. "Take me through what happened."

"I told you I don't remember what time I got home."

"Do you remember someone coming to your door? Breaking in?"

Annika hesitated, then nodded.

"Who?"

"It was Reverend Roundhouse. And she had Nick LaSalle with her."

Bernadette sat up straight and blinked. "You're telling me *both* of them came to your door?"

"That's right."

Bernadette paused. A hundred questions swam through her head. *What were Reverend Roundhouse and Nick LaSalle doing together? Had Annika seen them together before? Had Roundhouse been involved in the payment to Nick LaSalle?* But she needed to stay on track with the timeline that Annika provided. She leaned forward. "I'm afraid I need more detail, Annika. Did they knock? Or did they simply come in?"

"I—uh, they knocked."

"And you answered the door?"

Annika licked her lips briefly. "Yes."

"Even though the reverend had been by your dorm room on Monday night, and you didn't want her there?"

Annika opened her mouth and hesitated.

"I'm having trouble picturing your version of events," Bernadette said.

"I answered the door without thinking," Annika muttered. "I'm still pretty sad about Tommy getting killed. My brain wasn't working right."

Bernadette cocked her head and looked at Annika's face. The young woman's upper lip, with the off-center beauty mark, was still. But Annika wouldn't meet Bernadette's eyes.

"Okay," Bernadette said, leaning back. "When you opened the door, who was in front?"

Annika blinked. "Who was in front?"

"Yes. Was the reverend standing in front of your door with Nick LaSalle behind her, or the other way around?"

"I—I, uh, I guess the reverend was in front of the door."

"Okay. What were they wearing?"

"Wearing? Um—they were both dressed in black."

"Were they dressed for the cold weather? Heavy jackets? Winter hats?"

"Ah—no. Neither one had a hat."

"What did you do?"

A confused look swept over Annika's face. "What do you mean?"

"I mean—"

"Listen," Annika snapped. "They surprised me. I opened the door, they pushed me into the room, then they put a hood over my head. The next thing I knew I was in that warehouse. I managed to get my arm free and then I pulled myself to the door."

"You didn't hear the reverend or Nick LaSalle talk about anything?"

"No."

"How did they knock you out?"

"I don't know."

"Did you feel pain? A bang on the head, or maybe a cloth over your nose and mouth through the hood?"

"I already told you, I don't know."

Bernadette leaned forward again, this time with her hands

on her knees. "You're saying you lost consciousness as soon as the hood went over your head?"

"I don't know. I guess so."

"Who put the hood over your head?"

"I don't remember."

"But when you woke up in the warehouse, you didn't have the hood on?"

"No."

"Who else was in the warehouse?"

"No one. I was by myself."

"Do you know—" Bernadette paused. "You told me in the warehouse that a man left an hour before I got there. The IT guy from the Freshie."

Annika stammered. "Yes. He was leaving when I woke up. I was groggy. Maybe he wasn't there."

"Was he there or not?"

Annika looked confused. "I—I don't know. I thought he was."

"Okay." Bernadette resisted the urge to fold her arms. Annika still wouldn't meet her eyes. Kep cleared his throat— Bernadette almost jumped in her seat; she'd forgotten he was there.

"You must understand," Kep said evenly and calmly, "that we are having difficulty piecing together these events."

Annika stared at Kep blankly.

"We can't establish a timeline that makes sense," Kep said.

"*None* of this makes sense!" Annika roared. Bernadette leaned back, away from her. "My boyfriend gets murdered and suddenly I wake up in a warehouse tied to a chair! Why are you treating me like *I* did something wrong? Those two psychopaths kidnapped *me!*"

Kep nodded slowly. "I can see that you're frustrated," he said. "I understand. We have a lot of conflicting information."

"I think," Bernadette said, "it's time for you to tell us what Reverend Roundhouse said to you on Monday evening when she came to your dorm room."

"She'll deny being there," Annika said. "It doesn't matter."

"It does matter," Bernadette said. "She kidnapped you."

"No one will believe me."

"We'll believe you."

Annika lifted her head and stared Bernadette in the face, then raised her chin as if to point to Kep. "*He* won't believe me."

Bernadette smiled. "Then you can tell him 'I told you so.'"

Annika frowned. "She told me to repent. That I was destroying the natural order of things. That I was using the sacred iboga for worldly gain." She paused. "She told me I'd be sorry if I didn't 'heed her warning.'"

Bernadette nodded slowly. "Did she mention anyone else she had to give this warning to?"

"Well—I told her that I was only an intern there. And she told me if I didn't make things right, I'd get kicked out of the church."

"But," Bernadette pressed, "did she mention anyone else? Kymer Thompson? Maybe Eddie Taysatch?"

"She said I was lucky that I had just started there. That I still had time to get out. That others had to make harder choices."

Bernadette clenched her teeth.

"She said," Annika continued, "that there would be a reckoning. That's the word she used, too. Like it would be the day of the rapture." Her voice broke, and she lifted her eyes to the ceiling. "I have to get out of here. Tommy's anchor ceremony is in a few hours, and I can't miss it."

"I'm not sure—"

"A word, Becker?" Kep said.

Bernadette looked up at Kep. His eyes were creased at the corners, his mouth set in a hard line.

"No problem," Bernadette said.

They both stepped out of the hospital room and closed the door. Officer Chesapeake glanced at Bernadette.

"What is it, Kep?" Bernadette murmured.

"I have doubts about Annika's story."

Bernadette nodded. "The timeline of the kidnapping."

"In addition, we haven't uncovered any evidence even hinting that the reverend was working with Nick LaSalle."

"But," Bernadette said, "Reverend Roundhouse doesn't have a good alibi for *anything*. She could have killed Kymer Thompson. She could have shot Eddie Taysatch. She could have stolen the TFM from Douglas Rheinstaller's shed." Bernadette shook her head. "If Annika had told us about her conversation with Roundhouse earlier, we would've had a motive. And maybe we'd have picked up Roundhouse before she kidnapped Annika." Bernadette sighed. "We may have our doubts, Kep, but we can't ignore what she said. You heard her—'there will be a reckoning.'"

"The reckoning happened already, though, didn't it? With all the lampreys killed—surely that was the reckoning."

Bernadette shook her head. "The man who was behind all of this—all of the need to make money off the 'sacred iboga'—he's still out there. Jude Lightman."

"No one's even tried to kill him yet."

"Maybe that's because we've had an officer on him." Bernadette tapped her chin. "Do you think maybe someone will try to kill him during the anchor ceremony tonight?"

"Lightman will be there?"

"Of course he will. One of his top researchers was killed. He can't miss the memorial service."

"True."

"I'm not confident I'm right. But I don't think we can ignore the possibility."

Kep pushed his glasses up on his nose. "What about the payments from the shell corporation that's owned by Parr Medical?"

"I agree," Bernadette said, "that doesn't fit. But it's a long way from corporate espionage to murder. You said so yourself."

"If Nick LaSalle accepted a bribe to install the keylogging program on Kymer Thompson's PC, why would he also work with Vivian Roundhouse? I fail to see a plausible scenario."

"Not from where we stand," Bernadette said, "but maybe there's something to tie all this together."

Kep exhaled sharply. "I don't like this."

"You mean you don't trust Annika."

"No, of course I don't. You shouldn't either."

Bernadette put her hands on her hips. "I'm skeptical of everything she says," she said in a low voice.

"Could have fooled me."

"Good. Maybe that means I fooled her too."

A nurse hung up the phone at her station, stood, and walked toward Kep and Bernadette. "Excuse me," she said, trying to slip past them into the room.

"Hold up," Officer Chesapeake said.

The nurse turned to look at him. "The doctor is releasing Miss Nakrivo. I'll need to get her ready."

"How soon will she be leaving?" Bernadette asked.

"And you are?"

Bernadette pulled out her identification.

The nurse scanned it and nodded. "I've called for a wheel-chair. That usually takes at least forty-five minutes." She opened the door.

Officer Chesapeake stepped over to Bernadette. "She's been talking about leaving for that memorial service ever since I arrived. It'll be hard to protect her in a crowded chapel."

"Did you tell her that?"

"Yes. She said she doesn't care."

Bernadette shook her head. "I'll talk to Maura, but I don't think we'll be able to prevent her from going to her dead boyfriend's anchor ceremony."

"Do you know anything about this ceremony? A big crowd? Will there be low lights and candles at the front of the chapel?"

"What? Low lights and—"

Chesapeake cut in. "We need to see what we're supposed to be protecting."

Bernadette thought for a moment. "I wonder if Annika's statement gives us enough to arrest Vivian Roundhouse before the ceremony."

"If Roundhouse is the one who wants Annika dead," Kep said, "she won't be able to touch her while she's conducting the ceremony."

"But if Roundhouse is paying off someone like Nick LaSalle to kill people for her, she won't have to do it herself. And," Bernadette continued, "we need to tighten security on Jude Lightman as well."

Kep rubbed his chin. "I'm not sure that we have enough to get an arrest warrant for Vivian Roundhouse."

"We have a victim's statement."

"Yes, but the victim has only specified that Roundhouse was at her door. We can't prove that Nick LaSalle involved anyone else in the kidnapping."

Bernadette pursed her lips. "I think we have enough to pull her in and hold her for forty-eight hours."

"Right before she leads the memorial service of the murder victim?" Chesapeake shook his head. "That would be a bad look for CSAB—even if people think Agios Delphi *is* a cult. And you know the Milwaukee Police Department would get blamed for it. We'd be accused of religious persecution."

"Then," Bernadette said, "we have to keep Annika Nakrivo from showing up at the ceremony tonight."

"And I'm telling you that won't happen," Chesapeake said. "There's no way she'll stay away."

Bernadette pulled out her phone. "Damned if we do, and damned if we don't. I only know that we can't have anyone else murdered on our watch."

The phone buzzed in her hand.

She glanced down at the screen, then covered her mouth with her hand.

"What is it?" Chesapeake asked.

Bernadette swallowed hard. "Eddie Taysatch. He died about a half hour ago."

Chapter Twenty-Four

IN THE DIM LIGHT OF THE CLUMPS OF CANDLES PLACED around the chapel, Bernadette could barely make out the shape of Jude Lightman's head in the third row on the right-hand side. Annika Nakrivo was across the aisle, in the second row from the back—an odd place for the girlfriend of the deceased to be. But it was far from Vivian Roundhouse, and if Bernadette didn't expect her to be so far toward the back of the chapel, she doubted Nick LaSalle—or anyone else who wanted to hurt Annika—would look there either.

Officer Chesapeake had been clairvoyant: the low light and candles—and the packed service—weren't conducive to keeping either Nakrivo or Lightman visible, let alone safe.

In front of the pews, on the stone floor, a four-foot tall metal anchor—it looked like dull silver or brushed nickel—was fastened to a large stand made from five thin black poles. The anchor hung off the ground, the bottom a few feet from the floor, the top of the anchor uncomfortably close to the ceiling of the chapel.

On a stool at the side of the right pews, a young woman played a guitar and what sounded like an old Tudor-era hymn.

And Kep had been right, too: the anchor ceremony was a big draw, and the media surrounding the murder hadn't hurt attendance. Bernadette glanced up to the front of the sanctuary. Vivian Roundhouse was sitting, head bowed.

The hymn finished, and Vivian Roundhouse stood and took her place behind the lectern. She took a breath.

"*Like as the armed knight,*" Roundhouse recited, her voice strong in the small stone church, "*appointed to the field, with this world will I fight, and faith will be my shield.*"

"*And faith will be my shield.*" About twenty voices rose around Bernadette to repeat the last line—she almost jumped in the pew.

When the voices ended, it was silent. Bernadette suppressed a shiver.

"In this life," Roundhouse said, "we are often unmoored, adrift. The tides of this secular world push and pull us, throwing us into reefs, pitching us into dangerous waters." She looked around the room, the candlelight casting eerie shadows up from below, almost like a flashlight illuminating a camp counselor telling a scary story around a crackling fire. "We are here to anchor the life of Kymer Thompson to this church, as he was a shelter from the storm, an oasis of smooth water in the terrible yawning maw of the ocean."

Thunk.

This time, Bernadette *did* jump in her seat as the heavy metal anchor dropped about eight inches on its stand with a loud metallic noise. She wasn't the only one shocked by the sound; several other people, including Jude Lightman, were looking around in mute alarm.

Bernadette gritted her teeth. As if it weren't difficult enough to keep Nakrivo and Lightman safe in the candlelit chapel, she had to deal with a metal-on-metal boom that would drown out a gunshot, never mind a deadly injection of ibogaine.

"*Faith is that weapon strong,*" Roundhouse continued, "*which will not fail at need. My foes, therefore, among, therewith will I proceed.*"

"Therewith will I proceed," repeated a smattering of people in the pews, although more voices joined in this time.

"Faith is the strongest weapon that Anne Askew possessed," Roundhouse said. "It allowed her the strength to go on even when her body was tortured and broken. And faith allowed Kymer Thompson to go on, even though the pull of worldly riches beckoned."

Thunk.

No one jumped in their seat this time. Bernadette looked across the aisle to Annika Nakrivo. She stayed seated. A man in front of Bernadette leaned forward, temporarily blocking her view of Lightman.

"*More enemies I now have than hairs upon my head,*" Roundhouse declared. "*Let them not be depraved, but fight now in my stead.*"

"*But fight now in my stead,*" repeated the congregation, and Bernadette found herself chanting too—and then she looked up at Roundhouse.

Who held a jeweled dagger over her own head.

Two torches, one on either side of the pulpit, burst into flame.

Where did those come from?

Roundhouse let loose a scream.

And the congregation screamed with her.

"Make me a double-edged dagger of a cubit length," Roundhouse screeched. The fire of the torches reflected in her eyes. "Gird it under a raiment upon my thigh."

The anchor dropped again with a louder *thunk* than before.

"I have a secret errand unto thee, O King," Roundhouse shouted. "Do not beseech me to keep silent."

"O King!" went up a yell from about twenty people in the pews.

"And I did take the dagger from my thigh and thrust it into the King's belly, and the haft went in after the blade, and the King could not draw the dagger from his stomach."

"And the dirt came out," said Roundhouse with the congregation.

The congregation kept chanting. "And the dirt came out. And the dirt came out. And the dirt came out."

The blood thundered in Bernadette's ears, as if beating drums were assaulting her. The words reverberated in the small space.

And the dirt came out.

And the dirt came out.

And the dirt came out.

"*I am not she that lists,*" Roundhouse yelled above the cacophony, "*My anchor to let fall!*"

The chant changed and grew in volume. "*My anchor to let fall. My anchor to let fall.*"

Thunk.

Roundhouse's voice carried above the chant. "My brethren, remember Kymer Thompson. Remember his passion for seeking the truth. For being strong through the cruel spite of his fears. For now, he is meeting his God and delighting in His presence."

"*My anchor to let fall. My anchor to let fall. My anchor to let fall.*"

"My anchor to let fall!" screamed Roundhouse, and with one last, ominous, grinding *thunk*, the anchor dropped to the last level.

The torches went dark.

Bernadette's head whipped around to see where Annika was. The seat in the pew—

—was empty.

Bernadette jumped over the back of the pew and raced across the aisle, the chill shooting up her back. She whirled her head around, her eyes adjusting to the low light, but with all the people crammed into the chapel, she couldn't find Annika.

A scream from the front—and several people in the second pew rushed to their left, away from the side aisle as the lights in the chapel came up.

In the seat next to the aisle, a tall, lanky bearded man with horn-rimmed glasses sat slumped. Bernadette rushed forward, and she saw the slumping man's face.

Nick LaSalle—eyes open and unseeing.

THIRTY MINUTES LATER, AT THE STATE STREET administrative building, Bernadette leaned over Lesley Gill's chair and stared at her screen. Kep sat in a guest chair against the wall a few feet behind her, while Maura sat on a tall stool on the other side of Lesley.

"So you lost Annika?" Maura asked.

"Yes," Bernadette said, clenching and unclenching her fists.

"Six police officers and two of my best investigators sitting in the chapel with her. And you lost her—and we have another dead body."

"It was unexpected," Kep said. "Torches of fire as the only light source in the chapel, and loud noises as the anchor dropped. Both the leader and the congregation were chanting. The ceremony was intended to induce a trance-like state in the attendees."

Maura folded her arms. "Do you have a theory about who killed Nick LaSalle?"

"CSI is onsite now," Bernadette said, lowering her eyes. *Another person murdered on my watch.*

"Do you know how he was killed?"

"CSI hasn't said yet, but I didn't see a wound. I told the crime scene tech to check for a needle prick and ibogaine." Bernadette rubbed her forehead. "So it follows that whoever killed Nick LaSalle also murdered Kymer Thompson and Curtis."

Maura hopped off the stool and paced behind Lesley. "We've been thinking of Annika Nakrivo as a victim all this time. Sounds to me we need to put her on the suspect list."

Kep rested his chin in his palm, his elbow on the arm of the guest chair. "Given her proximity to Nick LaSalle's dead body, I can't disagree."

"Were you able to assess the murder scene, Dr. Woodhead?"

"I stood close to Mr. LaSalle's body." Kep dropped his eyes to the floor. "I detected ibogaine, likely on the corpse, though I wasn't able to determine the exact location." He sighed. "Unfortunately, I identified too many conflicting scents in the chapel and near the body. I can suggest no additional areas of inquiry for us."

Bernadette looked at the floor. "Based on our suspicions, it's possible that LaSalle tried to get to Annika and she turned the tables on him." She closed her eyes. "But it also could be that she's behind everything." She rested her hand on the back of Lesley's chair. "Once CSI arrived, I came back here so we could find Annika Nakrivo. If she's the new prime suspect, she might be on the run. And if she's still being victimized by the killer, we still have to locate her. That's my top priority."

"I agree," Maura said.

"Uniforms report that she's not at her dorm or at the Freshie," Bernadette replied. "I thought we could dig through her past and that might give us a clue. Lesley, can you bring up Annika Nakrivo's records from Miami?"

"As soon as I heard what happened at the chapel, I began to

pull her information." Lesley pointed to the screen. "Annika Nakrivo was only in Miami for two years. She didn't grow up there. I can find no trace of her in Miami after October of last year."

"You already told us you suspected she was on a chartered jet when she left Miami."

"That's correct—Miami to Cleveland."

"Where Parr Medical is headquartered," Maura said.

Bernadette scratched her temple. "We're assuming Annika's plane was chartered by Parr Medical?"

Lesley clicked on another screen, then squinted and shook her head. "I haven't found proof yet. I'm following a couple different money trails." She clicked another window. "I also found something else."

"What?"

"The photo of Annika Nakrivo on the escort website isn't the way she looks now."

"Right—I saw it."

"That got me thinking. I started searching medical records —plastic surgeries in October with missing insurance codes, or that had been scheduled with less than two weeks' notice." She tapped her keyboard and another screen popped up. "And here's what I found. Dr. Jeffrey Watermaker. Rhinoplasty, collagen, botox. Unnamed female patient, twenty-eight years old, two days after Nakrivo's plane landed in Cleveland."

"Wait—did you say twenty-eight?" Bernadette asked. "She said she was nineteen. She *looks* like she's nineteen!"

Lesley nodded. "I assume that's the plastic surgery." She tapped again, and another screen appeared. "Parr Medical has a contract with the Erie Fairfax Circle Hotel, two blocks away from their campus, and there's a guest who checked in the same night Nakrivo's plane landed in Cleveland, and who stayed for almost two months. Name on the room is *Parr Medical Guest*."

Bernadette stood up straight, her back cracking loudly.

Lesley glanced up. "Do you want a chair?"

"I need to stand and think. So—you've got a rough timeline from the financial information you've uncovered?"

"Emphasis on the *rough*," Lesley replied. "But I'll go over it. First, in mid-August, Parr Medical made a verbal offer to Eddie Taysatch to lure him away from the Freshie project. But he said no."

"Right."

"The next week, a keylogger program appeared on Kymer Thompson's computer."

Bernadette and Kep both nodded in agreement.

"And after the Labor Day weekend, we know the keylogger is on his home machine too."

"Oh—I didn't tell you," Maura said. "We found fan letters from Kymer Thompson on his home computer."

"To Mariska Sikmo?" Bernadette asked.

"Yes."

"Typical gross stalker stuff?"

Maura grimaced. "Religious discussion, actually. Talking about the meaning of Anne Askew's writings, almost as if he believed Mariska Sikmo had written her own lines in *Six Wives*."

Bernadette tapped her chin. "So we think the keylogger continuously reported all of Thompson's keystrokes to Parr Medical?"

"Again—no proof," Lesley said. "It's all being transmitted to a server address, but that's where the trail goes cold."

"When were the fan letters sent?"

"The first was September nineteenth. A few had been saved, but not sent."

"And what about the spreadsheets on the lampreys?"

"Transmitted starting September seventh, from the work PC."

Maura clicked her tongue. "How does the motive of corporate espionage look?"

"Lucrative," Lesley said. "I ran the numbers in a couple of different simulations. If Parr is able to sell their cancer treatment without competition—"

"Competition funded by Eponymous Pharmaceutical," Maura interrupted.

"—it's worth over thirty-five billion dollars," Lesley continued. "That's billion with a B. We're talking about making most of the major shareholders obscenely wealthy."

"Did one of your simulations include Eponymous beating them to the market?"

"Yes," Lesley said, "and they were still profitable. But prices would have been lower to be more competitive. Parr's medication would be prescribed less often—and since they wouldn't have first-mover advantage, they couldn't price themselves at the top of the market. Maybe sixty million over the course of the next three years after release. Like I said, still profitable for the company. But not an obscene amount of money for any of the stakeholders."

Maura took a deep breath and rubbed her forehead. "How long before Vivian Roundhouse is processed?"

"Dunn said it would be a couple of hours." Bernadette folded her arms.

"What's wrong?"

"The optics," Bernadette said. "Nick LaSalle was dead in his seat, and the woman who led the service was arrested the second the ceremony concluded. Everyone in the church knew the reverend hadn't done it."

Maura sat up straight on the stool. "I don't care. If she planned or coordinated these killings, we need her in custody. If Milwaukee's finest get bad press out of it, they can blame us.

Everyone already thinks the Feds are heartless assholes." She pointed at Lesley's screen. "Besides, we have evidence that Vivian Roundhouse was involved with the murders—it was her van, she has a weak alibi, and she had motive to eliminate the mass-produced ibogaine."

"But nothing that connects Roundhouse to Parr Medical's activity." Bernadette shook her head. "And no evidence that she was anywhere near the Freshie the night—" Bernadette hesitated. "The night the lampreys were all killed."

"And LaSalle is the one who had the knowledge to disconnect the alarms in the aquarium. The theory makes sense if the two of them were working together." Maura hopped off the stool and leaned forward to look at the spreadsheet on Lesley's screen. "I can't believe that it's a coincidence that a corporation trying to protect thirty-five billion dollars isn't connected to the murderer of Kymer Thompson and Eddie Taysatch."

Bernadette glanced over at Kep, who was staring at the floor.

"We must have *some* footage of Vivian Roundhouse," Maura said, her voice cracking slightly.

"The security cameras at the dorm had been tampered with and the recordings were missing," Lesley said.

"Nick LaSalle had the know-how to turn those off," Kep mused. "The camera and alarm systems are all administered by computer systems that he could access. We should check LaSalle's logs—if he used his key cards in that building, or his login information for the aquarium control unit in the laboratory."

"I believe that's the connection," Maura said. "Nick LaSalle was working for both Parr Medical *and* Vivian Roundhouse."

"That's a big leap." Bernadette rubbed her eyes. The pieces weren't falling into place yet. "They were certainly working toward the same goal, I suppose, but who got him to do what? And how does Annika fit into all this? If we suspect Nick LaSalle was working for Parr Medical based on the payoff of his student loans, we must suspect that Annika works for them too."

"Or works for Roundhouse," Maura said. "Remember, Annika said the reverend stopped by her dorm the night Thompson was killed."

"I can keep digging in Annika's financials," Lesley said.

"Can we get to financial information from the other side?" Bernadette asked. "Can we get the records from Parr Medical?"

Maura shook her head. "Not yet. We've started the process, but their lawyers are fighting it. We'll sort it out. It's a bundle of red tape." Maura walked around the table. "I know it's late, but you're right, Bernadette. Top priority is finding Annika Nakrivo —and figuring out if she's a suspect or a victim."

Kep closed his eyes and leaned back in his chair. "We must move her to our suspect list."

Maura hesitated. "Let's not get ahead of ourselves. Whether she's a victim or a suspect, we need to find her. The last thing we need is another dead body."

Another dead body. Yes, the torches and the anchor and the chanting had distracted her, but Bernadette was supposed to be a professional. She should have seen LaSalle. She should have been closer—even though Annika made it clear she wanted to be left alone.

Maybe it would have been better if she'd been fired after the holiday party. If Maura hadn't given her one last chance.

Losing her job would have made it hard for everyone, especially Sophie—oh, who was she kidding? Sophie would have been fine. Bernadette would have been the devastated one. Her money situation would have been horrible, and she wouldn't have been able to afford a divorce lawyer. Barlow could use her job loss against her for custody. She shut her eyes tight—she had to think positively. She still had time to find Annika. She still had time to solve this case. And if she did, maybe the demotion to case analyst could work out. Maybe it was a blessing in disguise.

She straightened up.

In disguise.

Everything clicked into place. Annika Nakrivo wasn't a victim at all. She was the murderer. And Bernadette could prove it.

"Lesley," she said, "did CSAB give you access to all the files and footage we went through?"

"I think so."

"Can you pull up the footage from Monday night? The recording from the security camera at the gym across the street from the Freshie?"

"Um—yeah, I think so. Give me a minute." She began clicking the mouse and typing on the keyboard.

"What are you thinking?" Maura said.

"Annika gave us an alibi for Monday night—she'd said Roundhouse visited her, but she was so reluctant to tell us about it that we didn't question it. But Roundhouse was never there. No footage or witnesses back up Annika's statement."

Maura grimaced. "You're right. You're saying she fooled us?"

"And that's not the only trick she pulled. She's already shown that with a fake beauty mark and a little plastic surgery, she could transform herself into a Mariska Sikmo lookalike. She'd have to do more than look like Mariska; she'd have to act like her, move like her, talk like her. And she pulled it off—well enough to become Kymer Thompson's girlfriend." She glanced up at Maura. "So what other disguises could she pull off?"

Maura's shoulders slumped. "She's our prime suspect now."

"She's also got the knowledge of the Agios Delphi ceremony," Bernadette continued. "I saw how muscular she is in the hospital—she'd have enough strength to—" Bernadette shook her head, trying to avoid Maura's eyes. "We've been taking what she's said as evidence, but all she's done is throw blame on Vivian Roundhouse and Nick LaSalle."

Lesley turned from her computer screen to look at Bernadette. "Are you saying she staged her own kidnapping?"

Kep gave a short, derisive laugh. "She absolutely did."

Bernadette tilted her head and looked at Kep.

"That's what was bothering me about the smell in the car. The scent of Annika's perfume was stronger in the front seat, particularly on the driver's side."

Bernadette set her mouth in a line. "Annika was driving the university's Camry." She glanced at Maura. "It would also explain why nothing was broken in her dorm room and why she had one arm free when we found her."

Maura looked up at the ceiling, eyes losing focus, and exhaled long and low. "It's a nice story. It might even be true. But we have very little hard evidence."

"Not if I'm right about the footage from Monday night," Bernadette said.

"There's no one on this recording but Rhonda with her shopping cart," Lesley said as the footage unspooled on the monitor in front of her.

Bernadette leaned forward. "Zoom in."

"On what? Her shopping cart?"

"Her face."

Maura squinted. "It's dark, Bernadette. I can't make much out."

"Forward the recording until she turns toward the camera." Bernadette watched carefully.

"It's too dark."

"She's about to walk under that streetlight. There." The

tape paused as the woman was illuminated by the sodium streetlamp. "Now zoom again."

The scarf, draped around the woman's neck, covered her mouth but dipped below the woman's nose.

And peeking above the edge of the scarf, off-center and perfectly circular: a beauty mark.

Chapter Twenty-Five

❧❦❧

"That's Annika Nakrivo," Bernadette said.

Maura rubbed her forehead. "How did she wind up in a homeless woman's clothes pushing a shopping cart?"

"The pile of clothes in the shopping cart must be Kymer Thompson," Lesley said, squinting. "It's a bigger pile than when she—well, when Rhonda first appeared."

"I don't follow," Maura said. "I get that I'm watching Annika push our murder victim in a shopping cart. What I don't get is how Annika wound up being the killer. We don't have a motive. We've assumed that she was a victim until the ceremony ended in Nick LaSalle's death. Now we're looking at evidence that she's the killer."

Bernadette nodded, her heart racing. "Look at the timeline again. Two weeks after Kymer Thompson sends Mariska Sikmo the fan letter—"

"And the keylogger program tracks it all," Lesley put in.

Bernadette nodded. "That's when Annika Nakrivo left Miami for Cleveland. Had plastic surgery—"

"To look more like Mariska Sikmo," added Maura.

"Bankrolled by Parr Medical."

Lesley clicked on another screen and a spreadsheet popped up. "The flight information, hotel check-ins, and medical records. Yes—that all matches up."

"Then Annika Nakrivo enrolled at Kilbourn Tech and got an internship in the lab."

"So Annika, in a striking resemblance to the Anne Askew character from *Six Wives*," Maura said, "gets the religiously obsessive Kymer Thompson's heart all aflutter, and she—what?"

"She must have been on Parr Medical's payroll this whole time," Bernadette said. "That was her motive. She was hired to stop the research project." It wasn't for love, it wasn't for jealousy—Annika was essentially a hit man. "She convinced Thompson to share some information about the lampreys. Especially how they were protected."

Lesley swore softly.

"What is it?"

"I checked Annika's cell phone records and location for this week. Her phone was in her dorm the Monday night of Kymer Thompson's murder and during the shooting of Eddie Taysatch, so I didn't think any more about it. But I didn't check where it was two weeks before the murder." She opened a screen and began typing.

"Two weeks before?" Maura asked.

"Of course," Bernadette murmured. "Fond du Lac. Annika was at the Wildlife Specialties in Fond du Lac, wasn't she?"

Lesley clicked twice more, then nodded and pointed to a line of digits on the screen. "Yes, right here. I'd have to double-check, but I think this is the same time as Douglas Rheinstaller and Cecilia Carter were there."

Another click in Bernadette's head. "The Justice for Oceans brochures in Annika's dorm—I bet Annika went to a few Justice for Oceans meetings and convinced Cecilia Carter that she and Rheinstaller needed to work together—against a common enemy." She started to pace. "We were so busy thinking Annika was a victim in all of this. But she coordinated everything."

"But you saw Nick LaSalle with the tote bags," Kep said. "The ones I smelled TFM in."

"Nick was paid handsomely for going behind the scenes and helping out," Bernadette said. "Installing the keylogger. And I bet he's the one who disconnected the cameras and stole the footage at Juneau Hall—and probably disconnected the alarm system."

"So—" Maura scratched her scalp with both hands. "Who killed all those lampreys?"

"Annika must have killed the ammocoetes," Kep said. "If Bernadette is correct, Annika also persuaded Carter and Rheinstaller to purchase the TFM." He sucked in air through his teeth. "I identified TFM in the trunk of the Camry—because Annika is the one who pilfered it from Rheinstaller's shed."

"But why kill Tommy and Eddie?" Maura asked.

"In a very literal sense," Bernadette said, closing her eyes and talking with her hands, "she killed two birds with one stone. Both Kymer Thompson and Eddie Taysatch were on call. They were the ones alerted when the aquarium was compromised. Plus, they both had the most institutional knowledge of the science behind the development of the medication."

"And Thompson found out?"

"Or maybe he interrupted Annika during a dry run," Bernadette said, opening her eyes. "That would explain why he was killed instead of—I don't know, distracted or knocked out. It also explains why he called the campus police to ask the cost for adding overnight security. He wasn't afraid for his life. He was afraid for the project—he was talking about the *lampreys* getting killed."

"Annika had access to the concentrated ibogaine," Kep said.

"We took her word as gospel, yet she kept feeding us bad information."

"And we fell for it," Bernadette said.

Maura nodded. "But that doesn't get us any closer to where Annika Nakrivo went after the anchor ceremony."

"But this might," Lesley muttered. The screen in front of her had changed to flight paths.

Maura squinted at the monitor. "Is she in the air? Where is she headed? Are you tracking her that way?"

"Not quite." Lesley pointed at the screen, at a plane over the southern part of Lake Michigan, heading west. "This is a small jet with the same aircraft registration number as the one that flew Annika Nakrivo from Miami to Cleveland. It took off from Cleveland about an hour ago and according to its flight plan, it's headed for Milwaukee."

"The Milwaukee main airport?" Maura jumped up.

Lesley traced her finger to a line on her monitor. "No. Timmerman. The executive airport. About five miles north of downtown." The screen changed; lines of dark green text appeared. Lesley smiled. "There it is. Scheduled to land in fifteen minutes."

❦

As Maura turned on the SUV's engine, Bernadette slid into the passenger seat, Kep in the back. "If we can catch Annika before she gets on that plane," Maura said, "she might give us the leverage we need to get that Parr Medical warrant unstuck, too."

"Want me to contact airport security to hold the jet there?" Bernadette asked.

Maura clicked her tongue as she turned on the lights. "I

thought about that, but I don't want to give Parr Medical any warning that we're about to arrest Annika."

"Won't they already think the feds are on to them based on the subpoena?"

"I hope their lawyers think we're going on a fishing expedition," Maura said. "Besides, we didn't suspect Nakrivo until now. They might think we're still chasing Vivian Roundhouse."

"I'll keep in touch with Lesley. See where the plane is."

Twenty minutes later, Maura pulled the rental SUV into the Timmerman Airport parking lot and idled in front of a large building with off-white vinyl siding with a sign reading *Maintenance and Services.*

"And what about the jet?"

"Lesley says it's sitting on the tarmac. Pilot called in needing to refuel."

"Crew?"

"Besides the pilot, just a flight attendant. And Lesley just sent me this." Bernadette tapped her phone screen and a news article from *The Miami Observer* appeared. "The article is about Hester McCall, who was about to testify in a class action lawsuit against Parr Medical. Murdered in an attempted carjacking in Ft. Lauderdale. That was three weeks before Annika Nakrivo pulled her disappearing act to Cleveland."

"Are you suggesting," Kep said from the back seat, "that she's a killer-for-hire for Parr Medical?"

Bernadette set her mouth in a line. It was exactly what she believed, though she had no proof. "If she's not, it's a big coincidence."

Maura drove the SUV around the corner of the maintenance building. Directly in front of them, parked diagonally across two spaces, was a light blue van.

"So much for the APB," Bernadette muttered.

"What's the end game for Annika?" Maura asked, pulling

into a space near the main building. "She escapes on the plane after killing four people and thousands of lampreys, and what does she get?"

"Money, I assume. Maybe another assignment. A new identity."

"Without being able to talk to anyone at Parr Medical," Kep said, "it's impossible to know."

A Milwaukee police cruiser, lights off, turned in behind the SUV. The driver and passenger doors opened at the same time, and Dunn jumped out and ran to the SUV. Maura lowered her window; the crisp breeze cooled down the car almost immediately.

Dunn stood at the driver's-side door. "We've gotten word that a woman matching Annika Nakrivo's description has boarded the jet on the tarmac."

"They refueled already?" Maura asked. "That was fast."

Bernadette cocked her head. "I don't think they had time. Do you know how long it takes to fuel a jet that size?"

Kep nodded. "At a small airport like this, refueling usually takes at least a half hour."

Dunn screwed up her face. "They haven't been on the ground that long, have they?"

"No," Maura said. "Ten minutes, tops."

"That's weird," Bernadette said. "Why—" Then a thought struck her. "What if Parr Medical isn't planning to get Annika Nakrivo off the ground at all?"

"What are you saying?" Dunn asked.

"Bear with me for a second. Nick LaSalle was killed, and he's the one who hacked Kymer Thompson's PC, disconnected the alarms, destroyed the camera footage. He knew too much."

Dunn nodded. "Or they didn't trust him to keep his mouth shut."

"What if," Bernadette continued, "like Nick, Annika knows too much? Or they don't trust her?"

Kep pushed his glasses up on his nose. "Parr Medical set a trap for her, and the company plans to have us unwittingly execute it."

"Do you mean," Maura said, "that Parr Medical thinks law enforcement will kill Annika Nakrivo?"

Bernadette ran her hands through her hair. "Maybe it ends with us in a shootout. Or with Annika arrested. Or with the plane blowing up. But if that plane hasn't refueled, it's about to play out on the runway."

Maura's phone rang.

"Lieutenant Stevenson," she said. "Yes. We're here. Uh huh. Detective Dunn—is anyone else coming?"

"We've got two other officers," Dunn said. "They were about five minutes behind me."

"But no SWAT team?"

Dunn shook her head. "We didn't have one at the salt warehouse, and we don't have one here. There's no hostage situation. Looks like we need to board the plane and make arrests."

"Annika Nakrivo might act in ways you can't predict," Kep said. "We don't have her complete background. We know she isn't a nineteen-year-old university student, but, as Becker inferred from the Miami article, she could be the world's most ruthless murderer-for-hire. If she believes she's cornered, she could be lethal."

"She's already been lethal," Bernadette said.

"We'll be right there," Maura said, and ended the call. "Come on—we've got to meet the security manager on duty."

THE FOUR OF THEM WALKED AROUND THE RIGHT SIDE OF THE building, the piles of dirty snow solidifying in the freezing night. As they came around the corner, they saw a small white jet on a strip of asphalt leading off one of the runways.

A heavyset Black man wearing aviator glasses, a black Timmerman Airport cap, a black down jacket, and khaki trousers met them. "Lieutenant Stevenson?"

"That's me," Maura said, stepping forward and shaking hands.

"I'm Carlos Costa," he said. "Head of security here. The jet is still on the ground. It doesn't seem like it's going anywhere."

"Has the jet refueled?"

"Not yet. Haven't called in to refuel either, which is a little unusual before they take passengers on."

"Do we know for sure that the passenger is Annika Nakrivo?" Kep asked.

"We've got the security footage," Costa said, taking his phone out. He tapped the screen and held it out to Maura.

Kep looked over her shoulder. "It's definitely Annika."

Maura nodded. "So do you have protocol we need to follow?"

"This is a police action, so we've shut down the runways."

Maura cast a nervous look at Bernadette. "We don't know what we're walking into."

"No," Kep said, "but I'll get as close as I can and smell for explosives."

"Explosives?"

"Certainly," Kep said. "If Parr Medical doesn't want Annika Nakrivo captured alive, there's a possibility they will kill her on the plane."

"But they wouldn't—" Maura closed her eyes for a moment. "Fine. Go out there and smell for explosives."

Dunn raised her eyebrows. "I heard C4 smells like almonds."

"The scent is more akin to tar," Kep said. "It can smell like plastic or vinyl when it's warm."

"Which it's not," Maura said.

"Correct." Kep rubbed his chin. "I will be able to smell explosives at approximately twenty meters from the plane. However, with the jet fuel and the asphalt, it will more difficult to distinguish certain explosive materials. Anything that's fertilizer-based or plastic-based, though, I'll be able to detect. I can warn you if there's danger."

The radio on Costa's belt buzzed. "Hold on a second," he said, taking a few steps away from the group.

Two officers appeared from around the corner of the maintenance building: Officers Lamar Chesapeake and Lance Schroeter. Bernadette did a double take, then caught Chesapeake's eye. He smiled and touched the brim of his police hat, and Bernadette took a few steps away from the group.

Chesapeake walked up to Bernadette. "We have to stop meeting like this."

"If I didn't know better, I'd say you were following me."

He laughed. "Like I said, I need all the overtime I can get."

Bernadette smiled. "I see. It's all about the overtime."

"It looks like my long working days might be coming to an end after tonight. Would you like to have dinner with me before you leave Milwaukee?"

Bernadette turned toward the white jet on the tarmac. "I should probably see if we both survive this first."

Chesapeake nodded. "Yeah. It won't be a straightforward arrest, will it?"

"Probably not." Bernadette's phone rang; she looked at the screen. A 754 area code.

"Seven-five-four?" she asked. "Where's that?"

"South Florida," Chesapeake said.

Bernadette answered the phone. "Bernadette Becker."

"Ms. Becker?" It was a woman's voice, not low, not high. Calm. Familiar.

"Speaking."

"It's Annika Nakrivo."

Chapter Twenty-Six

Bernadette waved wildly. The team stared at her, and she put her finger to her lips. Confusion washed over their faces, but Bernadette put the phone on speaker.

"I didn't expect to hear from you, Annika. I didn't even think you had my number."

"You gave me your business card when you came to my dorm room in Juneau Hall, remember?"

"Ah, yes," Bernadette said. "So I did. Why are you calling me?"

"I can see you from the airplane window. Take me off speakerphone."

"Why?" She started sweating despite the cold and unzipped her puffy purple coat.

"Because you'll be the only one getting on this plane."

"You must know that we're here to arrest you."

Silence.

"Are you still there?"

"I thought you arrested Vivian Roundhouse."

"We did. But then we saw you on camera. With Tommy's dead body in the shopping cart."

Silence.

On the tarmac, the door to the jet swung down slowly.

"Hey!" Annika yelled. "What are you—"

Two women, both in uniforms, jumped from the plane, then dashed across the asphalt.

"The pilot and the flight attendant," Dunn exclaimed.

Costa, hand on his belt—was there a holster under his jacket?—hurried toward the pilot and flight attendant. A female figure appeared in the door, holding a phone to her ear.

"You promised that you'd believe me," Annika said. "I guess that was a lie."

"No—wait—Annika!"

The line went dead.

The door to the jet, as it reached the bottom of its descent, began to rise slowly.

Then the plane jerked forward—toward the runway.

She'll try to take off anyway. And she doesn't know there's not enough fuel. She'll crash into downtown Milwaukee.

Bernadette broke into a sprint.

Surprised shouts came from Dunn, Maura, Officer Lance Schroeter—but a glint was in Kep's eye as she darted past him.

The door was almost halfway closed now, but she was racing toward the plane, and if she timed the leap right, she could make it.

The pounding of her boots against the pavement, the whine of the jet engine as it tried to turn onto the runway—was Annika a pilot in addition to a killer-for-hire, a scientist, an escort, and a chameleon?

The plane turned and Bernadette changed her angle. It was closer now, the door still partially open.

Twenty yards.

Ten. Five.

She leaped.

Her head and shoulders flew through the open space in the door, her bruised hip crashing painfully into the corner of a seat. The pain seared for a moment—she might have dislocated her shoulder, too—but she had the presence of mind to pull her knees up. Then the door was closed. And the plane was still moving.

Panting and in pain from her shoulder and her hip, she scrambled into a crouching position on the small jet.

The plane sped up. She looked out the window and the group of people—Kep standing halfway between the maintenance building and the tarmac—were receding. The jet was on the runway, accelerating.

She reached for her gun in her holster.

It wasn't there.

Shit. It must have fallen out when she jumped into the plane.

She rubbed her forehead. What was she going to do?

The plane kept speeding up. If she didn't decide soon, she and Annika would be crashing the plane into a city block or two.

She closed her eyes and took a deep breath.

She rushed into the cockpit and jumped forward.

Her elbow connected squarely with Annika's temple. Annika's head snapped to the side, then she turned back, growling.

A movement across Annika's torso—

Bernadette jumped backward and heard the sound of ripping fabric. She looked down—Annika had sliced through her puffy coat. She couldn't feel any cut on her skin—but she didn't have time to check.

Annika reached up, the knife glinting from the cockpit lights.

Bernadette rushed under the blade, the top of her head hitting Annika's chin.

A clatter of metal on metal—Annika had dropped the knife.

Bernadette jumped onto the throttle control and pulled it hard, all the way back, and the plane jerked suddenly, slamming to a stop. Bernadette lost her balance and fell into the instrument panel, smashing her injured shoulder. She heard a bang, then a bump: the tire on the landing gear blowing out.

She barked in pain, then scrambled to her feet as the plane rocked to a stop.

Annika was standing in the small cockpit too, a crazed look in her eyes.

"I didn't think you'd try to stop me," Annika said. Her lip was cut and blood dripped down her chin.

"I didn't think you were the killer," Bernadette said.

"I wasn't supposed to kill anyone."

"Then what happened, Annika? You've killed four people."

She snarled. "It's all your fault."

"*My* fault? You killed Tommy before I even got into town."

"If you hadn't chased Nick down the street," Annika said, ignoring Bernadette, "we would have killed the lampreys *that* night. We had to abort because of you."

Bernadette remembered what Lightman had said. "You and Tommy were both on call on Tuesday."

"Yeah, that's right. But we had to switch to the next night instead. And Eddie was on call then. We couldn't risk him getting the alarm notification." She frowned. "Then your cool-as-ice co-worker had to follow me from my dorm to the lab." Annika's nostrils flared. "I thought I was pretty good at losing a tail, but I wasn't thinking straight." She gave Bernadette a withering stare. "If you'd stayed where you were on Tuesday night, no one else would have died."

Bernadette kept eye contact. Where did the knife go? She wished she hadn't dropped the gun on the runway.

Sirens. Surely Annika heard them too.

Then Annika drew her hand up—holding the knife. She launched herself at Bernadette with a scream.

Barely sidestepping the blade, Bernadette felt it catch the inside of her puffy coat.

But this time she was ready. Bernadette jerked her torso—her shoulder screaming in pain—and her arm came clear of the sleeve, the blade still embedded in the coat. Annika's face contorted.

Bernadette kicked out and caught Annika's leg.

Annika fell forward, face right onto the wall separating the cockpit and passenger area and collapsed onto her stomach.

Bernadette jumped onto Annika, a knee between her shoulder blades, and pulled her hands behind her back.

She was shaking from the exertion, sweat pouring off her brow. She took a deep breath, her heart pounding, and pulled herself completely free of her shredded coat.

It was over.

Bernadette let out a long, slow exhale.

"Annika Nakrivo, you're under arrest for murder."

The sirens were louder now, right in front of the door to the plane.

"Anything you say can be used against you..."

As she finished the Miranda rights, Bernadette reached over the narrow cabin, knee still in Annika's back, and pushed the button for the door release.

The hydraulics whined as the door with the built-in stairs slowly lowered. Two police cruisers were fifty feet from the jet, and Officer Lamar Chesapeake was inside the cabin first, handcuffs already out, cuffing Annika's hands behind her back. He pulled her to her feet, then turned to Bernadette.

"You okay?"

Her heart pounded and her hands shook, but she nodded. "Yeah. Yeah, I'm okay."

"You're sure?"

Bernadette gave him a weak smile. "Give me a minute."

Chesapeake nodded and led Nakrivo down the stairs.

Then Bernadette was alone on the jet. The plane was eerily quiet. There were no sounds from the runway.

She looked down at her ruined puffy purple coat, Annika's knife caught inside it, and briefly wondered if she could expense a new winter jacket.

She sighed and closed her eyes. Would Maura think she was worthy of becoming an agent again after this? She'd certainly gone above and beyond. Although running onto the plane put herself in danger—and it didn't serve to protect Kep either.

Bernadette opened her eyes, steeled herself, and turned toward the airplane door—a fresh wave of pain shot through her shoulder as she started down the stairs. She'd have to go to the hospital.

Chapter Twenty-Seven

ARM IN A SLING, BERNADETTE STOOD IN FRONT OF THE Outsider Hotel. The sun was out, but it was far too cold without her coat, which would stay in evidence for a long time. She looked across the street: a thrift store stood next to the bagel café; maybe she'd run over there and buy a cheap winter jacket.

Her phone rang in her purse and she looked at the screen. Sophie.

"Good morning, sweetie."

"Hi, Mom."

"You're not in school."

A short laugh. "Mom, it's Saturday."

"Right. Sorry—sometimes when I'm working a case, I forget what day it is."

"Did you catch the bad guy?"

She thought of the faceless people at Parr Medical who had paid for the murders—but at least Annika was in custody. "Sure did."

"Good. Does that mean you're coming home?"

"In a few more days. I hurt my shoulder. The doctor won't let me back on a plane until he sees the results of the x-rays."

"Oh."

"Everything okay?"

"Well," Sophie said, "I guess."

"How's your dad doing?"

"Oh, *he's* fine. Couldn't be happier." Sophie's voice was thick with disdain.

"What's the matter?"

Sophie clicked her tongue. "Nothing, really. I, uh—Lisa doesn't like food she says is unhealthy."

"Oh. Well, you're old enough to make your own meals now. I can—"

"And the way she *chews*. I want to strangle her." She paused. "When are you coming home?"

"Monday, I think. If the doctor lets me go."

"Okay. I miss you."

"Me too, Sophie." Bernadette looked up to see Maura's rented SUV pulling in front of the hotel. "Okay—my boss just got here. I have to go."

"You have to work on a Saturday?"

"I know, being an adult sucks sometimes. I love you. I'll see you soon."

Kep got out of the passenger's side, opening the rear door for Bernadette, and she climbed in to find a paper bag with *The Elegant Doughnut* printed on it.

"What's this?"

"A present," Maura said. "It's not much, but you put yourself in danger so that Annika wouldn't crash that plane into a neighborhood. The least I can do is get you a lemon-pistachio old-fashioned donut. There's a maple-glazed croissant donut in there too. The woman behind the counter insisted I get one of those for you."

"Only because it was the most expensive item on the menu," Kep said, "and yet I can still smell the sodium hexametaphosphate, which is decidedly not real maple." He sighed. "I hope the Wisconsin old-fashioned donuts taste better than the Wisconsin Old Fashioned cocktails."

"Don't let the locals hear you say that." Bernadette took a bite of the lemon-pistachio. It was delicious. "You sure you don't want one?" she said, holding the maple-glazed donut out to Kep.

"Oh, thou lump of foul deformity," Kep muttered.

"*What* did you say to me?" Bernadette tilted her head.

"The donut," Kep said quickly, "not you."

In the rearview mirror, Bernadette saw a smile touch the corners of Maura's mouth.

Bernadette sat back. "I don't see why I have to be there for this today." She took another bite.

"Annika asked to speak with you," Maura said. "I don't understand it either, but she won't give up the name of the person—or people—who hired her. I don't know if she's scared for her life, but we're already giving her in-prison protection. Not a whole lot more we can do. Maybe she'll talk with you in the room."

"And you have to talk to her before her transfer to Taycheeda Correctional," Kep said from the passenger seat, "unless you want a two-hour drive on snowy roads instead of a ten-minute drive through downtown."

"It's fine," Bernadette said, and took another bite.

Her phone rang. Was that Sophie again? No—it was a 414 number she didn't recognize.

"Becker."

"Hey, Bernadette. It's Lamar."

"Oh—hi." Bernadette stole a glance into the front seat, but

Kep and Maura were talking to each other, not paying attention to Bernadette's call. "This is a nice surprise."

"I was planning to visit you in the hospital, but you'd already gone."

"Yeah. They didn't even keep me overnight. Just an ER visit. Got x-rays and a sling, another appointment in two days."

"Oh. Good."

"Good?"

"Not that you're injured, but that you're—uh—still in town. Are you free for dinner?"

Was he asking her on a date? She couldn't remember the last time she'd been on a date. Even a night out with Barlow seemed like a lifetime ago. "Uh—yeah. Yeah, I'm free. Maura and Kep are leaving this afternoon. I hadn't planned anything but sitting around my hotel room, trying to entertain myself until Monday's doctor's appointment." She realized she sounded a little overeager and evened out her tone. "You know how it is, though; a girl's gotta eat."

"Good—I know a couple of great restaurants by your hotel. Any dietary restrictions? Vegan? Gluten-free?"

"Food I can eat with one hand."

"Right. I know the perfect place. How does seven o'clock sound?"

"Great."

"See you then."

Bernadette ended the call and caught a glimpse of herself in the rear-view mirror. She looked—not exactly happy, but like she was finally getting her feet back under herself.

When the SUV pulled into the facility's parking lot, Maura killed the engine.

"Want us to come in with you?" Maura asked.

"I think I'll be okay."

"Great. Let us know if it'll be longer than an hour. We'll

need to get to the airport." Maura looked at Kep. "So what do you think? Ready to do this again when we have another poisoning murder for you?"

"Yes."

"Any concerns? Travel arrangements? Personnel?"

Kep turned his head and looked at Bernadette, his gaze serious but soft. "No concerns."

Bernadette gave him a slight nod.

Kep turned back to stare through the windshield.

Bernadette opened her door and, eyes inquisitive, tilted her head at Maura, who rubbed the back of her neck.

After checking in at the front, Bernadette was led into a small room with eggshell walls and a metal table with four straight-backed metal chairs. The furniture was cold to the touch. She sat, sending a jolt of discomfort through her arm, but it wasn't nearly as bad as it had been the day before. Of course, the drugs probably helped with that.

She'd had a dream the night before of getting on a plane—a commercial airline, not a private jet—and all the passengers attacked her with knives and crowbars. She'd awakened in a cold sweat.

Now she sat on the frigid metal chair and waited for her attacker to come greet her.

After what seemed like an hour, the door opened. Annika Nakrivo, in handcuffs and ankle cuffs attached to each other, appeared. A guard let her through, seating her opposite Bernadette, then stood next to the door.

Annika glared at the guard, then turned to Bernadette, then back at the guard. "Can we talk in private?"

"Without the guard? No. You tried to run me over with a stolen van. You killed four people, including one of my co-workers. You attacked me with a knife."

Annika looked at the guard, then back at Bernadette. "I can't tell you what I need to tell you with a guard here."

Bernadette could feel the pain medication begin to wane as her shoulder began to throb. "The guard stays."

Annika shook her head. "I'm sorry. I cannot tell you with anyone else in the room. I'll go back to my cell."

Bernadette had not come all this way, doped up on painkillers, to have Annika go back to her cell. She looked at the cuffs and the chain hooked to the table.

"Wait," Bernadette said. "How long do you need?"

"Five minutes."

Bernadette looked at the guard. "Can you give us five minutes?"

The guard nodded. "Five minutes." She turned and walked out of the room, closing the door behind her.

"Okay," Bernadette said, "you got me alone. You going to shiv me? Because with the amount of painkillers running though my sys—"

"I'm sorry about everything," Annika blurted.

Bernadette looked at her, then burst out laughing—and stopped when the pain radiated down her arm. "Ugh," she said, "I don't believe you. I think you're only sorry you were caught."

"You have no idea what they made me do."

"I think I have *some* idea," Bernadette said. "We've been doing some research on your background."

Annika cast her eyes down.

"They flew you to Cleveland and made you get plastic surgery to look like Mariska Sikmo. They sent you to Milwaukee to kill thousands of lampreys so rich people could get even richer. They had you get two activists who hate each other to buy a hundred pounds of TFM. Then they had you steal it. They told you to kill the lampreys and anyone who got in your way."

She leaned forward, taking care not to tax her shoulder. "Including Curtis." She leaned back in the hard metal chair. "We want to know who 'they' are. Who put you up to this?"

Annika swallowed hard, then looked up at Bernadette, eyes wet. "They have my sister," she whispered.

Bernadette's eyes went wide. "What?"

"You have to help her," Annika murmured. "It's too late for me, but I won't talk. Not until my sister is safe."

Annika stood up and shuffled over to the door, then banged on it awkwardly with both hands. The guard opened the door. "We're finished."

The guard stuck her head in. "You need anything?"

Yes! I need to know who her sister is! I need to know where she's being held! I need to know who 'they' are!

Bernadette managed to smile. "No. Thank you for your time."

The door closed behind them.

Bernadette ran her hands through her hair and exhaled slowly. The seconds ticked by.

The photo on Annika's dresser in her dorm room—that must have been a younger Annika and her sister. She'd have to go back there. It might be the only lead she'd be able to get.

She slammed her fist on the table, then winced at the pain shooting up her shoulder.

She got up and left the room.

Want more Woodhead & Becker?
Get Book 2: The Bridegroom Murder

Cast of Characters

THE CORE TEAM

- **Dr. Kep Woodhead**: A forensic toxicologist in his early fifties, Dr. Woodhead is both an expert in poisons and a "super smeller"—he can detect and specify scents far beyond the olfactory range of most humans. His brusque manner rubs many people the wrong way, including...
- **Bernadette Becker**: A recently demoted case analyst who has been assigned to manage Dr. Woodhead on relevant cases. Becker is Woodhead's sixth "handler" in the last twenty-four months. Freshly separated from her husband of nearly fifteen years, Becker is trying to get back on her feet both personally and professionally.
- **Lieutenant Maura Stevenson**: Becker's immediate supervisor runs the CSAB Homicide Liaison Unit and joins Woodhead and Becker on important cases, greasing the wheels with local law

enforcement agencies, cutting through red tape, and getting needed resources.

- **Curtis Janek**: A young, enterprising tech analyst and researcher for the CSAB unit. Janek is a computer whiz and wants to climb the ladder at the bureau.

THE CASE

- **Kymer Thompson**: Found dead in a reconstructed fifteenth-century chapel on the Kilbourn Tech campus. Grad student working on a cancer research project.
- **Detective Kerrigan Dunn:** The Milwaukee police detective assigned to the case, now the liaison to CSAB.
- **Officer Lamar Chesapeake:** A Milwaukee police officer.
- **Officer Lance Schroeter:** A Milwaukee police officer and Chesapeake's partner.
- **Carlos Costa:** The head of security at the Timmerman Executive Airport.
- **Lesley Gill:** A tech with the Milwaukee police department who helps the CSAB team.
- **Jude Lightman**: Thompson's advisor and research leader. His project uses a local species of silver lamprey to harvest two types of enzymes which react with ibogaine and can destroy cancer cells. Brilliant and handsome, and he knows it.
- **Rev. Vivian Roundhouse**: Leader of the local Agios Delphi church, tracing its origins back to

Anne Askew, of which Kymer Thompson was an elder and Thompson's girlfriend was a member.

- **Suzanne Thao**: Another member of Agios Delphi, she is involved with Roundhouse.
- **Annika Nakrivo**: Thompson's girlfriend; recent transfer to Kilbourn Tech, majoring in chemistry and working on the research project as an intern.
- **Eddie Taysatch**: Thompson's fellow grad student and peer on the cancer research project.
- **Zadie Michaels**: Another intern working on the cancer research project at the Freshwater Sciences lab.
- **Cecilia Carter**: An activist with the local Justice for Oceans group, who oppose the cancer research project for harvesting silver lampreys for their liver enzymes.
- **Douglas Rheinstaller**: Head of the local Lake Shore Piscary Association, which opposes the cancer research project for encouraging the population of lampreys in Lake Michigan and its feeder rivers.
- **Nick LaSalle**: An IT specialist at Kilbourn Tech, he sets up and maintains the lab computers.
- **Barlow Finnegan**: Bernadette's estranged husband and soon-to-be ex.
- **Sophie Finnegan**: Bernadette's twelve-year old daughter.

More by Paul Austin Ardoin

The Woodhead & Becker Mysteries

Book One: The Winterstone Murder

Book Two: The Bridegroom Murder

Book Three: The Trailer Park Murder *(coming soon)*

The Fenway Stevenson Mysteries

Book One: The Reluctant Coroner

Book Two: The Incumbent Coroner

Book Three: The Candidate Coroner

Book Four: The Upstaged Coroner

Book Five: The Courtroom Coroner

Novella: The Christmas Coroner

Book Six: The Watchful Coroner

Book Seven: The Accused Coroner

Novella: The Clandestine Coroner

Book Eight: The Offside Coroner

Collections

Books 1–3 of The Fenway Stevenson Mysteries

Books 4-6 of The Fenway Stevenson Mysteries

Dez Roubideaux

Bad Weather

Sign up for *The Coroner's Report,*

Paul Austin Ardoin's fortnightly newsletter:

http://www.paulaustinardoin.com

Subscribe to Paul's Patreon, with several levels of members-only goodies:

https://www.patreon.com/paulaustinardoin

I hope you enjoyed reading this book as much as I enjoyed writing it. If you did, I'd sincerely appreciate a review on your favorite book retailer's website, Goodreads, and BookBub. Reviews are crucial for any author, and even just a line or two can make a huge difference.

Acknowledgments

Many thanks to my editors Max Christian Hansen, Melissa Crandall, and Jess Reynolds; to my proofreader Lisa Lee; and to my cover designer Ziad Ezzat of Feral Creative. This book is much better because of you.

Thank you to all the early readers and reviewers. Special thanks to Beverly Ange, Dana Luco, Michelle Damiani, Siobhan Ordorica, and the Wordforge Novelists group in Sacramento, whose critical eyes and tough love were invaluable. Thanks also to Dr. Christina Bellinger, Devin McCrate, and IshKiia Paige. I also appreciate Robb Moore and Robyn Sarty taking the time to provide invaluable airplane and small-airport details.

Thanks to my patrons, including J.W. Atkinson, Stan Peters, Janice Webber, and Donna White.

Special thanks to Cheryl Shoults, who has been invaluable creating, organizing, and maintaining my author newsletter, website, reader teams, promotions, and a million other items.

To my wife, my children, and my mother: I'm deeply grateful for your encouragement and support.